MARIE TAYLOR-FORD

Wedding Bells at Lilac Bay

LILAC BAY
SERIES
BOOK 4

No part of this book may be reproduced in any form or by any electronic or mechanical means, including information storage and retrieval systems, without written permission from the author, except for the use of brief quotations in a book review.

This is a work of fiction and all characters in this publication are fictitious. Any similarity to real persons, living or dead, or actual events, is purely coincidental.

Text Copyright © 2023
Marie Taylor-Ford
All rights reserved

Cover design by Ana Grigoriu-Voicu

—

Author note: This book is set in Australia, and therefore uses British English spelling.

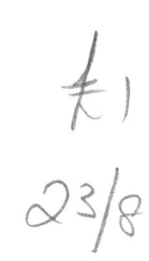

For my babies. Everything is for you. Always.

1
SATURDAY: EIGHT WEEKS TO THE WEDDING

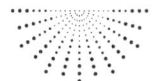

Amy wasn't going to say anything to the tween girl staring open-mouthed at Lyra as they browsed bridesmaid dresses at the boutique.

But Marley was. At seven months pregnant, Marley's swollen belly was making her uncomfortable and irritated, even inside the temperature-controlled shop. As Amy and Lyra sipped from champagne flutes, Marley harrumphed around, tsking at any price tags she saw. Amy had no idea why costs would be bothering Marley so much, especially since she wouldn't be the one paying for the dresses. But her friend looked uncomfortable, so Amy was biting her tongue. And honestly, her list of wedding to-dos was so long, she didn't care what her two bridesmaids ended up wearing. She could make any colour work with the rest of the scheme.

Amy questioningly lifted an emerald green pleat number that would accommodate both Marley and Lyra's body types. Marley was tilting her head at it when her eyes landed on the girl.

"Can we help you with something?" she asked sharply.

The girl flushed bright red and moved back to her

mother, standing on tiptoe to whisper in her ear. The woman turned to glare at Marley.

"My daughter is allowed to look at you," she said crisply.

"She's not looking, she's *staring*," Marley said. "It's rude."

"Marley, it's fine." Amy gently laid a hand on her friend's arm. She smiled at the store owner, Jacqueline, who looked wary, toying with her pearls and smoothing her elegant blonde chignon.

"Uh, what is happening right now?" Lyra asked, turning around.

"That girl was staring, that's all," Marley said, flapping her hand dismissively.

Lyra glanced at the girl who blushed again. Her mother nudged her forward. "Ask her," she said encouragingly.

The girl cleared her throat, taking a tentative step towards Lyra. "A-are you the singer Lyra?"

"Oh. Yeah, I am," Lyra said warmly, shooting a quick glance towards Amy to check whether an interruption would throw them too far off schedule.

Amy shook her head, a wide grin splitting her face.

"Do you think ... maybe I could get a selfie with you?" The girl's voice wobbled nervously.

"Sure!" Lyra said. "What's your name?"

"Montana."

As Lyra slipped her arm over a beaming Montana's shoulders, the girl's mother snapped several pictures. Montana wanted one with the peace sign, one with their tongues out—Lyra played along, then fell into easy conversation with the grateful mother once they were done.

Amy heard Lyra's phone pinging in their changing room and she jerked her head to let Marley know she'd go check on it. She guessed it was Lyra's boyfriend, Alex, checking how much longer they'd be. He and Lyra were booked to view a house they were considering buying, and Amy had promised to deliver her friend back in plenty of time.

The changing room was really a suite, though the décor was a little bland for Amy's taste. Warm, flattering light diffused over outsized mirrors, plush carpet, thick curtains and an over-stuffed white armchair. Amy found Lyra's phone face down on the armchair. She set her champagne on a low white shelf and tilted Lyra's screen towards her.

Jake: Came up with a sweet opening hook for Undone.

Jake: Hit me up when you get this. I def know this will make you smile ...

Jake: I love your smile ;)

There was something intimate about the messages that made Amy shiver with a sense of foreboding. Lyra was madly in love with Alex, there was no way that she'd do anything to jeopardise that. But *Jake* might not have gotten that message. Amy sighed, biting her lip as she frowned at the screen, hoping her best friend's keyboard player wasn't going to stir up any trouble.

"Hey," Lyra said, appearing behind her with two more dresses on one arm, her champagne in the other. She glanced down at the phone. "Oh, was it going off?"

"Sorry, I didn't mean to pry, I thought it might be Alex."

"It wasn't?" Lyra frowned, then her features registered recognition. "Let me guess then, Jake?"

Amy nodded. "Is he kind of ..."

"Into me?" Lyra asked, laughing. It was the kind of thing Amy would never have dreamed she'd hear her friend say, even a couple of months ago. But as Lyra's music career had taken off, Amy had been pleased to notice that her confidence had grown as well.

"I guess that's what I meant," Amy admitted with a sheepish grin.

Lyra's brown ponytail swung. "Not even a little. He's just like that. A natural flirt, I guess. Totally harmless."

"Well, he has a new *hook* for you," Amy said, gesturing to the phone.

"Cool, I'll get back to him later. I don't want to think about that right now. We're down to the last two months and we still don't have our bridesmaid kits!"

"Excuse me, we are *going* to talk about the fact that you had your first fan recognise you!" Amy said, beaming.

Lyra pursed her lips, her eyes twinkling.

"Ohhh," Amy said, realising. "That's not the first time is it?"

"Nope. But weirdly it tends to be teenage boys that spot me first. I would have thought I was too old!"

"Are you *kidding?*" Amy squeaked, pointedly looking her friend up and down. "If this was the eighties, poster versions of you would be seeing *sickening* things in teenage boys' rooms right now."

Lyra laughed. "Alright, back on task." She lifted one of the dresses draped over her arm. "I kind of like this pale pink one, but Marley isn't keen on it. I'll let you two decide, of course. I'll turn up in a hessian sack if you want."

Marley entered the changing room holding up a deep fuchsia dress. Jacqueline trailed her, with an armful of similarly bright, jewel-toned dresses.

"Lyra, what about this one?" Marley held it up.

Lyra wrinkled her nose for a second. "I mean, it's *loud*. But if you like it ... Ames?"

Amy shrugged. "I'm so happy to be finally marrying him. And with you guys by my side."

"Alright," Marley said, the slightest note of impatience in her voice. "Lyra, we have to choose. I'm voting fuchsia."

Lyra side-hugged Amy and nodded at Marley. "Fuchsia. Sure thing."

2
SATURDAY

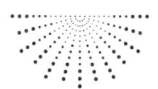

"You really look good, Marley," Amy said, as the three of them sat down to ice-cream floats at a little cafe on Ocean Avenue after shopping. The weather was crisp, but they had braved it to sit outside. "Although I realise you might not feel it," she added, as Marley shifted uncomfortably in her chair.

"I feel like an absolute balloon," she sighed, tugging at the green, oversized jumper Amy was positive had been made for Nordic fishermen. "Went up a shoe size and can't fit any of my rings. And I've still got two months to go. I'm grumpy as anything and my hips constantly feel like they're dislocated. But ... when I feel the baby move," she closed her eyes dreamily. "It's beyond worth it." She beamed at them, affectionately rubbing her bump.

"I'm going to get all teary," Lyra said, stirring her float with a paper straw. "My besties—knocked up and getting married."

"Only one of us is knocked up," Amy clarified quickly. Her phone was open in her lap, and she discreetly scrolled through her various checklists to the one labelled "Wedding".

Her anxiety spiked at the sight of it, and checking off "buy bridesmaid dresses" wasn't the relief she had imagined it would be. Mainly because it triggered a whole sub-set of to-dos that she hadn't started yet.

"And only one of us is getting married," Marley added, just as hastily.

"And you're looking at buying a house with Alex, plus your career has taken off," Amy said, clicking her phone off and managing a smile. "I can't believe you'll be gone three weeks on tour."

"I know. Me either, sometimes. I keep pinching myself."

They let out contented sighs.

"It doesn't get better than this, does it?" Lyra said dreamily, then flinched as Marley swatted her.

"*Why* are you jinxing us right now?" Marley's expression was stern.

Amy flapped her hand at Marley. "Don't be so superstitious. We're allowed to revel in the good times. And of course we know there will always be bad times to level it all out. It's not bad luck to appreciate it when things are easy."

"How are you and Finn doing anyway?" Lyra asked Marley.

A frown flickered across her forehead. "We're good. Good, good."

Amy tilted her head. "You know you can talk to us," she said gently. "If you want to."

Marley heaved a sigh. "I feel horrible talking about him behind his back. But… he's still renting his other apartment even though he's staying with me most nights."

"Tell him you want him to give it up!" Lyra said.

Marley bit her lip. "That's the thing. *I* want him to keep it. So I'm afraid to start the discussion in case he says he wants to give his place up. But I feel bad and manipulative at the same time."

Amy nodded slowly, seeing the dilemma. "You're pretty close to the due date now …"

"I know!" Marley wrung her hands. "But we've still been together less than a year!"

Lyra shot Amy a concerned look. "Do you suspect it's bothering him?" Lyra asked.

"I don't know," she admitted. "He hasn't said anything. But it's Finn. He wouldn't say anything even if it was. It's such a huge leap. I … I don't know."

Amy placed a reassuring hand on Marley's arm. "What about the nursery? How's that looking? We haven't seen any pics! Do you need help with it?"

Marley stirred her drink with the straw.

"You haven't started yet?" Lyra asked in alarm.

"Not yet."

"Do you want me to design something for you?" Amy asked kindly. "Porter Lucas would take you on for free, of course. Maybe it's easier if it's out of your hands?" Amy's offer was genuine, but she found herself secretly hoping Marley would turn her down—she was already up to her ears in lists.

"I don't know." Marley tilted her head. "Thanks so much for offering, but … I want it to feel like it's really *ours*, you know?"

The girls both knew Marley was nervous about something going wrong with her pregnancy. Her family also didn't have a great history where relationships were concerned, and Lyra and Amy were immensely proud of her for pushing past all that to start dating Finn. Still, it seemed some mental barriers remained.

"Sure," Amy nodded. "But I will point out, that's actually the *purpose* of an interior designer. Sometimes we can find a look that's more *you* than even you could ... not to toot my own horn," she added with a grin.

Marley looked thoughtful. "Let me talk it over with Finn."

"Sure, no pressure at all," Amy said, sucking a big gulp of her float down. "By the way, why do we call these 'spiders'?" She pointed to her drink.

Lyra frowned. "I thought we only called it a spider if the drink is creaming soda and the ice-cream is vanilla?"

"No, no," Marley said firmly. "It's any ice cream flavour and any fizzy drink. When it starts to fizz up, it looks like a web."

"That makes *no* sense. Language is weird," Lyra said, chuckling. Her phone pipped and she flicked the screen on. "Oh. Alex is going to come get me from here if that's okay? He'll be here in a minute."

"Sure," Amy said. "Did you send us a link to the place so we could have a look at it?"

"I haven't even seen it," Lyra said, reaching for her wallet to toss a few notes onto the table. "It's a surprise, apparently."

"A surprise viewing?" Marley made a sceptical face. "He should at least have sent you a link. What if it's an outright no from you?"

Lyra laughed. "If he wants me to see it, it's not a no." She smiled happily. "He knows me pretty well by now." She stood, spotting Alex's car and waving him towards them. She ducked to kiss both girls. "We nailed the dresses, ladies." She high-fived them both. "Now we just need to finish planning the hen's party!"

Amy inwardly sighed with relief, knowing at least *that* wasn't her responsibility. "Don't forget Marley's baby shower," she added. "Although that's almost all planned."

"Can't we combine them somehow?" Marley asked.

Lyra and Amy exchanged a glance. Combining a drink-

WEDDING BELLS AT LILAC BAY

free baby shower with what they hoped would be a wild hen's night didn't exactly sound like a great idea.

"I'm kidding," Marley said on a sigh. "Or, at least I wasn't until I saw your faces. Amy, I'll be there with bells on. Cow bells," she added jokingly, examining one puffy hand.

The girls grinned. Alex pulled into a parking spot right outside the cafe and rolled down the window, leaning out. "Hello ladies, was the trip a success?"

"Yes," they chorused.

Amy looked at Lyra. Her face was split wide into a smile, her eyes trained on Alex's handsome face as her cheeks pinked.

"Alright, get out of here!" Amy said, tapping Lyra's backside playfully.

Lyra grinned and jogged towards the car, leaning in through the window to kiss Alex slowly. The smile on his face was so dazed when she finished that Amy was worried he wouldn't be able to drive.

"Get a room!" Marley hollered.

"That's exactly what we're off to do," Alex said, grinning. He tooted the horn as they zipped away.

"Can you take me home?" Marley yawned soon after. "I need a second nap."

"Sure," Amy chuckled. "That baby really is giving you a hard time."

"It's stealing my energy, my looks and about half my brainpower, and giving me the water retention of a hippo in return."

"I have to disagree," Amy said. "You still look absolutely beautiful."

Marley grinned, rubbing her belly. "You're sweet for saying so. But I don't. And I wouldn't have it any other way."

3
SATURDAY

"How'd dress shopping go?" Pam asked Amy when she rustled through the Ford household living room with her bags.

"Well, thanks," Amy replied coolly. She was bristling—and not for the first time—at the fact she still had to ring the doorbell to come in. She stayed with Pam and Rick at their family home most nights, but Pam wouldn't let her have a key. Rick had tried to ask a few times but for some reason Pam ended up in tears whenever he pushed. Amy's Bondi Beach apartment wasn't accessible for the wheelchair Rick still needed a lot of the time. The strength in his legs was coming back, but recovery was an unsteady science.

"You chose the dresses, then?" Pam persisted, trailing Amy into the house and towards Rick's room.

"Yep," Amy threw over her shoulder, surprised Pam wasn't getting the hint that she didn't want to talk.

"Amy, stop."

Amy gave herself a moment to school her features into a neutral expression, then turned to Pam.

"Could I see the dresses, please?"

"Sure." Amy thrust the bag towards her. "I'll go say hi to Rick."

She found Rick on his bed, laptop open. The frown of concentration on his face made Amy's heart squeeze. She leaned against the jamb, soaking up the sight of him—her gorgeous *fiancé*. His hair hung over his forehead a little and it was tucked behind his ear on one side, revealing both his dimple, as he bit his lip in concentration, and the scar that Amy had come to love so much. He glanced up from the screen and grinned at her, making her stomach flip.

A second later, Pam clogged beside Amy in the doorway, the bag of dresses crashing into Amy's leg with a pointy end. Amy pressed her nails into her palm to keep her irritation down.

Rick closed his laptop. "Both my women," he said.

Pam beamed. "You want some lunch, honey?"

Rick tilted his head. "Ames?"

"Thanks, but I already ate." She hadn't had anything aside from the ice-cream float, but right now she didn't feel like being around a table with Pam, making polite conversation. She wanted to flop onto Rick's bed and have him rub her shoulders while she heard about how his project was going. She had a ton of work to do as well. Just the thought of it was making her itchy.

"Then I'm good, too, Mum," Rick said. "I'll have something later."

Amy sat beside Rick on the bed and smiled at Pam, hoping she'd take that as her cue to leave them alone and close the door.

Instead, Pam pursed her lips. "Richard. You need to eat."

"Mum, I'm fine. I ate a huge breakfast." He turned pointedly to Amy. "How was the shopping trip, Ames?"

"Breakfast was hours ago," Pam persisted, before Amy could open her mouth.

Rick smiled patiently at her. "Mum, I'm not going to starve to death."

"Amy, please. Could you tell him to eat?"

Amy felt her blood pressure rising. She shot Rick a *help me* look, not wanting to get caught between the two of them. He closed his eyes, exhaling. "Okay, Mum. I'll have, I don't know, a sandwich or something."

"Good. I'll make three." She turned and rustled off down the corridor with Amy's bridesmaid dresses, leaving the door wide open.

Amy groaned softly, heaved herself off the bed, and closed it—resisting the urge to slam it.

"Sorry," Rick said, biting his lip as she returned to the bed.

And there was the problem. If Amy lost her temper at Pam, it was Rick she hurt. If she made it known how frustrated she felt, it was Rick who felt guilty, Rick who got irritated with the slow pace of his healing. At the same time ... she didn't know how to keep things from him. Since they'd managed to overcome that big hiccup in their past—where Rick had lied about what he did for a living—they'd sworn never to have secrets between them. Still ... she was determined to keep her growing irritation with Pam to herself, though she was finding it harder and harder.

"It's fine," she said, suddenly weary, and leaned over to kiss him. At least that would make her mind go suitably blank and stop her having to formulate any further response. When they broke apart a long moment later, frustrated and breathless, it was in time to hear Pam calling them from the kitchen.

"Tell me later how the trip went?" Rick asked, swinging his legs off the bed and into his chair. Amy marvelled at how comfortable and dexterous he looked doing that now. It had been a slow, clunky movement at first. Now it seemed second nature.

WEDDING BELLS AT LILAC BAY

Pam had set out ham, cheese and tomato sandwiches and mixed up a fruit cordial for each of them. She'd cut Rick's sandwich in half, a detail that set Amy's teeth on edge.

"So, the colour of the bridesmaid dresses is ... an interesting choice," Pam began once they were all seated. She washed a bite of her sandwich down with the juice, holding Amy's gaze.

Amy bit heartily into hers to buy herself some time. "The girls chose them," she said with a shrug. "And they're the ones who have to wear them, so it's fine with me." She chose not to mention that she was drowning in her to-do lists. For work, the wedding and house-hunting. Things were in danger of overwhelming her, and now she'd *finally* crossed bridesmaids' dresses from the list.

"Hmm." Pam appeared to contemplate this. "You've still got the receipt though, so if something better comes along, you could return them, right?"

Rick's eyes darted to Amy.

"I don't think I'll be returning them." Amy kept her voice impressively level. "It's hard to get both girls together now, and Lyra's on tour for a lot of the lead up to the wedding."

"But you know her size, don't you?"

"Excuse me?"

"I mean, in theory, you could get her something else ... Just *if* you found something better. She doesn't really need to be there to try it on."

Amy slowly sipped her drink. Pam's face was bright and open, her gaze studiously unassuming. Amy wasn't fooled for a second. "Pam, I like the dresses. I'll keep them. So there's no need to worry about Lyra's size."

"No, I'm only saying. For instance if we found something in a nice mint colour that would go with the flower arrangements a little better."

"The flower arrangements can easily be tweaked. I'd

much rather do that than try and get the girls back together and force a pregnant Marley out dress shopping again."

Pam's lips pressed together in a thin line. "I have a friend who has an online store, she had some beautiful dresses in there. The mint green really--"

Rick lowered his sandwich and spoke firmly. "Mum, if Amy's happy with the dresses, then she's happy with the dresses."

Pam held her hands up dramatically. "I'm just saying, that's all! There's no need to bite my head off."

"He didn't—" Amy began, but Rick laid a silencing hand on her leg under the table.

Amy counted to five, drawing in a long breath as quietly as she could. Then she smiled at Pam. "Thanks for thinking of it, but really, we're good with the dresses."

"It'll be hard to get a pocket square for the groomsmen in that colour."

"I'll ask the store. Maybe they have more fabric."

Pam made a face like, *it's your funeral* and picked up her sandwich again. "You'll put Lauren next to me, at the wedding dinner table, won't you?"

"Probably not actually," Amy said, surprised. "You'll be in the bridal section of the table, and there won't be room for Lauren there."

Pam frowned. "But she's dating the Best Man."

"Who'll be sitting beside the Maid of Honour," Amy pointed out mildly.

Pam frowned. "Well, that doesn't seem right, does it, Richard?" She shot her gaze to Rick for support. He drew a breath, but before he could answer, Pam continued. "Lauren somewhere down the table by herself?"

"She can sit by Finn and Alex, or with the girls from work," Amy said. "They're easy to get along with, and it's only for the duration of the dinner."

Pam considered. "What about if I'm down the end of the bridal section, and then Lauren's the first person in the non-bridal section?"

"Maybe … you wouldn't really be near us, then," Amy said.

"If you show me the seating arrangements, I'm sure I can make it work."

"Mum, please," Rick said, struggling against his temper. "Is it that big of a deal if you don't sit next to Lauren? Would it be so horrible to sit near your son and daughter-in-law for an hour-long dinner?"

"Oh, Richard, of course I don't mean that," Pam said. "Amy's parents will be there, and I'll be …" She broke off, her chin wobbling as she swallowed audibly. "Your father …"

Rick made a sympathetic noise and Amy felt a wave of guilt wash over her. She hadn't considered that aspect of things. It must be difficult to think of watching your youngest son get married without his father present. Dane Ford had passed away several years earlier and Amy knew it was still a raw wound—for both Rick and Pam.

"Pam, my parents aren't together," Amy began gently. "It's my mum and stepdad, and they'll be as far from me as I can politely put them, and then my Pop and his girlfriend. Maybe we could organise a dinner with those two ahead of the wedding, so you can get to know them."

"Percy's awesome," Rick added.

"And then of course we can find a way to sit you by Lauren anyway," Amy finished.

Pam sniffed. "Are you sure?"

"Yes." Amy reached her hand across the table, covering Pam's with hers. "Of course. Sorry for not having thought of it."

Pam nodded, pulling her hand back to dab her eyes with

her napkin. "What about your father?" Pam asked. "Didn't you say he'd be coming?"

"Yes ... he'll be there somewhere. That's ... I have to find a way to keep him and my stepfather apart. I *was* going to sit him beside my Pop, but ..." Amy's phone rang at that moment with a video call from her father. "Oh! Speak of the devil. Do you mind if I quickly grab this?" Pam and Rick shook their heads and Amy stood from the table. She wouldn't normally have been so keen to talk to her father, but it was a good excuse to quickly wrap up an awkward conversation.

Video calls from Sean were still a rarity, but slowly becoming more common—though it had been five weeks since their last one. After he and Amy had reconnected, their relationship had gotten off to a sputtering, faltering start. He'd still been gambling; a fact Amy had found almost unbelievable after everything it had cost him and their family. She'd worked long and hard on trying to let her anger go, but his delusions still annoyed and upset her. He was convinced he was close to a "winning streak", and all Amy could do was avoid the topic. It was that or cut him back out of her life, and she didn't have the stomach for that again.

She swiped up to answer the call and sucked in a sharp breath when she took in his face. "Oh my *god*, Dad. You look amazing!"

On screen, Sean Porter beamed into the camera. When Amy had first seen him again after the long years of estrangement, he'd been a mess. Totally unkempt, bloated, all the light gone from his face. He'd remained the same since then—until now, that was. The man onscreen looked *sharp*, if slightly flushed and sweaty. His blue eyes were bright and alert, he was outside, and his face had hollowed back out to reveal the chiselled features so long hidden.

He laughed, and there was true happiness in it. "You don't

need to sound so surprised," he said. "I just finished a run. Doing my cooldown walk and I thought I'd give you a call."

Amy settled onto the sofa in the living room, tucking her legs up beside her. She grinned into the camera. "Wow. You've started jogging?"

"Yep," he beamed. "Wanna see what a difference it's making?"

"I can already see it in your face!"

Sean held the camera up high and panned down over himself. He looked trim and toned—much more like the version of himself Amy had known before everything went bad. There was something about it that made her feel odd and stirred up traces of memories she thought were long gone, though she was happy for him.

"You look great, Dad," she said, only a hint of a wobble in her voice. "What inspired you?"

He blinked at her as though she was being dense. "Your *wedding*, of course! Can't have your father looking sloppy in front of all your friends, can we?"

"Dad, you didn't need to—"

He held up a hand, shaking his head. "I should have done it years ago, Baby Girl. I feel *great*. And … I've kicked the gambling too. Or, at least I've learned enough to know that I'll always be a gambler," he clarified, his expression earnest. "But consider me 'sober'. Couple of weeks now. I've been going to a group."

"Oh, Dad," Amy breathed. "That's wonderful." Amy silenced the part of her brain that screamed *too little, too late*, and focused instead on the fact that it was positive news.

"Yeah." He smiled shyly as though he was a little embarrassed and Amy's heart swelled. "Where are you? Doesn't look like your place?"

"I'm at Pam's place. Rick's mum. They're in the other room eating, so I won't talk long."

"Ah. Do you fancy flashing my face at them, so I can say a quick hello? We're going to be, what, joint parents-in-law?" He grinned.

"Oh, I don't …"

"Bring him in!" Pam called from the dining room.

Great. So they'd been able to hear all that then. Amy's face grew heated and she pushed herself up from the sofa. "I'll show you for a very quick hi, okay? And then I have to run."

"Sure."

Amy re-entered the dining room with the screen turned to face Pam and Rick. She hovered near the edge of the table as Rick shot her a sympathetic look and Pam squinted towards the camera.

"Hello, Sean," she said lightly. "It's lovely to meet you finally."

"You too, Pamela," he replied. "Sorry, I've been out running and I'm not at my best. Promise I'll scrub up better for the rehearsal dinner."

Pam flapped her hand at the screen, a coy smile teasing the corners of her mouth. "Oh, hush. You caught us here all scruffy-looking, eating our snack."

"Well, you could've fooled me," Sean said.

A silence fell and Amy realised with alarm that Pam and Sean were grinning at each other. Rick was studying his mother's face, clearly as aware of the pink tinge spreading across it as Amy was. He looked mildly horrified.

"Okay, Dad," Amy said quickly, swivelling the phone back to her. "I'd better head off."

"See you later, Mr Porter."

"Oh, please! Call me Sean!"

Rick swallowed and Amy waved a quick goodbye, hanging up the call. She settled back into her spot around the table, picking her sandwich back up and trying to steady her nerves. She was shocked to see her father like that. Looking so well. Looking … *handsome* again. And as though he was actually participating in life.

After a moment, Pam cleared her throat, eyes trained firmly on her empty plate. "Maybe it would be nice if we organised that dinner you mentioned, Amy? Perhaps we can better discuss the seating arrangements once we all know one another a little more."

Rick glanced up sharply at his mother, then darted his eyes towards Amy, realising she'd noticed the look.

"All good, Rick?" Amy asked pointedly.

"Yep," he replied, not entirely convincingly. "All good."

4
SATURDAY

"Wow, I already love it from the front," Lyra said, turning to beam at Alex as they pulled up to the unassuming brown-brick single-story in Sydney's Inner West. The lawn was neatly-kept and the front balcony gleamed. The trim looked freshly painted and the neighbourhood was quiet and green.

Alex grinned back at her. "I hoped you would. Shall we go in?"

Lyra frowned slightly, looking at the house then back at Alex. "This surely can't be in our budget though?"

"Come on." He unclicked his seatbelt, beckoning her out of the car. "Let's just go check it out before we worry about that."

The real estate agent waiting for them introduced herself as Alicia, and Lyra was surprised to realise they were the only couple visiting the place. Usually viewings in Sydney meant sharpening your elbows and stalking the competition like prey, doing anything to commandeer the agent's time. There must be something wrong with the house, if no one else had bothered to show up. But ... Lyra couldn't find the flaw from the outside, if there was one.

"There's a hidden sprinkler system through the lawn, and you'll notice the plants are natives, so it's very low maintenance," Alicia said, then held open the front door for them.

"Wow," Lyra breathed, as they entered a small sunroom that ran the length of the front of the house. It was fitted with comfy-looking armchairs and deep-pile carpet. Filtered sunlight streamed in and potted plants brought life to the space.

Lyra's eyes widened and she looped her arm through Alex's, pulling him close. He grinned down at her, squeezing her arm back—obviously as excited as she was.

From there, they were led into an open-plan living-kitchen-dining area, with high ceilings and skylights that added an outdoor feel. It was bright and airy, modestly but tastefully furnished. But what Lyra noticed most was the quiet. She felt her shoulders relaxing as Alicia guided them through the large master bedroom—complete with small walk-in-robe that led to a tiny en-suite—and two smaller bedrooms off a little corridor. The laundry was generous, with a deep sink and lots of storage space. The main bathroom was fitted with pale peach tiling and had a deep tub that Lyra could picture herself soaking in.

She realised she hadn't let go of Alex's arm since they'd arrived, clenching it in enthusiasm with each new thing they saw. When they reached the back door and she looked out at the small, tidy yard with the picturesque little wooden shed, she clamped down so hard on him that he yelped.

"Sorry!" she said, easing her grip. He smiled down at her, pleased that she was so delighted.

They pushed through the door into the yard and Lyra breathed in deeply. The scent of mulberries filled the air and she spotted two bushes heavy with fruit. The grass was plump beneath her feet, and tall hedges screened them from the neighbours.

"Perfect for a bunch of kids," Alex sighed, looking around with a soft smile.

Beside him, Lyra froze. When their eyes met, she could see the horror in his features. He clearly hadn't meant to say that out loud. She cleared her throat, tearing her eyes from Alex as heat rose to her cheeks. It was a discussion they hadn't had in a while, and she was aware it was long overdue. But now was definitely not the time.

"How come we're the only ones here?" she asked Alicia quickly.

The agent blinked before smiling politely. "There are ... perceived issues in the surrounding area that have kept some people away."

Lyra's shoulders slumped. She knew it was too good to be true. All those months of looking, they'd never seen anything this nice that was remotely in their price range. "What issues?"

Alicia bit her lip. "There's a home for refugees nearby, in a converted warehouse."

They waited for further explanation. None came.

"And?" Lyra prompted.

Alicia shrugged. "That's it. But we've seen the values in this area fall significantly since it opened."

"That has to be a joke, right?" Lyra frowned.

"I wish it was," she sighed. "In any case, that's the only thing that speaks against the house. There's a current building inspection that declares it structurally sound. The crime rate hasn't increased, which seems to have been the main concern, and there's no damage to anything surrounding the group home. There is a high security fence around the building, but I believe that's more about keeping the people inside safe. Or, at least I'd like to think."

Lyra's mouth was open in disbelief. "But that can't be all there is to the lower price?"

"As I explained to your partner, there's something psychological about it," Alicia said. "People in the area have been worried about it devaluing their properties and it becomes a self-fulfilling prophecy because they hurry to get out before the values fall. The owners of this place aren't leaving because of that, they're joining a retirement village, but the asking price has been significantly pulled down by recent sales in the area. Honestly, I've been struggling to even find viewers for this place. And in the current climate, it's unheard of."

Lyra turned her eyes to Alex, who was frowning, his jaw tight. She couldn't tell whether he still felt weird about his earlier comment about children, or whether he was upset at what they were hearing about the neighbourhood.

"That's pretty sickening," he said. "People being ostracised in the community where they're supposed to find safe haven."

Lyra pulled him closer. "This place is a *dream*," she sighed. "Not too big and not too small. And so peaceful."

"You know you're not supposed to look so eager in front of the agent?" he joked, but she could hear the tension in his voice.

Alicia grinned. "Who has time for games when you're standing somewhere like this?"

The buzzing of Lyra's phone interrupted them and she pulled it from her pocket. "It's Jake. Can you give me one second? Just one."

A muscle popped in Alex's jaw at the mention of her band member, but he quickly cleared his expression and nodded. "Of course."

Lyra stepped inside. "Jake, what it is?"

"It's this hook."

"Yeah, I saw the message about it. Can it really not wait? I'm in the middle of—"

"No, it absolutely can't. This will be super quick! Even Mags agreed this one couldn't wait."

"Okay," Lyra relented. "If she told you to, then play it really quick, okay? …"

Alex turned to peer at her through the glass back door and Lyra rolled her eyes, mouthing "sorry." He gave her a tight smile.

Jake set her on speakerphone and played the notes for her. The melody was short, haunting and catchy. Lyra's eyes lit up in surprise. "Wow," she breathed. "I *love* that! That's absolutely perfect. Were you thinking of it for the …"

"Yep, for *Undone*."

"Yes! Same! Does Maggie have a bass line for it yet?"

"Yes, I do!" Lyra heard Maggie say.

"You're there, too?"

"Yup!"

"And Kit?"

A short drumbeat sounded and Lyra giggled. "I can't believe you're all there without me."

"Well, we did try!" Jake yelled

"Okay, okay. Are you all staying there for a bit? You know it's the weekend, right?"

"Waiting for you!" they chorused in unison.

"You're all nuts," Lyra grinned. "I'll be right there."

She quickly stepped into the back yard.

"Alex, I am *so* sorry. Can we …?" She glanced around, frowning. "I don't want to let this place go, but I need to get to the studio."

"On a Saturday?" His voice was flat.

"I know. Only for a few hours."

Alicia looked at Lyra with sudden recognition. "Oh, I *thought* you looked familiar. You're Lyra, aren't you? I'm a big fan."

"Yes, that's me." Lyra blushed. "Thank you."

"You really need to head in?" Alex asked, and Lyra hated the note of disappointment in his voice.

"This song," she explained, "it's all coming together. And everyone's available right now, it's … we *have* to get this down. I feel really inspired. We leave in three weeks and we can test this out on a live audience if we get it right. Please don't be mad?" Lyra made her eyes round and pleading.

He puffed out a breath. "I can never be mad, so you can put those puppy dog peepers away."

"We can continue the discussion, or negotiation," Alicia added, with a note of hope, "online or over the phone, now that you've seen the place in person."

"Okay, phew." Lyra glanced around the backyard again. It really was perfect.

"I'll definitely be in touch," Alex told Alicia, as they headed for their cars.

As they drove out of the Inner West towards the city centre, Lyra sighed. "Gosh, that place is perfect. And it's so close to the studio as well."

"Yeah, I really liked it, too. As soon as I saw it online, I knew I wanted us to look at it. I definitely thought there was a mistake with the price though."

"It's so ridiculous."

"Yeah," Alex said grimly. "I can't imagine anyone disagreeing with a facility in principle, but I guess no one wants it in their own backyard. Oh well. We win." As they pulled up outside the studio, Alex shut off the engine and turned to her, looking serious. "About what I said in the back yard…"

Lyra flapped her hand. "It's totally fine. Let's talk later? Okay?"

He held her gaze, then nodded. "Sure. Good idea." She leaned to kiss him goodbye.

"You want me to pick you up?"

Lyra beamed at him. "You wouldn't mind?"

"Of course not. What time?"

Lyra glanced at her watch. "Two hours?"

"I'll give you three," Alex grinned.

Lyra pulled him close, giggling. "You know me too well." She searched his face with worried eyes. "You're definitely not mad with me?"

"Nah." He tucked a strand of hair behind her ear and kissed her hard.

Lyra's face was flushed as she watched him pull away before entering the building. She hated being away from him, hated that following her passion often meant sacrificing time with her love. And she was also dreading the baby conversation. She knew how badly Alex wanted kids, and how hard he tried never to mention that to her, in case she felt pressured. She wanted them too, but now wasn't the time. Not when her career was in top gear. She toyed with the locket she always wore—the one that had been her mother's—as she strode through the main hall, wondering how long she could ask him to wait.

Then the notes Jake had shared with her rang through her head and she practically jogged the rest of the way to meet up with her band.

5
SATURDAY

As Lyra entered the studio, even Maggie was smiling—a beam that lit up her normally poker-faced features and made her freckled nose crinkle prettily. The smile took Lyra's pride in their song to a new height.

She'd badly miss Alex, her brother, her girlfriends and Mick—her previous keyboard player who was more like a father figure. But she was also getting excited for her band's upcoming tour. This would be their second stint on the road, but their first as a complete outfit instead of with the temporary keyboard player they'd used last tour. Lyra knew she worked well on the road with Maggie and Kit—"Yep, my name's Kit and I play drums. I *guarantee* I've heard the joke you're about to tell". They had good chemistry on stage and all enjoyed retiring to the cramped tour bus for a casual drink or two to unwind before a sensible, early-ish night. Jake was more of an unknown quantity, but he had slotted into the band with such ease that Lyra felt sure the dynamic would be just as good on the road.

"That was fine," Maggie said, nodding. "I liked it."

"Someone call the press," Jake joked. "Maggie said it was *fine*."

"I say nice things all the time." Maggie shrugged, taking a swig from her water bottle. "Just not to jerks."

Jake grinned, knowing full well that was a Maggie-compliment, and Kit jubilantly flipped a drumstick in the air. Their producer, a hyperactive, bespectacled Scot named Julian Pillard-Ffinch, was pacing around the space, nodding.

"Yep," he said finally, almost to himself. He waved his forefinger erratically, as though tapping to a beat none of them could hear. "Yep. Yep. Ready."

Lyra raised an eyebrow at Maggie who widened her eyes.

"Everyone's dismissed," Julian added, flapping his hand.

The four of them exchanged a glance. They hadn't even been summoned, in order to be dismissed. They were there because they'd wanted to rehearse.

"Wait," Julian added. "Lyra, Jake, please stay back."

Lyra clenched her jaw to keep from sighing as she glanced at her watch. Alex would be outside waiting. She was feeling very protective over the little time they had left together before her trip, especially as she'd interrupted their house-hunting to come in.

"So, not *everyone* dismissed then?" she couldn't help saying.

"Huh?" Julian snapped his eyes to hers, seeming genuinely not to have heard her.

"Nothing," Lyra mumbled.

Once the others had left, Julian spent a long moment sizing her and Jake up. Jake didn't seem the least bit worried, but internally, Lyra was squirming. She wasn't sure what this was about, but she hoped it was quick.

"Lyra, I understand you're in a relationship?"

"Yes?" Lyra frowned at him, her head reeling back slightly. Beside her, Jake cocked his head.

"You?" Julian asked him.

"Single. Are you allowed—"

"How serious is it?" Julian demanded of Lyra, his eyes already back on her.

"*What?*"

"With you and your … boyfriend? Girlfriend?"

"Boyfriend. And very. I'm *super* taken," she emphasised. "Why?"

Julian twisted his mouth.

"Where are you going with this, man?" Jake asked.

"Selena and I have been talking."

"And …?" Lyra prompted, after a long moment of silence.

"You and Jake test well together. We want you to have a *thing*. Or, be *believed* to be having a thing."

Lyra genuinely thought she'd misheard. Then she thought she must have misunderstood. "A thing? We have a thing. We have the band?" She flicked her puzzled glance to Jake, found him watching her intently. She held his steady gaze for a moment, realisation dawning. Her mouth fell open in disbelief.

"Why?" Jake asked, turning back to Julian, before Lyra could ask anything else.

Lyra held up a hand. "Sorry. That's not the question here. The question is *are you actually crazy?*"

"No, we're not." Julian held her gaze levelly. "It'll boost your numbers. Also gets people excited. They want to see if they can catch some of that frisson on stage. A shared moment, a little hint, a small display of affection. You two can do radio interviews together. Pretend to be reluctant to talk about it, you know, all giggly and shy," he mimed covering his mouth like a schoolgirl, "but drop enough that people are panting for more. You're both very good-looking, young and talented. The key demographics would *eat* it up. You two as a couple tested only slightly behind Lyra and

Maggie. But we're still playing on the wholesome image so we're not going to stray into queer territory … Oh, and they'd like it even more if Jake *fell first*." Julian made air quotes around the phrase. "And most important is showcasing a situation where Jake has to protect you. We're thinking," he waved his hands through the air, as though grasping for inspiration, "a crazed fan running on stage and he leaps to your defence, or … I don't know, a stalker or something. What's really working well right now is caveman protectiveness. Like he'll *kill* someone who hurts you. That stuff is off-the-charts effective."

Lyra blinked, her brain reeling. The moment was equal parts surreal and nauseating. She'd be laughing if she wasn't so shocked. If Alex even heard them discussing this … Never mind Alex, *she* didn't want to hear another word of this stupidity. Lyra strode to the corner of the room and heaved up her backpack. She swung it onto her shoulders, then returned to face Julian and Jake, both of whom were staring at her.

"I'm going to say this once," she said carefully, looking back and forth between them. "The answer is a hard, *hard* no. And if this ever gets brought up again, I will walk away from everything."

"Oh, you can't do that," Julian said calmly, with a small shake of the head. "You'd be sued for breach."

"He's right, Ly," Jake added. "Listen, let's talk about this. It doesn't need to be real."

"Of course it won't be real," she snapped. "It won't be anything at all!"

He held up his hands. "I'm only saying we talk about it."

Lyra's gaze was fiery. "You *cannot* be serious."

Jake turned his palms up. "It never hurts to explore all options. This doesn't have to be weird. Especially not if Alex is in on it."

Lyra stared at him, open-mouthed. "You want me to tell the man I love that I'm going to fake-date the guy I'll be on the road for three weeks with?" She laughed sarcastically. "Even if he lost his mind and was okay with it, I. Am. *Not*."

"Not good," Julian said, shaking his head rapidly. "Selena didn't really *suggest* this." He paused, and Lyra's brain filled in the gap. She didn't suggest it—she ordered it. "The tour photographer is primed. An 'inside source' will drop a hint to the gossip rags and music press. We're still figuring out the details of the whole touch-her-and-you-die thing, but we'll get there."

"Call it off," Lyra said angrily. "Call *everything* off. This is not a circus. I'm not an actor, I'm a singer. I do not agree, I do not consent. I won't do *anything* of the sort. If Jake tries to touch me, I'll crack his jaw. On stage, off stage, I don't care. If a crazed fan comes up, I'll tell the crowd they were hired. I am not joking. About *any* of this. Do you hear me?"

Jake was chewing his lip. "Ly. Let's not give hasty answers right now." He tipped his head meaningfully towards Julian, raising his eyebrows as if promising her they would discuss it rationally once he was gone. "Let's just think it over? Okay?"

Lyra took a step closer to him, until their noses were almost touching. She heard Jake's breath hitch and then quicken, but he didn't back off.

"No," she said loudly. Then she turned her head, caught Julian's eye and repeated herself. "Absolutely, one hundred and fifty percent, *no.* See you later."

She walked out of the room, down the hall, through the big lobby and out through the revolving doors into the fresh evening air.

It was only once she saw Alex waiting in the car that she realised how much she was shaking.

6
SUNDAY

"It's definitely better in the burnt umber," Ernie said, eyeing up the sofa in the furniture showroom. "Don't you think, Si?"

"Yeah, it's great." Silas shrugged. They'd been looking at sofas for hours—Ernie was apparently indefatigable in his ability to stalk through showroom after showroom in mall after mall. Everything had started looking alike to Silas approximately six shops ago. He'd started the day determined to reign Ernie's spending in. Now, Silas was ready to wave his credit card and eternal gratitude at whomever could get Ernie to actually *buy* something.

"What? Why are you shrugging? Why are you saying it so dismissively?" Ernie squinted at him in concern. "Shrugging isn't good. You like it, don't you? I know it's not *black*, but you weren't being serious. We can't have a black sofa."

Silas bit his tongue to keep from saying he'd be happy with a plank of wood or an upturned bin at this point.

Ernie turned to the saleswoman in alarm. "You said this was limited edition, right?"

She nodded blandly. She was exactly the kind of sales

assistant Silas usually loved. One who didn't say anything unless she was asked, and didn't push a purchase on them. Now, he was silently wishing she had even a spark of commission hunger in her.

"If it's limited edition, we should definitely get it," Silas said quickly. "You wouldn't want to miss out. This is the one you've been most enthusiastic about. And you've been enthusiastic a *lot*."

Ernie's shoulders dropped. "Si, this is our first big furniture purchase together. We have to both absolutely love it. Can you tell me what you *really* think of it?"

"I think it's a brown couch."

"It's *burnt umber*," Ernie groaned.

"Right."

Ernie peered at Silas for a moment before his expression softened. "You *do* like it don't you? You're trying to torture me. You're the *worst*. Admit it."

Silas decided to play along, for the sake of closing a deal. He slung his arm over Ernie's shoulder and pulled him closer. "I love it. It's comfortable and you're happy."

Ernie let out a small squeal and hugged Silas tightly. "I *knew* you couldn't really be so blasé about such a perfect shade. We'll take it," he said, gesturing to the sales assistant, who smiled placidly again.

She gestured them towards the counter and they trailed her, Ernie's grin lighting up half the store.

"You know we have to wait five weeks for delivery if we're getting that shade, right?" Silas asked.

"Can you really put a timeline on perfection?" Ernie shot back, digging Silas's ribs with an elbow.

"That's your idea of perfection? A brown couch?"

"I said it's *burnt* … grrr." Ernie pulled Silas's arm to bring him to a stop as the sales assistant moved ahead. Then he dropped his voice, staring Silas in the eye. "And *no*. I'm looking at perfection right now."

Silas rolled his eyes and shoved Ernie lightly, ignoring the ripple of goosebumps that spread down his spine. He could never let Ernie know how much he secretly loved his over-the-top declarations of affection.

"Okay, okay. Let's go get this done. You're bankrupting me, you know that?"

"And again I ask you, can you put a price on perfection?"

Silas chuckled. At the counter, he gave their address to the assistant, who slowly keyed it in and took his credit card.

"I think you owe me a beer after this," he said, expecting Ernie to be by his side. He wasn't, and Silas glanced around in surprise. He spotted Ernie a few feet away, eyes glued to his phone and a grin spread from ear to ear. "Erns? You 'gramming it already?"

"Huh?" Ernie snapped his head up and quickly clicked off his phone, pocketing it with a slightly guilty expression. "What were you saying about beer?" He closed the gap between them, looping his arm through Silas's.

Silas had never seen Ernie squirrel his phone away like that. Usually, his boyfriend was excited to share *any* titbit of his news, filling silences with more details than Silas cared to either hear or remember. For a split second, Silas contemplated asking what Ernie had been doing on his phone, but decided to savour the peace and mystery instead.

"You owe me a beer," Silas repeated. "Maybe—"

"What about somewhere on Darling Harbour?" Ernie asked quickly.

"Meh." Silas wrinkled his nose.

Ernie made pleading eyes. "Come on. Can't we get dressed up and go out properly? I hardly ever get to show you off."

"At a place that costs like eighteen bucks a drink?"

Ernie groaned. "I'm paying, remember?"

"Because you owe *me*." Silas countered. "Shouldn't it be my choice?"

Ernie's shoulders slumped. "You're going to make me take you to that dingy little place down the road that shows the greyhound races on that old cathode ray TV, aren't you?"

Silas bit his lip. "Oh, alright," he relented. "If you want to go *out* out, we can."

"Okay, sounds good." Ernie bounced a little on the spot. "Let's invite Mick and Kathryn? And maybe see if Lyra and Alex are free?"

"That's not a bad idea. It's been a while."

"Right? And Mick's birthday is coming up. Lyra's on tour then, so we need to take him out then, too. But it would be great to see him before that."

Silas grunted, but inside he felt almost unbearably squishy. Ernie had claimed Silas's family as his own and was often the one to bring them together as a group. Ernie had zero chill, and if he was in, he was in one thousand per cent. He was like that with everything—an endearing if exhausting trait—but Silas especially loved that he was like that with his family.

One of the store's salesmen slowly cruised by the till, pointedly trying to hold Silas's gaze as he did so. The man was well-built, with a thick thatch of golden-brown hair and a chiselled jawline stubbled just-so. After he passed, he glanced back over his shoulder at Silas, biting his lip in a display so obvious that Silas fought to keep from laughing. Ernie noticed, and distractedly tightened his grip on Silas's arm as he peppered the saleswoman with question about caring for the couch fabric. They were both used to this kind of thing now—the double-takes Silas got from both men and women. Silas wasn't blind to his own good looks. When people realised he and Ernie were a couple, they automatically thought Ernie was punching well above his weight.

But Silas knew the truth—he was lucky beyond measure to have this man at his side.

Burnt umber couches and all.

7
SUNDAY

Marley stirred awake as Finn set a steaming cup of peppermint tea on the coffee table with a gentle clack.

"Oh God," she groaned. "Did I really fall asleep again?" She wiped the corner of her mouth and struggled to sit up.

Finn grinned and helped her upright, before sitting beside her and slipping an arm over her shoulders. "Yeah. Shopping for dresses yesterday must have wiped you out! But I've always found snoring and dribbling cute, so don't worry."

She swatted him, her mind still groggy with sleep. "I hadn't realised how much stuff there was to do with a wedding until I went out with Amy." She blinked dramatically. "I'm glad we're not having one."

He smiled at her and leaned to rub her tummy. "How's the bean today?"

"Active as anything." She placed her hand on top of his, guiding it to where she could feel the baby wriggling. "It's so reassuring to feel it."

Finn's face lit up as he pressed his hand gently against her mid-section, and he swallowed to try and cope with his emotion. He got overwhelmed every time he felt that movement inside of her—growing stronger every day. Before he could get too sentimental, she poked her knitting bag with her foot.

"I need to get cracking on that little set of booties I'm making."

Finn laughed. "I really didn't know it took so long to knit such small things."

"Hey!" Marley said, mock-defensively. "If you think you can do better, be my guest."

He held his hands up in surrender. "They're beautiful. And quality things take time." He generously neglected to mention that the booties were hideously misshapen and that they would likely never be used, unless they duct-taped them to the baby's feet.

"I'll get better. *Surely*. Ouch!" she yelped, when the baby pushed up into her solar plexus suddenly.

Finn leaned down to her belly, a stern look on his face. "Baby Mayberry, you listen to me. You stop giving your mother grief, okay?" He glanced up at Marley as he felt her freeze. "What?"

"I, uh ... Baby Mayberry? It'll be a Phelps."

It was Finn's turn to freeze. He slowly straightened up, eyes wide as he looked at her. "Wow." He puffed out a breath and pushed a hand through his thick black hair, the deep pools of his blue eyes turning murky with worry. "God. How have we not talked about this?"

"I don't know," Marley said sadly.

Finn frowned as he processed it. "But ... yes, of course. You're," he swallowed, shaking his head, "you're giving birth, so ... yes, I think that's right. It should—it should be a Phelps."

Marley was instantly upset for him. "No, Finn, we can

discuss it." She reached a hand out to his, shifting her position to look at him square in the face.

Finn rubbed her knee, lost in thought. "I could change my last name?"

"Even if we're not married?" Marley asked, frowning. "You use it for work! And … oh, God. You'd be Finn Phelps."

"Well, if you changed yours you'd be Marley Mayberry."

"We both sound like cartoon characters. We can hyphenate."

"Baby Phelps-Mayberry? Baby Mayberry-Phelps? I guess so. But let's give the kid a fighting chance…"

Marley couldn't help but smile at that. "Mayberry could be the middle name? It's not a bad name for a child."

"It's not a *good* name either," Finn said. He smiled at her, a trace of sadness in it that pulled at Marley's heart. "I think what we both need is some chocolate chip ice-cream."

"Oh, you read my mind," Marley said, melting into him. "You always know what the baby is demanding."

He leaned to put an ear to her belly, pretending to listen. "What's that? You want extra Ice-Magic on your scoops?"

Marley swatted him again and he rose, chuckling. Her eyes tracked him as he left the living room for the kitchen.

She loved him. More than she'd thought possible. Certainly her previous, ill-fated marriage had never taught her about a love like this. She hated that her love was still tinged with fear and reservation. It wasn't Finn's fault that her marriage to Hayden had been so disastrous, and she constantly felt guilty that he was paying the price for that. His patience was endless and she often felt like she was taking advantage of it, but that didn't stop the hesitation she felt. She scrubbed a hand over her face, wondering if she should squash her reservations and tell Finn to give up his apartment. But she knew she couldn't do it. She still needed that safety hatch and there was no point trying to ignore it.

Finn returned a moment later, proffering two bowls of ice-cream drizzled with caramel sauce. Marley took them both, set them on the coffee table and pulled him close.

"What's happening?" he asked, his eyes turning heavy-lidded as Marley leaned in to kiss him.

"Finn, will we figure this out?" She rested her forehead on his.

"Hmmm, keep kissing me, I think that's helping," he whispered, stroking this thumb along her jaw.

She laughed, then turned serious. "No, Finn, really. Will we fix this?"

"Of course we will," he said, toying with her hair. "It's not a big deal, really, in the scheme of things. It's *our* baby, no matter what it's named."

A silence fell, and Marley's thoughts swirled. She didn't want Finn to have to sacrifice anything, but if she thought of *not* giving her child the same surname as her, tears instantly pricked at her eyes. She sighed, trying to think of a way around things. But it was hard with Finn's hands running through her hair. She was relaxing despite herself, the tension leaving her shoulders, her neck, her head...

A moment later, she was sound asleep. Finn smiled, pulling her close as their ice-creams melted on the coffee table.

8
SUNDAY

For the family dinner he'd managed to pull together at short notice, Ernie chose the Lilac Bay Sailing Club. A small, relatively unassuming venue, it was framed on three sides with floor-to-ceiling windows that let in the stunning view of the waterfront beyond. The clientele were generally the yacht and skiff owners who lived in the area, but the club was open to all and served ultra-fresh seafood at reasonable prices. It was a favourite of Ernie's, not least, Silas knew, because he had a *thing* for all those rugged, outdoorsy men milling around. Silas pretended not to, but he didn't mind the view either.

"Mick!" Ernie cried, practically flinging himself at the older man, as he and his girlfriend Kathryn wove their way through the tables. Silas noted, not for the first time, how contrasting their looks were. Mick's hair was short and thick, but looked like it hadn't seen a brush for a couple of days. He was dressed in black jeans and his favourite leather jacket. Kathryn held his arm proudly, her lips slicked with a pearlescent pink that matched her twin set. But despite the contrast in their looks, it was clear they couldn't keep their hands off one another.

"Hey," Mick said, breaking into a grin and slapping Ernie's back as they hugged. "Si," he added, shaking Silas's hand firmly.

Silas wanted to hug him too. But he'd missed the moment, and instead wrapped Kathryn in a brief squeeze. The four of them took their seats at the table.

"What do you want to drink, Mickey? I'll go to the bar. Are you two alright?" Kathryn asked Silas and Ernie, who nodded.

Once she disappeared with Mick's order, Silas broke into a grin. "*Mickey?*"

Mick smiled sheepishly, rubbing his hand over the grey stubble on his chin. "Oh Mickey you're so fine. You know how it is?"

"I do know your luck's changed since you met her," Silas said. "No more lightning strikes at least."

Mick's eyes trailed Kathryn across the room, a smile playing on his lips. "She's been good for me, that's for sure."

"Well, good enough that you turned down a recording contract for her!" Ernie piped up.

Mick had been Lyra's keyboard player from the moment she'd realised she wanted to sing. They'd gigged together in all sorts of crappy places, until they finally played the gig that landed Lyra a recording contract. The label had wanted Mick, too. But he'd turned them down, arguing he was too old to do things like go on tour. In reality, he'd recently met Kathryn. His wife had left him several years earlier—for his younger brother—and Kathryn had not only changed his luck, she'd made him believe in love again.

"Ah, the kid needed fresh blood anyway," Mick said. "Didn't need some past-his-used-by-date holding her back."

Silas felt a flicker of guilt when they talked about the

recording contract. For a long time, he'd pushed Lyra to leave Mick and find a younger band to support her. He'd meant it in the best possible way—had wanted nothing but success for his sister. But he still struggled to cope with his guilt over the fact he'd been relieved when Mick stepped down. Especially as it had broken Lyra's heart.

"Oh stop it," Ernie gushed, playfully tapping Mick's arm. "Men like you only get better with age!"

"Are you honestly hitting on my dad right in front of me?" Silas joked, then froze. He'd never said that out loud. Never called Mick his *dad*, even though the man had taken on the role of father figure to him for more years than he could count. He felt his face flame and flicked his eyes to Mick's, finding them bright with emotion. He saw the older man take a deep breath as if to steady himself.

"Ohhh," Ernie cooed gently, touching a hand to his heart in reverence. "I'm *so* glad I was here for this moment."

"Shut it," Silas said quickly sharing a sheepish smile with Mick.

"What did I miss?" Kathryn asked, setting down Mick's schooner with a clack and taking her seat beside him.

"Nothing," Silas said quickly, trying to snap them all out of the emotional mood. "Anyone know what time Lyra and Alex are getting here?"

Kathryn checked her phone. "According to my nephew, Lyra woke up from a nap twenty minutes ago. They're on their way in."

"Love a good Sunday nanna-nap," Ernie said.

"I think it's because she's been working so hard." Silas scratched his chin. He was concerned for his sister, but he was also aware that she was living out her dreams. He'd always wanted this for her, and it felt *right* that she was being taken seriously now. Still, he worried about how hard she worked. And he knew Alex did too.

"Apparently another band member made up some kind of," Kathryn squinted at her phone. "*Riff.* And she was at the studio for a long time yesterday."

"Ah." Mick nodded in understanding. "Maybe we can get some starters before they get here, eh? Don't know about anyone else but I could eat a scabby horse between two bread vans."

They ordered prawns to share and were all two drinks deep by the time Lyra and Alex finally arrived.

"I'm so sorry," Lyra cried breathlessly, running straight to Mick and looping her arms around him.

Silas bit the inside of his cheek. He'd always been envious of the easy relationship the two of them shared. Mick had even listed Lyra as his next of kin—needing someone to sign for him during those all-too-frequent hospital trips. They made each other laugh, knew each other inside out, and Mick was the one Lyra went to when she needed advice or help figuring something out. He thought it was kind of neat that Lyra's boyfriend was also Mick's girlfriend's nephew—if a tad incestuous.

"So tell us about this incredible riff then," Mick said, once they were all seated, with orders placed and drinks in their hands.

"Well, it wasn't ideal to go in on a weekend, of course," Lyra began, shooting a glance at Alex.

"Especially in the middle of checking out that house," Ernie added, and Silas glanced at him in surprise. But of course he knew what they'd been doing, the man made it a personal mission to be tangled in the weeds of Silas's family's business.

"Right," Lyra beamed. "But we about finished a new track and part of another in a couple of hours. It was *really* good. You know those moments where everything is just working out?" She turned to Mick. "Like basically every single time I was on stage with you. We tweaked some of the lyrics, and we have this awesome bassist, I'm kind of half in love with her—don't worry, only have eyes for you," she added with a grin when Alex clicked his tongue. "But I'm *really* getting jazzed about this tour." She brought her hands together in a gesture of amazement, a little shiver running through her.

"When do you leave?" Kathryn asked.

"In three weeks. I mean, of course I will *hate* being away for so long." She squeezed Alex's arm. "But … the venues we're playing, they're all still small enough to feel a little intimate, but not so small that you can see all eight people from the stage, you know."

"No Rusty's Bar, is what you're saying?" Mick said with a chuckle.

They all laughed, thinking back on one of Lyra and Mick's earlier gigs, where a fight that broke out had landed him in hospital.

"God no. But I miss those days, too," Lyra said, a touch of sadness in her voice as she pouted at Mick. "I'm done trying to get you to change your mind, but remember, you *only* have to say the word and I'll turf that keyboard player right out."

Kathryn looped her arm possessively around Mick's shoulders. "My man isn't going anywhere, thank you!"

Silas smiled at the display of affection, shifting his eyes to Ernie, who he was certain would be swooning. Instead, he found his boyfriend surreptitiously typing on his phone, which he held under the table. Silas frowned, and Ernie looked up at that moment. He quickly clicked his phone off, slapping it face down on the table and leaning over to Si.

"If I have *any* more to drink I'm going to start behaving inappropriately," Ernie said, and Silas smiled.

"Best we check on those orders then."

"Oh good," Lyra said. "I am *starving.*"

The evening went far too quickly, Silas feeling a tug of

something almost like nostalgia for a moment he was currently living though. He took in the gentle touches between Kathryn and Mick, the fire in Alex's gaze when he stared at Lyra, and the starry-eyed look on his own boyfriend's face when their eyes met. He felt lucky to be part of a family filled with so much love—though he'd rather have sliced his own tongue from his head than said such a thing aloud. He watched Mick joke with Ernie and had to swallow a lump in his throat. His biological father wouldn't have even accepted the fact that he was dating a man, let alone instantly welcomed Ernie into the family with open arms the way Mick had done. Mick caught his eye and they shared a smile.

As the sun sank below the horizon, everyone ordered cake and coffee, seemingly reluctant for the night to end—stretching it out in any way they could.

Eventually, Lyra started yawning and Kathryn followed suit.

"Alright," Mick said, leaning to plant a kiss on her temple. "Let's get you home, missus."

Kathryn beamed tiredly at him, and Lyra and Silas shared a happy smile. They loved seeing Mick so doted upon, so happy after his long streak of bad luck.

At the sailing club entrance, everyone hugged tightly as they said their farewells before the three couples headed off to their separate cars. There was something about the scene that sent chills down Silas's spine, and he made sure that he properly hugged Mick.

"I meant what I said," Silas said in a low voice, when he was sure no one else was listening.

Mick squeezed him tighter and clapped his back. "I know you did, son." His voice shook with emotion. "I know."

9
MONDAY

"Huh," Kristina said with a puzzled frown, punching the button to end her call.

"Kristina, it's Monday morning," Amy croaked, looking up at her from over the rim of her steaming cup of coffee. "That better have been a *good* huh and not a bad one."

The three employees of Porter Lucas were in the front room of their Lilac Bay offices—an area Amy had originally intended as a showroom for client meetings. But since the company had grown to include the three of them, they'd realised they hated being squirrelled away in individual offices. Not to mention Martha still didn't really have one. So they'd improvised and added a long bench to the space, fashioning it into a small open-plan office. The other rooms were reserved for private or difficult phone calls, as well as storage, or for when they needed to concentrate and work uninterrupted.

"That was Evertree Bakeries..." Kristina said.

Amy's attention was instantly and mercifully diverted from the difficult client floorplan she'd been hunched over.

Trying to figure out how to include the eight-seater sofa they'd requested was giving her a headache. Unless she took the roof off and stacked it vertically, it simply wasn't going to work.

"Rebecca?" she asked Kristina.

The Evertree Bakeries account—and its owner Rebecca—had caused a rift between Kristina and Amy when they'd first begun working together at their previous employer. Their old boss, Beaumont, had taken Amy's long-term client and given it to Kristina, who'd been unaware of the history. They'd worked hard—and successfully—to overcome all that. Amy was gratified to realise that the name didn't even cause her heart rate to rise.

"Yeah," Kristina said, staring at her phone. "She's leaving Edgerton's."

"What?" Amy straightened up, and Martha shifted slightly in her chair, lowering her coffee mug to give Kristina her full attention. "Actually, lots of clients are leaving..."

"What? Why?" Martha asked.

Kristina raised her eyes to them, a frown creasing her forehead and her huge brown eyes looking haunted. She tugged on one of her braids, a gesture Amy knew meant she was nervous. "Apparently Beaumont is in a coma after a stroke."

Amy sucked in a sharp breath, glancing to Martha, who paled.

"Is he okay?" Amy asked. She'd fallen out quite dramatically with her former boss, but could still remember a time when he'd acted as a mentor to her. The idea that he was lying in some hospital bed didn't bring her any joy.

Kristina shook her head. "He's ... Rebecca said he's not expected to pull through."

"This is ghoulish," Amy protested, as the three of them stood in front of the whiteboard wall in the back office, a hastily-scrawled client list running its entire length.

"It's *practical*," Martha sighed. "I know it doesn't feel good, but if we don't strike and get these clients, some other firm with fewer scruples is going to."

"Realistically, what are we going to say?" Amy asked, playing with the pussy-bow on her sapphire silk blouse. She mimed picking up a phone. "Oh hey, we heard Beaumont's in a coma so we thought you might want to jump ship?"

"Amy, of course not," Kristina said. "We don't bring Beaumont up at all. We were planning to contact a lot of these clients anyway, now that we're close to the end of our non-compete clause with Edgerton's. This is stuff we would have been getting around to. We're just … bringing it forward slightly."

"It's icky."

"It's *prudent*," Kristina said, and Martha nodded.

Amy sighed, tapping her manicured nails crisply on the Formica desk. "Who do we think is going to take on all this work, anyway? We already have clients coming out of our ears."

Her own portfolio was bulging. Before starting the business with Kristina, they'd both agreed to keep the client list curated. They'd agreed not to say yes to every single project that came along. The last thing they'd wanted was to get overwhelmed with work the way they had done at Edgerton's. They knew that way of doing business meant sacrificing workmanship, and they wanted Porter Lucas to be synonymous with good quality. Still, they'd pushed themselves to their limits recently and Amy was worried this would take them beyond—something she didn't feel up to. Especially with the way her workload was already keeping her up at night.

"It's a good chance for us to bring on new staff," Martha said with a shrug. "Another part-timer at least, to cover my off days. We've needed to do that for a while."

"I know," Amy agreed. "But there's a lot of work involved in bringing on new staff, making sure they're a good cultural fit, having them shadow us for a while, doing performance appraisals ..." She was trying to remain upbeat, but the very thought of so much additional work was making her itch.

"Well," Kristina said slowly, and Amy narrowed her eyes, realising the tone. She wasn't going to like whatever Kristina said next. "We might be able to nab a few designers from Edgerton's ..."

Amy gasped. "He's not dead! Don't you feel bad, picking over his bones like this?" Kristina and Martha shared a look. "What?" Amy demanded. "What was that?"

Martha bit her lip, gently patting Amy's arm. "We know that at one point, Beaumont was ... I don't know, a mentor to you."

"This has nothing—"

"It does though," Kristina cut in firmly. "I know it's all murky. I'm truly sorry. But Amy, we have to look at what's good for our business. Beaumont was about to throw you out before you left. Do you remember him asking you to take a pay cut? Remember him telling you you were skating on thin ice? That you weren't contributing?"

Amy's shoulders slumped. "Yes," she admitted, her voice low.

"He would be doing this if we were on the chopping block somehow," Kristina said with a shrug. "And we're not doing anything wrong. It's a chance for Porter Lucas to take a big step up. Really enter the game."

"We're *in* the game," Amy pointed out.

"This could *change* the game," Kristina persisted, and Martha gave Amy a pointed look.

Amy pressed her fingers to her temples. She was prone to stress headaches and was starting to feel one coming on. "I can't take on any more work, you guys. I'm trying to plan my wedding, I'll need to take a break for my honeymoon, I'm house-hunting with Rick … not to mention I'm trying to perform an actual miracle in my current project."

"We got you," Kristina said.

"And we really should think about talking to others from Edgerton's," Martha added. "People who got fired. Or were about to be. We might even start needing support functions. Like proper IT and not that on-call guy we have who doesn't know his bum from his bicep."

"Okay, that is *not* a saying," Amy chuckled, relenting.

"Hope's coming back from maternity leave soon. Maybe she'll only want part-time," Kristina said, mentioning the former IT Manager from Edgerton's, who'd taken a year off after giving birth to twins.

"And Amber was really good," Martha reminded Amy.

"Not Kyle, though," Amy and Kristina said in unison, naming the former colleague who'd snitched on Amy for violating contract terms and tried to pass it off as Kristina's doing.

Martha and Kristina fell silent, both watching Amy. They'd agreed early on that all decisions affecting their firm needed to be unanimous between them.

Amy looked back and forth between them, seeing the same inspiration and steely determination written on both their faces. Finally, she held up her hands.

"Okay. Alright. We can make a *couple* of calls. But let's do it with dignity, and no one mention Beaumont."

Martha pulled her into a side-hug and Kristina grinned, immediately turning back to the whiteboard.

"Right," she said, instantly all business. "Let's split this list up and hit the phones."

10
WEDNESDAY

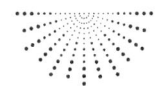

"Earth to Amy Beth," Rick said.

"Hmmm," Amy murmured, her face smooshed into Rick's blanket, where she'd fallen face first when she finally arrived at Pam's place. She heard him close his laptop—he'd been sitting in bed, busily working away—and felt his fingers run along the back of her neck.

"Do you want something to eat?" he asked.

Despite her bone-tiredness, his touch sent sparks of desire through her. She rolled onto her back, catching his hand and threading her fingers through his.

"Can we get takeout?" she asked.

"Whatever you want."

"Can we eat it in bed?"

"As you wish."

"Can it include pizza?"

"Ames, it can even *be* pizza."

"I need to do some work. Actually, I have a fair bit of work to do. But can we ... snuggle afterwards?" She arched an eyebrow at him. His eyes narrowed wolfishly and he bared his teeth at her, making her giggle. "I honestly don't know how you manage to look hot doing that."

"Excuse me, I look hot doing everything," he said, grinning.

"Actually, you really do." Her voice turned dreamy. "My future husband."

"My future wife," he echoed, pride shining in his eyes as he leaned forward to give her an upside-down kiss. The warmth of his face against hers, and the softness of his lips mixed with the rough brush of his stubble had butterflies stirring in Amy's stomach. She hummed, pulling him closer to her. Then her phone rang in her bag and she groaned, breaking off the kiss as she sat up to look for it.

"It's Dad." She saw tightness flicker through Rick's face.

"You want to answer that and I'll phone in for some pizza?" he asked. "I'll ask Mum if she wants some too."

Amy nodded, and swiped to answer the call. "Hey."

"Heya, baby girl," Sean said. It was too dark on his end to make out his face properly. All Amy could see was a faint glow.

"Are you out running again?" She squinted and brought the phone closer.

"Just finished boxing class, actually," Sean said, and flicked on a light. Amy could see he was at home, but when the camera panned over the living room, it looked much different to how she remembered it. It was neat as a pin, brightly lit and her father was standing in the middle of it, his face red and beaming when he flicked the camera back to himself.

"Boxing?" Amy shook her head with a smile. "Why do you need to learn that?"

"I don't. Or, at least, I hope I don't," he said with a cheeky smile. "One of the guys in this neighbourhood used to be a semi-pro heavyweight. Runs a free class for kids around here. Figured I might as well help out and learn a bit at the same time."

Amy smiled tightly. She wanted so badly to believe in her father's transformation. But it was so sudden and dramatic that it was hard for her to trust it was real … or lasting. She felt bad for the thought, but she knew it was partly self-preservation and she couldn't be angry at herself for that. After all, he'd let her down in the biggest way. And not just once. And not just her …

"Anyway, how's work?" he asked, interrupting her thoughts.

"It's good," she said brightly, pushing aside thoughts of her mammoth to-do list. "Lots of opportunities on the horizon."

"I'm so glad you decided to strike out on your own. I check out your website every couple of days. You girls are doing a stellar job. I even signed up for an Instagram account so I could follow you. I love those before and after reveals some of your clients do."

Despite herself, Amy felt a glow of warmth. It was yet to be seen whether her father had truly transformed, but at least he cared about her work. Which was more than she could say for her mother.

They chatted for a few more moments and then Amy went to search for Rick. She was exhausted, wanted nothing more than to eat pizza in bed with Rick and talk about their days. She also needed to go through some spreadsheets for work—she, Martha and Kristina had chunked down the admin involved with bringing on extra hires, and needed to produce lists to cross-check with each other. She'd been hoping to do it in the peace of his room.

She found Rick in the kitchen with Pam, deep in

conversation about pocket squares for his wedding suit. They broke off when she arrived and Amy chose to pretend she hadn't heard.

"You look exhausted," Rick said. He checked his watch. "Pizza should be here any moment."

"I'll set out some plates," Pam said quickly, springing up to head for the cupboard.

Amy inwardly groaned, and Rick shot her an apologetic look. They couldn't very well leave Pam sitting on her own in the empty kitchen and take their pizza back to Rick's room, much as they might want to. Amy wished for the thousandth time that Pam had more friends, or enjoyed getting out more often. Or that Amy and Rick already lived together in their own place. She drew a deep breath, reminding herself that day would come. She loved that Rick was close to his mother—he was a good son. She only wished her own relationship with Pam was less fraught. And less close-quarters.

"You know, you don't have to hide away when your father calls," Pam said casually, once the pizza arrived and they were tucking in. "I want you to feel completely comfortable here."

But not so comfortable that I get a key, Amy mentally added. "Sure," she replied out loud.

"How's he doing anyway?" Pam asked.

"He's…" Amy studied Rick's face, finding it neutral. "Apparently he's taken up boxing."

"Oh?" Pam said, in an interested tone.

Rick flicked his gaze to her, then to Amy, who was watching him. He looked quickly back down at his pizza, seeming riveted by it.

"Yeah. Some neighbourhood thing to keep kids out of trouble or something."

Pam lowered her slice. "Well, what a wonderful way to give back to the community."

"Oh, I don't think *he's* running it. He's--I don't really know. Helping out or something. Joining in."

"Well, that's lovely. Sounds like he's not doing it for the glory. The people in the background are often more selfless than the ones taking centre stage."

Amy made a noncommittal noise, hoping for a change in subject. Pam's enthusiasm made her feel guilty for not taking her father's newfound lifestyle at face value.

"I wonder whether they need some help."

Rick stared at his mother. "What, you're going to start boxing?"

"It never hurts to be able to defend yourself," Pam said, her cheeks pinking prettily. "But no, I was more thinking ... I don't know, with fundraising or support or something."

Amy scratched her neck. "He didn't mention needing that."

"Well, sometimes people are a little afraid to speak up," Pam said, eyes firmly on her pizza. "These grassroots things always need support."

Rick tongued his teeth, a frown creasing his forehead. "I thought you were thinking about volunteering at the library again?"

Pam shrugged one shoulder. "I never committed to that."

"Well, anyway," Amy said. "I'm genuinely not sure they need anything."

"You ask him though, will you?" Pam asked, holding her gaze. "I'd like to be of some use if I possibly can be."

"Okay," Amy agreed. She felt torn. Rick clearly didn't want his mother near her father—a fact they'd need to unpack at some point—but at the same time, it might be a good way to get Pam out of the house. A silence fell.

"How was work, Ames?" Rick asked.

"Yeah, good," she replied. "And you? Were you working on something with Alex?"

Amy hated having this conversation with her fiancé in front of an audience. She wanted to be alone with him, preferably horizontal. She felt like their relationship was on show for Pam, and up for judgement.

"Yep," Rick replied. "It's a house we're fixing up a little."

"You're not pushing yourself too hard, are you?" Pam asked sharply. "Lauren said you have to be careful."

"Mum, *please*." Rick closed his eyes. "I know I'm at home, but I'm a grown man. I was in the army most of my life. I know how to take care of myself! *Stop* smothering me."

Pam's eyes welled and she looked down at her plate as Amy stopped chewing. She glared at Rick, jerking her head towards Pam to prompt him to say something.

"Sorry," he muttered, a moment later. "Mum, I didn't mean to snap."

"It's okay." Pam waved her hand. "Why don't you two finish eating in your room. I'm sure you're dying to have some time alone without me." Without waiting for an answer, Pam took her plate and left the room.

"That was a bit harsh," Amy said finally, gently.

Rick scrubbed a hand over his face. "I know. But I'm going crazy cooped up in here. Ames, we *really* need to find a place. And soon. I hate the idea of Mum being alone in this big house. But even worse is the idea that us staying here is going to damage my relationship with her."

Amy twisted her mouth, nodding slowly. She didn't want to say she thought the same thing. She felt bad admitting how much she missed her own place. She needed to spend more nights in the week there, even if it meant being away from Rick. Otherwise she was likely to say something she'd regret. And she had the feeling her presence drove a wedge between Rick and his mum.

But most of all, she didn't want to say that she suspected the reason Rick had lost his temper was because Pam had showed an interest in Sean.

11
WEDNESDAY

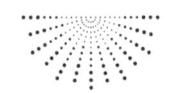

The phone was face down in Ernie's armchair, pinging just infrequently enough to drive Silas insane. He took a deep breath and buried his nose back into his book, trying his best to ignore the dings.

Since Lyra had moved out, Silas had initiated Ernie into the weekly family tradition of reading books in silence while sipping their favourite drinks. Ernie's comic book was spread open on his chair, an espresso martini on the small table beside it, but Ernie himself was nowhere to be seen. He'd sat down once, turned a single page and then sprung up, announcing he'd forgotten to water his plants. He always thought of a thousand things to do before he finally settled down to read his book in relative silence.

As the phone pinged one more time, Silas growled and slapped his book shut.

"Erns!" he called, as loud as he could. No response. He was probably in the small backyard, fussing over his ... dilly buttons? Hydrapannies?

Silas grabbed the phone and fumbled to flick the volume button to mute, as another message came in. The sender was listed in Ernie's phone with no name, just four heart emojis, and the message preview mode had been disabled. Silas frowned. He was sure in the past Ernie's phone had been set to show message previews. In any case, four-hearts apparently had a lot to say to Ernie tonight.

Silas gritted his molars, fighting the urge to snoop. He knew Ernie's passcode, but he'd never used it. He hadn't even wanted it, Ernie had forced him to memorise it when they started dating, saying he didn't want secrets between them. Funny that he was the one keeping a secret now. Silas tossed the phone onto Ernie's chair and sat back down. But after reading the same paragraph six times, he finally admitted defeat.

He got up and stomped to the back door, pausing to watch Ernie through the fly screen. Ernie was merrily humming away to himself in last of the evening light, measuring small amounts of water onto his beloved plants. He was always so *happy*.

For the first time, Silas wondered whether it was an act. What if Ernie was actually unhappy with him? With their relationship dynamic? What if he wanted someone ... sunnier? Brighter? More like himself?

Silas couldn't bear the thought of losing his boyfriend, and the very idea that there was someone else out there sending him sweet messages made Silas feel sick.

How had it never occurred to him that if he wasn't more bubbly and affectionate with Ernie, he'd start to look elsewhere for those things? Silas took a deep breath and plastered a huge smile on his face, banging through the door to cross the yard to Ernie.

"Hey, Si!" Ernie said brightly. He did a double-take. "Whoa. What's wrong with your face?"

"Nothing," Silas said, keeping the smile in place as he tried to echo Ernie's light tone. "I'm smiling. Can't I smile?"

"Sure, but that looks ... you look like you're in pain." Ernie pulled a cloth from his back pocket and began to polish, actually *polish* the leaves of one of the plants.

"Well, I'm not. Those are nice," Silas added.

Ernie's hand froze mid-swipe and he eyed his boyfriend suspiciously. "You're complementing my flowers? Last week you threatened to pour concrete over the whole back yard."

God, had he really said that? Silas was annoyed at himself. No wonder Ernie was texting other guys, if that was how Silas behaved. Worse, he didn't even remember saying it. He straightened his spine and dialled the smile up a notch. "Well, not anymore, I think they're ... so pretty. We should bring them inside and, uh, display them."

At that, Ernie abandoned his leaf-polishing and stood upright. "Okay, what gives?"

"Huh?"

"You're creeping me out with that jack-o'lantern smile, and now you're talking about bringing *flowers* into the house?" Ernie scanned Silas's face for a moment, then gasped. "Did you break my favourite coffee cup?"

Silas frowned. "What?"

"The speckled one from my mother." Ernie placed a hand on his hip. "The one you said looked like a deformed duck egg."

Dear *lord* what was wrong with him? Why was he programmed to be so mean to his sweet, loving boyfriend? Well, no longer, Silas swore to himself. From this moment onwards, Ernie wouldn't recognise him. He'd be kind and happy and pampering to a fault. It was no less than Ernie deserved. Silas wouldn't let his boyfriend go without a fight. Four-hearts wouldn't know what hit him.

"I haven't smashed anything at all. I was missing you, that's all."

"I know, I know, it's reading night and my bum isn't in the chair and I'm not being silent. I'm almost done."

"No, that isn't—"

"I've got about three more plants to take care of and then I'll be in."

"Take your time," Silas said, still wearing the smile.

Ernie looked at him for another moment and then shook his head. "Okay, please stop doing that, it's actually creeping me out."

"You don't like my smile?"

"I love your smile. Your smile is hot. It's so rare that angels practically sing when it happens. What you're doing with your mouth right now is … *not* that."

His pride wounded, Silas let the forced grin slip from his face. "Alright. Well…" He turned to head back inside, then turned back. "Can I help?"

Ernie's head reeled back a little. "No. Thank you." He was frowning at Silas as though trying to puzzle something out, and Silas's heart sank a little.

Maybe things were already too far gone. Maybe he'd been a grump so long to Ernie that there was nothing he could do to make up for it. Here he was, trying his heart out, and Ernie was rejecting him cold. Well, no matter. This was a fight Ernie wouldn't win. Silas was ready to dial it up a notch, heck *seven* notches, if that's what it took.

This was a little set-back, nothing more.

12
WEDNESDAY

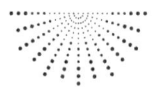

"Thai?"

"We had that last week."

"We had everything last week," Lyra countered.

"We have everything *every* week," Alex volleyed back.

"*One* of us should really learn to cook." She nudged him as they leaned with their elbows on the small kitchen counter, poring over the plastic display folder of local delivery menus.

"I never get sick of Italian," he said, by way of response, eyes trained on the folder as he struggled to suppress a smile.

"I don't either. But I should probably get something less carby. I might need to watch what I eat, because in case you hadn't noticed, I'm kind of a big deal right now," she joked.

"I can see the headlines." Alex flicked quickly to a salad menu. "Is Lyra Beck letting herself go? Take our quiz to find out."

Lyra groaned. "You laugh, but that's basically what it's like for women."

"Oh, I know," Alex said, shaking his head. He hooked his finger under her chin and stood, bringing her up with him and staring her in the eye, his expression deathly serious. "If anyone talks smack about you, I *will* come for them."

Lyra tensed, guilt rippling down her spine. She hadn't told Alex the stupid idea Julian had approached her with, about faking a relationship with Jake. She had rationalised that it was pointless to upset him, since she'd rather cut off a finger than participate. She'd meant what she'd said to Julian —she was willing to walk away from it all if they tried to force her into something. Nothing was worth hurting Alex for. And that was all it would be if she told him—hurt.

She looked into his eyes now, her heart rate quickening as she sank into their grey-gold depths. "You'd come for them?"

"Yeah."

"What would you do?" She hooped her arms around his waist and melted herself into him, enjoying the firmness of his body against the softness of hers.

"It would start with their fingernails," he said darkly.

Lyra couldn't help laughing. "You're kind of freaky when you talk like that."

He shrugged. "They mess with my girl, they get the horns."

Lyra hugged him tighter. "Isn't that saying about a bull?"

"I don't care." He leaned down and kissed her slowly, leaving her tingling all the way to her toes. "They will all pay," he murmured.

When they'd first moved in together, Lyra had expected some of the spark to slowly disappear between her and Alex. Not in a bad way, in a way that signalled comfort and security. To her surprise, it had only become more intense and more passionate. Most days, they couldn't keep their hands off one another, and as their relationship had deepened, so had the intensity of the attraction between them. Now, it was only their hunger levels that kept them from the bedroom, as they finally voted on Indian and sat to wait for the delivery at their tiny dining table. They were two-thirds the way through a puzzle of a classical painting portraying a woman emerging from a bathtub—a hand-me-down from Amy's grandfather.

"What are we going to do about that house?" Lyra asked, testing out a few puzzle pieces with no success. She kept her eyes glued to the pieces, knowing that talking about the house meant they were getting close to the *other* issue that had come up that day. The talk of children.

"Did you really like it?" Alex asked, and Lyra could hear the tightness in his voice.

She sighed dreamily. "Yeah, I did. Didn't you?"

"A lot. It was actually pretty perfect. I can't pick a flaw with it."

"Me either," Lyra agreed, sipping the Diet Coke they were splitting. "I still can't believe the price. I feel like we'd be crazy if we let it go."

"Same," Alex said, a note of excitement creeping into his voice. "Are we really going to do this?"

Lyra grinned at him. "I think so? Right? I mean, pending everything being in order with the bank and all that. I hope it works out, although I don't exactly hate your place."

"Me either," Alex said. "But this is a bachelor pad. You fit, or you do as long as you lay off the pizza," he winked, "but —"

Lyra froze, her hand over a cluster of dark orange puzzle pieces. She slowly lifted her eyes to Alex's. He looked stricken. She knew what he'd been about to say. There wasn't enough room to raise a family.

"We never did finish this conversation …" Lyra said slowly.

"I know. And we don't have to now, either. It slipped out that day when we were viewing the house. I want you to know that. We didn't talk about it when you got home, and I didn't want to push. I meant for the future."

Lyra twisted her mouth, straightening in her seat. "Are you ready now?"

Alex held his features still. "I'll be ready when you're ready. Not before."

Lyra tipped her head. "Alex, please. Be open with me."

His shoulders dropped. "I mean, I think about it all the time. But it's not a good stage in your life right now. I know that, and I respect it."

"Well, I don't know if there ever is a perfect time."

"Right, but I mean … things just started happening for you. I can't imagine you want to take a bunch of time off right now, or have to go around touring while pregnant."

Lyra nodded slowly, considering. "I'm also not getting any younger." Alex immediately scoffed, but she held up her hand. "I know women get pregnant into their forties, but I also know how hard it gets, and how quickly the chances decrease. I … I want to have a family with you, Alex. But you're right. The timing right now isn't fantastic. I was thinking …" She toyed with a puzzle piece, trailing off as he held up a hand.

"To be perfectly clear, there is *no* pressure from me. I know how much a pregnancy asks of you and your body. I promise you, I wouldn't have raised this if you hadn't asked me to be honest. I'll wait as long as it takes. I know you want them too, that's more than enough for me. I swear it."

Lyra put a hand on his reassuringly. "I know. But after it came up at the viewing, I did some thinking. I was kind of considering getting my eggs frozen."

"Okay." Alex frowned. "Is that something that's painful for you?"

Lyra shrugged. "I really don't know anything about it. But

I think it might be a smart thing to do, you know? As a kind of insurance."

"Right."

"You don't sound enthusiastic."

"Not because I don't think it's a good idea. But I think that's a big deal for your body. The hormone injections or whatever. I don't even know how they get the eggs out. Do they have to cut you?" He sounded worried.

"I don't think so? We can do more research into it if we think it's a good option."

"Ly, look at me."

She raised her eyes to his. His jaw was set, his eyes narrowed in focus. "I do not want you to have to worry about this right now. If the time comes for us and it doesn't work, there are a million other ways to make a family. There's fostering, adoption, I don't know, egg donation or surrogacy and I bet there's more I'm not thinking of."

Lyra felt tears pricking her eyes. Why had she met the man she wanted to spend her life with and make a family with at the exact same time that her career had taken off? If she was still working in The Pie-ganic and gigging with Mick, she'd have been over the moon to start a family with Alex. Now ... her music dreams had finally come true. She was heading off on tour, she was recognised, she had an awesome band. Okay, so her label sometimes kind of sucked, but still. It really was not a good time to stop things and have a baby. She knew that. But that didn't stop it from hurting.

"Thank you, my love. I know. But thank you for saying it."

Their dinner arrived and they abandoned the puzzle to scarf it down in front of the TV. By some unspoken mutual agreement, they dropped the topic altogether, and instead talked about the house during lulls in their show. Lyra snuggled into Alex, loving these long lazy evenings with him.

But her thoughts kept straying back to their conversation.

Had he been waiting for a child all this time? That must be so hard, and he hadn't breathed a word until that day at the house—had been nothing but supportive of her and her career.

She burrowed herself even more tightly under his arm, and he squeezed it around her. At least they'd decided on a house now. That was a big step.

It would have to be enough ... for now.

13
THURSDAY

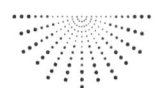

Marley shifted uncomfortably on her office chair, remembering a time in the not-too-distant past when it had seemed like the most luxurious seat ever made. Now, her hips felt like they were on fire, her back was pinched, and her legs swelled if she sat still for more than twenty minutes. She was crotchety, and she was taking it out on the patients. And Dr Martelle. And poor Finn, whenever he came out of his office to ask her for anything.

When the door burst open and a man full of aggressive energy strode in and demanded an immediate appointment —as though Marley was a robot built to serve—it didn't take long for her to crack.

"As I explained, we're booked out for weeks," she said huffily, struggling to her feet after telling him for the third time he couldn't simply walk in and be seen.

The patient, a bulky man with an angry set to his jaw, practically growled at her. "I told you I need to see the doctor. Isn't it your job to find me a slot? What else do you do if not that?"

"Oh, I don't know," she snapped. "Run the office? Manage

patient files? Deal with *idiots?*"

As soon as the words were out, Marley knew she'd gone too far. The man's face purpled.

"What did you say to me?" he asked, his voice dangerously low.

Marley summoned all her remaining willpower and drew a deep breath. "I apologise for speaking that way to you. But you're not presenting as an urgent case, and if you were, I'd send you to A&E at the hospital. Dr Martelle is seeing her last patient for the day. You're not even on our books, which are closed to new people right now. I've been polite, I've been patient, I've explained as clearly as I can why I can't help you."

"I'm not going to stand here and be backchatted by some *bimbo*," the man began.

Finn's door opened and he led out his latest patient, laughing easily with her as they headed to the reception desk. At the man's tone, and on hearing the word "bimbo", Finn's head snapped to Marley, then to the man. He crossed the room and placed himself in front of Marley's desk, blocking him from her.

"Can I help you with something?" Finn asked, perfectly composed and casual. They were similar heights, and though Finn was more muscular, the man was far chunkier.

"I'm talking to the receptionist here, *mate*."

"What were you talking to our Office Manager about?"

The man sighed, and shifted his weight. "Seems she can't work her computer enough to get me an appointment."

Without turning, Finn spoke to Marley. "Do we have any appointments available, Marley?"

"No."

"And did you already inform the gentleman of this?"

"Several times."

"Then, sir, I think you'd best be on your way. Also, FYI,

it's not your best look, intimidating and insulting women."

"Pregnant ones especially," Finn's client chimed in, her arms crossed as she glared at the man from where she stood outside Finn's office door.

The man grunted and heaved a sigh. "Bloody idiots," he mumbled as he walked towards the door. But Marley noticed he said it under his breath and only when he was a decent distance from Finn.

She swallowed hard, resisting the urge to run around her desk and pull Finn into her arms. "Can I help you with a new appointment?" she asked his patient politely.

Once that was done, and Finn had locked the door behind her, Marley crossed the office to meet him. She smiled up at him, her heart tripping as his blue eyes crinkled at the corners.

"You didn't have to rescue me, Finn Mayberry. But I love that you did."

"It was hardly rescuing," Finn said, bending towards her to press their foreheads together. Marley breathed in his heavenly scent. Slightly spicy and woody. "I was merely pointing out where his manners were lacking."

"Oh yeah?" her voice was breathy, her arms cinching tighter around his waist.

"Marley, you're carrying my baby, and even if you weren't, you're carrying my heart. Do you honestly think I'd stand there and watch him insult you?"

She looped a hand behind his head and pulled their mouths together, melting at the softness of his lips and the skill of his tongue. They sprang apart when Marley's boss, Dr Elizabeth Martelle, cleared her throat.

"Sorry!" Marley said, straightening her top and pressing her lips together in a secret smile at Finn.

"Need I remind you this is a professional workplace?" Elizabeth said. "Should I introduce a code of conduct?" Her tone was mock-stern, but her eyes were sparkling as she struggled to suppress a smile.

"That same code will apply to you and Don … and that supply closet," Finn said.

Elizabeth blushed and reached forward to playfully slap his arm and Marley caught sight of the huge, glittering diamond on her boss's finger as she did so.

"I still *cannot* believe you and Don eloped and didn't tell us. I'm tempted to uninvite you to my baby shower."

She was joking, and Elizabeth grinned down at her bling. Her eyes took on a misty focus. "It's hardly eloping if you invite a bunch of people."

"Well, we still want to see pics," Marley said.

"Soon as we get them back," Elizabeth reassured her. "You'll be the first to know. Now you two head off, I'll close up."

Marley shut down her computer and she and Finn threaded their fingers together and set off on the short walk to Marley's apartment. Peak hour traffic clogged King Street and they took the shortcut through the oval, stopping to watch a flock of sulphur-crested cockatoos swarming over a yellow box eucalypt, picking fallen nuts from the ground and stripping the branches as they squawked raucously.

"Finn, I was kind of rude to that guy," Marley admitted.

Finn was silent for a moment. "Well, I'm sure he drove you to it. But let's forget about him. I've noticed that you're getting tired at work and I … I wanted to talk to you about it."

"Okay?" Marley said cautiously. "Did I do something wrong?"

"Of course not." Finn shook his head. "I just … you know I earn more than enough money to take care of us both. I hate the thought of you forcing yourself to come in every day when you could be at home relaxing instead."

Marley tensed, staring at the birds in front of her instead of meeting his eye. "Finn, I could never," she said gently. "I appreciate the offer, but ... it's not even something I'd consider. I have the money from the house sale in Darnee. If I wanted to, I could use that and stop working. But I don't want to whittle it away and have nothing to show for it. Besides, I want to keep paying into my retirement fund."

Finn nodded beside her. "I thought you'd say that. But I wanted to offer, and I want you to know that I'm sincere. There'd be no strings attached."

"I know," she said, squeezing his hand and gazing up into his eyes. "I know."

"What about reducing your hours a little?"

"No." She shook her head firmly. "I'll only get eighteen weeks of maternity leave. I'll want more. I need to be saving for that now."

"I get it." They walked in silence for a few moments before he spoke again. "You know, I'm staying most nights at your place. I could ... start kicking in some rent."

Marley froze, realising what he was really asking. He bit his bottom lip as her eyes ran over his face. His expression was hopeful, and she felt a piece of her heart break off.

"Finn ... I ..."

He searched her face, then nodded once, shifting his gaze to the birds. "I know. Don't worry. Forget I said anything." He pulled gently on her hand as they started walking again, and Marley's chest felt tight.

She hated this block. Hated so much that the thought of him moving in with her permanently made her feel itchy and claustrophobic. It wasn't fair on him and she knew it. She just didn't know how to get over it.

"I'm sorry," she whispered, tears filling her eyes.

He pulsed her hand with his but made no reply.

"I'll get there, Finn. I promise. I'm trying. And once Petunia's here--"

Finn burst out laughing, but the laugh died on his lips as he took in Marley's expression. "*Petunia*? Wait … did you open the envelope from the midwife without me?"

The hurt in his voice was more than Marley could bear. She vehemently shook her head. "No! Of course not. And it's … we can discuss it."

Realisation dawned in Finn's eyes. "That was your GamGam's name, wasn't it?" he asked softly.

Marley nodded. "Yeah. But I'm not saying it has to be that. I mean, we might be having a boy. Do you hate the name, Finn?"

He opened and closed his mouth, looking pained. He clearly wanted to give her one answer, but it was just as obvious that would have been a lie. Marley's heart squeezed.

"Listen, let's wait till we get back to your place. I'll cook us a nice meal, and we can have a chat about it all. There's nothing we can't get over. I promise."

Marley swallowed against the lump in her throat. "Okay," she said finally, as he pulled her into a tight hug in the middle of the field.

She buried her head into his shoulder, feeling his strong arms around her as she tried to breath out the sting of his reaction to the name she'd wanted to give her child her whole life. *He's giving up a lot too,* she reminded herself.

Why wasn't it easy? Why wasn't it as simple as two lives merging with no one having to compromise on something that was so important to them? She knew that wasn't a fair thought—she was the one hesitant to give Finn some of the things he so clearly wanted and needed. And she knew beyond all doubt that he deserved a say in their child's name.

She just wished the one she'd already chosen wasn't so important to her.

14
FRIDAY

"It's been way too long since we were here together, hasn't it?" Amy said sadly, glancing around the Whistle Stop that Friday night. In the past, the three best friends could be found at the dingy bar most nights a week. But those days were long gone now, especially with Lyra's career having taken off, Marley's pregnancy heading into the late stages, and Amy running her own business. It was rare they'd all had a Friday free, and had decided on a spontaneous meetup.

"Yeah, it has," Lyra agreed. "But this place hasn't gained any charm in the meantime."

They chuckled. They were squished into one of the vinyl booths near the door, their "usual" barrel having long since been surrendered to others.

"It really hasn't," Marley said dryly, her gaze coolly assessing the surroundings. She was dressed in a flamingo-print men's shirt and an elasticated-waist maxi skirt, her belly straining at the buttons around her middle.

Lyra looked around at the staff. "Ugh, this place makes me think of Miles," she said, a sour look on her face.

"Don't do that," Amy admonished. "It was the birthplace of Margot. And therefore your career."

"To dear Margot," Lyra agreed, raising her glass.

"Wherever she is," Amy added, chiming her glass against Lyra's. Marley didn't bother to join in, shifting uncomfortably in her seat.

"Do you guys ever worry that when you have kids, you'll have to start compromising on stuff you never thought you would?" Marley blurted.

Lyra and Amy exchanged a startled look.

"Uh, we've pretty much decided not to have kids so, no. But … is this about the name?" Amy asked carefully. Marley had texted her after Finn's reaction.

"What name?" Lyra asked immediately.

Amy knew Marley wouldn't have minded her mentioning it in front of her, and her hunch was right.

"I want to call the baby Petunia if it's a girl," Marley said, lifting her chin.

Amy discreetly tried to squeeze Lyra's knee under the table.

Lyra's eye twitched like she had something in it, but before she could open her mouth, Marley sighed.

"I know. It's not a popular name. I know not many people will like it. But it was my grandmother's name and I always wanted to use it. Ever since I was a girl. But I accidentally told him about it and his reaction was to laugh."

"Oh dear," Lyra said sympathetically, shooting a grateful glance at Amy for the warning leg squeeze. "Well, you know sometimes those old names come back into fashion."

"Not Petunia," Marley said sadly. "I checked. It bottomed out in like 1903 and it's never coming back."

"Oh."

"Yeah. He wanted to talk about it when we got home, but I managed to … distract him." Marley averted her eyes, as the girls caught her meaning. "But it's not exactly a question we can put off forever." She gestured at her bulging belly.

The girls were silent. Then Lyra leaned forward. "This isn't only about the name, is it?"

Marley puffed out a breath. "If we have such different opinions on names, how will we do with the actual parenting? What if we have completely different styles? What if he gives up his apartment and we realise we don't work as a co-parents? What if—"

"I think you can tell a lot about how raising a kid will go, by how they are as a partner," Amy said quickly, sensing Marley was spiralling. "And whether you have similar values. I can't imagine Finn being such a loving boyfriend and then, I don't know, wanting to spank your kids or something."

"God no." Marley's eyes widened in alarm. "He would never. But ... I don't know. These are the things I'm starting to worry about.

"I can totally get that," Amy said finally. Then she slid a hand across the table, squeezing Marley's arm. "Finn isn't like your ex-husband, Marley."

"Yeah," Marley said quietly, her eyes welling. "I know. I know that. My heart knows that. I just wish my head would get the message."

"Have you thought about talking to someone?" Amy asked.

"What, like a shrink?"

"Sure."

Marley tilted her head. "No. I don't really want to spend that kind of money when I'm already going to be off work for a while."

"I wouldn't think of it as spending," Amy said. "Think of it as an investment in your own mental health, and in your relationship with Finn. And that's worth it."

Marley nodded slowly, the frown on her face making it clear she was considering Amy's words.

"Anyway, one of the games for your baby shower next weekend is guessing the sex," Lyra said, trying to brighten the mood.

Marley groaned. "What kinds of games are there? Please don't tell me we're going to play pin the sperm on the egg?"

Lyra's eyes bulged. "That's a *game?* I'm in charge of games, and I haven't heard of it. I'm going to try and track it down!"

"What does the winner get?" Amy asked, as Lyra jotted in the little notebook she always kept with her.

"A candy appendage."

Marley coughed. "Lyra, you'd better mean an arm. My *boss* will be there."

"Your boss is a doctor!" Amy pointed out. "She's seen every kind of appendage before."

Lyra palmed her forehead. "I just realised I can only give the prize to the winner once the baby's born. But I have more for some of the other games."

Marley dropped her head to her hands.

"Alright. Change of subject." Lyra snapped her notebook shut. "We might need your company's help, Ames," she added with a secret smile. "We're *hopefully* going to put an offer in on a house."

"Finally!" Amy said. "It's taken you two long enough."

Lyra arched an eyebrow at her, smiling. "You of all people know how hard it is to house-hunt in this town!"

"Touché!" Amy said, holding up her hands. "Tell us about it!"

"It's in the Inner West—"

"Oh, you'll be near me!" Marley said happily. "An on-call nanny."

They all laughed.

"And it's cute and cosy and neat and quiet. It's perfect for us."

"You don't want somewhere louder, so you can, I don't know, *rock* out in the garage?" Amy asked.

"Ha! No." Lyra firmly shook her head. "The amount of time I spend at the studio, I need the peace and quiet for my mental health."

A shadow flickered briefly across Lyra's face at the mention of the studio, and Amy made a mental note to follow up with her later.

"Maybe you can get a dog," Marley added. "I always wanted one but we never got one. I miss the animals from around Darnee. I could feed the wallabies whenever I wanted."

"I'm not that much of an animal person," Amy admitted, wrinkling her nose. "But I'll absolutely love your pets. And your kids," she added, beaming at Marley. "I can't believe your due date is getting so close."

"That means your wedding is too," Marley pointed out. "What do you have left to do?"

Amy pressed her fingers to her temples. "A ton of stuff, but most of it's small. Finalising playlists, paying some of the invoices, choosing guest gifts, we haven't set up the registry yet, Rick's suit is still on order, I don't have proper shoes, we need to prepare a run sheet, set up a playlist … the list goes on. But it's hard to find a big chunk of time together to do it. Especially as we're expanding the business."

"Wow," Marley said, impressed.

"I know you turned me down, but I'd still have a job for you there," Amy added, looking at Marley. "Part-time if you wanted."

"Thanks. I'll think about it."

"Ames, that's so awesome," Lyra grinned at her. "I'm so happy your business is booming."

"Yeah, me too …" Amy's forehead creased as she traced her fingernail through a groove in her whisky glass. "My old boss is in some sort of coma. So it does feel a little like I'm profiteering from his misfortune."

Lyra frowned. "But Beaumont was horrible to you. He drove you out. He'd been running the business into the ground for a long time, from what you said."

"I know, I know," Amy agreed. "But still—"

"Hey!" Marley bellowed, leaning forward to glare at a teenage boy trying to not-so-secretly snap a picture of Lyra. "If you want a picture come up and ask her like a *human*."

Lyra flinched at Marley's tone, instinctively turning her head away from the kid, who beat it when Marley tried to struggle to her feet.

"Thank you, Marley," Lyra said softly.

Amy sighed. "You guys, I don't want to be the first one to break this up, but I *do* have to get home before Pam goes to bed. I'm still not allowed a key. I've put off begging Rick to secretly cut me one, because I already feel like I'm causing issues between him and his mum. Anyway, if Lyra's getting recognised here …"

"I want to go, too," Marley admitted quickly. "My feet are ballooning and I'm so tired I'm starting to hallucinate."

"And I've been at the studio way too many hours this week," Lyra finished. Her gaze shifted from Amy to Marley. "Is this what we've become? Old women pigeoning home before we turn into pumpkins?"

"I guess?" Amy admitted. "But to be honest, I'm kind of okay with it."

"Me too," Lyra and Marley said in unison.

"Come on then." Amy scooched out of the booth, helping Marley get stiffly to her feet.

As the three of them headed for the exit, Amy saw Lyra take a last, lingering look into the pub.

"Weird to think we might not come here much anymore, right?" Amy whispered to her.

Lyra nodded. "But it means we've all come so far. So many of our dreams coming true."

As the teenager lift his camera screen towards them again, Amy grabbed Lyra and marched her out.

15
FRIDAY

Rick was sipping a beer, looking at the backyard through his huge bedroom window when Amy arrived. The very last traces of light were fading from the dark purple sky, and the ghostly shapes of squawking cockatoos were barely visible in the lone acacia tree.

"I missed you," he said, moving over to kiss the top of her head as she flopped onto his bed.

Amy relaxed and let out a soft sigh as his fingers gently began kneading her neck. "I missed you too." She shifted to look up at him. "Rick, do we tell each other everything?"

"I hope so. Why, what secrets are you keeping?"

"None. I was thinking of Marley. She's finding it so hard to let go of her stubborn independence and let Finn in. And it sounds like he's trying so hard and being really patient."

Rick was silent for a moment, his fingers still on Amy's neck. "It must be a big adjustment for her …"

"Yeah," Amy agreed. Then she widened her eyes. "Wait. What was that tone?"

"What tone?"

Amy sat up. "The Rick-wants-to-say-something-about-Amy tone."

He grinned. "Am I that transparent?"

"Yes!" She elbowed him. "So what gives?"

"You're forcing me to say this, remember that."

"Depends on what you're going to say!"

Rick rubbed his jaw. "I was going to say … maybe it's not just Marley that finds it hard to change?" He winced.

Amy frowned. "Meaning?"

"Ames, you're doing *everything* for the wedding by yourself. And most things for the baby shower—"

"Lyra—"

"Yeah, yeah, I know. You let her do the games or whatever."

"*And* prizes. Which may have been a mistake after hearing what she's bought," Amy added.

"You haven't let me do a single thing. For *our* wedding. And I've been begging. So has Mum."

Amy was silent. He wasn't exactly wrong. In the early planning stages, Pam had been overly enthusiastic. But her ideas had clashed completely with Amy's. Pam favoured a cutesy, country homestyle over Amy's vintage aesthetic. They could rarely agree on anything, from location to food choices to music to decor. Amy *should* have surrendered a little control, if only for greater harmony. But it wasn't in her nature. She was a perfectionist and possibly a control freak, and if she was being forced to have a wedding—where she and Rick would instead have happily eloped—she at least wanted the wedding to feel like *hers*.

But Amy's style also wasn't Rick's style, and it was his wedding too…

"Shall I walk you through the checklists?" she asked. "What would you want to be in charge of?"

"I don't know. I don't even know what there is."

Amy grabbed her laptop and sat beside Rick on the bed. "This is my master spreadsheet. And this tab is for the wedding. I store it in the cloud, so if you want, I can give you the password."

"You'd do that for me?" he joked, then his eyes bugged as he took in the sheet. "Ames, this is like …"

"Two hundred and eighty lines. I know. But it's clustered into categories."

"What do the colours mean?"

"It's a basic traffic light system," she explained. "Stuff in green is done, we can forget about it. Stuff in orange is underway, and this column," she tapped the screen with a red lacquered nail, "shows what I'm waiting on to close it off."

"Red means what? Nothing done yet?"

"That's right." Amy nodded.

"There's a *lot* of stuff in red."

"And now you see why I'm a bit stressed."

Rick leaned forward to peer at one of the lines. "This one says 'customised cookie icing'. What's that?"

"Oh, I'm having little individually-wrapped cookies made with our portraits on them as part of the favours. I'm looking at a few different companies, and it's orange because I'm waiting on the quotes."

Rick twisted his neck to look at her. "You go into *this* much detail?"

"Of course. How else would I keep track of all these things?"

"No, but I mean … does the detail itself need to exist?" He blinked at her. "I kind of thought we were done once we picked the venue and our clothes."

"Really?" she asked flatly. "You didn't think we'd need to choose our food and drinks? Have cutlery?"

"I thought *they* sorted all that out. The venue."

"I'm sure they'd throw *something* together."

"You said it was relaxed and casual."

"Do you know how much effort goes into relaxed and casual?" Amy said with a laugh.

He shook his head at the spreadsheet. "This must be driving you nuts."

She shrugged. "This calms me. Turning the little orange and red squares to green is basically therapy. So, what were you thinking you might want to tackle?"

"What about …" Rick peered at the screen. "Does this cell say the *Pantone* colour of napkins?"

"Yes. Oh, I can move that to green now, because we have the bridesmaid dress colours. I'll match the napkins to the girls." Amy tapped away. "Oh, and we can change the pocket square cell to green as well, because they'll match the bridesmaid dresses."

"Okay, then what about … Wait, why is *Persian rug* listed here?"

"For the outdoor lounge area after dinner. There'll be some furniture like lounge chairs and floor cushions, the venue provides those. But I want to tie them together with an area rug. It also gives people another place to sit."

"Oh, that's a cool idea. Could I help with that?"

Amy bit her lip, staring at the blinking cursor. "Well, I have a really good idea for that one. And I have lots of supplier contacts because of work. That one's an easier one for me I would say."

"Right. Um …" Rick trailed his finger down the screen. "Glassware? Really?"

"They have options."

"Then I'll pick one."

Amy twisted her mouth. "Okay."

"You've blown me away with your enthusiasm."

She tried to laugh. "I was thinking that whoever's doing

the whole table layout should do that one. It needs to all go together. But …" She hesitated. "Sure. You do that one."

"Great." Rick turned back to the screen. "This one says balloons. Surely I could do that?"

"Oh, well … yes, technically. But it's for the arch we'll get married under. So it kind of … I'll do that one."

"Ames …"

She heard the warning in his tone. "This is how I work!" she said defensively. "You should see my tab for the business."

"Go on then."

Amy flicked between the tabs and Rick burst out laughing as she scrolled downward. "It doesn't end!"

"Definitely feels like that to me, too," Amy agreed.

"Go back to our wedding one," Rick asked, then squinted, shaking his head. "Now that I've seen this, I have to say I'm *very* surprised you let the girls choose their own dresses."

"I'm not Bridezilla," Amy sniffed.

Rick flashed his heart-stopping smile, dimple showing. "Well, I seem to have picked ones that aren't convenient to share. Why don't you tell me which ones Mum or I could do?"

Amy felt itchy at the thought of handing over the reins. Even a little. She scrolled up and down the list, twirling a strand of her hair. A long silence fell. "Well, you're doing the glassware. So I guess … you can choose the plates as well? I can show you the mood board."

"Ames, I'm worried about you," he sighed. "I mean it. I think you've even lost a little weight due to all this stress."

"Don't tell my mother," Amy said darkly. "She'll be over the moon."

Rick sighed, throwing his hands up.

"Oh hey," Amy said, pointing to a microwave perched on top of Rick's dresser drawers. He glanced in that direction and she quickly closed her laptop. "That's new!"

"I thought we could make popcorn in here sometimes, watch a movie or whatever."

"That's a great idea! Shall we start right now?"

"Don't think I don't know you're trying to distract me."

"I'll think about what else I can delegate, I promise. Right now I need a shower."

Once the popcorn was ready, Rick turned down the lights and Amy snuggled beside him in her robe, dipping her hand into the bag as the opening credits of the movie came on. Rick yawned dramatically and snaked an arm over her shoulders. She twisted her head to look at him.

"You know you don't have to try and be smooth, right? I'm kind of a sure thing."

"Oh, are you?" he replied, arching his brows as he reached to open her robe a little, his fingers brushing the skin on her decolletage.

"Hmmm," she said, the popcorn paused on its way to her mouth. "I am indeed. And that kind of manoeuvre is probably going to end *very* well for you."

"Is it now?" Rick's voice was husky and breathy in her ear, and Amy shifted to give him better access.

"Knock, knock!" Pam said loudly from the other side of the door.

Popcorn flew over the bed as Amy jerked her robe closed and sat bolt upright. Without waiting for an answer, Pam pushed the door open and flicked on Rick's bedroom light. "I smelled popcorn and I thought you guys might be watching a movie or something."

"Uh-huh," Rick said, squirming to pull a corner of the blanket over the tell-tale signs of his enthusiasm.

"Well, I thought why don't we all watch it together on the big TV in the lounge room? I'll meet you in there in a couple of minutes. Just need to top off my wine."

Once she was gone, Rick shot Amy a mortified look.

"We *really* need to get her a hobby," Amy hissed.

"I'm so sorry," he said, face in hands.

"If we watch this movie with her, you *are* coming to brunch with my mother tomorrow."

"Any idea what it's about yet?"

Amy shook her head. "Can't even imagine. But being in love means suffering together while we find out."

Rick groaned. "Why is this my life?"

16

SATURDAY: SEVEN WEEKS TO THE WEDDING

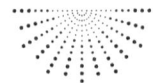

"I'll have a cobb salad, no dressing, thank you," Diana said, snapping the menu closed. "And a cup of hot water with lemon."

Amy took a subtle, calming breath before smiling up at the waiter. "Veggie burger and a coke, please."

"Side of fries or salad?"

"Fries," Amy answered. She sensed rather than saw her mother stiffen, but when she looked up, Diana was smiling blandly. In the end, they'd decided Rick shouldn't join her for this morning's visit, and Amy had to admit that the cafe was far from accessible for his wheelchair. It was close to the beach—Diana had made the unheard-of concession of meeting Amy at Bondi—and the owners had rammed it with tables to fit in as many customers as possible.

Amy had decided to combine the brunch with a check-up on her apartment. She needed to collect mail anyway and hadn't been home in about a week. And after being forced to watch a movie with Pam, then being admonished for working on her laptop during it, she was happy to put a little distance between herself and the Ford household.

"How's the wedding planning coming along?" Diana asked, once the waiter had left.

"Good," Amy lied brightly. "Pretty much everything is done and taken care of."

Diana leaned forward, elbows on the table. "Tell me about the dress."

"It's a surprise," Amy said hesitantly. She was on high alert. It was the first time in a long, long time that her mother had proactively reached out to her and asked to meet up. She hadn't gone about it the best way—trying to guilt Amy by dropping some not-so-subtle hints that she felt abandoned by her daughter—but the suggestion had come from her in the end. Amy couldn't quite figure out why.

"But you can tell your mum, can't you?" Diana prompted.

"I won't show you a picture or anything, but I can tell you that it's vintage."

A frown flickered across Diana's face. "You're wearing something second-hand to your wedding?"

"Vintage."

"Isn't that technically … Never mind. I'm sure it will be beautiful, darling."

"Thanks. It is. Anyway, don't they say 'something old, something new'?"

"Traditionally, the jewellery is old. But anyway!" Diana plucked a napkin from the pile in a small container on the table, folding it neatly in half. "It's good you're still letting yourself have an occasional day off from your wedding diet, too," she continued, seeming pleased with herself for the sentiment.

"There isn't a wedding diet," Amy said flatly, her eyes glued to her mother's face.

Diana's head tipped back slightly in shock, but she pressed her lips together in something like a smile. "Well, good for you," she said weakly.

The waiter appeared with their drinks, and Diana wrapped her bony fingers around the steaming mug. Amy leaned to sip her coke.

She found the silence awkward, but there was obviously something on her mother's mind, and she didn't have the patience to slowly tease it out of her. If Diana had something to say, she was going to have to come out and say it.

"So, your father will be walking you down the aisle, I presume?"

"No. Pop will."

Diana's eyes widened. "Really? You don't … you don't want your father to do it?"

"Mum, I only just started talking to him again. We're building this from the ground up. I lived with Pop for longer than I did with you or Dad. Of course he'll walk me down the aisle. Or, what there is of an aisle anyway."

"Isn't that very upsetting for your father?" Diana continued, frowning.

Amy held up her palms. "That isn't really my problem."

"Well, Amy, how can you say that?"

Amy blinked. "Pretty easily, actually. Look, if you're here to question the choices I've made, I'm not interested."

"No, no." Diana quickly flapped her hand. "My apologies if you got the wrong end of the stick. Of course that's not my intention."

Her mother never said *I'm sorry*, like a normal person. And it was always a qualified statement that stuck the blame squarely back with Amy. *What a shame* you *took it* that *way.*

Amy swallowed and held her mother's gaze. "Then what is your intention?"

Diana averted her eyes. "Do I need an intention?"

"Of course not. How are things with you and Bill?"

"Wonderful, thank you."

Amy knew her mother could have discovered a cellar full of hostages and would still give the same answer.

"Glad to hear it."

Amy let a silence fall. It stretched out as the waiter returned with their meals. Amy picked at her fries, her appetite muted. Diana crunched down some lettuce in silence, before swallowing a sip of her lemon water and placing her hands on the table.

"Tell me about Rick's family?" she asked, trying to sound casual.

Amy frowned. "His father passed. And his mother is … she's nice. I spend a bit of time there since my flat isn't accessible for Rick."

"Oh, okay. So she's nice, the mother? Pamela—that's her name?"

Amy didn't remember ever having mentioned Pam before, so she was surprised Diana knew her name.

"Yeah, Pam." Amy shrugged. "And she's nice enough."

Diana swallowed, staring at her plate for so long Amy was worried she was glitching. "Do you … have any pictures of the three of you? I'd love to see the family you're marrying into."

Amy's eyes snapped to Diana's face. "You want to see a picture of Pam?"

"I mean, she *will* be my," Diana waved a hand through the air, "some kind of in-law, I presume."

"I might have a picture of her and Rick?"

Diana nodded. "I'd love to see it."

"Okaay," Amy said slowly, reaching for her phone, wondering why on earth Diana was interested in a picture of Pam. And then it hit her, and her fingers froze over the screen. She raised her eyes to her mother, who was studiously focused on her plate. Amy resumed scrolling through pictures, and kept her tone light. "What do you think about Dad starting boxing?"

"I guess it can't be bad for him," Diana said with a shrug.

"So, you guys talk quite a bit?"

"Oh, you know ... As often as we always have."

Amy found a picture of Pam and Rick, playing a game of cards in the living room. Pam was laughing, her bobbed blonde hair spraying out around her. She looked girlish, natural and beautiful. For a moment, Amy hesitated to show her mother the picture. Especially now that she had a good idea why Diana was curious.

"It's a good shot of her," Amy said.

Diana was practically leaning across the table in her haste to grab the phone—the most eager Amy had seen her about anything. Amy turned the screen around and watched as Diana scanned the image, her breath coming shallow and a frown creasing her forehead. "I suppose she's nice looking enough."

"Nice-looking? Enough? For what?"

Diana's cheeks grew warm. "I only mean ... she doesn't look awfully like Rick, does she?"

"Not really, I guess."

Diana's eyes roamed over the photo again, her jaw setting. "So, you sometimes have chats with your father, when Rick and his mother are around? You've certainly come a long way."

There it was.

Sean must have mentioned Pam to Diana, and something about the way he talked of her must have set Diana's radar on full alert. Amy knew her mother still had strong feelings for her father, despite having left him years ago, and despite having long been remarried.

Amy had also thought her father was carrying a torch for Diana—he'd admitted as much the first time he and Amy had reconnected. But he hadn't mentioned her in a while ... not in any of their conversations, now that Amy came to think of it. And Diana was worried enough about it that she'd actually reached out to Amy, organised a cafe lunch, driven out to Bondi and found a way to bring up Pam in conversation.

Amy didn't know whether to feel sorry for her mother, or irritated that the only time she actually called to see her daughter was when she was checking out competition for her ex-husband. For a moment, she wondered whether she should mention the pre-rehearsal dinner meet up. Perhaps Sean had mentioned it to Diana, and Diana was testing her to see if Amy would invite her mother and stepfather.

But the last thing Amy wanted was to have to spend extra time in Bill's company. Especially when Amy knew he couldn't be trusted not to make snide remarks about her father.

Once Diana had seen the photo she so clearly came for, she wrapped things up rather quickly. After an air-kiss goodbye, Amy saw her mother to her car and headed up the hill to her flat.

It felt good to be there after so many nights away. Too good. She kicked off her heels at the door and wiggled her toes into the plush carpet, then flung open the windows to let in the sea air and trailed her fingers over the marble in her luxury bathroom. She loved the way every stick of furniture and decorative item had been styled to perfection. It was her oasis, her sanctuary, an extension of herself. She missed it.

She opened the doors to the Juliet balcony off the dining room, and stood, taking deep breaths of the clean, salty air. Then she called Rick.

"Would you hate me if I stayed here the next couple of nights?"

Rick paused. "Of course not. I'll definitely miss you though."

Amy sighed. "Yeah. Me too. I just feel the need to be here for a little bit."

"Are you trying to motivate me to do more house-hunting online?" he joked.

"Do you need more motivation?" Amy closed her eyes and tipped her face to the sun, drinking in the warmth.

"God no. There's not a lot coming up in our price range."

Amy's shoulders collapsed. "I know. What about if we started looking for blocks of land? Then we could build something exactly the way we want? We need to get something accessible. Even when you stop needing a wheelchair, we're both going to get old. Although, I'm not sure how close to the city we'd be able to find anything."

Rick was silent a moment and when he spoke, Amy could hear the smile in his voice. "I love the idea of getting old with you," he said.

She sighed dreamily. "Yeah. Me too. Ugh, I don't want to be away from you!"

"Take a couple of days. It will make it that much better when we see each other again."

"And by *it*, you mean…?"

Rick puffed out a breath. "Amy Beth Porter, you're corrupting me."

Amy closed her eyes and smiled. "I wish I could corrupt you right now."

"Okay, stop," Rick begged and Amy chuckled, showing mercy.

"See you in a few days then."

"Love you, future wifey."

"And you, future hubby."

Amy hung up the phone and decided to head down to the ocean for a dip, before taking a long soak in her bath. She knew she should probably be worried about Diana's possessiveness over Sean, but she pushed the concern to the back of her mind. There was too much other stuff competing with it. Besides, they were adults. Surely they could take care of themselves.

17
TUESDAY

Amy looked up and smiled as Kristina walked in. It was the first time she'd beaten her co-owner to work and Kristina's surprise showed on her face.

"Everything okay?" Kristina asked, shaking out the braids she'd pinned up under her motorcycle helmet and shucking her leather jacket.

They worked in a kind of unspoken shift pattern—Kristina started earlier and left earlier, Amy started later and worked later. It meant the office was staffed for longer, and also allowed them both to work to their natural rhythms.

"All good," Amy said. "I'm staying at my place in Bondi for a few nights, and it's nice to do the drive in from there instead of Pam's place. I went for a swim yesterday morning, but the weather today was a bit off-putting."

"Ah," Kristina said, nodding out the front window at the gloomy, windy day. "You and Rick okay?"

Amy noticed the tightness in Kristina's voice and smiled at her. She knew it was hard for her colleague to ask personal questions. Mainly, Amy suspected, because she didn't want them asked back. They'd been working together well for over a year now, and Amy still knew very little about her. She also had the sense Kristina wanted to keep it that way, so she didn't pry. They had an excellent working dynamic and shared a crystal-clear vision for their company. That was more than enough for Amy, but she did appreciate Kristina's attempt to check in on her.

"We couldn't be better," Amy said reassuringly. "Thanks for asking. I *might* have needed a small break from his mum."

"Oh." Kristina winced knowingly. "Boyfriend's mums can suck."

"Especially when you have to spend so much time with them," Amy sighed. "Anyway, I've called everyone on my former client list now."

Kristina moved to the little kitchenette to make herself a coffee. "Yeah, me too."

"And?"

Kristina grinned over her shoulder at Amy. "About seventy percent on board."

"Similar for me!" They beamed at one another in a silent celebration. Then Amy turned thoughtful. "Okay, now we *really* need to start hiring more people."

"I know." Kristina turned her back to Amy as she fiddled with the machine. "Have you given any more thought to …"

"Trying to poach people from Edgerton's?"

"Well it's not really poaching, but that's what I meant, yeah."

"I have," Amy said slowly.

"And?"

"I think I've come around to it. We probably should start putting out feelers. I can't get over the fact that they don't think Beaumont will wake up."

Kristina sipped from her coffee, coming to take a seat opposite Amy at the long bench table. "It is odd. I do sometimes feel bad for the way I left. He seemed to have a lot of faith in me."

Amy nodded. "Yeah, he did. I don't know if this info makes it worse or better, but he often told me how impressed he was with you."

"Sorry," Kristina said, her mouth twisted.

Amy waved a hand. "It's totally fine. It had been me once, but he was also the reason I stopped trying so hard. Besides, he really did me a huge favour. If he hadn't been so mean to me, we wouldn't be here now."

Kristina smiled. "I'm really glad we are."

"Me too."

"Alright then, shall we wait until Martha gets in and then start planning our expansion?"

"Expansion?" Amy said with a grin. "I think you mean world domination."

"Wow," Martha said breathily, standing back from the whiteboard. "Have I mentioned how glad I am that I accepted the offer to join you guys here?"

Amy slung an arm across her shoulders. "Not as glad as we are."

Kristina uncapped a red marker and circled the remaining projects on the list that hadn't been allocated to one of the three of them. "Now we need to cluster these and figure out how many people we need to hire to cover them."

"We definitely need Amber," Amy said quickly. "If we can get her."

"She could probably tackle these," Kristina underlined four of the projects.

"Walter?" Martha asked.

"Eh. I could take or leave him," Kristina said.

"Do you have any contacts from your previous company?" Amy asked her.

She looked thoughtful. "Yeah, maybe one. Jessamyn."

"Only one?" Martha grinned at Amy, knowing they were sharing a thought. Kristina was a harsh judge. It made them both that little bit prouder that she'd picked them to work with.

"Mm-hm," Kristina said, deep in thought as she stared at the whiteboard. She turned abruptly to stare at them. "If we bring two or three new designers on board, plus maybe Hope for IT part-time, we need to move out of this building. We have to factor that into our decisions as well. It will mean a big outlay."

Amy crumpled into a chair. "One more thing for me to deal with."

"Well, *us*," Kristina said.

"No, that's not what I meant. I know we'll split the work, but … I mean, are you two honestly okay with me taking on a little less over the next couple of months?"

They'd already reassured her, but it didn't feel quite fair. She'd still be pulling the same wage, the same cut of the profits. And if they needed to factor in a move and more hires, it felt even more unjust.

Kristina locked her gaze onto Amy's. "We'll all have periods where we need each other to pick up some of the slack. If it becomes a problem at any stage, and we think one of us is taking the mickey, we'll have that chat."

"Thank you," Amy said solemnly. "We definitely can't fit three more people in here, huh? Even if we got Rick and Alex to knock down the walls, so we have more open space?"

"Or if we cram into the front room in the beginning?" Martha said with a shrug.

Kristina tugged on her braid. "I think it will be a mistake

not to move right away. But since all decisions need to be unanimous ... let's decide once we see who accepts our offers. I'll call Jessamyn, one of you call Amber and the other call Hope. I don't think we'll need her full-time. See if she'd do consulting and we could pay her in blocks of her time. We'll definitely still need one more person. It would be good if we knew them and didn't have to advertise."

"This cluster here," Amy said, pointing. "It's mainly industrial clients. Who was good at that? Doug?"

"He left to start his own thing, remember," Kristina reminded her.

"I'll call Amber," Martha said. "I was the last to come on board, so I think I can be the most convincing. Maybe we can ask her if there's someone else she's been working well with?"

Amy bit her lip, scanning the list. They definitely couldn't take on all that work. And it was also a big gamble to double their size so quickly. Still ... someone else could snap up the staff and clients they didn't. And hadn't this always been the goal? For them to grow and expand? Who knew when they'd get another chance like this.

"Okay, let's ask her," Amy said finally. "If there's no one she immediately recommends, we'll just have to put an ad up."

"Agreed," both women said and Amy felt a smile begin to spread across her face. She chose not to think about the additions to her to-do list.

18
WEDNESDAY

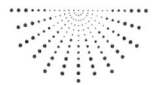

"How did you know?" Marley groaned, sinking into the sofa with a giant smile as Finn presented her with a warm cup of peppermint tea when she emerged from the shower. It had been another long day at work, and she was exhausted. He sat beside her, pulling her feet onto his lap and pressing them. Marley closed her eyes and practically melted as his fingers found the most painful places and began to gently ease away the ache.

She peeked at him through her lashes, his glossy black hair falling forward as those other-worldly blue eyes, the ones she'd fallen in love with, were trained with concentration on her feet.

"I want to find out what we're having," Marley said.

His eyes snapped up to hers and his fingers paused on her feet. She could see him fighting to keep his expression neutral. "Really?"

"Yeah," she smiled. "I do. I know you don't like the name I want, and I won't pretend it doesn't hurt. That's one of the things I never thought I'd have to compromise on. But, we're in this together. It's your baby too, and I don't want to give it a name you hate."

"It's not that I *hate* it, exactly," Finn said carefully. "And I don't even necessarily have another name to propose. I sort of feel like it's maybe not the best name for a little girl growing up in this day and age."

"Well, I disagree," Marley said, trying to remain calm. "I think it's a beautiful name for a girl in any era. But ... maybe we can avoid this whole thing if we find out we're having a boy."

Finn's brow furrowed. "You ... you wouldn't want to call a boy Petunio or something?"

Marley couldn't help bursting out laughing. "No!"

Finn joined her. "Okay, well, I'm really glad we had this chat, and I'm so excited we get to find out what we're having. Where shall we open the envelope from the midwife? Where even is it? I'll go get it."

"I was thinking maybe we have a nice little cafe lunch somewhere and do it?"

"That's a good idea," Finn said, agreeing easily.

Marley nodded. "I spoke to your office manager and she's blocked a long lunch slot for you next week."

"Next *week?*" Finn yelped.

Marley couldn't help but laugh. "Okay, okay. you're right. Shall we do it tomorrow?"

Finn scratched his neck, looking at her with a sheepish smile.

"Right *now?*" she asked.

"I can't believe you can wait any longer! I've been *desperate*."

Marley blinked. It was as though only now that she'd agreed to get the envelope out, was Finn expressing his true feelings. He'd been so eager, but he'd hardly said anything to her before now. The realisation made her chest hurt. This man loved her so much, he was putting his own desires after hers, without even hinting at the sacrifice of it. On the one hand, it made her sad to think he was holding things back from her. On the other, she could hardly blame him. *She* was the one who'd created an environment where he didn't feel comfortable telling her. She was the one asking him to always keep a little something back from her, so that she could go at her own pace. She made a decision right then to find a psychologist, and soon. Amy was right. She needed to speak to someone. Finn and the baby were the best things happen to her in a very, very long time. She shuddered to think she was risking things with Finn in any way.

"I'll go get the envelope," she said finally. The look on his face was so overjoyed that Marley leaned forward to grab his hand, threading their fingers together. "And we should probably finally get started on the nursery after that," she added.

She'd expected him to be delighted, but she felt him tense again. Then she realised why ... they were skating close to that other issue they had yet to overcome: their living arrangements once the baby was born. She pressed a quick kiss to his cheek and went to the stationery drawer to get the envelope. Everything would be fixed once she spoke to someone. Surely.

She sat back down, watching as Finn struggled to keep his breathing even.

"You open it," she said, thrusting it at him. "I'm too scared to look."

He took a deep breath and clutched the envelope in his hand. Instead of tearing it open as she thought he would, he dropped it to his lap and pulled her close. She watched his Adam's apple bob and felt the familiar clench of desire as she breathed in his smell.

"Whatever it is," he whispered, "we'll figure it out. I promise you."

He swept a hand through her hair and she felt herself melt into him. She was a crazy person for not accepting this man entirely into her life. And she vowed to work through her issues so that she could.

Finn tore into the envelope and then froze, his eyes skimming the paper and then meeting hers. She knew what that look meant even before he said the words.

They were having a girl.

19
WEDNESDAY

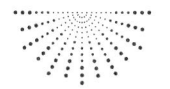

"How on *earth* did you get tomorrow off, for both of us?" Ernie asked as he and Silas boarded the late afternoon ferry on Sydney Harbour. Silas had hoped to keep their destination a secret, but he could hardly march a blindfolded Ernie up the gang-plank without attracting a lot of attention. Still, the ferry had multiple drop-offs and he hoped to keep his boyfriend guessing until they disembarked.

"Dan and Jenny are covering for me tomorrow," Silas said, leading Ernie to the upper deck so they could watch the city disappear. He tucked the single suitcase he'd packed for them both into the bench in front of them, taking a deep breath of the salty air. From this point, he could almost see his food truck.

He and Alex's cousin Jenny had merged their side-by-side vans—Jenny's vegan *Meat is Murder* and Silas and Lyra's *The Pie-ganic*—around a year earlier. They'd bought a bigger truck and rebranded as *The Good Food Stop.* They were enjoying huge success and though Lyra no longer worked for Silas, she kept her ties to the business as an investor. Jenny and Silas worked well together, and he enjoyed his days down at the waterfront with both her and Dan, the staff member they'd hired and split the costs of. They'd maintained separate suppliers, and were careful to keep all utensils and equipment strictly segregated. Since Jenny offered vegan food and Silas's pies were mainly meat, keeping things separate gave customers peace of mind. Silas had sweated over the decision to merge, knowing he didn't always play well with others, but he and Jenny had slid seamlessly into a good routine.

"And what about my work?" Ernie asked, nudging him.

Silas winked. "I have my ways." He wasn't about to tell Ernie that his "ways" had included practically begging Ernie's boss and promising her free pies for two weeks. It shouldn't have been such a big deal to get him a day off he was entitled to, but Ernie's boss had sniffed Silas's desperation and pounced.

As the ferry rocked away from the harbour, Ernie leaned into Silas's side and closed his eyes to the sun.

"How lucky are we to live here?" he asked dreamily. "The smell of fresh seawater, gorgeous warm days, not a cloud in the sky. Seriously, ours is the most beautiful city. And the *aquarium* is right there ..." He paused and stared at Silas, who made no reaction. "Dang. Not the aquarium. But isn't the *Opera House* looking stunning? Would be great to see a show there one night ..."

Silas bit back a grin at Ernie's obvious attempts to find out where they were going.

"The Rocks looks beautiful as well," Silas pointed out, mentioning the quaint, historical old part of Sydney Harbour. "And don't forget Manly Beach. We haven't been there in ages."

Ernie thrust his bottom lip out dramatically and Silas fought the urge to lean down and nibble it.

When the only stop left was Taronga Zoo, Ernie let out a squeal. "Oh my god. Are we doing that thing where you stay overnight at the zoo? And the room looks into the animal enclosures? And you can feed the animals and stuff? And will I *finally* get to hold a koala?"

"You might," Silas grinned.

Ernie clapped his hands together. "Argh! You are the best boyfriend in the whole entire world!"

He hid his smile as Ernie looped his arms around his neck, drawing a lot of attention and almost choking Silas in the process.

That was certainly the reaction he'd been aiming for.

"Si, this *room*," Ernie breathed, pressing a hand to his heart and spinning in a circle as he took it all in. Floor to ceiling windows ran the length of the suite and overlooked the forest sanctuary, with glimpses of the harbour all the way out to the Bridge. A four-poster was pushed up close to the window so that they'd be able to see the view when waking. A cosy sofa, armchair and coffee table created a separate space for relaxing, while an open en-suite area with a deep tub and glass-walled shower meant there was nowhere in the room from which the view wasn't visible. The carpet was plush, the lighting mellow and flattering, and the linen obviously expensive.

"I don't even know what to do with myself first," Ernie said. "Flop on that bed, pour a bath or keep staring at that view!" Silas smiled and Ernie crossed the room to slip his arms around him. "Thank you for this," he said, gazing adoringly up at him.

"You're welcome. We're also having dinner at the treetop

restaurant," Silas added, "but before that, we get a private tour."

"Are you *serious*? And I really get to hold a koala?"

When Silas nodded, Ernie released him to do a silly little jig. "And is dinner fancy?"

Silas shrugged. "I don't know. A bit maybe?"

"But I've only got my shorts," Ernie said in despair, looking down at his clothing. He was dressed in a crisp lilac polo t-shirt and tan shorts.

"You look fine. But I packed more clothes for us. What you're wearing is perfect for the tour, and if you want, we can dress up for dinner later."

"When does the tour start?"

Silas glanced at his watch. "Actually, we'd better get going now."

"I don't want to leave this room," Ernie pouted.

"There are elephants."

"Meh."

"Baby elephants."

"What are we waiting for?"

The tour was a dream come true for Ernie, who peppered their guide—a friendly young man named Jack—with questions on everything from the dietary habits of each and every animal, to their mating rituals. Jack took it all in his stride and answered as much as he could. It helped that Ernie was spellbound by every single fact he offered.

"Male lions can weigh over a quarter of a tonne."

"*No.*"

"Sun Bear tongues are almost as long as a standard school ruler."

"Ew. But also, wow."

"There are only four hundred Sumatran tigers left in the world."

"Oh, that's *shocking*. Don't you think, Si?"

"Huh? Oh, yes. Shocking."

Silas wasn't really an animal person, but there was something about meerkats that made him want to bundle one up and take it home. He tried to linger by the enclosure, but the koala encounter was next up so Ernie was tugging on his hand. He waggled his fingers goodbye at one of the meerkats who stood tall and alert, staring at him—those intelligent, dusky eyes trained on his.

"Did you just fall in love with an animal?" Ernie asked.

"Shut it."

"Oh, you big softie."

"No one will know if I toss you into the lion enclosure tonight."

Ernie tsked, beaming at Silas, and hooked their arms together, practically dragging them to catch up with Jack.

It was during the koala encounter that Ernie slipped. Jack had handed them over to a startlingly young, apple-cheeked woman named Emily, who would accompany them during the encounter. Ernie was reaching out to take a fluffy koala from Emily, his arms outstretched and his expression one of pure joy. As he put one foot forward, he hit a slick patch and went down hard. Silas immediately moved to help him up, but Ernie's face crumpled as he realised what he'd slipped in.

"I am *covered* in koala poo!" he gasped.

Silas bit his lip to keep from laughing and Emily blanched.

"I'm so sorry!" she said hastily, the koala still clinging to her. "Someone is supposed to come through and clean all that up regularly. I'll get them right away."

She turned and fled, the koala looking sleepily over her shoulder at Ernie.

"Si, what am I going to *do?*" Ernie wailed. The entire back of his shorts was smeared and he seemed afraid to touch them to dust anything off.

"We'll go back and get changed. Do you want to wait and have a photo taken with the koala?"

Ernie seemed torn, devastated to be so close to fulfilling his dream but also clearly desperate to change. "Take *one* picture of me with it, then we go back and get changed?"

"Of course."

When Emily returned with a red-faced employee who immediately set about scooping up the remaining mess, Ernie reached for the koala and Silas primed his phone camera for a picture. Ernie held still for approximately four seconds, squeezing the koala so tight that Emily panicked.

Back in their room, he got to work rinsing his shorts in the shower.

"I cannot *believe* that happened," he complained, over the noise of the running water.

Silas had been trying hard not to laugh at the memory of it. The look on Ernie's face as he'd slipped had been priceless. But he knew better than to be caught laughing. Ernie would never laugh at him in a similar situation. Instead, he unzipped the suitcase to get out fresh clothes for his boyfriend … and froze in horror. There was Ernie's crisply-pressed shirt. There was a pair of black slacks and a black tee for Silas himself. There were both sets of pyjamas … But he hadn't packed Ernie's trousers. He gulped, heat rising to his face, and swore under his breath.

"What?" Ernie asked. Silas had forgotten his boyfriend's supersonic hearing.

"Nothing."

Ernie shut off the water, draping his sopping shorts over the top of the glass shower door. "No, really. What?"

Silas stood frozen in horror as Ernie glanced back and forth between him and the suitcase. His face fell. "You forgot to pack my clothes, didn't you?"

"Not all of them."

"Please tell me you forgot the top."

Silas was silent.

"Oh, *Si!*" Ernie huffed. "What am I going to wear to dinner?"

"You can wear my trousers?"

"You're like two sizes bigger than me. And *much* rounder in the seat. I'm going to look like a boy dressed in his dad's clothes. And what will you wear?"

"My pyjama pants?"

Ernie made a sceptical face. "You're going to wear red and black check *flannel* pants that are obviously from a pyjama set to a fancy dinner?"

"It's not *that* fancy," Silas said lamely.

"I seriously cannot believe this! Do they have a gift shop that sells clothes? Can you run and buy me something? Do we have time to ferry back into the city and get something?"

"You'd have to go in your underpants," Silas pointed out as he checked his watch. "Also, I don't think we'll make it."

Ernie crossed the room and flung himself dramatically onto the bed.

"Come on, it's not that bad," Silas tried. Ernie lifted his head enough to shoot Silas a withering look over his shoulder.

"Show me those pyjama pants on you," he said, grudgingly.

Silas stifled a grin, and changed into them, turning this way and that for Ernie, who had flipped onto his side and was propped up on one elbow.

"You'd wear them to dinner to make me feel better?" Ernie asked, with the hint of a smile.

"Yeah. Who cares?"

"I know *you* don't, but I'm going to look like I raided the dress-up box."

"We'll be ridiculous together," Silas shrugged.

A slow grin broke over Ernie's face. "Say that again."

"We'll be ridiculous together," Silas repeated, trying not to smile.

"You, the regal and *impossibly* beautiful Silas Beck, would make yourself ridiculous for little old *me*?" He fake-swooned onto the bed.

"Shut it."

"You love me *that* much?" He raised his eyebrows at Silas, who did his best to frown.

"What did I warn you about the lion enclosure?"

Ernie beamed, sitting back up. "Give me those trousers of yours. And something to punch a new hole in your belt."

"You're going to maim my belt on top of all of this?" Silas asked, aghast.

"Well, unless you want them sliding off me as we enter the restaurant, I think that's all we can do."

Silas sighed dramatically. "What about we skip dinner? I'm not that hungry anyway."

"Uh-uh. Not a *chance* mister."

Silas had to practically carry Ernie back to the room after dinner. Ernie had spent the evening convinced that every single person who laid eyes on the pair of them was secretly assessing their clothing. Maybe even live-tweeting the horror of it. It didn't matter to him that one couple had wandered in in their bathrobes, before being politely turned away at the door. Or that another couple were both dressed in ripped jeans and sloppy old band t-shirts. For Ernie, that was simply the end of decorum. He held the two of them to a different standard. But no one had batted an eye at their attire—certainly not the waitstaff, who were minutely attentive to their needs. Particularly to Ernie's constantly empty wine glass. The food had been first-class, the view breath-taking. And the wine apparently far too strong and plentiful.

As Ernie tripped over the threshold and giggled, Silas caught his arm to steady him.

"At least there's no koala poo in the bedroom," Ernie hooted.

Silas rolled his eyes indulgently.

"Ooh! I'm going to pour us a bath!" Ernie declared. "With *so* many bubbles. You'll get in there with me, Si, won't you?"

"Are you sure hot water is a good idea when you're this …"

"Drunk?" Ernie supplied, then sputtered out a laugh through his hand. "Yes! You'll make sure I don't drown, won't you?"

He patted Silas's arm and then set about trying to figure out the taps, while pouring entirely too much bubble bath into the tub.

"There won't be any room for water if you keep going like that," Silas said. He tossed his phone onto this bed and it bounced beside Ernie's. The screen lit up and Silas saw that it was filled with messages. From *four hearts*, of course. He swallowed hard and turned his head away from the phone, finding Ernie watching him with a silly grin on his face.

"I can't believe you spoiled me like this," Ernie said, having upended the bubble bath bottle into the tub. "There couldn't be a better boyfriend than you."

"Really?" Silas asked, tilting his head at Ernie.

"Well, I mean there *could* be," Ernie admitted. "Maybe one who didn't threaten to throw me to the lions all the time."

"Oh yeah?" Silas forced a light-hearted laugh out, his chest squeezing at Ernie's words. "What else would he be like?"

"Umm," Ernie twisted his mouth as he pondered. "He *definitely* wouldn't have laughed when I slipped into koala crap."

"You saw that?" Silas winced.

"Of *course* I did. But I have to admit now … maybe it was funny."

"Kind of wish I'd caught it on camera."

Ernie waggled his finger at Silas. "See, he wouldn't say things like that. Oh! And he definitely wouldn't be in love with a *meerkat* of all things. Why couldn't you like a normal animal?"

"Meerkats *are* normal!"

Ernie shut the tap off and dipped his hand to test the water. "Perfect," he purred. He slipped into the tub and heaved a sigh of contentment. "Come on in."

"I'm honestly not sure it's big enough for the two of us," Silas said.

"We'll fit."

Silas doubted it, but was willing to try. "*He* wouldn't have forgotten your trousers, would he?" he asked, continuing the discussion about the theoretical better boyfriend.

"No!" Ernie laughed as he slipped deeper into the bubble bath, cupping a handful of the foam and blowing it. A second later, a puzzled frown crossed his face. "Wait. Who are we talking about?"

Silas flinched. He felt like he'd tripped Ernie up and his boyfriend had admitted that there *was* someone else. Someone far more organised than Silas, who wouldn't have messed up the packing and gone to a fancy dinner in his pyjama bottoms. All this effort, and he was still somehow falling short. But when he glanced over at Ernie in the bathtub, his cheeks pink from the warmth and the alcohol and a silly, giddy grin on his face, Silas decided all that could wait for another day.

20
WEDNESDAY

"Amy Beth, you're dancing 'round something, and I'm not getting any younger," Pop said huffily.

Hazel put her hand on his arm. "I'll stop giving you coffee so late if this is what it makes of you," she admonished.

Amy grinned. "I love how she keeps you in line, Pop," she said, leaning to take a sip of the half-finished mug of coffee Hazel had smuggled her. She glanced discreetly down at the phone in her lap, open to the to-do spreadsheet. She'd had an idea for her client's unsolvable sofa riddle after seeing the set up in Pop and Hazel's joint room. It was easily double the size of the one Pop had lived in when he was alone. There was even an actual bedroom with a closing door, although Amy knew it contained practical twin beds. But the living space was much roomier and they even had a little kitchenette.

"You've been glued to that thing all night, too," Pop said, as Amy typed the note down.

"Sorry." She clicked off her phone. "It's my to-do lists."

"On your phone?" Pop frowned.

"You have a smart phone. You know what they're capable of."

"I know it means you never seem to switch off!"

He had a point, Amy had to concede. She looked up to find the two of them watching her expectantly. She slipped her phone into her bag and held her hands up in surrender.

"I wanted to talk about Dad ..." she admitted finally.

Percy's features froze, and he nodded his head slowly. "Going to need some Clinkers for this conversation," he said, naming the candy Amy usually brought with her on visits.

"Oh, I forgot—" she began, but Hazel held up a hand and moved to a little cupboard, tugging open a drawer to reveal a stash of the candies. Amy gasped.

"You're both going to die of a heart attack," she said.

"Gotta be something, I guess," Pop shrugged, holding his hands out for the bag. Hazel deftly tossed it to him. "So, what about your father?" he asked, when they were settled again.

Amy slowly shook her head, trying to find the words. "I wonder ... I wonder whether it can be real? His turnaround, I mean? I want to believe but ..."

Hazel glanced towards Percy, then pushed herself up from the table. "Excuse me dear, I have some admin to take care of," she said, and quietly left the room.

"Well that wasn't a good sign," Amy noted wryly.

Percy shook his head. "I've told her she can stay for conversations like this. But she feels it's not her place." He bit into a chocolate, cracking it in two and crunching it down. "And I don't know, is the answer."

Amy's shoulders slumped.

"I will say, this is the most convincing attempt I've seen," he continued gently. Amy raised her eyes to his. "He's definitely running with a new crowd—which seems a strange thing to say for a man his age. But that's the thing about Sean. He does tend to mould himself to the group he's in with at the time." Pop sighed. "It's not a wonderful trait, I grant you. But in this case, it might be a good thing."

"But then ... then it hangs on these friendships, right? And if they disappear, or he falls out with them, he might go right back to how he was before."

Pop nodded sadly. "Amy Beth, my job as a parent is different to yours as a kid. Mine's to never give up on him, no matter what. No matter how many times he falls short or messes up. I'm going to keep believing that *this* time is the time."

"I get that."

"But you're his kid," he continued, placing a hand on her arm. "Your job is to protect yourself. Protect your heart. That man's let you down in a bigger way than I can ever really understand. I know I was there for it, but I don't know what it did to you deep inside. What kind of mark it left. If you need to keep your walls up, you keep them up. You've got plenty of people in your life that love you like mad. You don't need him, too. 'Less you want him."

Amy felt herself tearing up. "He's my Dad," she said, swallowing against the lump in her throat. "I don't want to keep punishing him."

"It's holding him accountable. It's protecting yourself. There's a difference."

Amy twisted her mouth, grabbing one of the candies from the bag and toying with it. "But you think it's genuine."

Pop sighed so heavily Amy felt it in her hair. He was silent a long time as he glanced down at his empty coffee cup. Eventually he nodded. "That's what I'm choosing to believe. Yes."

"Could you repeat that, Dad?" Amy stood on her Juliet balcony in her bathrobe later that evening, her heart pounding. After her visit to Pop, she'd headed back to her flat for a nice, relaxing bath. Now, her father was making her tense again.

On screen, Sean looked as close to blushing as Amy could imagine. "I know you heard me, baby girl ... I want Pam's number."

Amy's mind unspooled as she thought of the many different ways Rick might react to the news she'd passed on Pam's contact information. None of them were good. Then again, Pam was a grown woman, and she *had* expressed an interest in helping Sean out ... Not to mention that if she had an interest outside the house, Amy might get more time alone with her fiancé.

"Dad, it's not that I don't want to. Maybe I could ask her first? See how she feels about it?"

"Yes, of course. I don't want you to do anything you're not okay with. Or make an advance she doesn't want."

"I'll be back there in a couple of days and I'll bring it up with her then."

"Your Pop also mentioned there was an idea floating around about getting the two families together ahead of the rehearsal dinner?"

Amy sighed. She was going to have to take another relaxation bath at this rate. Perhaps live underwater entirely. "It was mentioned at some point, I think." She was reluctant to add that Pam herself had requested it. It wasn't actually the worst idea ... at least she would know what she was up against with the two of them. And there would be no need to invite Diana and Bill.

"I think it would be great," her father continued. "I'd love to come. If you'd have me."

"Let me talk to Rick. It'd be Pop and Hazel there, maybe you and Pam as well. I'm a little busy at the moment, so it might not happen this week or next."

"We're in countdown mode!" Sean looked genuinely delighted, and again, Amy was forced to compare his enthusiasm with Diana's uptight digging around and talk of wedding diets. Her father came off looking better and better these days. And Amy wasn't sure how she felt about that.

"Yes, we are."

"Are you excited? I've only met Rick over the phone, but he seems perfect for you. He gets my seal of approval, if that means anything."

Amy felt a warm glow in her chest. "Thanks, Dad. It does. And he is. Absolutely perfect. We've worked so hard to get to this point. And honestly, with what we overcame, I think we're pretty much rock solid."

Hours later, Amy was going slightly cross-eyed sitting up in bed, staring at her to-do spreadsheet. The wedding tab was a lattice of green, red and amber cells. Nothing felt like it was moving—she'd been staring at that same pattern for what felt like weeks. There were still a thousand tiny details to sort out. Nothing she'd allocated Rick had yet turned green, but she knew it was probably a bit soon for that.

Work was even worse. With her list of projects, the items that had been added around hiring, the new clients they'd have to onboard and draw up contracts for, not to mention potentially find new office space ... she felt like Porter Lucas was a ship out at sea—one that was rapidly getting away from her. Worse, there was nothing she could do but plough through the work to get it done. She knew Kristina was doing the same. But as far as she knew, Kristina didn't have a wedding to organise on top of that.

Nor a house to find. That tab was entirely red. Amy heaved a sigh and opened a new browser window, typing her house search criteria in for what felt like the thousandth time. Sort by: New Listings. Nothing. She was going to be trapped as a visitor in Pam's house for eternity.

Amy slapped her laptop closed. The last of the caffeine from her visit to Pop was leaving her system, and her eyes felt gritty. Glancing at the clock, she realised it was already one am. She groaned, sliding the laptop to the other side of the bed as she shut off the light. But her mind whirred for a long time and she could see the first streaks of dawn before she finally fell asleep.

21
FRIDAY

Amy woke up alone on Friday morning. Still half-asleep, she rolled over, sliding her hand across to the cool side of the bed, instinctively seeking Rick. Then she blinked her eyes open, realising that for the fifth morning in a row, they were apart.

She growled in frustration and grabbed her phone, video calling him.

"This sucks," she croaked when he answered.

"You're telling me," he replied. His hair was dishevelled with sleep and Amy's fingers ached to run through it.

"I stayed up until one last night looking for houses for us."

Rick shook his head, already knowing the outcome. "You can't keep doing that. Ames, are you sure you don't have a long lost relative on their deathbed, who just so happens to be going to leave you a three-bedroom single-storey somewhere along the shoreline?"

"If I do, they're hiding out with the same relative from your side of the family."

He laughed. "Please tell me you're coming back to me tonight?"

"Can't stay away from you a moment longer," Amy confirmed. "Besides, turns out that when I don't have you to tell me to go to bed, I stay up far too late."

"You'll be a wreck at work today," Rick admonished.

"I know. But I *have* cleared off a lot of my to-dos. For work at least. Going to drag my carcass down to Icebergs for a swim. Then I'll get a bunch of espressos at work and I should make it home to you in time for a nervous breakdown."

"I'll catch you."

"You always do," Amy said tenderly, touching his face on screen.

"Get your butt to the pool. I need to know you're not going to crash the car on the way in. Text me once you arrive."

She blew him a kiss and flopped back into the bed. When she caught herself drifting off, she sprang up.

The water was brisk and Amy shivered as she dipped in a tentative toe. But she lowered her goggles and dived in anyway, the icy shock of it making her breath catch. She pounded out laps—seven without stopping—and headed in for a warm shower. As her body slowly heated back up, she sipped a coffee on the bottom deck of Icebergs and gazed out over the aquamarine waters of the Pacific Ocean. She watched the waves break, wild and rhythmic, and breathed the salt mist deep into her lungs. By the time she drove into work, she was feeling refreshed.

She was greeted with chaos. Kristina and Martha were mid-argument as Amy pushed through the door. It wasn't terribly heated, but Amy hadn't heard them so much as raise their voices at one another before.

"What's going on?" she asked, frowning as she hooked her handbag on the rack.

"They've all accepted our job offers. Hope, Jessamyn and

Amber," Kristina said, ticking the names off on her fingers. "We still need another hire, too. Amber didn't know anyone, so we have to advertise. And we're discussing where everyone's going to fit."

"Discussing?" Amy raised a brow.

Martha stomped to the espresso machine. "Okay, we were arguing," she sniffed. "Kristina thinks we need to move out of here. But we've already discussed it, and we'd decided not to, right? It's too much of an expense when we don't know if we'll retain all these clients long-term."

"We've never lost a single one!" Kristina cried.

Amy dropped into her seat, spinning in a slow circle as she surveyed the room around them. The very idea of having to do *anything* to the space, let alone look for new offices, made her feel bone-exhausted despite the swim and coffee. She spun back to find Kristina and Martha watching her expectantly.

"What if we knock out the offices?" she said, sounding tired even to her own ears.

"Open spaces don't work," Kristina said firmly. "It's been proven. It only works for us now because at least two of us can have a quiet office if we need it."

Amy closed her eyes, a slow breath leaking from her. "There *has* to be a way around this."

"There is," Kristina said flatly. "We move."

"Let's knock out one wall only," Martha suggested. "It's a quick fix, we maintain at least one quiet space, and we gain enough room to add two more desks. Maybe Hope doesn't actually need a place?"

"What, you want her to stand?" Kristina asked.

"Didn't we say she'd consult?" Martha frowned.

Kristina shook her head. "She wants stability now that she has kids. A permanent part-time contract. And I don't blame her. She'll go up to full time hours as we grow, and as her twins get older."

"Then … what if we also knock out that kitchenette and coffee section?" Amy said. "We could fit another desk there?"

Kristina's jaw clenched. Martha froze with a coffee halfway to her mouth and an expression of pure horror on her face. She glanced around at the area as though it was in danger of disappearing at that exact moment.

"I don't get why you guys can't face up to the fact that we need to move," Kristina said. "Our lease is coming up soon anyway." She crossed her arms at their blank looks.

"Well, do *you* have a solution?" Amy asked.

Kristina hid a smile. "As it happens …" She held out a stapled booklet to Amy. "I do."

"What's this?"

"Our new offices. If you agree, of course."

Amy flicked her eyes to Kristina, then back down at the booklet. She heaved a sigh and sat down to examine it. Martha peered over her shoulder.

"This isn't in Lilac Bay," Amy said, her eyes snapping back to Kristina as she took in the address.

"No. We have to move. Just two suburbs. I know it sucks, but there's nothing else around here. But look at those offices."

Amy leafed to the next page. It showed a bright, airy office space that could easily hold a huge collaborative working area, with a row of glass-walled offices along the windows. Each of them could have their own quiet office in which to work, but they could also easily come together as a team.

"Keep flipping," Kristina said.

The next image showed a large boardroom, and Amy imagined client meetings in the impressive space. A small bathroom and a kitchenette with lunch area completed the space. The square meterage was perfect for them, and if the figures on the booklet were right, rent was a little over a third more than they were paying now—completely doable. The lobby of the building was impressive, floored with marble and lined with greenery.

Much as Amy despised the idea of leaving Lilac Bay, she had to admit it ... these offices were absolutely perfect.

She raised her eyes to Kristina, who was doing her best not to look too triumphant.

"When can we move in?"

"It's available immediately. We'll need to snap it up quick."

"Bloody hell." Amy rubbed her temples. "What do we need to do?"

"Talk to our landlady. See if we can get released a little earlier. If not, we'll need to manage the double rent, but it'll only be for three and a half months. I ran the numbers. It's tight—real tight—but we can do it. Sign the lease on this place. Move. We'll have to get Hope to come in some time before the others officially start. Pay her extra."

Amy threw herself back in the chair, covering her eyes with her hands. Behind her, Martha hissed out a breath.

"We have to do it, don't we?" Martha asked glumly.

Amy nodded. "Yeah. We do."

Kristina grinned. "Do you want to go see Mrs Beckwith? Or shall I?"

Amy rubbed the corner of her eye. "I was the one who drew up the lease, so it should come from me."

"Oh, and now may not be the time to mention this, but we might want to get an HR consultant on retainer," Kristina added. "We're okay with just the three of us, but there's always a potential for things to go pear-shaped as we add more. It would be good to know our legal obligations and rights and stuff."

"Kristina, please," Amy said firmly, pressing her fingers

together in a closing gesture. "No more bombshells for at least forty-five minutes."

Kristina laughed, mock-saluting Amy, who hadn't been entirely joking.

"There is one more that I need to tell you," Kristina said, her voice soft as Amy turned to leave. Amy glanced over her shoulder, eyebrow raised. "Beaumont died."

Amy shut the door to the office behind her and closed her eyes. Beaumont being dead felt impossible. She'd assumed he'd be one of those men who kicked on forever, tormenting people. She searched her feelings as she scrolled through her phone for Mrs Beckwith's number, and realised that below her indifference, there was a tiny grain of sadness. Her first few years at Edgerton's, Beaumont had been a different man. An encouraging one who saw her talent and spurred her on and paid for additional courses and gave her the best clients. He had been kind and patient and Amy had felt seen, for what had felt like the first time. There was no doubt he'd had a huge impact on her professionally. But it had also extended to the personal—Amy's career was one of the great joys of her life, and had given her a confidence that had spilled over into her private life.

However, Beaumont had more than overwritten those fond memories with nastier ones as he'd slowly seemed to morph personalities right before her eyes. The last words they'd spoken to one another had been when Amy dramatically marched out of his offices for the last time.

She allowed herself a moment's silence for him, out of respect for the past, and then moved on with her day.

Mrs Beckwith's landline rang for a long time. Eventually, it was answered by a flustered sounding woman. "Yes, hello?"

Amy was taken aback at the unfamiliar voice. "I was looking for Mrs Beckwith?"

"May I ask who's calling?"

"Amy Porter. I'm her tenant in the property at Lilac Bay. Well, I run my business there."

"Ah," the woman said softly, and Amy heard a squeak and a puff like she was sinking into a chair. "I've been looking for your number. I'm Lydia's niece, Alona. I'm sorry to let you know she's passed away."

"Oh no," Amy whispered. "I'm really sorry for your loss."

"Yes, thank you. What was it you were ringing about?"

"Uh, actually, we don't wish to extend our lease here. I was ringing to ask if there was a way to get out of it earlier. But that seems … inappropriate now."

Alona heaved a sigh. "I was rather hoping you'd keep going in there for a while. I've a heck of a lot of paperwork to get through, and that will be one more thing to deal with." She tsked and broke off as though she'd caught herself. "Sorry, dear. That's not actually your problem. But I'm afraid I won't be able to release you earlier. We'll need at least your notice period to figure out what to do with the place."

"I understand," Amy said, hearing the tension in Alona's voice. "What do you think you'll do with it, if you don't mind me asking?"

Alona paused. "I really don't know. I think probably try and sell it. That seems the easiest thing to do. I'm the executor of her will and there are several … *interested* other parties, if you know what I mean. I suppose selling it and splitting the profit will be the easiest way to go about it."

"Right. Well … I'll send over the formal paperwork with our notice in writing. And I wish you the very best of luck with everything."

"Thank you," Alona said.

They hung up the call and Amy heard a horrible niggling voice in her head. *People always die in threes* ... First Beaumont, now Mrs Beckwith.

She shivered, and then pushed the thoughts from her mind. There was enough to do without worrying about stupid superstitions.

22
FRIDAY

Alex lowered his fork, nodding slowly as a grin spread over his face.

"I can definitely wait a year," he said. "*Definitely*."

"Really?" Lyra eyed him anxiously, pushing her Pad Thai around the plate as they sat at their little dining table that Friday evening. Her appetite was gone. She'd been thinking about the baby question since their last chat. A year had seemed like the right timeframe. Not too soon, not endlessly far away. Although in the back of her mind she worried that *starting* in a year might not mean getting pregnant for two, or even more.

"It feels like a long time to me," she said, watching his face. "So I can imagine it does to you, too. But … I think that's enough time to really have my name established and have another album out. And then it won't matter so much if I'm off for a few months."

"Will you be happy with a few months off?"

Lyra considered. "I don't know. I never necessarily imagined myself as a stay-at-home mum, but I think that was mostly because I wasn't sure I wanted to be a mum at all. I guess if I did hate the idea of going back, I could delay it a little longer. Maybe I can have enough stuff pre-recorded so that the label could slowly release songs while I was out? I don't really know how it works."

"Me either," Alex agreed. "But I would happily stay home. When you're on tour, or if you preferred to go back full time."

He'd given himself another home haircut, and for some reason there was nothing more endearing to Lyra than noticing the little pieces he'd missed when he did so. He was also getting more muscular, thanks to the renovation work he and Rick were often doing together. It was still odds and ends, mostly for friends and nothing formal. Still, it was having a physical effect on him. If Lyra thought about having this man's baby, her insides turned instantly to jelly and she had to force herself not to climb across the table.

"And if it's only a year, I thought we wouldn't have to worry about freezing my eggs or anything," she added.

Alex's eyes shone with relief. "I would have supported you one hundred percent, if you wanted to do that. But I did a bit of research after our last chat and it seems like a pretty big deal. There's a risk of overstimulation from the medication, and—"

Lyra cut him off, grinning. "You researched it?"

He frowned. "Of course I did. If the love of my life's going to go through it, I need to know a little bit more about it."

"Alex, *I* didn't even research it."

"Well, no matter, because I did."

Lyra dropped her cutlery and stalked around to his side of the table, pushing his chair back and plonking herself in his lap. "Do you know how adorable you are?" she murmured, running her hands through his hair.

"Adorable is puppies, Ly." He ran his hands softly over her hips. "No man wants to be *adorable*."

"No? What do you want to be then?"

"Manly. Competent."

"Do you have any idea how manly and competent you are?"

"Are you done eating?" Alex growled. "Because if you are, I'm going to throw you onto this table right now and have my wicked way with you."

"I'm leaving the week after next, I think we'd better stock up—" Lyra began, and then squealed as Alex easily hoisted her by the waist and set her onto the table.

"So, ummm, I saw this thing," he said later, as they sat curled on the sofa watching *Stranger Things*.

"What thing?" Lyra asked distractedly, her attention glued to the screen.

"About you…"

Lyra turned to him, taking in his serious expression. She clicked pause on the remote. "What thing about me?"

Alex seemed hesitant to answer. "I was on social media…"

"Okay?"

"Umm, and I typed in your name."

Lyra's eyes widened. "Why would you do that? I don't do that!"

"We've established that I do a lot of things you don't do."

She smiled. "Ha-ha. Well, what did you find?"

"Some teenage boy made this video about …" Alex swallowed. "About the things he'd like to do to you."

She blinked. "What, like bad things? He hates my music? Don't worry, he's not in my target demographic."

Alex shook his head. "No, no. It was like … sex stuff."

Lyra blanched. "Oh no."

"Yeah, it was …" He let out a shaky breath. "It was pretty intense. I had a full-on meltdown in the comments and flagged it as a community violation but the report came back saying it was fine."

"Of course it did," Lyra muttered darkly. "I'm sorry you saw it."

"I wondered … does the label protect you from stuff like that? Do they have staff out there making sure you're not being, I don't know, cyber bullied or cyber … assaulted or something?"

Lyra turned to face him, tucking her feet up beneath her on the sofa. "I don't think so." She took his hands. "Honestly, the easiest thing to do is just not look."

"But that's not fair," Alex said earnestly, tracing his thumbs in circles around her own thumb joints. "You should be able to go wherever you want on the internet without seeing … *that*."

She tipped her head, nodding. "I agree. I should. *Everyone* should. But … it isn't like that. Social media brought all the village idiots together and gave them a platform. They're all finding one another with hashtags or sub-groups or whatever, no matter where they are in the world. It can kind of feel like there are more of them than there probably are. Thank you for flagging it, that was sweet."

His face was troubled. "I worry that they need to do more. I wonder if they even promote stuff like that, or encourage it or whatever, for publicity for you."

Lyra swallowed, her mind swirling back to Julian's pitch about a fake relationship with Jake. Maybe they were capable of doing something as sickening like that. After all, they'd apparently "tested" the idea of her and Jake being together, *and* her and Maggie. Who was coming up with ideas like that? When? And who were they testing them out on?

Lyra felt her skin prickling, the beginnings of something

like anxiety stirring. Now that she knew what they had in mind for her image, she wouldn't put anything past them. They'd casually expected her to disregard her boyfriend's feelings, as well as her own. Was she the idiot in that situation? Was she supposed to calmly tell Alex it came with the territory? Julian hadn't mentioned it again, but she knew better than to think the subject was truly forgotten.

She forced herself not to think about any of that now. She needed to comfort her boyfriend first.

"Alex, I'm a woman living out my dreams in a public forum. There are things that *shouldn't* come with that, but they seem to. I just ..." She shrugged with one shoulder. "I don't know, try to ignore it as best I can. I think you should too," she added gently, pulling him forward so their foreheads touched. "Besides, there's no one else I want to make a baby with, regardless of how many videos they share about me."

"In a year," Alex added, and his eyes crinkled with his smile.

"In a measly little year," she agreed, enjoying the warmth and tingles where their skin touched. Sometimes she felt like it was impossible to get physically close enough to him. "You know, minus tour dates, and with all the stuff we'll need to do to our house if that goes through, it's basically only a couple of months."

"And take out weekends and public holidays, and it's basically *a* month," Alex added, getting into the spirit. Lyra saw the tension easing from his shoulders.

"Right. And Marley's baby shower is tomorrow, so I can use her as a guinea pig to figure out what I want for my own baby shower."

Alex chortled. "Yes, I'm sure that's what your role as best friend is!" He shoved her playfully backwards. Then he drew her close again and she nestled into her favourite place in the world, the crook under his arm. They sat in contented silence for a few moments, a cheeky smile spreading across Lyra's face.

"So, this guy in the video. Was he cute, or—"

"Too soon, Lyra Beck!" he bellowed, smacking her with a cushion and making her break out in a fit of giggles.

And for the rest of the evening, all was right with the world.

23
SATURDAY: SIX WEEKS TO THE WEDDING

On the morning of her baby shower, Marley woke up to a sharp kick in the solar plexus. She gasped and Finn shot awake.

"Is it happening?" he asked, springing out of bed and trying to pull on trousers with his eyes half-closed. He shoved two feet into one pant leg and fumbled for his glasses. "I'm ready."

Marley burst out laughing. "You're absolutely not!"

"Huh?" Finn croaked, blinking at her. "It's ... you're not...?"

Marley shook her head, wiping tears from her eyes.

"Oh thank god," he said, collapsing face first onto the bed.

"But it's good to know that's your response," Marley added. "You're all over it. The baby and I are in great hands."

"Don't tease me," Finn said, his face smooshed into the bed. He kicked off his trousers and crawled back under the blankets beside her, putting a hand onto her belly. "Was it kicking again?"

"Yep." They lay there in silence for a moment, Marley enjoying the gentle stroke of Finn's fingers against her taut skin, the baby shoving a foot towards him in response. "I'm imagining all the presents we'll get. Which, let's be honest, is the *real* reason I'm doing this." Marley pointed to her belly.

Finn smiled indulgently. "There's what, three people coming? I wouldn't expect too much."

Marley felt a prick of annoyance at his words, and bit back an irritated response. He couldn't know that having so few friends was a sore point for her. Or that she was proud of the fact there were even three guests. There was a time in her life when she couldn't have imagined anyone showing up. Amy, Lyra, and her boss, who Marley had *finally* started calling Elizabeth. A small gang, but a good one. Marley hoped they'd all get along and there wouldn't be long, awkward silences. She had no idea what the girls had planned for her, but she hoped it was relaxed, and fun. Amy was coming to pick her up around midday to drive her to a secret location.

Marley nudged Finn with her foot. "What was that you said? Pancakes for breakfast?"

Finn grinned at her and her heart caught. She still sometimes struggled to believe they were really together. Though she'd matured a lot since her teen days of thinking that a man's good looks were his greatest asset, there was still a shred of that girl in her that swooned over Finn's handsomeness. His tanned skin, his muscular physique and strong hands, the blue of his eyes and the softness of his dark hair …

"I remember a time when you wouldn't even be in the same room as a lemonade you were so afraid of sugar," he joked.

"That was before I was actually pregnant and realised how much of a sweet tooth your baby would give me!"

"Pancakes it is," Finn said. "Healthy ones or junk?"

"Make them healthy," Marley decided. "I'm sure there'll be treats at the baby shower."

"Alright. Give me a second. That wake-up was quite draining."

At the thought of him springing chaotically into action, Marley smirked.

"I wonder if I'll get any decorations for the nursery as a present," she mused.

"That reminds me," Finn said. "I was thinking of painting it while you were out. That way there won't be as many fumes when you get back."

"Oh, that's a good idea, thanks. I love the colour we chose."

"Me too." They shared a smile, thinking of the long trip to the hardware store where they'd haggled over paint colours before both spotting a beautiful rich green and reaching for the sample chip at the same time.

"It's a shame your Mum and sister couldn't make the baby shower," Marley added.

"I know. They're devastated. But they'd had that girls' trip planned for ages. And I know for a fact they have tons of guilt-induced goodies for us, so maybe it works out in our favour."

"It's so nice how excited they are for you," Marley said, entwining their fingers. She felt a deep ache at the fact that her GamGam would never get to see her child. Never get to hug it. Never get to see how well things had turned out for Marley.

Finn seemed to sense what she was thinking and reached a hand up to brush his thumb over her cheek. "She can see you, you know? I'm sure of it."

Marley blinked back tears, nodding as she swallowed a lump in her throat. "I like to think so. I read this thing once about how a woman is born with all the eggs she'll ever have.

So in a way, I was also in GamGam's womb, when I was an egg in my mother's body before she was born. But … this baby misses out."

"That's a beautiful thought," Finn said gently. "And this baby would have been held in your mother's body before it was born. Not to mention it carries those genes. I also heard something nice the other day, from one of my patients. She's pregnant and her mother has passed away. She said she likes to think that her mother is holding the baby now, caring for it until it comes earthside." Finn looked at Marley tenderly, his finger still stroking her cheek. "Maybe your mum and grandmother are doing that right now, with this one."

Marley's eyes blurred as the tears fell, and she pulled Finn tightly towards her. She felt so lucky to be doing this with him. He always tried so hard to understand what she was feeling, and always managed to say the exact right thing.

"Besides," he added now. "Their blood flows through you. And all your actions, thoughts and beliefs—your GamGam helped shape those and you'll pass them on to our baby."

Marley nodded, letting Finn stroke her hair. She felt both lighter and heavier after the conversation. As though she'd been forced to acknowledge what she'd lost and what her baby would miss, while at the same time being comforted by the idea that somewhere, on some plane of existence, that love carried across.

A moment later, her stomach let out a loud rumble. It broke the tension and she and Finn both sniggered.

Finn tenderly planted a kiss on her lips, then sprung out of bed for the second time that day.

"Pancakes for my love, coming right up!"

"Are we going to Lilac Bay?" Marley asked, as Amy steered the car past the Darling Harbour exit.

Amy pursed her lips. "You'll have to wait and see."

Marley groaned, wriggling in her seat with anticipation. "At least the weather is nice."

"It's perfect," Amy agreed on a contented sigh.

"We *are* going to Lilac Bay," Marley said confidently, and Amy grinned at her as they headed over the Harbour Bridge.

The tar beneath the wheels thrummed as they drove over each section of bridge, and Marley craned her neck to look at the dark grey arches high above their heads. On both sides, the water of Sydney Harbour fanned out, glittering and blue and reflective. It was dotted with yachts and ferries and jet boats and streaked with their wakes—little scars that quickly dissolved into the blue surface. The sun glinted off the ivory tiles of the Opera House sails.

Marley felt a deep sense of contentment. Her best friend was driving her to a secret location to meet her other best friend, so they could spend some time together in a setting they'd dreamed up specifically for her. She might not have a huge girl gang, but the one she had was awesome.

"I can't wait to see how it all looks set up!" Amy said. "Ly and I are probably more excited than you are."

"I seriously doubt that," Marley said with a smile.

They parked the car at the top of the slope of Lilac Bay and walked the few short blocks down to the waterfront, passing the Secret Garden as they did. When she spotted a white sunshade canopy in the middle of the open field area, Marley squealed with delight.

Lyra waved an arm high overhead once she caught sight of them, a wide grin splitting her face.

"It looks *great!*" Amy yelled excitedly as she and Marley

WEDDING BELLS AT LILAC BAY

reached the canopy. Lyra hugged Marley tightly, and Marley looked over her shoulder at the beautiful scene before her.

Atop a natural fibre rug sat four high-backed wicker chairs with round, earthen-toned cushions. A low wooden table draped with a beautiful, cream-coloured macrame runner held a snack platter that ran the length of it. Marley's eyes ran over artfully-arranged cheeses, grapes, crackers, breadsticks, dips, olives, pesto and fruit skewers, and caught on the napkins and plates. They were a rich deep green that she instantly recognised as the nursery paint colour. Clusters of pearlescent balloons in ivory and the same green shade festooned the corners of the canopy. Three frosted glass drink dispensers beaded with condensation, and Marley spotted iced cucumber water in one, lemon and berry water in the other two. A deep copper bowl held bottles of alcohol-free sparkling wine packed in ice. At each of the four place settings, a small, pale green succulent sat in a woven basket, a calligraphy tag scrawled with the guest's name peeking out. A small, mouth-watering cake frosted in pale green graced the centre of the table. To the side, an easel showed a hand-written sign saying "Welcome to Marley's baby shower!" It was perfect, shaded from the sun yet outdoors and with a gentle breeze rippling through.

Marley's eyes filled with tears. "You guys," she whispered. "This is *so* incredibly beautiful."

Lyra clapped her hands together. "Wait till we get to the games part!"

"She's only saying that because she was in charge of games," Amy laughed.

"This set up here has Amy written all over it," Marley said, sweeping her arm to indicate the scene before her.

The bay was like glass, smooth and glittering with reflected light. The air was fresh, with the last crisp tangs of winter hanging on the breeze. The lilacs were starting to bloom and their scent would soon fill the entire bay and drift gently through the suburb. The view out to the Harbour Bridge was uninterrupted, the air so clear Marley could spot the miniscule forms of the bridge walkers on top.

Lyra nodded. "You had the best working on it, that's for sure!"

Amy beamed. "Shall we grab seats?"

"Sounds good," Marley said sinking gratefully into a cushioned chair. "Oh, there's Elizabeth!" she said, heaving herself back out and calling out to her boss, arms waving high. Lyra and Amy exchanged a smile, delighted to see their friend so happy.

Marley returned to the canopy, beaming as she led her boss by the hand. "Girls, this is Elizabeth. My boss."

"Nice to meet you," Elizabeth said awkwardly. She didn't look entirely comfortable being there, but Amy and Lyra had been forewarned on that point. Apparently Dr Elizabeth Martelle worked hard, but was less successful with the "play" aspect of her life, counting very few people in her social circle. As they took their seats again, Elizabeth reached out a hand to touch her succulent and Amy caught sight of the enormous, glittering diamond on the doctor's ring finger.

"Oh," she breathed. "That ring is exquisite."

"Oh, thank you." Elizabeth blushed. "I recently eloped with my ... I guess husband now." She let out a small laugh. "Sounds kind of braggy to say that."

"Congratulations," Amy and Lyra chorused.

"Her husband is a famous YouTuber," Marley added.

"Oh?" Lyra asked, interested.

"Well, I'm not sure I'd use the word *famous*," Elizabeth said, clearly bursting with pride. "But definitely popular."

"Lyra's famous, too," Marley said, her eyes sparkling as she looked at her friend.

"Not sure I'd go that far either," Lyra clarified quickly. "Just at the beginning of my career, really."

"What career is that?" Elizabeth asked.

"She's a singer," Marley said, before Lyra could answer. "You've probably heard *The Right Notes* and *Struck from Above* on the radio."

"Oh, yes, I have!" Elizabeth said. "That's you?"

"Yeah," Lyra nodded.

"How wonderful. I should get an autograph for Don, my husband. He's a big fan of yours."

"I'd be happy to oblige," Lyra said smiling. "But first, we have a game to play. Worst date ever. Elizabeth, since you're recently married, I think you should go first."

"Come on Marley, you have to share, after my story," Elizabeth said, leaning forward in her chair.

Marley groaned. "I honestly don't have any worst dates to share! I'm basically two for two in guys that I've dated versus relationships."

"Well, that's boring," Elizabeth slumped back in her chair.

"I can definitely add something here," Amy piped up, chuckling. "I think my worst date was a guy who told me that he was deliberately choosing, and I quote, *chubbies,* off dating apps so he could drum up clients for his personal training business."

"*No!*" Lyra cried, as everyone else gasped in shock. "I can't believe I've never heard that one before."

"I'm pretty sure I told you. Maybe we were both drunk. Believe me, I *needed* a drink after that."

"Oh god." Lyra put her head in her hands. "I don't blame you."

"I can't believe he actually *told* you that," Marley said, aghast.

"I hope you beat him up," Elizabeth added viciously, stabbing her cake with her fork.

Amy grinned. "No. But I definitely got him back."

"How?" Marley asked.

Amy chuckled at the memory. "I told him I could help with his website for free—"

"Oh, I *do* remember this!" Lyra yelled in glee.

"Yep," Amy nodded. "And once he gave me the login credentials, I changed *everything*. The headline said 'I'm a pervert who preys on women', and I changed the mission statement and the entire About Me section to tell my story."

The women hooted with laughter.

"That is *perfect*," Elizabeth said, bringing her hands together. "What did he do?"

"Oh, he flipped out," Amy said, delicately wiping tears of laughter from her eyes. "I said I'd only undo it if he disabled all his dating profiles and deleted himself off the apps. And that I'd know if he ever tried to slink back on."

Elizabeth's mouth dropped open in awe, as Marley and Lyra beamed at their friend.

"Never saw him back on there," Amy added. "Not that I'd know now anyway." Her expression softened as she thought of Rick.

"Your turn, Lyra," Marley said a moment later, sipping her cucumber water and grabbing another slice of the sugar-free cake, which had turned out to be surprisingly delicious.

Lyra tapped her chin. It was clear what her worst "date" was, but she didn't really want to talk about it. It was definitely with the sleazy bartender named Miles from the Whistlestop. It couldn't even really have been called a date, but the misunderstanding it led to had broken up her and Alex before they'd even had a chance to get started.

Especially when it transpired that Alex's ex-girlfriend, Alison, had cheated on him with the very same guy. It had all been an ugly mess that Lyra shivered to remember.

"What about that idiot bartender from the Whistlestop?" Marley said. "Who basically told you he'd only let you play a gig if you put out."

"Yeah. That's virtually the whole story," Lyra said wryly, sipping her drink.

Elizabeth gasped in horror. "I can't imagine Don having to put up with anything like that. Ugh. Also, I'm so glad I don't have to date anymore!"

They ate cake in comfortable silence for a while before Amy prompted Lyra that it was time for the guessing games.

Lyra jumped to her feet. "Yes! We're doing the usual ones," she said, walking towards the easel and flipping back the welcome note to reveal a chart. "But we also have a few new ones thrown in, as you can see here." She drew her hand down the left-hand side column.

"How many times Marley swears at Finn while in labour," Marley read aloud, then blushed. "Lyra!"

"Oh, just wait till you see the others," she smirked.

Once the games had been played—much to Marley's embarrassment—and the gifts had been handed out—much to her delight—the picnic started to wind down. Lyra was staying behind to help the catering company pack up, and Amy would drive Marley and her gifts home.

The girls were bidding one another farewell when Lyra locked eyes with someone walking down the hill to the bay. She froze, Amy's arms still around her.

"What's going on?" Amy whispered quickly to Lyra.

Lyra twisted her mouth. "That's Alex's ex." Amy tried to turn, but Lyra held her in place. "Don't you dare!" she hissed.

Alison had come to a standstill several yards away, clearly unsure whether she should approach Lyra or not.

"Is she going to recognise you?" Amy asked.

"Yeah," Lyra nodded, releasing her friend. "She knows me. She used to call me all the time when Mick went through that horrible streak of getting injured really often. Get Marley out of here quick. She's heading over."

Amy did as she was told, making a *call me* gesture to Lyra as she led Marley and Elizabeth up the hill.

Lyra's nerves were jittering and her palms were instantly slick with sweat as Alison drew near. She wasn't entirely sure what her feelings were about the other woman. They'd enjoyed a friendly relationship before they knew about their common interest in Alex. Lyra was mad with her for having hurt Alex, but at the same time grateful they'd broken up—giving her the chance to get together with him.

Alex himself had always spoken highly of the woman he called Allie, making sure that Lyra knew he didn't blame her for their breakup. But there was something odd about being in the same place as her boyfriend's ex. Especially since it had been sprung on them both.

"Lyra, do you have a sec?" Alison asked, once she was close enough for Lyra to see that she was blushing.

"Yes, of course. Hi, Alison."

As the catering crew swooped in to clear up the picnic, the two women stood beneath a shady fig. Lyra told her herself not to be nervous, but couldn't help reaching up to stroke her palm over the trunk of the tree. She concentrated on the roughness of it, trying to keep her breaths slow and even.

"How … how are you doing?" Alison began, and Lyra could detect a slight shake in her voice.

"Good. Thanks. And you?"

Alison drew a deep breath. "I know you're with Alex. I know you're living together and I also know he's completely nuts about you."

Lyra's eyes snapped up, scanning the other woman's face. For signs of what, she wasn't sure. "You talk to each other?" Lyra asked.

Alison shook her head, then appeared to reconsider. "Well, a couple of times since … We had some things to sort out."

Lyra frowned. "Okay."

"I guess I wanted to say … what happened between he and I, it was completely my fault. And, as I'm sure you know, we hadn't been good together for a long time before it happened. He's a really good guy, I'm glad you're together and I'm not any kind of threat. Not that I think you think I am," she added hastily, when Lyra opened her mouth. "This isn't coming out right."

"I know what you mean though," Lyra said. She felt surprisingly calm, and she realised it stemmed from how secure she was in her relationship. How certain she was that Alex was in love with her and that she was it for him. "And I appreciate the thought."

They fell silent.

"I hear you on the radio sometimes," Alison said. "In the nurse's station or in the car on my way to and from work. You have a beautiful voice."

"Oh. Thank you." Lyra took her palm from the tree, letting it dangle by her side. "Have you … are you dating? Is that odd to ask?"

Alison's mouth twisted, an expression of pain flickering across her features. "No it's not odd. But no, I'm not dating. I don't really want anything else right now."

Lyra frowned. "I remember the day at hospital when you

told me about the breakup," she said gently. "I know you were mad at yourself. I'm sure he's said this to you and maybe it's even weirder for me to repeat, but it wasn't your fault."

Alison didn't answer, just looked down sadly, stubbing the toe of her sneaker into the fig tree root.

"I hope you don't punish yourself," Lyra said. As soon as the words were out, she knew she'd crossed a line. "God, *sorry*," she added quickly, covering her mouth with her hand.

Alison smiled crookedly. "If it's okay, I don't really want to talk about it?"

"Of course—"

"Things were friendly between you and I in the past. I don't think we'll run into each other often, but I really wanted to clear the air between us just in case. Sydney sometimes turns out to be smaller than you think. Case in point," she added, sweeping her hand to indicate their meeting.

"Thank you. I really appreciate that." Lyra smiled. "Air all clear."

Alison managed a smile. "Great. Well, enjoy the rest of your day."

"You too," Lyra said, stepping forward to give her a quick, awkward hug. Then she joined the others to help clear up.

24
SATURDAY

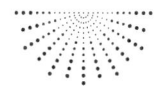

"Hey, how was the shower?" Alex asked as Lyra walked in the door. He pulled her close for a kiss, and for a moment she forgot her irritation at him, kissing him back. Then she pushed him gently away.

He frowned. "What's wrong?"

"Umm," Lyra stalled for time, kicking off her shoes and heading to the bathroom to wash her hands.

"Ly? Talk to me please." He stood in the bathroom doorway, his arms crossed and his brow furrowed.

Lyra towelled off her hands, facing him. "I don't think I have a right to be mad," she began carefully. "But I ran into Alison after the shower today, and … she said you guys still talk sometimes."

"Alison? As in Allie? My ex?"

Lyra nodded, scraping her bottom teeth across her top lip. "Yeah."

"Oh." Alex rubbed a hand through his hair. "Okay, let's get a cup of tea and talk about this."

Lyra nodded, trailing him to the kitchen. Her stomach was in knots. She felt stupid for worrying about their connection—after all, she spent long hours with the two other men in her band, and there was nothing at all between them. But she'd been stewing on it since Alison had told her, and she needed to get it off her chest before it festered.

Once they were settled on the sofa with steaming cups of tea, Alex started talking.

"She was in a really, really bad place when we broke up. She blamed herself so badly."

"I remember. She kind of had a breakdown on me at the hospital one time I was there visiting Mick."

Alex nodded. "And, don't get me wrong, she messed up. But that's all it was. Human error. The way she punished herself, the way she punishes herself still ... I worry about her."

Lyra sipped her tea. "I can see that. She told me today she still doesn't want to date anyone."

"That's just it. She really wanted a family. She wanted kids, picket fence, the whole deal. I guess I might have been dragging my feet a little on that ..."

"Why?"

Alex took a deep breath. "I knew she wasn't it for me. I ... we'd been together a while, but it wasn't ... like this. Like us. And *this* was what I wanted. *This* was what I knew was possible."

Lyra ducked her head, not wanting to show her smile.

Alex reached out and crooked a finger under her chin. "Look at me, my love."

She raised her eyes, blushing.

"You *are* it for me. You know that. I know you know that. You can talk to me about this stuff, but please. Never, ever be jealous."

Lyra leaned forward, touching her head to his chest. "I'll try," she whispered, smiling. Then she looked up again. "Do you think she's going to be okay?"

Alex wrinkled his nose in thought. "I really hope so. But it's been a while and still I get the feeling she hasn't let it go. Not *me,* I mean. Her mistake."

Lyra frowned. "That's horrible." She released a long sigh. "Okay, I feel completely better. Sorry for being weird about it."

Alex shrugged. "I should have mentioned it. It's my fault. From now on, whenever I talk to her, I'll tell you. I never want us to hide things from one another."

Lyra looked into the depths of her tea, nodding slowly. Her conscience pricked, but she swallowed it down. Stuff at the label was different to stuff in real life. There was no reason to tell Alex anything. Her band—including Jake—would be over at their place for a barbecue the following day. If anything came up naturally, she would deal with it then.

25
SUNDAY

"Mags, you always bring something, and I always tell you not to!" Lyra said, delighted and dismayed as her bandmate proffered a bottle of top-shelf tequila at the door.

"Are you going to let us in, or not?" Maggie joked, deflecting.

Lyra pulled first Maggie, then Kit, into quick hugs and opened the door wide. She'd recently started a tradition of having the band over to Alex's place for a barbecue once a month. Jake had never previously made it, but would apparently be putting in an appearance tonight. However, he hadn't turned up with Kit and Maggie. Lyra wondered whether they'd purposefully travelled in together, or simply met by coincidence outside. But she knew better than to ask.

"Hey guys," Alex said, looking up from the kitchen counter where he was chopping tomatoes for the salad.

They greeted him casually, already at ease in his presence, and pulled out chairs around the little dining table as Lyra served them both glasses of white wine.

"You ready to let her go for a few weeks?" Kit asked Alex.

He pulled a face. "Don't think I have a choice, do I?"

Lyra slipped an arm around his waist. "I told him I could get him VIP tickets for every single show, but there was a lot of blah blah about having to work."

Maggie grinned. "I offered the same thing to my stepdad. But I think his reluctance is more to do with the fact we're not a death metal band."

"We could throw in a surprise song for him?" Lyra joked.

"You have great vocal range, but I don't *quite* think it goes that far," Maggie said, tilting her wine at Lyra.

"So how did a girl raised on a diet of metal end up in a pop band?" Kit asked, squinting at Maggie over the top of his glass.

"I could ask you the same thing, little drummer boy," she hit back.

"Your parents were also into metal, Kit?" Alex asked. "Were mine the only ones not?"

Lyra laughed, shaking her head. "I can *guarantee* mine weren't."

"It was only my stepdad," Maggie said. "Mum's way more into gospel."

"No way," Kit said, incredulous.

Maggie nodded. "She's very religious."

"Are you?" Kit asked.

Maggie swirled her wine, a thoughtful expression on her face. "In some ways, I guess."

"Well," Kit breathed, shooting a puzzled look at Lyra. "The Maggie mystery deepens."

"Huh? What's mysterious about me?"

"Oh, come on, Mags," Lyra laughed. "We barely know a thing about you! And you pretty much *never* give away whether you even like our music."

Maggie shrugged, tipping her head back to sip her wine. "I'm here, aren't I?"

They all laughed. "I think that's probably the deepest answer we're going to get from her," Kit said, and Maggie air-toasted him, grinning.

"So, do either of you have partners also being left behind on this trip?" Alex asked, sprinkling the chopped tomatoes over the lettuce. "I realised I don't know that about you."

Lyra thought she saw Kit cast a sidelong glance through his lashes at Maggie. She knew Kit was single, but of course, had no idea about Maggie's love life.

Maggie cleared her throat. "You need a hand cutting anything?" she asked Alex, getting to her feet and deftly avoiding the question. Kit's shoulders slumped slightly.

"Uh, sure," Alex said. "Can you dice that avo for the salad? I'm about to fire up the barbie. You said Jake was coming?" He glanced at his watch. "Should I wait for him?"

"No," Maggie said firmly. "If he gets here late, he deserves cold sausages."

"Ouch," Kit said, shaking his hand as though it had been burnt. "Brutal. I'm glad I got here on time."

The doorbell rang at that moment and Kit got up to answer it, bringing Jake back into the kitchen a moment later. Lyra was used to seeing her keyboard player standing tall, with squared shoulders and an air of confidence. He looked almost bashful as Kit led him back into the room, his gaze on the floor and expression flat.

"Jake! It's great to see you," Lyra said, hoping to make him feel more at ease. "This is my boyfriend Alex. Alex, this is Jake."

Alex wiped his hands on his apron and extended one to Jake, who shook it firmly. "Nice to meet you."

"You too," Jake said, eyeing him. "Good to finally put a face to the name."

"Would you like some wine?" Lyra asked, when Jake's gaze lingered almost critically on Alex.

"No thanks, I don't actually drink," Jake replied.

"Coke then?" Lyra asked, not wanting to probe into the reasons for his sobriety. She firmly believed drinking was a personal choice and after having grown up with an alcoholic father, respected people who stayed out of the potentially destructive path of drink. Not that she managed to.

"Sure, that would be great. I got you these chocolates," he added, almost shyly, proffering a box to her. From the corner of her eye, Lyra saw Maggie and Kit exchange a glance. Beside her, Alex cleared his throat.

"Thanks so much," she said, feeling heat rising to her cheeks. "Maggie brought tequila, too. Although I'm not sure we'll be opening it tonight."

"Yes we will," Maggie piped up, and Lyra laughed. She handed Jake a glass of soda and pulled out the third chair around the table for him.

"Alex is about to start the barbie," Lyra told them. "Food shouldn't be too long."

"Oh, you want help?" Jake asked, getting to his feet again.

"All under control thanks, mate," Alex said, heading out onto the little balcony with a tray of meat. "Ly, that garlic bread timer's going to go off in a minute. Why don't you stay here with these guys and I'll take care of the food."

"Thank you," she said, standing on tiptoe to press a kiss to his mouth. When she turned back to the others, she found Jake's eyes on her. He quickly looked away.

"So, how has everyone spent their weekend?" she asked brightly, filling the fourth and last seat around the table.

"This and that," Maggie said.

"Of course *that's* the only answer we're going to get," Kit said.

"Well, what did you do?" she asked.

"This and that," Kit said in a mocking tone.

"Okay, Maggie," Lyra said, grinning and holding up a hand. "What *can* we talk about?"

Maggie tapped her chin. "When we're opening that tequila."

The sun had already set and the mosquito coils were burning when Lyra started yawning. Beside her, she could almost feel Alex's tiredness. Kit and Maggie, however, were apparently just getting started. They'd all had a pleasant dinner together out on the small balcony, watching the sunset and chatting amiably. A few possums danced in the gum that reached Alex's second-storey balcony, their round hazel eyes looking beadily at the feast.

And then Maggie had opened the tequila. A couple of shot glasses in and Lyra's stomach was burning, but her cheeks hurt from smiling. Everything had taken on a fuzzy, warm quality, although it hadn't exactly done wonders for her tiredness.

Maggie held up a shot glass to get everyone's attention. "I can see that our hosts are dead on their feet," she said, grinning merrily, "but are *far* too polite to ask us to leave. So, I propose we play one round of 'ask me anything', and once each person's had a turn, we three head off and leave our hosts in peace."

"I don't know this game?" Alex said, scratching his neck. His cheeks were slightly pink from the tequila, his hair mussed. He looked so handsome that Lyra was having a hard time keeping her eyes off him.

Kit's face lit up. "It's where each person asks a question to the group, like a truth question. And you have to answer, or if you don't, you have to do a shot."

WEDDING BELLS AT LILAC BAY

"Like truth or dare but the only dare is a shot," Maggie clarified.

"And what do I do?" Jake asked.

"You have to …" Maggie glanced around. "Do a shot of tabasco sauce." She lunged for the little bottle as Jake shook his head.

"That is *so* unfair."

"I agree!" Lyra said, coming to his defence.

"He can do it," Alex said, slipping his hand into Lyra's and giving Jake a challenging look across the table.

Jake ground his back teeth, then nodded once. "Condition accepted."

"Okay!" Maggie said, holding the bottle aloft. "I'll go first. My first ask me anything is … tell us about your first kiss?"

"That's a good one," Lyra said. "Mine was with Alex and it was about a year and a half ago."

"Liar!" Maggie shouted, and Lyra dissolved into giggles.

"No, I don't know," Lyra said truthfully. "I think it was with James Blanker in the back oval? I would have been like … sixteen? Memorable, obviously."

"Oh, you were so innocent," Kit laughed. "Sixteen is really late!"

"Well how old were you then, Mister Experienced?" Lyra asked.

"Thirteen. And it was with Lorna Parks, and she was my *best friend's mother.*"

"Ew!" Maggie shouted, her eyes wide. "I'm pretty sure that's illegal!"

"Me too," Kit said, nodding. "I was taken advantage of."

"Mine was when I was fifteen," Maggie said.

"And?" Kit prompted. "Who was it with?"

"Helena Summers."

Kit fell silent, processing the news. Jake laughed at the slightly dazed look on his face.

"A girl?" Kit asked.

"No, genius. A boy called Helena. *Yes*, a girl."

"Wait, are you …?"

Maggie slapped his arm. "I *kissed* her, I didn't marry her. And I don't like labels. Jake, over to you."

Jake grinned at Kit's bewildered expression. "Uh, I think sixteen as well, actually. A girl from this camp I went to for maths nerds. I forget her name though."

"You went to *maths* camp?" Lyra asked, impressed.

"I use those skills to count our beats," Jake said, winking at her.

Beside Lyra, Alex straightened up. "And mine was at thirteen," he said loudly. "With Missy Baker. In detention."

"My bad boy," Lyra sighed dreamily, leaning onto his shoulder. She gazed up into his gold-grey eyes, loving how they crinkled at the corners when he looked at her.

"My turn!" Kit said. "I gotta break these two up before they sneak off to the bedroom!" Lyra giggled, holding Alex's arm tighter. "Okay, uh …" Kit drew a deep breath, his eyes glued to the bottle of tequila. "Would you date anyone in the ba—anyone you worked with," he corrected quickly.

"I would," Lyra said, grinning. Jake hissed in a barely audible breath. "Well, I *did*," Lyra corrected. "Alex and I actually met when we were working together along Lilac Bay!"

"Oh, that's sweet," Maggie said, tilting her head at them.

"And I guess my answer's the same," Alex added with a secret smile at Lyra. "Would and did. Only once though. Kit?"

"Yes," he said quickly. "Yes, I would. Uh, Jake?" It was clear he wanted to ask Maggie, but couldn't summon the courage.

"In theory, sure," Jake said, shrugging. "But the options are kind of limited right now."

Maggie sniggered. "True."

"It's your turn, Maggie," Kit said finally, his voice an octave higher than usual.

Maggie lifted her eyes to his and Lyra realised Kit was holding his breath. Maggie tilted her head at him, something in her gaze softening as she did so. Then she raised her full glass of tequila, winked at him, and chugged it back.

"Cheat," Kit said softly.

"Those are the rules, actually," Maggie countered with a smile. "Okay, Lyra. Your question."

Lyra ran a finger over the rim of her glass, feeling everyone's eyes on her. She pressed her lips together, then raised her eyes hopefully to the group. "Do you believe in heaven?"

"One hundred percent," Maggie said quickly.

"Really?" Lyra asked, lighting up.

Maggie nodded firmly. "My mum's got stories. We should talk about it one night."

"I'd love that."

"I do, too," Jake added quietly, not meeting anyone's gaze. Lyra felt as though there was a story behind his conviction, but it wasn't exactly the place to pry.

"I don't," Kit said. "I'm really sorry. I know it would be good to believe, but … sorry."

"I *hope* there's such a place," Alex said gently, stroking Lyra's arm. "And who are we to say whether there is or isn't?"

Lyra nodded, gazing up at him. "I think there is." He squeezed her arm in response.

"Your turn, Jake," Maggie said quietly, and Jake considered for a moment.

"What's your best quality?" he asked finally.

"That's easy," Kit said. "My resilience."

"Had a hard life, have you?" Maggie asked. "Being loved on by two caring parents? Being a good-looking white male?"

"You admit I'm good-looking," he said triumphantly, and Maggie rolled her eyes. Then Kit turned serious. "You have no idea what goes on for people behind the scenes though, Mags. You don't really know as much about me as you like to think," he added.

Maggie frowned. "You're right," she said, penitently, reaching across to touch his forearm. "I'm sorry. Mine is of course my mysteriousness."

They all laughed, lightening the mood.

"I don't know mine?" Lyra said, shaking her head. "That's a really hard question."

"I can suggest one," Alex said. "Your ability to light up every single room you enter."

Lyra, Maggie and even Kit sighed dreamily. Lyra melted, leaning over to look into his eyes and kiss him. "Thank you," she whispered.

"Brownie points?" he whispered back.

"All of them."

They turned back to find Kit and Maggie grinning at them, and Jake sipping his coke, staring elsewhere.

"Alex, what's your strength?" Kit asked. "Aside from flattering your girlfriend, of course."

"It was the truth!" Alex laughed. "Okay. Maybe how hard-working I am? At least, I feel pretty good about myself after my business partner and I finish something."

"He does *amazing* work," Lyra added proudly. "Okay, Jake. Your turn."

Everyone fell silent as Jake pondered the question, rolling his lips together. Then he looked directly at Lyra, holding her gaze. "I'm an eternal optimist," he said quietly.

"Alright!" Maggie clapped her hands together and stood, rounding up the glasses from the table. "I think we should all get out of their hair. Thank you both, so much for having us. I love these barbecue nights!"

"Me too," Kit added, moving to help Maggie clear the table. "I promise we won't stay as late next time."

Lyra yawned, getting to her feet and leaning on Alex's arm. She waved her hand at the others. "Leave the mess, we'll get it. Or the possums will. And Mags, no tequila next time, for god's sake."

Maggie saluted her and turned to head inside. She made a final trip out to the balcony, swiping the almost empty bottle of tequila. "I'll take this off your hands then, shall I?" she winked at Lyra.

Jake was the first one out the door, barely stopping to say goodbye. Kit and Maggie lingered, giving Lyra and Alex several rounds of tight hugs. It was the most physical she'd seen Maggie, and she liked this version of her usually stern bandmate.

Once they were all gone and Alex had closed the door behind them, Lyra turned to him.

"I realised you didn't get to ask your question!" She looped her arms around his waist and tipped her head up to look at him. He was smiling down at her, clearly tipsy. "I'm sorry," she added, putting her ear to his chest to hear the rumble of his voice.

"It's fine," he said reassuringly. "And my question is, do you realise how into you Jake is?"

Lyra froze, then titled her head to look at him. He was serious, frowning at her with a dark expression on his face.

She shook her head, not breaking eye contact. "Honestly … I really think that's his personality. Anyway, it doesn't matter." She cinched her arms more tightly around him. "As it happens, there is only one man in the entire universe that I have any interest in whatsoever. And it's going to stay that way for a very long time. Maybe even forever," she whispered.

Alex reached down, gently tucking a strand of hair

behind her ear. "Is it James Blanker from high school?" he asked, and Lyra giggled, glad the tension was broken.

"Yes. You found me out." She stood on tiptoe and pressed a kiss to his lips, the alcohol making her tingle and sigh at the contact.

"How about those brownie points?" Alex whispered, running a hand down her spine. Goosebumps broke out over her skin where his hand trailed.

"Hmm," she replied, closing her eyes and leaning harder against him. "You can cash them in right now if you like."

In a single move, he'd swept her off her feet and into his arms like a new bride. "Deal," he said, grinning, and Lyra squealed as they headed for the bedroom.

26
TUESDAY

Marley sipped her herbal tea as Finn drained his latte macchiato practically in a single gulp. The crowded cafe was loud and people bustled around them, but Finn seemed lost in his own world. They'd just come from a scan, where everything looked perfect with their little girl.

"I'm not ever going to be able to say no to her," Finn sighed. "Let's get that clear right now."

Marley grinned. "I don't think I'll be able to either. That little *thing* she did with her hands like she was shielding it from the sonogram?"

"I almost launched myself at your belly right then."

They fell silent again. Finn's eyes sparkled as he shook his head in amazement. "You're doing the most amazing job with her. She's absolutely perfect."

They fell into a comfortable silence, until Marley found herself curious about something.

"What did you imagine calling a girl if you had one?" she asked.

Finn blinked. "I … It doesn't matter. I'm not carrying her. You are. And you've had a name planned out your whole life."

"Just tell me."

"Elise," he said quickly.

Marley kept the smile plastered on her face. "Elise…" she repeated. "Does it have any special significance?"

Finn drew a deep breath. "There was this girl in our neighbourhood when I was growing up. She was an incredible skateboarder. I mean, she kicked *all* the guys' butts. She was funny as heck, super cute and she didn't give a fig what anyone thought of her. She was kind of my hero."

Marley tilted her head. "So you wanted to name your daughter after your schoolboy crush? Is that a wise thing to tell your heavily pregnant girlfriend?" She kicked him playfully under the table.

Finn's eyes clouded. "She was hit by a car when we were twelve. Killed instantly. Drunk driver. I always …" He fiddled with his cup handle. "I always thought I'd use that name as a way to honour her."

Marley's eyes went round with horror. "How horrible for her parents."

"Yeah," Finn nodded. "I don't think they ever got over it. I was in touch with them for a long time afterwards. They didn't have any other kids. Elise was their everything."

"I already can't stand the thought of something happening to our baby, and she's not even here yet." Marley placed a protective hand over her swollen stomach.

"I know," Finn said quietly. "It's nightmarish."

Marley slumped back in her chair. "I feel like that name is cursed."

Finn jerked one shoulder. "I can see why you would think that, I guess. I don't feel that way though. To me, it was better that she lived, even for a short time, than that she never did. It would have spared us grief, but it would have robbed us all of the joy of knowing her. Anyway," he shook his head, "it doesn't matter. I'm only telling you because you asked me, that's all. I'm not trying to change your mind."

Marley heaved another sigh. "Whose name usually goes first if a kid has two surnames?"

"I have no idea. But Marley, she doesn't have to have my name. She's mine, and she always will be. Besides, I detected the Mayberry profile on her. I've left my mark."

Marley smiled. "I guess we still have a while to decide." She stirred her tea slowly.

"What are you thinking?" Finn asked her. "You've got that look in your eye."

"What look?" Marley asked.

"The one when you've got something on your mind."

"Do I really have a look?"

"Yes," he said, holding her gaze. "I know all the Marley expressions. And I love them all."

She smiled at him through her lashes. "That was pretty cheesy."

Finn shrugged. "I *am* cheesy. My girls better get used to it."

Marley placed a hand over his. She loved the tanned roughness of his hands. Their size and strength were comforting. She hadn't intended to get used to being taken care of, but she often found herself feeling grateful that Finn was so well-built. Opening difficult jar lids, taking out the garbage, rubbing her feet and her shoulders, carrying things they bought for the baby … holding her up against walls …

Some of those were things she *could* do on her own, of course. But it was nice not to have to.

"I guess I'm a bit worried about you meeting up with Bess tomorrow night," Marley admitted. The thought of them together made her uneasy. She knew Finn wasn't about to get back together with his ex, but she also knew Bess felt like she had unfinished business with Finn. Or at least, that was what she imagined. That he was *the one who got away.* That's how she'd feel about him if she was stupid enough to mess things up.

Finn's expression softened. "This should be the last time we need to meet."

"You know she'll keep finding reasons though," Marley said, eyes on her drink. She hated how jealous she sounded.

Finn put his hand on her arm, the contact sending tingles through her. "You have absolutely nothing to worry about, Marley. From anyone."

"Are you ... are you going over to her flat?"

He shook his head. "We're meeting at a restaurant."

Marley gulped. "You're never very happy when you get back from seeing her, you know?"

"Can you blame me?" Finn asked. And honestly, she couldn't. Finn hadn't been a great version of himself with her. He'd given up everything, including his dreams, to help her along with hers. He'd virtually put his life on hold, and he hadn't exactly been rewarded for it. There was a tiny voice in the back of Marley's mind that worried she was doing the same thing with him. Not letting him completely move in, not giving him a say in their child's name, not being ready to throw herself in, lock stock and barrel. She hated that tiny voice, but she couldn't deny the truth of it.

She opened her mouth to say something, but Finn's phone pipped. He glanced at it, his eyes going wide. "Oh, that baby shop we walked past is having a sale!"

Marley frowned. "What, do you have an alert set up or something?"

He grinned sheepishly. "With every baby store in town."

"You're tragic," she said lovingly, grinning at him. "Also, we have to get back to work."

He gave her a secret smile. "I told Elizabeth we were taking the afternoon off. She called in backup. Besides, it's twenty-five percent off."

Without thinking, Marley struggled to her feet and snatched up her handbag. "Well, what are we waiting for?"

27

WEDNESDAY

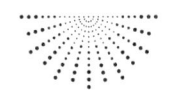

"Lots of men love flowers," Silas said defensively, holding out the small bunch to Ernie who was frowning suspiciously as he flicked his gaze between the flowers and Silas.

"It's not that I don't like them," Ernie said, relenting a little as he looked longingly at the bouquet. "They're actually really beautiful. I don't even know where you managed to find dahlias at this time of year, or how you remembered that I love them."

Silas had found them at a little florist in Lavender Bay, and had simply chosen the most expensive small bunch. As for Ernie loving them … pure dumb luck, though he was happy to let Ernie think otherwise.

"It's just … you've never done anything like this before," Ernie added.

"Well, I can start, can't I?" Silas said gruffly. He shook the bunch. "Take them before I throw them in the bin."

At that, Ernie's face split into a grin. "There you are," he said, leaning forward to place a tender kiss on Silas's lips. "Hi." He snatched up the little bouquet and rifled through the kitchen cupboards for a vase.

Silas watched, annoyed with himself. He hadn't meant to turn crotchety again. In fact, the flowers were only the next step of him trying to turn over a leaf where his relationship with Ernie was concerned. And he'd managed to snap at his boyfriend only seconds into the whole thing. Was there any hope for him at all?

Ernie selected a vase and turned to the sink to fill it with water, humming a happy little tune as he did so. It was so adorable that Silas couldn't keep himself from tentatively snaking his arms around Ernie's waist and slowly leaning his head on Ernie's back. As soon as his ear touched Ernie's spine, Silas felt his boyfriend freeze beneath him. He was roughly shoved back as Ernie spun to face him, sloshing water over the floor.

"What was that?" Silas yelped in surprise, jumping back from the small puddle.

"Are you cheating on me?" Ernie snapped, his knuckles white from clenching the vase so hard. His eyes bored into Silas's.

Silas's mouth fell open in shock. "*What?* How can you even ask that? I brought you flowers!"

"Exactly!" Ernie said, his voice shaking slightly. "You never buy me flowers. Or take me away on spontaneous trips to the zoo. And here you are hugging me, which is *another* thing you don't do unless you have … ulterior motives!"

Silas blinked, his cheeks reddening. God, another score against him. "Ernie, I promise I'm not cheating on you," Silas said mournfully. "I'm sorry that you even think that's a possibility."

Ernie was silent, still glaring at Silas suspiciously. "See, even that!" he said finally, shaking his head.

"Even what?" Silas threw his palms up.

"Answering me *so* politely." Ernie's tone was mocking.

"You'd usually tell me I was being an idiot or laugh in my face or something."

"Would I really?" Dear Lord.

"*Yes*. You're kind of freaking me out."

Silas's shoulders slumped and he took a deep breath. "I don't mean to freak you out. I promise you, there's nothing going on with me."

"Would you really tell me if there was?" Ernie grumbled, turning back to the sink.

"Would *you* tell *me?*" Silas retorted, before he could stop himself.

Ernie whipped back around, frowning. "Is that a serious question?"

Silas bit his lip. He didn't want to mention to Ernie that he'd seen the three messages come in from four-hearts when he'd gotten up to use the bathroom at two am that morning. Ernie's previews were still switched off and his phone had been charging beside the sink. Silas's fingers had itched, actually *itched* to check the messages. But he'd resisted, crawling numbly back into bed and lying awake until daybreak, planning ways he could hang onto the man snoring so adorably beside him. The flowers had been step two. And so far, step two was a bust.

"I guess not," Silas said finally. Ernie seemed to be challenging him, and if there was something to know, he didn't want to hear it yet. He wasn't done fighting, not by a long shot.

Silas grabbed a roll of kitchen towel and busied himself sopping up the spilled water, as Ernie filled the vase and unwrapped the flowers in silence. When he was done, he set the vase down in the middle of the dining table with a clack.

Silas looked up from the floor to find Ernie watching him. "What?"

"Nothing," Ernie said with a frown. He twisted his mouth.

"You can leave that, I'll do it later. And thanks for the flowers."

He stalked out of the room and Silas sank irritably to the floor, hurling the wad of kitchen roll across the room where it stuck to a cupboard with a wet thack.

He was going to have to try harder, do better. *Be* better. The problem was, he didn't really know how. He'd never had to work at this before. Men just kind of … fell at his feet, much as he hated to admit it. He was always the one who kicked them on their way. Always the one being worshipped, the one being chased. Even the beautiful ones, and they had mostly been beautiful, had all fallen hard.

These feelings were all new to him and he kind of hated them. But Ernie was the best thing that had ever happened to him. When he thought about his boyfriend's slightly gangly frame, his wide, earnest eyes, his cheap haircut—Silas's heart swelled. He had it bad, and he wasn't going to give up easily.

Surprise getaways, flowers and hugs apparently weren't going to cut it.

Then he sat bolt upright. Those things might not work, but he had a good idea what might …

28
THURSDAY

As soon as Finn came home from his meeting with Bess, Marley could tell something was wrong. The usual light was gone from his eyes, a deep frown in its place.

"What is it?" she asked, greeting him at the door with a cup of tea.

He toed off his shoes and chewed the inside of his cheek. "Nothing," he said, but his tone told her it wasn't the truth. He took the cup from her and immediately set it on the dresser by the door. Then he took a deep breath. "No, not nothing."

"Okay," Marley said anxiously, scanning his face for signs of what was to come. "Are you two getting back together?"

He puffed out an incredulous breath. "Is that a joke? Of course not."

"Okay, sorry. You've got me nervous, that's all."

"Let's go sit down in the living room."

Marley's heart was galloping as they took seats beside one another on the sofa. Finn seemed reluctant to start the conversation, and stayed silent so long that the words burst out of Marley. "If you're breaking up with me, tell me now."

He scrubbed a hand over his face, then fixed her gaze with his earnest one. "I'm not breaking up with you. But … I do need to take a little time."

"What does that mean?" Marley said, her voice high and tight.

He rolled his lips together. "Seeing Bess again … It made me I realise that I have a habit of putting my needs last. In every situation. And you're not *remotely* the same as Bess, I'm not saying that. The problem is me. And how I kind of … feel like I'm doing it again. Making the same mistakes."

"Finn," Marley breathed, the wind going out of her at his words.

He held a hand up to stop her. "I'm not trying to pressure you into anything. The opposite, in fact. But I have realised that I maybe need to do a bit of work on myself. Figure some things out, like about why I'm not good at saying what I want, what I need. I think … I'm going to go and stay at my flat for a little while. Take a bit of time alone. I hate the idea of leaving you so far along in the pregnancy, but you *know* I'm only a phone call away."

Marley squeezed her eyes shut, a fat tear plopping onto her lap. She gazed down at her hands, the knuckles white from where she was kneading them so tightly together. Part of her wanted to beg him to stay, to throw herself at his feet and give him anything he asked for. But she had a feeling the time apart would be good—for both of them. They each had things they needed to sort out.

"I understand," she whispered.

He sat for a moment longer, before pushing to his feet and heading to their bedroom. Theirs. It was theirs, as much as this apartment was theirs, as much as this baby was theirs. She knew that, but she hadn't shown him that. And now she was going to pay the price.

Nothing prepared her for the scrape in her heart as she

heard him going around, opening closets and closing drawers as he filled his duffel bag. Marley pushed her fingernails into her palm to keep more tears at bay. She didn't want him to think she was manipulating him with her tears. He needed to go and she knew it.

It was only when he'd kissed her goodbye and she heard the door to her building bang closed that she let the tears fall.

29

FRIDAY

Amy had never seen Marley look as distressed as she did right now, pacing around her living room.

"You told me to see a shrink before it turned into a big deal," Marley said sadly. "And I meant to, I really did. But I didn't get around to it. And now I can't sleep at night and I don't know when he's coming back."

Amy made a sympathetic noise as she tucked her legs up beneath her in the armchair. She was crawling out of her skin with to-dos, but at Marley's distress flare, she'd allowed herself a single moment of closed-eyed panic, then hopped in the car.

"It's not like it's *over* though, right?" Amy asked.

Marley shook her head, swallowing. "But ... I feel like I've damaged something."

Amy slowly slid a manicured nail around the rim of her water glass. "Even if you did, it's something that can be fixed. I *know* it is. Look what Rick and I came back from. Or Lyra and Alex."

Marley nodded. "Your enormous messes definitely give me hope."

Amy flinched, then decided not to take offense at Marley's phrasing. "Do you think you've worked anything out since he's been gone?"

Marley frowned. "What do you mean?"

"I mean, as to why you're still keeping him at arm's length. I know it can't just be because of your past. Or maybe it is. But I think you should figure it out before it's too late."

Marley was silent. "You know when you have a dream for so long?" she said finally, her features downcast.

"Sure," Amy said. "But I think our dreams are different. You mean having a baby?"

Marley nodded. "I waited so long, Amy. *So* long. And in that time, I figured it all out. Everything was planned."

Amy nodded, but kept her mouth closed.

"And then Finn came and it was all messed up. I couldn't *not* have him be part of my life, once I'd met him. I guess I was kind of in love with him for a long time before I let myself actually admit it. But …" Marley leaned forward and grabbed a carrot stick from the little serving tray on her coffee table. She didn't eat it, just toyed with it. "But I think I've assumed that I'll still be able to have it both ways."

"What do you mean?" Amy encouraged, even though she had a good idea. She knew her friend needed to talk things through out loud.

"I wanted Finn, but I wanted my space. I wanted a relationship, but I needed an escape hatch. I wanted a father for the baby, but I still wanted to do everything the way *I'd* imagined. I wanted him, but without compromise. Including with the name. I wanted a family, but I still want my independence. And I'm glad to be sharing the costs and responsibilities of parenthood, but … I still want to make sure I never get trapped. Not that I ever think Finn would try and trap me, but—"

"That part is smart," Amy said firmly. "Actually, a lot of

that is smart. *Especially* the financial stuff. And after the life you had with Hayden, I don't really blame you for any of the rest of it. I don't actually think that's the issue though."

Marley's mouth twisted. She got to her feet, pacing painfully, with her hands in the small of her back. Amy watched her, frowning. Pregnancy looked awful and Amy secretly vowed to talk to Rick about getting a vasectomy. Or to her doctor about having her tubes tied.

"Then what *is* the problem?" Marley asked.

"I guess … maybe that you don't think he's worth taking a leap of faith for?"

She froze. "Amy, I'm having his freaking *baby*," Marley burst out. "What's more leap-of-faithy than that?"

"Does he know if he's allowed to live here when the baby's born?"

Marley spun to her. "What?"

"Well, it's his kid too, right? But it must be pretty sucky to think at any moment he might be sent away from you both. Imagine yourself in his shoes. He's already nuts about this baby."

"We both are."

"Imagine how you'd feel if you didn't know whether you'd actually get to live with it. Imagine not even being on the same lease as your baby."

Marley's shoulders slumped. "I hadn't thought of it like that."

Amy pressed her lips together, not wanting to push further.

"Oh god," Marley groaned a moment later. "I've been horrible."

"You haven't," Amy said. "You absolutely have not. But you *might* have made him feel like he's on shaky ground. Partnerships are *hard*. They take work. They make everyone feel insecure at times. But you *do* have to show him that you're committed. You *do* have to prove that you're all in, even if it means you'll get hurt later. And unfortunately, you *do* have to compromise. Once the baby comes, there'll be so much pressure on both of you. You need a rock-solid foundation so you can get through it."

Marley's huge eyes were glued to Amy's, and they were starting to well. "I can't sleep without him anymore," she whispered.

"I know. I can't without Rick, either."

"And I don't like the apartment when he's not here," Marley continued, her voice wobbling.

"It's weird how that happens, isn't it?" Amy got slowly to her feet, crossing the room to pull her friend into as tight a hug as Marley's belly would allow.

"I think you've got a phone call to make," Amy said, smoothing her friend's honey-coloured hair.

"Being wrong sucks."

Amy chuckled. "Yep. But you're strong. You can admit it."

Amy called Rick from the road. "How's Marley?" he asked, as soon as he answered.

"She'll be fine."

"Okay. Are you going to stay at your place again? Is that why you're ringing?"

Amy smiled at the note of panic in his voice. "No. I'm ringing to tell you I adore you and I can't wait to see you."

"Well, snap," Rick replied, then dropped his voice. "And I have a surprise for you when you get here."

"If it's what I think it is, I can't wait," Amy said, switching lanes as she left the city and headed for the beach suburbs.

"It's even better," Rick said, lowering further to a whisper. "It's a lock on my door."

Amy burst out laughing. "I never thought those would be the hottest words I heard."

30
SATURDAY: FIVE WEEKS TO THE WEDDING

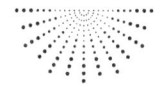

"I can't believe you'll be gone for three whole weeks," Alex said, pulling Lyra closer to him as the morning sun streamed in through their bedroom window and they snuggled under the blankets.

"I know," Lyra groaned, rolling into him and cinching her arm tightly around his broad chest. "Are you *sure* you don't secretly know how to mix sound?"

His laugh rocked her gently and she curled into his warmth, amazed for the millionth time at how quickly he'd become home for her. Every morning, she got to wake up to his handsome face, sometimes spending a few moments watching him as he slept. She knew he secretly did the same, and it melted her. She just hoped it happened when she looked beautiful, instead of drooling and snoring. But she knew he didn't care either way.

"How hard can it be?" he joked. "I'm sure half of those switches they slide up and down are only for show."

"They have to be, don't they?"

Alex squeezed her, growling a little. "I hate being without you."

She tilted her head to look up at him, her eyes tracing the thin scar on his chin—one of the first things she'd been fascinated by on his handsome face. The other was the grey-gold eyes that were watching her intently now. "You have no idea," she replied, scooching up the bed to press her lips to his. "But at least I have all those groupies on tour to keep me company."

"A warm body is a warm body, right?" he added with a shrug.

Lyra grinned. She loved the way he always matched her joke for joke. The way his calm confidence in himself meant he wasn't prone to jealousy. She loved that strength in him, and knew it was hard-fought. He'd gone through periods of self-doubt during all the problems with Alison. But since Lyra's singing career had launched, Alex had been pragmatic about the attention she got. And Lyra made it her business to show him exactly how much she loved and appreciated him, and how she only had eyes for him. It wasn't exactly difficult, since he was truly the only guy she ever thought about.

"What are you going to do today?" she asked him.

He traced his hand gently up and down her back, sending warmth tingling through her as he replied. She put her ear to his chest to feel the rumble of his voice. "Rick and I have to finish a job. And we also need to pull together a few quotes for enquiries we got."

Lyra loved that Alex and Rick worked so well together. And as Rick grew stronger and was able to stand without his wheelchair for longer periods, they were able to seriously consider taking on a broader range of projects.

"That's great," Lyra said, enthusiastically. "You guys are a fearsome duo. Can't wait till you can show me some pictures. You'll have to send me stuff when I'm on the road."

"Oh, you'll get pictures alright," Alex joked, wiggling his eyebrows.

"Stop it!" Lyra laughed.

She slapped him playfully and in one swift move he'd flipped her onto her back. Lyra smiled up into his eyes.

"We have a couple more hours," he said, leaning to kiss her neck.

Lyra closed her eyes and sighed, wrapping her arms around him. "Let's make the most of them then…" she whispered.

"That's really all you'll need?" Alex asked a few hours later, as Lyra emerged from the bedroom with a stuffed duffel bag. "For three weeks?"

"Well, the costume department take care of what I wear on stage. So it's just off-duty stuff. It's mostly a couple of pairs of jeans and t-shirts," Lyra shrugged. "I don't see a need for much else? Last time I had a few dresses I'd packed myself, but aside from being on-stage, I mainly had on my jeans."

Alex's eyes widened. "I hadn't realised there was costume department now."

"And makeup," Lyra added with a grin. "Which, thank god. My face is blown up to about a billion times its normal size on the screens in a couple of the bigger venues. And the best I can do for myself is lipstick."

"Well, you look stunning no matter what."

"Thanks for driving me in," Lyra said, grabbing his hand as they locked up the apartment and headed for the car. "It feels weird this time. I guess because it's longer and the venues are bigger."

"Or you're more in love?" He nudged her and she grinned, then hugged his arm.

"Also that."

They spent a long time kissing in the car outside the studio. Lyra was secretly hoping Selena or Julian, or even Jake might spot the two of them. She was feeling slightly anxious about the whole "discussion" again. She'd managed to push it from her mind, and it hadn't been raised again, though she'd seen both Selena and Julian multiple times since then. Selena had acted as warm and friendly as Lyra had ever known her to be. Which was to say distantly polite and with an aura of danger around her.

Surely there was nothing they could do against Lyra's will? She would just have to make extra certain that she kept her distance from Jake during the tour. Not an easy feat, considering they'd be crammed together on a tour bus most of the time, when they weren't sharing a stage.

"*Man* I'm going to miss you," she said, hugging him tightly.

"You have no idea," he said, pressing his forehead to hers.

"I'm so glad we've signed the contract on the house. Makes me so keen to get back and start making plans."

"I'm surprised it all worked out so smoothly. And I can't believe we might be buying a place together finally."

"Such a good one, too," Lyra added, her eyes dreamy as she thought of their new little home. Then she realised she'd better get moving. "I won't have my phone on me a lot of the time, but I'll check it every night after each show. I'll message as often as I can."

"Me too."

Lyra moved to open the door handle, then lunged back at Alex for one more, passionate kiss.

"Nice show," said Todd, the label's receptionist, as Lyra finally headed in through the revolving doors. Lyra realised he had the street-side security camera footage showing on his screens.

"Perv," she retorted, sticking her tongue out.

Todd mimicked her gesture good-naturedly. They'd gotten off to a rocky start when Lyra had made her first ill-fated appearance at the label. But over time, they'd become polite acquaintances, occasionally dipping into friendlier territory.

"What are you doing here on a Sunday, anyway?" Lyra asked, turning back before she headed down the hall to the others. "Don't you have a life?"

Todd shook his head, averting his gaze. "Oh, you know me. Live to work!"

Lyra found the comment strange, and stranger still was how busy several of the rooms were as she moved through the main corridor towards the rear exit to the back lot. The others would be waiting for her in the van.

A woman opened one of the meeting room doors and scurried out. While the door was open, the PowerPoint presentation on screen was briefly visible to Lyra. It was filled with charts and graphs she couldn't make out from so far away. Catching sight of what she thought was her own name, she came to a dead stop in the corridor and squinted at the screen. But another suit around the table caught her looking, smiled politely, and quickly kicked the door shut.

31
SATURDAY

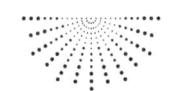

Amy's stomach was twisted in knots as she, Rick and Pam entered the small Returned & Services League Club for a pre-wedding, pre-rehearsal-dinner dinner. It had been hastily set up with Pam, Sean, Pop and Hazel as guests. Amy had secretly been hoping to get away with not having the dinner at all. But Pam and Sean had raised it so often that she'd started to worry they might go ahead and meet in secret—and that was the last thing she wanted.

They'd chosen the location as it wasn't too far from Pop and Hazel's retirement home, was along a bus route for Sean and was wheelchair accessible for Rick. That was the good thing about anything designed for returned servicemen and military personnel—accessibility had been heavily factored in.

Amy had no idea what to expect from the evening.

She couldn't help but notice that Pam had made quite an effort with her appearance. She was dressed in a baby pink blouse paired with fitted dark jeans that hugged her petite, slender figure. Red pumps, red lipstick and even mascara—something Amy hadn't seen her wear in the entire time she'd known her—completed the outfit. She looked much younger than her age. She looked great.

Rick's jaw had tightened when Pam had stepped out of her bedroom and announced she was ready. Amy could see the flicker of pain in his eyes. She knew he hadn't seen her dressed up in years—he'd often mentioned the fact she used to love getting made up to go out with his father. He'd managed to bite down any reaction he was having to the fact she was clearly dressed up for Amy's father. Amy had been proud of him for that.

If Pam had noticed anything in his reaction, she hadn't let on. She'd chattered happily the entire drive in, peppering Amy with not-so-subtle questions about the relationship between her parents. A short story as Amy told it—Sean and Diana married young, had Amy, got divorced when things turned sour. Diana had remarried when Sean was in prison. But the real story was much more complicated and fraught, at least where Diana was concerned. Amy knew her mother was still working through layers of complex and unresolved feelings about the marriage, and about her ex-husband.

Sean stood nervously at a table as the group approached. His dark hair was neatly combed, and his simple jeans and white t-shirt combo set off his tan and showcased what was quickly becoming an impressively toned physique.

He pulled Amy towards him once they were near, almost crushing her as though he had an excess of nervous energy to burn off.

"Hi, baby girl," he said, but his eyes were already straying to Pam.

He shook hands with Rick, who managed to make a smile-like shape with his mouth.

"Nice to finally meet the man who managed to snag my baby girl," he said, beaming. Amy felt a prick of irritation at his words. He made it sound like she'd been through a string of men and had tossed them all aside. She bit the irritation down. Sean hadn't seen her grow up—he needed to fill in blanks sometimes and make it seem that he knew her better than he did. So she let him have it.

"Best girl in the world," Sean added proudly, and Amy was glad she'd bitten her tongue.

"Don't I know it," Rick said, winking at her. Her insides melted.

Sean turned his attention to Pam, who was lingering back slightly. Her cheeks were flushed and she looked almost bashful as she extended her hand towards Sean.

"It's nice to meet you in person," she said, her voice an octave higher than usual.

"Likewise," Sean said, his eyes holding hers as he lifted her outstretched hand and kissed it lightly. Amy thought he managed to make the move look almost natural, but the expression on Rick's face told her otherwise.

"Oh, there's Pop and Hazel," Amy said loudly, hoping to break the odd spell between Pam and Sean, who seemed rooted to the spot, smiling at one another.

It was strange seeing Pop and Hazel outside of Sunnywoods, the retirement village where they lived. But it was a sight Amy hoped she'd see more of. Since they'd made the decision to room together, Pop had seemed fuller of energy than Amy could remember in a long time. It warmed her heart to see her grandfather so smitten with a woman after spending so long single after his wife, Amy's grandmother, had died. And Hazel clearly adored him right back.

"Look at these two lovebirds," Sean joked, chucking Percy on the shoulder.

"You're not too old to go over my knee, Sean," Pop retorted.

Hazel elbowed him. "This is an RSL, Perce. Keep your

kink shows out of it. I'm Hazel, by the way," she added, extending her hand to Pam. "And you must be Pam. I'm glad I get the chance to congratulate you in person for raising such a wonderful young man."

"Oh, thank you. Not sure how much credit I deserve. He's always been an angel." Pam beamed at Rick, who took both women's praise with a shy grin and a ducked head.

By unspoken agreement, everyone quickly took their seats. It seemed odd to loom over Rick, and Amy knew he was conscious of it. After spending most of his life as one of the tallest people in every room, one of the more difficult things about his wheelchair had been adjusting to the change in height.

He'd admitted it to Amy, in the dead of night when they were discussing his recovery in whispers. He'd been almost ashamed of worrying about such a seemingly trivial thing when his very life had been on the line. Amy had reassured him that it was far from trivial. Almost everything in his life had been turned upside down by his accident. He was allowed to mourn what he wanted, how he wanted.

"So, Amy Beth, am I walking you down the aisle naked or what?" Pop asked, and Amy laughed.

"I thought you had a closet full of tuxedos!"

"I can't do it without new threads. You promised me a shopping trip."

"And you said you'd rather swallow razor blades than be dragged around a mall and dressed like a doll."

Pop chortled. "Okay, you got me there. Still, we gotta pick something for me, less you want me turning up in track pants."

"Interesting," Amy said, tapping her chin thoughtfully. "Either I buy you a tux or you turn up in track pants. Don't you always tell me that kids these days dress like, what was it, homeless fishermen?"

Pop tksed. "I said that about your friend Marley, and I stand by it. How is she, by the way?"

"About eleven months pregnant and feeling every day of it." Amy was conscious of the fact that Sean might feel slightly left out of the conversation. He knew her friends' names now, but was yet to meet them. She briefly wondered if he was jealous of the relationship she had with his father. Then she decided it didn't matter. It wasn't her fault he'd ruined their family's lives.

Pop beamed. "Be good to see her again at the wedding. It's been a while since she stopped by."

Pam elbowed Amy with significance. "That'll be you soon, too."

"What will?" Amy asked, genuinely puzzled. Rick choked slightly on the water he was sipping, glass still raised to his mouth.

"You know. Pregnant," Pam said, smiling.

"Mum, we're not even down the aisle yet," Rick said quickly. "Let's get that done first."

Pam smiled a secret smile. "I'm already on bump-watch."

"Well, you don't need to be," Amy said firmly. "I can assure you, there's no bump to watch."

"Not yet," Pam said, and Amy once again dug her nails firmly into her palm to keep quiet. Rick mouthed "sorry" when she glanced at him.

"Kids don't suit everyone," Hazel said lightly, and Amy could have hugged her. "I never had any."

Pam tutted sympathetically, reaching past Amy to pat Hazel's hand. "Well, you have Rick and Amy now." Hazel smiled tightly, clearly thinking Pam had missed her point.

"Amy's the best thing that ever happened to me," Sean piped up, looking at Amy with such pride that she felt her cheeks pink.

"Okay, shall we order?" Amy said hastily.

"Good idea," Hazel said quickly. "I've been eyeing the poached snapper and I already know Percy's going to have a meat pie."

"And a coffee," Pop added loudly. "The jail we live in, they stop serving caffeine after three."

Amy grinned. "I happen to know you have a source who sneaks it to you whenever you want."

"Doesn't mean I'm not making the most of this night out," Pop said. "Getting ice-cream, too. You'll join me for that, won't you, Sean?"

Sean shook his head, patting his stomach. "Coach banned dairy."

"*Oh?*" Pam asked, sounding fascinated.

"Boxing coach," Sean said, by way of explanation. "He thinks animal products slow us down."

Pop snorted.

"Lots of the teens that come through had pretty bad acne before they cut it out, too," Sean said defensively. "I'm convinced it's bad for humans."

"Bad or not, I'm having a double scoop of chocolate," Pop said. "Couldn't care less if I had a breakout."

"It would make me feel young again, dating a man with pimples," Hazel added, and everyone laughed.

"Right, everyone give me your orders, this dinner is on Rick and I," Amy announced, getting to her feet.

"Lobster in that case," Pop quipped. "And oysters for Hazel."

Amy laughed, waving off all protestations from Pam and Sean about footing the bill, and headed to the counter to place the order.

She was seething at Pam and needed a moment to cool off. *Bump-watch?* What was this, the 1950s? First, why was Pam assuming they were even going to have a kid, and second, what was she thinking announcing that to *the entire table?* Amy stopped by the bar after swapping the food orders for a beeper tag, and ordered herself a huge glass of red wine along with some assorted soft drinks for the others.

She took petty delight in drinking deeply and flamboyantly once she was back at the table. Pam pressed her lips together and quickly looked away each time their eyes met over the glass.

The group naturally broke into clusters of two: Amy and Pop discussing when they'd have time to shop for his suit; Rick and Hazel talking business; Sean and Pam talking in low voices and with big smiles.

A few drinks in, Amy could feel herself relaxing, glad that Pam was driving them home. When Pop went to the bathroom, Rick squeezed Amy's leg under the table and she smiled at him, feeling a rush of love. The way his hair was starting to wave slightly at the longer ends, the stubble of his beard over his strong jaw. The dimple that had always driven her wild. And the scar across his face. The one that showed the world how very strong he was and how much he had survived and overcome, this man who only had eyes for her. Without thinking, she leaned towards him, planting a hard kiss on his lips.

"What's that for?" he asked, shooting a bashful glance towards Hazel, who pretended to suddenly be engrossed in her drink.

"I can't wait be your wife, that's all," Amy whispered.

Rick's face lit up, and he cupped her cheek with his hand. "You have no idea," he replied earnestly.

In the car on the drive home, Rick and Amy sat together in the back as Pam drove, Amy a little giggly from the wine. She felt like a schoolgirl, and even the way she and Rick were squeezing one another's hands seemed a little naughty.

Until Pam spoke.

"It was lovely getting to meet your father finally, Amy,"

she said in a tight tone, raising her eyes to Amy's in the rear-view mirror.

Amy's hand went still in Rick's and from the corner of her eye, she saw him frown.

"Hmm. Do you feel a little better about the wedding now?" she asked Pam.

"Oh yes. We've agreed to sit beside one another. The two parents without a partner."

Amy bristled at that, and vowed to have a word to Sean about it. She wasn't precious about the seating plan, but neither did she like the fact they clearly thought they could take it over without so much as consulting her.

"I see," she said finally.

Pam flicked her gaze to Amy's again in the mirror. The headlights of an oncoming car lit up both their faces, and Amy could see the tight edges of the other woman's eyes.

"I have to say, I find it a shame how many years your father missed out on with you."

"Mum," Rick said immediately, his voice a warning.

Pam's eyes widened innocently. "I'm just saying, that's all. What a waste of time it all was. You never know how long you get with someone, and spending all those years harbouring a grudge seems …"

"Seems what, Pam?" Amy asked, her jaw clenched.

Pam shrugged. "I don't know. Petty?"

It might have been the wines, but Amy wasn't sure she could have kept her temper at that, even if she'd been stone cold sober.

"It was *petty* to stop speaking to the man who gambled away my family home and went to prison after forging my mother's signature, so he could gamble even more money stolen from us?"

Pam was silent. "He's your father."

"Well he never acted like it," Amy snapped.

Pam drew a deep breath, as though Amy was trying her patience. "He tried very hard to make it up to you."

"Did he? Until a couple of months ago, he was *still* gambling. He told me he thought he could win my mother back." Amy knew she'd added that last point to try and wound Pam, but she didn't care.

She studied the other woman's face carefully in the mirror, and saw her flinch slightly. *Good.*

"Please don't do this," Rick said, his voice pained.

Instantly, Amy was chastened. Rick was always the innocent third party, and he'd forever be the only one wounded in any crossfire between her and Pam. The fight went out of them both, like a balloon being deflated, and no one spoke for the rest of the drive.

When they reached Pam's house, she shut off the engine and stalked inside. Amy retrieved Rick's chair from the boot and lined it up beside his door as he swung into it.

"I'm going to get a cab home," Amy said quietly, feeling suddenly sober as she stood in the brisk night air.

Rick looked up at her, his jaw tight and his eyes tired. "I completely understand," he said sadly. Then he reached for her hand. "But I wish you wouldn't. I don't know what's going on with her, but I'll speak to her tomorrow. I promise."

Amy's shoulders slumped. "Rick, that will only make it worse. Please leave it. And I've been thinking … let's increase our house budget. By, say, another hundred grand. The business is doing well, although we'll have a little liquidity problem for a while with the new hires and relocation costs. But I'll sell my flat if I have to. I don't want to, but it's getting painful now. I can't keep staying here with her. She hates me, and I'm going to lose it at her. Or we can rent. We haven't seriously looked into that option yet."

Rick looked down at the ground, a sigh escaping him. "I don't have steady work, Ames. I can't go any higher. I know

I've said I'm ready to consider a life outside the army, but Alex and I don't have anything regular. We can't bank on any set amount. It'll end up being a bigger burden to you if we borrow more. And you're already taking on so much."

"You have the payments from the army. It's not all on me. And I have complete faith that you and Alex will really be able to make a go of it."

Rick searched her face. "Okay. Okay, let's do that. Let's see what we can get for that, anyway. It seems ridiculous to be paying so much."

"It's Sydney. Everything's ridiculous. And let's also consider renting, okay?"

"The accessible options will be pretty limited."

"But there's still a good chance."

Rick nodded. Then his eyes crinkled, and Amy could make out the shine of something cheeky in them. "Why don't we head inside for now? I've got an idea for taking your mind off things."

Amy giggled like a teen, her tension momentarily forgotten. "Richard Ford. Are you trying to take advantage of my tipsy state?"

"Oh, absolutely," he confirmed, wriggling his eyebrows.

"I'm very inclined to let you."

32
SUNDAY

"Man that was a killer set," Jake said, flopping beside Lyra on the sand at Newcastle Beach, a parcel of hot chips in his hands.

They'd finished two hours earlier at one of the bigger venues in town, and after quick showers, had collectively decided to head to the local beach to relax. The sun had long since set and the moon was rising over the water, leaving a wavering, glistening white path in its wake. The roar of the ocean was relaxing, the sand cool beneath Lyra's bare feet. She had Alex's favourite cardigan wrapped around her. She'd stolen it from his wardrobe and stuffed it into her duffel, knowing he'd be touched once he noticed. She drew it to her nose and sniffed deeply, smiling secretly at the traces of his scent on it.

"It was pretty good, wasn't it?" she agreed. Jake unwrapped the package, and Lyra grabbed a piping hot chip. She bit into it and groaned. "These are amazing."

"Place called Scotties," he told her. "Tip from a local."

Newcastle Beach was a smallish crescent of yellow-gold sand and water that had looked bright turquoise patched with navy in the day, but now looked black. She and Jake sat between what locals had told them was called "Shark Alley" and something else known as the Canoe Pool—a ringed-off section of chest-height water. Not that Lyra was interested in going anywhere near the water. Once she'd cooled down from the physical high of the night's concert, a slight chill had settled into her bones. Behind them, a concrete lip ran the perimeter of the beach, and slightly beyond it lay their multi-storey hotel, alongside other waterfront properties.

They'd sleep nights on the road in the van, but since they were stationed here for two shows back-to-back, Selena had sprung for hotel rooms for them. Lyra had been sceptical at first, assuming she might "accidentally" be booked into a single room with Jake, but there'd been no such shenanigans. Lyra wanted to let her guard down. It had been one of those nights where things went brilliantly. No one made a single mistake, they'd had amazing chemistry on stage, the audience were enthusiastic and appreciative, and it had genuinely been a blast. Lyra knew as the tour ground on, the mood would sour. They'd be exhausted, they'd make mistakes, snipe at each other, get tired of living in a truck. But tonight, they were on top of the world.

Kit and Maggie were whooping up and down near the shoreline and Lyra and Jake laughed at them, feeling for a moment like the sensible parents witnessing their hooligan children.

Lyra's phone buzzed in her pocket and she shot off a quick text reply to Mick, then snapped a pic of the beach, though not much showed in the picture. She sent it to Alex, then clicked her phone to silent, wanting to soak up the moment.

"Do you reckon those two …" Jake trailed off, jerking his head to the shoreline, where Maggie and Kit were now roughhousing.

"Oh definitely," Lyra said quickly. "If they haven't already they will soon. I think that was pretty clear from the barbecue."

"Let's hope it's not on the bus then," Jake said, elbowing her.

Lyra smiled, and rubbed her arm where he'd touched her, pulling away slightly. He noticed and fell silent.

"So you didn't think any more about what Julian said?" he asked, a while later.

Lyra flicked her eyes to him, frowning. "I wasn't aware there was anything else to think of. I said no, I meant no. I meant it then, I mean it now."

Jake nodded, then stared out over the water for a long moment. "This band's the best thing that ever happened to me," he said quietly. Lyra stopped chewing, hearing a note of raw honesty in his voice she'd never heard before—wanting to respect it. Jake was the perpetual calm presence in the band, forever upbeat and indefatigably positive. Lyra had never known him to be this serious.

"I don't know if you know this," he continued, drawing a deep breath. "But I was in rehab two years ago. Actually, I've been in rehab three times."

Lyra lowered the chip that was headed for her mouth. "I would never have guessed."

Jake gave her a tight smile. "That's the best compliment, I guess. Thirteen months sober. Amphetamines. Kind of a rite of passage when you grow up where I did."

"Well … congratulations on your sobriety," Lyra said, feeling proud of him.

He nodded, looking proud himself. "This band has a lot to do with it. I love us. I don't mean you and me," he added quickly, when Lyra looked away. "I mean the four of us. What we come up with. How we do it."

Lyra nodded. "Same."

"It's almost like a family."

Lyra bit her lip. The band wasn't like a family for her. It was like a … band. Sure, it was magical, sometimes even otherworldly. But it was its own thing. Because she *had* family. Alex, Mick, Silas, Ernie, Amy, Marley. They were her family. Kathryn now, too. And Rick and Finn. Family was something separate to this, to the band, to their music. But she knew it might not be like that for Jake, so she dipped her head and picked up another fry.

"I'm scared if we don't go along with what Selena wants, she'll break us apart somehow. The band. Put me with some other group. With a singer who *would* be willing."

Lyra's pulse beat hard. It didn't feel as though Jake was trying to push her into something. It felt like he was being vulnerable with her, trusting her with his fears. She knew what he was asking—whether she couldn't *try* what Selena was asking.

She took a good long look at the man sitting in the sand beside her. In different circumstances, he was definitely someone she could have seen herself falling for. He was square-jawed and deep-voiced and well-built. He insanely talented. And obviously strong, having overcome what he'd just revealed. But no matter what, he left her cold. Every man did. Because there was only one man for her, and she already had him.

"Jake," she began gently. "You're so wonderful. Truly--"

"Ugh, don't," he said, with a flap of his hand. "It sounds too much like a rejection. I just want to say … you don't need to be into me. I'm enough into you for the two of us." He shot her a sad smile and she closed her eyes. She hated causing anyone pain, even unintentionally. "And I know you're in love with your boyfriend. I'd never forget that."

Lyra swallowed, her heart racing. "I could never," she whispered finally. "Maybe I'm dumb and naive and innocent.

Maybe this is what everyone has to do to please their labels or help with marketing or whatever ... But I could never. I'm sorry."

Jake looked away, nodding briefly. They sat in silence, both staring out to sea as he scooped handfuls of sand and let them pour through his fingers.

A while later, Kit and Maggie raced up the sand towards them, and each grabbed one of their hands, trying to haul them to their feet. Lyra sat firm, laughing in protest.

"I'm *not* going in the water, if that's what you're thinking!" she yelled, yanking her arm back. "And you're getting sand in the chips!"

"Oh, spoil sport," Maggie pouted. "Come on in!"

"Okay, one, we're apparently in Shark *Alley*, and two, we don't have swimmers!"

In answer, Maggie thrust her chin out. In a single motion, she'd whipped her long-sleeved, knee-length dress over her head. She stood before all three of them in her mismatched, silken underwear. Kit panted, dropping Jake's hands as his eyes lit on Maggie with laser focus. She gave him a coy side-eye glance through her lashes, then looked back down at Lyra.

"Are you *coming?*"

"Nope!" Lyra said brightly. "You'll have to convince someone else."

Without warning, Kit tore his shirt over his head and shucked his pants. Maggie grinned, turning to face the water as she unclasped her bra and let it fall to the sand. Then she took off, hoofing sand over Lyra's face as she raced to the shore. Kit was hot on her heels. Jake scrambled to his feet, laughing. He arched an eyebrow at Lyra, as his hands sought the bottom of his shirt.

"Absolutely *not*," she replied. "If you all get eaten by sharks, someone has to do the show."

"Your funeral!" He slipped off his shirt, dropped his pants and chased the others down to the sand on powerful legs.

Lyra laughed to herself as she watched the three of them squealing, splashing and diving under the water. They'd be blue when they finally got out, she was willing to bet.

Her band mates were nuts. And she absolutely loved it.

33
MONDAY

Lyra's phone felt hot in her hand. Everything felt hot. Her heart was pounding and she could barely believe what she was seeing.

Cheeky Lyra Beck goes late-night skinny-dipping with bandmates while on tour!

Her Instagram account had been tagged in a single tile on a gossip magazine feed. Worse, the caption accompanying the blurry photo of three bare bottoms along the shoreline appeared to be insinuating *she* was woman running naked along the beach between two equally naked men. After staring at it for several minutes, then frantically trying without success to untag herself, Lyra dialled Alex.

"Hey gorgeous," he answered croakily, on the fourth ring.

"I didn't go skinny-dipping," she said in a rush.

Alex paused, and Lyra could almost hear the wheels turning in his head. "Huh?"

She took a deep breath. "I'm tagged in some photo on social media that says I was skinny-dipping with my bandmates, but I was the *only* one who wasn't. I sat on the beach, innocently eating my chips, wearing your cardigan.

Maggie started it. She took her dress off, and then the boys, but I didn't even look and—Alex? Are you … *laughing?*"

He coughed to disguise it, and Lyra broke into a relieved grin. "Maybe?" he squeaked finally.

"Oh, thank *god,*" Lyra said, collapsing backwards onto her hotel bed in relief.

"You can skinny-dip if you want. I trust you completely, Ly. And you know I don't have Instagram, right?"

"Yes, I know. But you have other social media. And I thought maybe someone would have told you and you might be spiralling, and … I don't know. I freaked out."

"Who'd be calling me at six am but you?"

Lyra blinked, whipping her head to check the time on the hotel's digital alarm clock. "It's only six," she repeated on a groan.

"Yeah, nutbar. It's six."

"And I didn't go skinny dipping."

"And you didn't go skinny dipping. But you *did* steal my cardigan and *that* is adorable."

"I knew you'd like it. But women don't want to be called adorable, Alex." She used a mocking tone to throw his words in his face.

"Oh yeah?" She could hear the smile in his voice. "What do they want to be called?"

"Womanly and capable."

"Lyra," he said in a breathy tone, "you are so womanly and capable."

They laughed, and then he yawned. Lyra hesitated for a moment, wondering whether she should fill him in on the conversation with Jake. But that would involve revealing Jake's personal business, something she didn't feel comfortable with. Not to mention telling Alex the whole backstory. "Can I go back to sleep now?" Alex asked.

"Go back to sleep. I love you."

"I love you too. Talk later?"
"Yeah."
"But like, in two to three hours?"
She grinned. "Yeah."

They hung up and Lyra crawled back under the covers. But her mind wouldn't rest. Where had the photo come from? There was a photographer on tour with the band, but she hadn't spotted him last night. And surely he'd take a better shot than the blurry one she was tagged in. Sighing, she tossed her phone across the room. It was so incredibly frustrating to her that singing—doing what she loved and was good at—came with so much other *crap*. Why couldn't they simply let her do her thing? Yes, logically, she knew marketing had to be part of it, too. The world was awash with options and the label had the difficult task of making *her* music stand out from the crowd. But surely there were other ways to market? She vowed to be as boring as humanly possible for the rest of the trip. Okay, she might miss out on some fun moments with her band, and on exploring some great locations. But she could always come back to these places again. With Alex, or with friends. It wasn't like she'd never get another chance.

She pulled the covers up to her chin and focussed on her breathing. Eventually, she fell back to sleep.

34
TUESDAY

"Plainer," Silas said to the jewellery store attendant, who rolled her eyes to the replica frescos on the ceiling, as though patience could be found there. Her grey hair was pinched into a chignon and she wore heavy makeup that caked in her wrinkles.

"Without even the diamond solitaire?" Her tone suggested Silas had asked whether he could urinate in the store.

"Without a diamond at all."

"You said it was an engagement ring?"

"Yes."

"Sir, I'm happy to find anything that's to your taste. However, I would like to point out that the *majority* of women prefer a little … pizzaz to their engagement jewellery. The wedding ring is traditionally the plainer one. I've been doing this a long time, and I know what works." She pointed to her tag, which read "LILETH. MANAGER." in gold embossing.

Silas glared at her and she held up her hands defensively. "Plainer it is. Let me see what I have out back."

Lilith flicked her gaze to her colleague and though her

face was hidden, he was sure she'd rolled her eyes again. After she disappeared behind the curtain, the other assistant, a goth-looking younger woman with a lip piercing and glossy black hair, pushed herself up from the counter she'd been leaning against. Her label read "MONA. TRAINEE." and Silas thought that was a bit demeaning.

"It's not a woman, is it?" Mona asked Silas bluntly.

He shook his head. "I don't even care about correcting her. I want a ring and to get home."

"What's he into then?"

Silas considered. "He wouldn't want something too plain, I guess. But he also definitely doesn't want a diamond ... I don't think."

She nodded. "Gold or silver."

"Gold."

"I have an idea."

She crossed the room and pulled out a tray of gold bands. They were thick and beautifully carved, with swirling patterns textured into the gold. Silas was immediately drawn to one that portrayed two hands around a crowned heart. He picked it from the tray and held it up to the light, turning it over.

"A Claddagh," Mona said, obviously pleased with his choice.

"Bless you?" Silas pulled his gaze from the ring to frown at her.

She gave a small laugh. "It's an Irish thing. It's meant to symbolise friendship, love and loyalty. The purity of a relationship."

Silas stared at it a moment longer, then handed it to her. "I'll take it."

As Mona was punching the sale into the computer, Lilith brushed back through the velvet curtains, holding a tray of diamond-encrusted bands.

"You're *kidding,*" she said, her shoulders slumping. "Mona, we've talked about this! You can't steal my customers." Her voice rose to a whiny pitch.

"Mona clearly knows more about serving customers," he said. "You didn't listen to a thing I said, and she nailed it right away. Maybe *she* should be the manager and *you* should be the trainee."

Mona barely managed to suppress a smile, and Lilith blustered. Silas stalked out, swinging the glossy store bag and smiling to himself as he thought about how Ernie was going to react when he proposed.

The hours until Ernie finally arrived home from work stretched on and on for Silas. Ernie worked as a graphic designer for a print shop, and his shifts varied from early to late. Of course he'd be on the late shift that day.

Silas busied himself doing inventory for the truck, balancing his accounting books, filing his Business Activity Statements, checking in with his supplier, and brainstorming new pie ideas. He'd done all that and there were still two hours to go.

He dialled his sister, but her phone rang out as he knew it would. She'd be getting ready for her show, if not on stage already. He bit his lip and dialled Mick. He needed to share the news with someone or he'd burst. And he'd come to a strange realisation after having bought the ring. He wasn't doing it to try and keep Ernie. He was doing it because he genuinely wanted to be married to the man. On paper, Ernie was possibly the strangest choice of partner Silas had ever made. But it hadn't taken long before he was under Ernie's spell. Try as he might—and he'd definitely tried in those early days—no one could make him forget Ernie. It was Ernie's face he saw when he had a drink with someone else, Ernie he wanted to take home, Ernie he sweated over. He still had no idea why. Well, he did. And it was the horrible L word that still made him feel slightly icky inside.

"Silas!" Mick said, answering his call. "Nice surprise. You okay?"

"You sound so relaxed," Silas said enviously. He'd been pacing, but he took a seat in an armchair in the living room now.

"Might be because I'm sitting on the back deck watching the moon come up at Kathryn's place, having a little drink. Might be because you sound stressed. Want to tell me what's up?"

Silas smiled. Mick knew he hated beating around the bush. "It's Ernie," he said finally.

"Oh? You two okay?" Silas heard the ice clinking in Mick's drink as he took a sip.

"Yes. No. Well. Yes."

"Alright?" Mick let a silence hang between them. He wouldn't push, and Silas loved that about him.

"I think I'm going to propose," he blurted. "And I'm all of a sudden really scared he's not going to say yes."

Mick let out a slow whistle. "Big move, son. Wow. Gotta say, I didn't see that coming."

"Me either," Silas moaned, pushing a hand through his hair. "I sort of started off thinking I'd do it because I've been feeling like he's slipping away from me lately. But now …" Silas blinked rapidly before forcing the words out. "Now I *really* want this."

"You feel he's slipping?"

Silas sighed. "I can't explain it. I've seen messages on his phone here and there. I wonder if I'm nice enough to him. And it's doing my head in."

"These messages. Who are they from?"

"I don't know. I haven't actually read them, just seen a mystery number pop up."

"So could be, like, a female cousin or something. An aunt."

"The person's in his phone as four hearts."

"Right. Still. You could be five hearts."

"Mick," Silas whined, hating the sound of his voice. "Just tell me he's going to say yes."

Mick took another drink. "Can't tell you that. Much as I want to. Think the chances are pretty good though, if that helps? He's starry-eyed when he looks at you and I'm pretty sure he'd walk under a bus for you."

"Yeah. I thought that too. But lately …"

"He said something or done something?"

"No. It's just a feeling."

"So, in other words, a story you've made up for yourself. And I don't suppose there's any way you can *talk* to him about it?"

"No. Ugh, please stop making so much sense and like, trying to *work* through this. Surely a proposal and a ring fix everything? And it makes things pretty clear in any case. He says no, we're doomed."

"Why's that now?" Mick asked.

Silas opened and closed his mouth. "Because he would have *refused to marry me!*"

"Some people don't want to get married."

"I think he does."

Mick was silent. "Yeah, you're probably right. I think he does, too. When you doing it?"

"Tonight. I'm waiting for him to get home."

"And Murphy's law, he's delayed or something."

"Evening shift."

"Tough break. You got a drink?"

"Mick! I really thought you'd tell me everything would be okay!"

Mick chuckled. "Message me after you do it?"

"I will. Thanks."

"Anytime, son."

They hung up. It took another forty-five minutes for Ernie to arrive home and by then, Silas was practically feral. He yanked open the door when he heard Ernie coming up the drive, startling him so badly he dropped his keys.

"Christ on a ship, Si," Ernie said, clutching his chest. "What are you doing?"

"Sorry," Silas said, a little sheepishly. "I've been waiting for ages for you to get home."

"Oh?" Ernie frowned and stepped inside, kicking off his shoes. "Did I forget to tell you I was on the late shift?"

"No, I knew."

"Okay?" Ernie gave Silas a sidelong glance and headed to the bathroom to wash his hands. He started when he noticed Silas in the mirror. "Are you following me?"

"No. Yes. Maybe. I just …" Silas trailed off, unable to explain himself. "I'll be in the kitchen. You want a cup of tea?"

"Sure, thanks."

Silas rolled his eyes at himself and filled the kettle with water, feeling the weight of the ring box burning a hole in his pocket. He needed to keep himself together, or he was going to end up yelling the proposal out and terrifying Ernie.

"How was work?" he asked, when Ernie finally entered the kitchen.

"Meh," Ernie said, slumping into a chair. "Alright I guess. I can't wait till Lachie gets the boot. He mocked up literally the most hideous thing I've ever seen today. It was supposed to be a flyer for an estate sale, so you'd obviously expect it to be muted and classy."

Silas expected no such thing and barely understood what Ernie was saying. He nodded nonetheless.

"He made it *bright yellow and red* like a bargain basement ad for a grocery store. I don't understand why he's lasted this long."

Horror seemed the appropriate response here, so Silas made a suitable face.

"Right?" Ernie said indignantly, and as he droned on, the words lost meaning for Silas. He brought the steaming cup of tea to the table, unable to hear anything but his own heavy breathing and racing pulse ringing in his ears.

"So anyway, then I said to Liesl—"

"Marry me?"

Ernie burst out laughing. "*No*, that's not what I said." He slapped Silas playfully and wrapped his hands around the mug of tea. "I told her that she could either reassign the brief to me or we'd completely lose the cli—"

"No. I'm asking you. I … Ernie," Silas let out a shaky breath and pulled the little jewel box from his pocket, flicking it open. "Will you marry me?" He stood awkwardly beside the table as Ernie's mouth dropped open, closed, and open again. He looked back and forth between the ring and Silas.

"That's *gorgeous*," he breathed. "Can I look at it?"

"I'm hoping you'll do more than look at it," Silas said, with a half-laugh.

Ernie reverently plucked the ring from the cushion and examined it. "It's perfect," he said, tears shining in his eyes as he looked at Silas. "Sit down."

As soon as he heard those words, Silas knew Ernie was going to reject him. His breath came ragged and his heart played a staccato rhythm on his ribs. "You don't seem that happy," he said, fighting against the urge to wring his hands.

"It's not that," Ernie said quickly, glancing up from the ring before looking back at it again in awed bewilderment.

"Then what? Usually people say 'yes' when someone proposes …"

Ernie lowered the ring and looked at Silas, really *looked* at him. Silas had the feeling Ernie could see into the depths of his soul. It was extremely unsettling.

"I want to," he said finally, sadly. "You'll never know how bad. And maybe I can. But … I'm going to ask this once. I really want to trust that you can answer me honestly. Silas, *what* is going on with you?"

Silas paused, taking deep breaths and holding Ernie's huge, worried brown eyes. Could he tell him? That he was terrified he was losing him? That he was madly in love and didn't want to live unless it was with Ernie? That he had no idea when it had happened but there was no cure? That he was worried he wasn't good enough for him? He opened his mouth. But it all felt too much. Too weird and icky, too overwhelming. Too much like a soap opera.

"Nothing," he said finally. "There's nothing at all going on."

Ernie deflated. He took a last, longing look at the ring and then reluctantly handed it back to Silas. "Then my answer is no. I need to go take a shower."

Ernie walked quietly from the room. Silas thought he heard him gulping, as though fighting tears, but he had no idea what to say to comfort him.

So he sat, stunned, at the table. His palms were slick with sweat and his heart was racing. He couldn't believe it. Ernie had actually said no. And then left the room. Was that it for them?

Silas remembered his earlier words to Mick. "If he says no, we're doomed." Had he really meant that? Because now the moment was here, the only thing he found himself thinking was that he wanted Ernie to come back. Maybe they could forget everything—pretend the stupid proposal had never happened. Go back to how they were. But now he had his answer, plain as day. There was someone else, and Ernie preferred them.

He flicked open his phone and texted Mick. *He said no.*

Mick replied instantly. *Wanna come over and talk about it?*

Silas considered it. But it felt too overwhelming. Besides, he was currently glued to this spot, feeling slapped in the heart. He shook his head, running through their short conversation again, as he tried to figure out what the hell had happened. And where it had all gone wrong.

35
WEDNESDAY

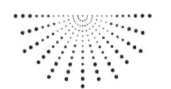

Marley paced her flat nervously in the twenty minutes before Finn arrived. They'd not spoken for almost a week, aside from pleasantries at work and his daily texts afterwards to ask her how she was doing. She knew they'd both needed their space, and she hadn't wanted to rush to tell him she'd changed her mind. She owed it to both of them to make sure it was what she really wanted, and not a reaction to missing him. But the week without him had been a living nightmare. She'd lain awake at night, wishing she could talk to him, wishing she could feel the warmth of his arms around her, wishing she could rest her head on his chest. In the morning, she missed them making one another cups of tea. She missed their playful fight for the shower to get ready, and missed slumping onto the sofa together in the evening. She missed his voice, his smell, his laugh ... *him*. And she was desperately hoping that they could sort things out tonight.

He rang the buzzer, which surprised her since he had a key. Maybe it was his way of letting her know he didn't feel comfortable using it. Or that he wouldn't be using it anymore.

"Stop overthinking," Marley muttered to herself, buzzing him in.

She opened her door and heard him coming up the stairs. He smiled at her as he reached her landing, and her heart flip-flopped. The effect of his good looks would never wear off for her. That inky, glossy hair, those other-worldly blue eyes and the thick lashes framing them, his white teeth, his chiselled bone structure, the way his skin tanned golden at the first sign of the sun, his huge hands, his toned forearms …

Marley stepped forward and slipped a hand behind his neck, pressing their lips together. He felt tense against her and she hated that, but he melted a little as she planted tiny kisses along his jaw. When she pulled back, his breath was ragged.

"Well, hello to you, too," he said gruffly.

She giggled, feeling very girlish, and shut the door behind him as he kicked off his shoes.

"I ordered your favourite," she said, grabbing his hand and pulling him into the living room. She gestured the spread on the coffee table.

"Lebanese," he smiled.

They stood awkwardly for a moment, then Marley gestured for him to sit down, taking a seat gingerly beside him. "You want a beer or something?" she asked.

"No, I'm good thanks."

Marley bit her thumbnail, staring at him. "How … how has your week been?"

He sighed, slumping back into the sofa. "Terrible, if I'm honest. I missed you so much."

The breath whooshed out of her and she sank back, tilting her head to look at him. "Me too. Like crazy. Seeing you at work was so hard."

"I know. But … I think it was right. I needed that time. And I did a lot of thinking."

"So did I," she said softly.

He nodded. "Good." Then he drew a deep breath and sat up straight. "Marley, I know I said I would go at your pace, and I've tried really hard to stick to my word on that. But I need to tell you what I want. It's okay if you don't want it too, we'll find a way around things—"

"Please," she said, raising a hand. "I'm going mad. I just want to hear it."

He let out a small laugh, like a sigh of relief. "I want to get rid of my apartment. I hate feeling like we're not permanent. Like when the baby comes I'll still have one foot out the door. I want to be with you both, all the time. No backup plan."

Marley nodded slowly, holding his gaze. "Finn, I want that too."

"You do?" The note of surprise in his voice made her chest squeeze.

She nodded firmly. "I do."

His face lit up, and she could almost see him gaining confidence. "Good. I also want the baby to have both our last names. But it's up to you," he added quickly, "as you're the one giving birth. I just had to get it out."

"I agree with that too. One hundred percent."

Finn swallowed, shaking his head in mild amazement. "Okay. And … I wanted to say that I'm fine with the name Petunia. I understand how important it is to you. I'm *hoping* we'll get to have other children," he winked at her, "and maybe I can take a shot at one of their names."

Marley grinned, but shook her head. "I've thought about that a lot. This baby has to have a name we both like." She rubbed her stomach, smiling at him. "Finn, I came into this with too many fixed ideas. I wanted to do things my way, but still keep you. I've realised how unfair that is, and I'm so sorry. We'll make lists, we'll buy books, we'll haggle over names like every other couple. But in the end, we both have to love it."

"Are you absolutely positive?" he asked hesitantly.

She sat up and shifted so she was facing him on the sofa. He mirrored her pose and she slipped an arm around his neck, pulling them close together. "Yes. I've never been more sure of anything. I'm sorry it's taken me this long. Thank you for being so incredibly patient. I didn't mean to ignore what you wanted, and I should have asked. I needed this push, too. Finn Mayberry, I'm all in. *All* in. I don't want you to ever spend a night away from her. From me. From us. Ever again. I want us to be a family."

One side of Finn's mouth turned up, and it was all Marley could do to hold herself back from jumping into his lap. "Well, okay then," he said softly, his voice rough with emotion. "It's settled."

He pulled her into his arms and crushed his mouth to hers. Marley leaned hard into him as their kiss deepened, until soon they were tugging at each other's clothes.

"Hmm," he said hoarsely, "maybe I should stay away more often." His voice was close to her ear, sending goosebumps down her spine.

"Don't you dare," she whispered sternly, pulling back to glare at him.

"No, ma'am," he agreed solemnly, and leaned back down to kiss her.

36
THURSDAY

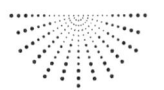

"What you looking for, Ly?" Maggie asked, frowning as she looked up from where she was journaling at the tour van table.

Lyra had torn the sheets off her bunk bed and now she balled them into the corner, shoving her hands down the cracks between the frame and mattress.

"My phone's missing."

Jake looked up from where he was leafing through a Mark Manson book opposite Maggie. Kit was outside smoking a cigarette. The concert was still two hours off and Lyra had been fighting a feeling of unease all day. She also wanted to read the "break a leg" or "knock 'em dead" texts from Alex and Mick. They sent them every day and she'd become superstitious about reading them.

"Where'd you see it last?" Jake asked.

Lyra threw her hands in the air. "It was by my bedside this morning. Or … in my bed? But since we went for the sound check, I don't think I've seen it."

"Did you leave it inside?" Maggie asked.

"No. I didn't even take it with me. It was here. I'm pretty sure I left it on the bunk."

"Well no one would have stolen it," Jake said quickly.

"I'm not suggesting they did," Lyra said, her eyes widening at the idea. "It's obviously fallen in a crack somewhere, or …" She trailed off, looking around.

"You can check my bunk," Maggie said, standing to help.

"Mine too," Jake added.

"What's going on?" Kit asked, stepping inside after finishing his cigarette.

Together, the four of them turned over every corner of the tour van, emptying everyone's duffels and checking under the small peels of carpet that lined the floor.

"I don't want to play tonight without it," Lyra said finally, giving up.

"You never have it on stage with you anyway, do you?" Jake asked.

Lyra shook her head. "But I need to speak to Alex beforehand. I usually at least exchange a message with him. And Mick."

"Do you know their numbers?" Maggie asked, holding her own phone out.

Lyra wracked her brain, frowning. "Maybe Alex's?"

"Want to try?" Maggie swiped to unlock the phone, and Lyra tried two numbers she thought might be right. Both were wrong.

"Why haven't I memorised them?" she moaned, dropping her head to her hands.

"I can remember the landline number from my first house as a kid," Kit said. "But I have to check even my own mobile number. No one remembers these days. You're not alone."

"I feel pretty dumb though. I'm definitely going to have to learn them off by heart now."

"Is Alex on any kind of social media that I could try to reach out to him on?" Maggie asked.

"I think so, but I think he's set to private."

They used Maggie's phone to scour the few networks Alex was active on. Finally, Lyra gave up. "I'll have to stop in a phone shop tomorrow," she said sadly. "I hope they don't think something's happened to me or that I'm ignoring them."

"I'm sure they won't," Maggie said comfortingly. "Why don't you head in for a shower to relax."

"I guess," Lyra said with a shrug. Then she slapped her forehead. "Email!" She grabbed Maggie's phone back and shot out a quick email to Alex. Then she headed in for a shower.

When she was gone, Kit stepped outside for another cigarette and Maggie rounded on Jake. "I thought I saw you with her phone earlier," she said, standing over him.

Jake looked up from the book he'd settled back down to read, seemingly bewildered that Maggie was talking to him. "What?"

Maggie put a hand on her hip. "I know you've got the hots for her. But if you did something to mess with her somehow, you'll have me and Kit to deal with."

Jake lowered his book, frowning at Maggie. "The fact you even think I could hurt her ..."

Maggie shrugged, then turned to look at Kit out the small truck window. "Love can make you do dumb stuff."

Lyra's hair was perfectly tousled, her dress clingy in all the right places, her lip-gloss slick. The venue was filling up—she could see it in the monitors backstage. She usually felt a kind of serenity in the moments before a show. But this time, she was distraught. Her phone still hadn't turned up. Maybe it was silly to obsess over it, but she had a horrible feeling something was wrong. She'd never lost a phone before. Not even once.

"Ly?" Jake asked, snapping her back into the room.

"Yeah?"

"You alright?"

Lyra forced a tight smile. "Don't worry, I'll be good once we're on."

As they walked out on stage, Lyra fixing a bright beam on her face like a pageant child, the crowd erupted into wild cheering and applause. The band members took their places on stage and Lyra gripped the mic, pulling it towards her. She glanced off to the side before she spoke, spotting Julian in the wings. She couldn't help a frown flickering across her face. Why was he there? He was never usually there. He glanced up from his phone and noticed her looking. Flashing a bland smile, he motioned for her to start the show.

She turned slowly back to the crowd. The lights dazzled and she felt the familiar flush of heat from their warmth. "Good evening, Taree!"

The crowd whooped, and Lyra grinned. Maybe it would end up being a good night after all. She continued smiling out at the crowd until the applause died.

Just as she opened her mouth to speak again, a single voice rang out crystal clear in the silence that had fallen. "Your friend Mick is dead!"

Lyra froze, her hand gripping the mic. She half-laughed in shock that someone would heckle her in such a cruel way. "Arsehole," she said crisply into the mic, and the crowd laughed awkwardly. She also heard gasps of shock, no doubt from parents who'd brought their kids along.

"No, he really is!" the voice insisted.

Was she being trolled? She'd talked about Mick in a few

of the interviews she'd given to music magazines since her career launched, so it wasn't surprising people knew his name or what he meant to her. But would someone really buy a ticket and turn up to a show to taunt her?

Lyra sucked in a breath, turning her head to look off stage to look at Julian. She tilted her head at him for a moment, wondering what about him was striking her as odd. He wasn't surprised. He seemed more irritated. Her phone disappearing... surely they wouldn't have—

"No," she said firmly, speaking to Julian. He dropped her gaze, clearing his throat and turning as if to leave. And then she knew it was true.

It seemed as though the entire hall fell silent as Lyra's rapid breathing echoed through the mic. She stared blindly out at the crowd, blinking in lights that suddenly seemed unbearably harsh and unforgiving. Her swallow was audible.

One person cried out her name, and for a split second, she was certain it was Alex. She squinted into the blackness, scanning for him. But it was impossible to make faces out, especially when her eyes were beginning to blur. And Alex couldn't possibly be there—she knew that.

Whoever it was, his shout seemed to break the spell and in Lyra's brain, it felt like chaos broke out at that moment. Phones started flashing, a sea of glinting cameras went up, trying to capture her reaction to this, the worst moment of her life.

She heard a noise behind her, remembered that she was on stage with her band, and slowly turned her head to look at them. Maggie was frozen to the spot, her mouth hanging open in horror. Kit had one arm in the air, where he'd been about to strike his drum and get things started. Jake was the only one moving, crossing the stage to her in quick steps and grabbing her shoulders to forcibly turn her from the crowd.

WEDDING BELLS AT LILAC BAY

He pulled her to his chest and wrapped his arms tightly around her.

"Ghouls!" he leaned to shout into the mic, Lyra pressed against his chest, numb. "Put your stupid cameras down!"

He released her and cupped her face with his hands, bringing his nose inches from hers and forcing her gaze to his. "Listen to me," he said, quickly and firmly. "I'm getting you off the stage, okay?"

Lyra nodded dumbly.

"They're going to try and get pictures," he continued, as though they were the only two people in the world, instead of before a crowd of several thousand people. "I'm not going to let that happen."

"No," she whispered, a coldness seeping into her core.

"I'm going to put my arms around you, you're going to face the back of the stage, I'm going to cover you, and we're going to head straight to the wings, okay?"

"Start the concert!" someone yelled into the void.

Jake gritted his teeth, leaning to the mic again. "I'll pay you back *myself* to get you out of here. The concert is *not* happening! You hear me? Go home everyone! Get out! There is no show. Not tonight. You can speak to the label about refunds," he added, with a dark glare at Julian.

He pulled Lyra back towards him again, and she didn't resist. The world had gone blank for her. *One foot in front of the other, that's all. Easy,* she thought to herself, as Jake shielded her and hustled her off the stage. Halfway across, Maggie and Kit joined them, the three of them forming a tight, protective knot around Lyra until they made it to the wings.

Julian blocked their path. "I'm sorry for your loss." Lyra blinked up at him, uncomprehending. "But don't you dare even think about not getting back on that stage."

It was Kit who swung at him. Dear, sweet Kit. His fist

balled and he jerked it back quickly, before lunging forward and connecting with Julian's jaw. A crack rang out and Julian stumbled sidewards. The band buoyed Lyra through the underground halls and towards the tour van. The lone bodyguard stepped aside in confusion as they approached, and once they were in, Maggie locked the door behind them, sliding a heavy box of drinks against the door.

"Um. My phone?" Lyra said dumbly, wiping at tears that had started to spill the instant they were safe in the truck. "God, I need to speak to Alex. I'm sorry, you guys. I didn't mean to ruin ..." She took a shaky breath.

Maggie grabbed Lyra's bag, rifling through it again.

"Don't bother," Jake said in an odd voice. Three pairs of eyes snapped towards him. "They have it," he added quietly.

Maggie launched herself at him, shoving him roughly backwards. "I freaking knew you did that. You *traitor!*" she spat.

"Mags," Kit said, pulling her back.

Jake covered his face with his hand.

"What?" Lyra asked, tears slipping freely down her cheeks. *"What?"*

Jake's jaw clenched. "I'll explain later. But ... I think I can make them give it back."

"Then *go!*" Maggie yelled. "Go!"

Lyra sank into a chair as Jake bolted out the door. "You guys, I'm so sorry," she said, her voice breaking.

"Ly, you don't have to apologise for *anything*," Kit said. He knelt before her, and Maggie took a seat beside her, slinging her arm tightly over Lyra's shoulders.

"What he said," Maggie added. "They can all go screw themselves if they think you owe them anything. Even if *you'd* wanted to play, none of us would have let you."

Lyra swallowed at the lump in her throat. She was seconds away from bursting into inconsolable tears—

holding it all back by a hair. All she wanted was Alex—with her, holding her, explaining everything to her. And telling her it was a mistake, or that it would be alright.

Maggie moved across the truck to her knapsack and rifled through it. Coming back to the seat, she pulled the cap off a pill bottle with her teeth and shook two tablets onto her hand, proffering them to Lyra with a small bottle of vodka.

"Mags, what are you doing?" Kit asked sternly. "That's not a good idea."

"I'm giving her a way out, for now," Maggie said. She turned her gaze to Lyra, her hands outstretched. "Ly, this is oblivion. It's what I do when things get too overwhelming." She ignored the bulge of Kit's eyes as she said it. "You can deal with everything tomorrow. You won't feel anything for a little while. You can shut down—"

"Maggie…" Kit said, hesitantly.

"I'm just *offering*. It's what I'd want."

"I want Alex," Lyra said, her eyes welling.

Maggie nodded, not breaking eye contact. "And when Jake the snake brings the phone back, we'll keep trying to get hold of him."

Kit's eyes were round and worried. "It's your choice, Lyra," he whispered.

Lyra sighed, leaning closer into Maggie, to the physical contact. She looked at her bandmates in turn. She read nothing but sympathy and concern in their features. Silently, she reached for the pills.

Maggie held onto her tightly and after a few more swigs from the bottle, Lyra felt the tears recede. She felt everything recede and the words to Pink Floyd's *Comfortably Numb* rang through her mind. Before the darkness stretched out its arms for Lyra, she replayed the moment she'd heard the news. The faceless voice in the crowd yelling out to her … about her friend.

Friend. It wasn't enough, wasn't the right word for the man who'd been by her side for over two decades. Who'd cared for her and protected her and helped her develop her talent. Who'd finally found happiness. And who, right now, she was convinced had left the earth not knowing exactly how much he meant to her.

37
FRIDAY

"What are you doing here?" Jenny asked, wide-eyed. Silas could tell she'd been crying, but she had a deft hand with makeup and had managed to cover most of the signs. A slight puffiness around her eyes, a hollowness to her gaze, her lips redder than usual—probably only he would notice those things, because he saw her so often.

He ignored her question, pulling his apron from the hook inside their van.

"Si," Jenny repeated. She laid a hand on his arm. "I mean it, what are you doing here?"

He froze for a second before shaking her off. "My job," he gritted out.

Jenny sighed. "It's hard enough for me," she said, in such a gently sympathetic voice that Silas felt a lump form in his throat. "I can't imagine how it is for you. And with your sister gone. Si, we only lost him *yesterday.*"

"You sound like Ernie," he said, picturing his boyfriend's broken-hearted face, puffy with tears, begging him not to go to work that morning. Ernie himself had called in sick. They weren't on the warmest terms after the rejected proposal, but for Ernie, none of that had mattered once he heard the news. Silas felt differently though, the hurt still fresh in his mind.

"I'm fine," he said finally, jerking his head towards the shoreline before turning away. "Customer."

Jenny drew a deep breath, before turning her charm full-force on the customer—a young woman obviously from the nearby office blocks. Silas saw her cast a few hesitant glances in his direction and realised his face must look like thunder. He deliberately tried to relax his features, and even attempted a smile. It mustn't have come out exactly right, because the customer averted her gaze and Jenny flinched when her eyes landed on him.

Fine, so apparently he didn't know how to smile. First he'd heard it from Ernie, now these two were spelling it out. He looked out at the waterfront.

It was good to be outside. The day was crisp, the breeze was running low along the water and ruffling it into small, choppy waves. The sky was a deep gunmetal colour, bruised in places with pale purple. It reflected his mood, and he felt like nature was being respectful of the world's loss. It shouldn't be sunny and hot. Not today. Not yet. Maybe not ever.

As a boat glided silently from Lilac Bay out into the harbour, Silas caught the relaxed grins on the faces of the blonde-haired family, all five of them, inside the boat. They looked like they belonged in a toothpaste commercial, and he was pretty sure they'd never experienced pain in their lives. Neither had the couple walking along, hand-in-hand, feeding each other fairy floss from the nearby amusement park and giggling at some secret. A stupid one, he guessed.

Once the customer was gone, Jenny turned to him again. He held up a palm.

"I want to be here."

"I already asked Dan to come in."

"Why?"

Jenny's mouth opened and closed. "I assumed …"

"Well, you shouldn't. I'm absolutely fine."

Jenny swallowed, then nodded. "Okay, sure. If you say so."

"I do."

"Should … should I call Dan and cancel him?"

Silas considered. Three of them together in the van would be pretty crowded. Even though it was double the width of his and Lyra's old truck, it was a hair narrower. They'd be tripping over one another. Then again, they'd have to pay Dan for part of the day anyway if they sent him back when he'd already set out. And Silas wasn't *entirely* confident he could really get through a whole shift. He'd needed a way to keep himself busy, after lying awake all night holding a sobbing Ernie at his request and biting back his own tears.

Silas shook his head wordlessly. Jenny gave a crisp nod, then busied herself stirring pasta in her huge stainless steel cooking kettle.

They fell into a silence, with Jenny serving most of the customers. Dan arrived about half hour later, tying on his apron at the same time as Jenny's phone rang.

"It's Mum," she said, her voice caught. "Do you mind?"

"Go," Dan quickly ushered her towards the back exit and down the wire steps. "Take as long as you need."

Silas liked Dan. He was a beefy guy in his late forties who apparently had no need of a full-time job after a filthy-rich ex-wife had cheated on him and he'd ended up with enormous spousal support payments. Dan had admitted to Silas that he donated a lot of that money to charity, and he'd been well set up even before he'd met his wife. He worked when he liked, gardened a lot, and donated vegetables to the local homeless shelter, where he also volunteered. He dated a *lot*, but was quite emphatic that he was never going to get married again. Silas secretly doubted it. Dan was a good-looking man-mountain, and women gravitated to him almost subconsciously.

Today though, Silas appreciated him for his calm air of competence and the way he completely took over without making Silas feel useless. It was like being around a grown up when Silas felt like a boy.

He heard Jenny sobbing from behind the van, and he reached for the little radio he kept on his side of the serving counter, twisting the volume knob up to drown out her tears. It would be hard enough to get through the day without thinking about Mick, but if Jenny was weeping, it would be pretty much impossible.

Dan was busy with another customer on Jenny's side when a cocksure, suited-and-booted office worker with a ridiculous fade haircut approached Silas. He was talking loudly into his Bluetooth headset and clicked it off for a micro-second to utter, "pie," before clicking it back on and continuing his conversation.

"Which type?" Silas asked, gesturing to the plethora of choices on the warming racks. Silas mentally dubbed him Jerkface, and considered that polite.

Jerkface frowned at Silas and shrugged, gesturing to his earpiece to imply he was in the middle of an important conversation.

Silas gave him a blank look in return. The song on the radio changed and Lyra's voice rang out—strong and clear. Silas gritted his teeth, suddenly feeling an almost overwhelming nostalgia for the days when he and Lyra worked their little van together. Her voice had developed so much in the time she'd been working for the label. He knew they'd invested a lot in her, with the voice coaching and the top-end producers. But her own raw talent shone through. Her songs were *good.*

Jerkface made a *hurry up* gesture with his hand at Silas, as he droned on about shorts or … shorting or longing. Silas didn't really understand.

"I need to know your choice," Silas said loudly, snapping the tongs together.

"Hold on a minute please," the guy said politely into his earpiece. He clicked it off. "Mate, I asked for a pie. Just put a friggin' pie in a bag with some sauce. How hard is that?"

"Plain? Liver? Steak and kidney? Cottage? Shepherd? Not hard at all, once I know what you want."

The guy tilted his head, going still in that way that all bullies did. A technique Silas was familiar with from being picked on in high school.

"*Obviously* plain," the man said, through gritted teeth. "If someone doesn't specify, it's got to be plain, doesn't it? Use your common sense, mate."

Silas slipped a plain pie into the bag, barely biting back a snide reply. The guy's tone had his hair standing on end. He'd lived his whole school life being made to feel small by bullies. Some of them apparently never grew up.

Jerkface clicked the earpiece back on. "Apologies," he said, and started yammering again.

Lyra's voice gave Silas goosebumps, and he briefly wondered where she was. No one had been able to get hold of her since the news broke. When her song ended, the DJ's soft, sympathetic tone took over. "Horrible news about Lyra Beck's family member passing away while she's on the road. Lyra, if you can hear this, we're sending—"

Silas quickly reached to slap off the radio, accidentally knocking the paper bag with Jerkface's pie off the slick waterfall edge of the display glass. Jerkface's nostrils flared as he looked down at the smashed pie and he clicked off the headset again.

"Are you reta—"

"Hey!" Dan said, clapping a hand on Silas's shoulder and

shoving him slightly behind him. "I suggest you watch your mouth. And educate yourself on what insults we're using these days. There's a *lot* to choose from, but we're done with the r-word."

"Not my fault he's an idiot!" Jerkface complained. "First he doesn't understand my order, then he friggin' throws it on the floor."

"I think you're done here, sir," Dan said, not breaking eye contact with the guy. "You can eat that pie there," he pointed to the ground, "on the house. Or you can go."

Jerkface was obviously intimidated and tried to cover it up with a blustering laugh. "What are you, his *boyfriend* or something?"

"And if I was?" Dan ever so casually leaned his elbows on the counter, extending forward. It was threatening without even trying to be. Silas was simultaneously impressed, touched and mortified that he'd needed saving, like a kid.

"Stick your pie where the sun doesn't shine," Jerkface muttered, spitting on the ground and storming away.

Once he was gone, Dan spun to Silas. "You doing okay?"

Silas took some deep breaths, then shook his head. The sounds of Jenny sobbing behind the van were louder. Silas almost rolled his eyes at the two of them. What a pair.

"You and Jen get out of here," Dan said. "Take her home. Take yourself home. Have Ernie give you a nice backrub or something. Take a bath. Don't come back for a few days. I got you both."

Before Silas could argue, Dan was lifting the apron over his head and shoving him down the back steps.

Jenny turned a tear-stained face to him. "They're not letting Mum make any decisions about Mick. He didn't get his paperwork updated."

Silas frowned. "But then Lyra's the next of kin. She'll do

whatever Kathryn wants, don't worry." Silas tried to sound reassuring.

"But that's the thing. No one can get hold of her. Have you heard from her?"

"Not yet." He clicked open his phone to check, carefully avoiding looking at the one he hadn't replied to.

Want to come over and talk about it?

Why hadn't he taken thirty seconds to reply? Silas closed his eyes, feeling overwhelmed.

"Let's get in a cab," he said, finally. "We'll go to your mum's and get Alex to meet us there."

"Alex is AWOL."

"Jesus. We'll figure something out."

"But the truck—"

"Dan's got it."

"Thank Christmas we hired him."

"I know," Silas agreed, flicking Dan a wave as Jenny dropped off her apron, grabbed her handbag and planted a kiss on Dan's cheek. "He needs a big pay rise."

38
FRIDAY

As soon as she woke, Lyra knew two things: it was late, after midday, judging by the harsh light streaming in through the van's shuttered windows, and they were on the move. Her mouth was clammy, her head pounding. The roiling in her stomach was overpowering and she let out a long, shaky breath as she tried to sit up.

She found herself pinned to the bed by a heavy arm.

"Alex, thank god," she whispered, rolling to face him, ready to fall apart in his arms as memories of the previous night flooded in. She came face to face with Jake, still fast asleep.

Lyra recoiled, flinging his arm off her to sit bolt upright, almost making herself sick in the process. He stirred, but didn't wake.

The tour bus was taking them home, Lyra assumed—and she squinted around for her phone, finally finding it wedged tightly down the side of the mattress. Thank god. Maggie and Kit were asleep in their bunks, an empty bottle of vodka in Maggie's uncurled hand.

As the bus jerkily rounded a corner, Lyra felt herself

heave. She just made it to the tiny bathroom before she was sick.

Throwing up had always made her cry, but she staunched the tears, knowing she had to hold it together until she found out where she was, what had happened to Mick, whether everyone was okay, and how soon she could see Alex.

After rinsing out her mouth, Lyra sat on the closed toilet seat and switched on her phone. It blinked at her for the code and the combination pricked her eyes with fresh, unshed tears. Mick's birthday. As it flickered to life, the phone vibrated with messages and calls. Forty-one missed calls, she couldn't even tell how many messages. From Alex, her brother, her friends … Kathryn. At the thought of Kathryn her mouth went dry. She needed to find out what had happened. An accident? Heart attack? Lightning again? Was he actually dead, or only in hospital, like he had been so many times before? She resolved one thing bitterly—Selena would pay for deliberately having taken her phone during this.

She dialled Alex. The call rang out. A flicker of panic burned in her stomach. Where was he? Why wasn't he there for her when she needed him most?

She scrolled to his contact. The most recent message made her stomach flip with nausea.

Today, 09:33: I guess you didn't need me there. I've just seen videos, after searching frantically for any news now that my phone is finally charged. Feel like an idiot driving all that way. But … hope you're okay, my love. Whatever you need to do to get through it, I'm okay with it. Truly. I forgive you.

What? Lyra sat up straighter, frowning.

Yesterday, 22:03: Last message I can try before the phone dies. I'll head home. I want you to know I tried. I tried to be there for you. I'm so sorry, darling.

Yesterday, 21:46: Dang, I didn't bring my charger. I don't have much battery left, just ran out the door and hit the road without thinking.

Yesterday, 21:03: Trying to find where the bus is, but I can't see it anywhere. Maybe it's in a part I can't get to. Trying to call again.

Yesterday, 20:27: They threw me out. I might have started something with the guy who shouted out the news to you. I know security know who I was. They won't let me see you. Can you answer your phone?

Yesterday, 20:18: I called out to you. For a second I thought you heard me, but I don't think you did. Your band are taking you off stage.

Yesterday, 20:16: Standing in the crowd, I can see you, you just came on stage.

"Oh no," Lyra whispered. "Nonono." She skimmed frantically through the other messages, her heart growing sicker with each one.

Yesterday, 20:11: Getting into the hall now. No one will let me backstage and you aren't answering your phone. I've had to sneak past security.

Yesterday, 19:47: Can't find parking without a ticket. Parking a few blocks away and walking. Call me when you get this.

Yesterday, 17:14: Past the halfway point. Stopped at a servo for petrol and water. Hitting the road again now.

Yesterday: 15:06: Getting in the car now. I'll see you in a few hours. Hold on.

Yesterday: 14:47: Silas just called me. I'm so sorry. My love, I'm so, so sorry. I'm lost for words, and can't believe it. About to hit the road to find you. Itinerary says you're in Taree tonight - should be there in 3.5 hours.

Lyra frantically hit the button to call him again. Again, the call rang out. She tried Silas.

"Ly," he answered. His voice was flat.

As soon as she heard his voice, the tears began again. Lyra

pressed a knuckle to her mouth for a moment, shaking. "Si. Oh my god."

"I know." He swallowed audibly, and she heard Ernie's gentle, sympathetic voice in the background. "I know."

"How?"

"Hold on. I'm going outside." She heard a door slide open and shut, then Silas let out a slow breath. "Uh, aneurysm, it looks like. It was quick, Ly. He didn't feel a thing. Where have you been? Everyone's been trying to get a hold of you."

"They had my phone ... Was he alone, Si?" Lyra asked desperately. "Please tell me he wasn't alone."

"He was with Kathryn, but ... she wasn't in the room. She found him ..." Silas broke off.

Lyra squeezed her eyes shut, tears now flowing freely down her face. She wiped her nose with the back of her hand, knowing she was a mess—not caring. "When?"

"Yesterday. Round lunchtime. Ly, we tried calling management from Teller's when we couldn't get through to you. I guess they didn't pass the message on."

"No," Lyra said bitterly. "No they didn't. Is ... is Kathryn okay?"

"I'm with her. Me, Jenny and Ernie," Silas said. "I don't know much else. We actually need you. You're listed as next of kin."

"I'm on my way home," Lyra managed. "I want to see him. Do you think they'll let me see him?"

Silas was quiet. "I really don't know. I don't know how this works. With Mum ..."

They'd been in the room as she'd taken her last breath. There hadn't been a need to find out what happened afterwards.

"I'll make them," Lyra said firmly, biting her lip. "They'll have to let me."

"I don't know."

"Si, have you seen Alex?" Lyra asked.

"Umm ..." The hesitation in his voice made her heart skip a beat.

"What? What? I just found a bunch of messages from him. Apparently he was here last night? He's talking about some videos?"

"Yeah. He jumped in the car and started driving like a madman. No one could stop him."

"I don't know why he couldn't get to me, but... I need to see him. I need to talk to him."

A long silence. Then she heard the door open and close again. Ernie whispered. *"Tell her."*

Lyra's stomach clenched. "Tell me what? Silas? Tell me what?"

"Have you looked on any music news websites? Or, umm ... any websites?"

"I just woke up. My bandmate gave me a bunch of pills last night. I guess I passed out before one of them got my phone back. Why?"

"You're kind of ... all over the gossip news. And apparently TikTok, too. And other sites I guess. You and ... Jake."

"What? Why are we on the news? What the hell?"

Silas sighed, and Ernie took the phone. "It's kind of hot, even though I obviously totally hate it." His voice was nasal and rough, like he'd spent a long time crying.

"What are you talking about?" Lyra practically growled.

"There's tons of video footage of Jake sweeping you off the stage, protecting you."

"The whole band did. I don't get what ..."

"And it's being shown together with a picture of you and Jake, umm..."

"What?"

"Snuggled in bed together? Like, under the blankets? With

him holding you? It's," Ernie's gulp was audible, "it's kind of going viral. The posts are saying he's your boyfriend and he was protecting you and comforting you when you got the news. I don't even know how these people edit so fast, but … Lyra it's kind of like a movie. People can't get enough of it."

"What!" Lyra's shriek hurt her head. "He's not! We didn't —nothing—"

"I know, Lyra. I know. It's a really sweet story, and people love the idea of it. And the video *does* make it look like …"

Lyra's stomach bottomed out. "Alex … has Alex …?"

"I think he has," Ernie said sadly. "Kathryn heard from him a few hours ago. He's on his way back here."

Lyra didn't wait to hear another word, hanging up the call and trying Alex again. The call rang out. Lyra swore.

She dashed tears away with shaking hands and forced herself to look at her TikTok account. She'd been mentioned hundreds of times. Closing her eyes for a second, she gritted her teeth and clicked on one.

Set to wistful music, the video started off with her stunned face beginning to crumple under the harsh stage lights, before—in slow motion—Jake closed the distance between them, pulling her into the safety of his arms.

"*She got the worst news of her life,*" the captions read, "*but he was there for her.*" It showed Jake leaning into the mic, his face twisted in fury as he yelled at the crowd, his words muted but his rage clear, as his arms tightly wrapped around her, her face pressed to his chest.

"*Protecting her …*" The video showed Julian going down with the force of the slug as he blocked their way. From the angle the video was taken, it looked as though Jake—still with Lyra pinned tightly to his side—had delivered the blow. "*Until they were alone, and she could fall apart in the safety of his arms...*" The music continued playing over a photo of the two of them in Lyra's bunk. She was curled tightly into his chest, her mouth open in the surrender of a pill-induced slumber. Jake's arms looped protectively around her, even in sleep—his chin resting possessively on her head.

"And she finally feels safe enough to rest." The teary-eyed emoji showed at the end of the sentence, and Lyra could practically hear women all over the globe ovulating in unison. It had even made *her* choke up for a moment, and she was the woman in it.

She clicked again and found more of the same. Some had millions of views. Ernie was right. They *were* sweet, and powerful, even if they were a complete fiction. Mick's death had handed Selena the opportunity to market her and Jake as a couple on a silver platter.

Lyra tossed her phone into the sink and growled, bursting out of the bathroom.

"Everyone get up!" she screamed. Maggie jerked up in alarm, almost smacking her head on Kit's bunk. Kit peeked down at Lyra in confusion and Jake opened one eye, frowning. "Wake up! Something terrible has happened!"

"We know," Maggie said gently, struggling to sit up properly. Her hair was a tawny bird's nest. "We remember."

Lyra sighed. "Yes, that. But … there's videos going around. Of—" She waved a finger back and forth between her and Jake. "Of me and you. In bed. Together." She turned to stare at Maggie and Kit, both of whom looked shocked and nauseated. "And my boyfriend saw them. Did one of you —"

"*No!*" They shouted in unison, and Lyra believed them.

"Well, someone did."

The three of them slowly turned their gaze to Jake, whose eyes widened in horror. "What are we doing in the video? Sleeping? How could I…?"

"Why did you sleep next to me?" Lyra groaned.

Jake reddened slightly. "You … asked me to."

"I did?" Lyra had no recollection whatsoever. Maggie's pills had really worked their magic.

"You did," Kit confirmed in a low voice. "We tried to talk you out of it, but ..."

"It wasn't like anything happened," Maggie added fiercely. "We wouldn't have let it."

"I would *never* have taken advantage of her," Jake shouted.

Maggie ignored him. "Kit and I stayed up drinking way too long," Maggie added. "You guys were just asleep."

"Well then who took the pictures?" Lyra asked.

Kit shook his head. "I honestly didn't see anyone come in."

"What time did you guys go to sleep?"

"Three?" Maggie guessed, scratching her head. "I think?"

Lyra glanced at her watch. "So there's quite a few hours where we were all passed out ..." A chill finger-walked down her spine as she suddenly remembered Julian's command from Selena. *And most important is showcasing a situation where Jake has to protect you.* They hadn't even needed to manufacture one. The news had come as she was standing on stage. Jake had rushed to protect her. Lyra's stomach churned. *And then she'd asked him to hold her through the night.*

She raised her eyes to Jake's and found him staring back at her, his eyes wide. "Do you think they—" he began.

"Yes," she spat. "*Yes*, I do."

"Um, what?" Maggie asked in confusion.

The bus slowly shuddered to a halt. "Fill her in," Lyra said, grabbing hold of the bunk to stop herself tipping forward. She made her way quickly to the door, yanking it open and blinking into the harsh early afternoon sunlight. Once her eyes adjusted, her head reeled back in shock.

"What the..." Her breath came in angry, shallow gulps as she felt the sting of betrayal and the frustration of helplessness.

A black SUV pulled up beside the tour bus. "Good morning, Lyra," Julian said, stepping out of it.

"We're not at home?" Lyra said.

"No." Julian shook his head firmly, and Lyra could see the beginning of what would be a shiner of a bruise under his left eye socket.

"Where are we?"

"Your next tour location. Lyra," he said tensely. "You've suffered a terrible loss and Selena is very sorry. But…" He spread his arms wide. "The show must go on."

39
FRIDAY

"They can't *make* us play," Maggie said bitterly. They were locked in a tense stand-off with management and had barricaded themselves into the van. Lyra was trying Alex on repeat. Dial, wait, hear it ring out, redial.

"Contractually, yeah they can," Kit said, flicking his lighter on a cigarette. Lyra raised her swollen eyes to his. "Sorry." He leaned and tilted open the bus window nearest him, holding the cigarette outside of it. "This okay?"

Lyra nodded. They were in Coff's Harbour, a solid five and a half hours from Alex if he really had headed home. She felt the distance between them as a physical ache.

She didn't even let herself think about the fact that with every minute she was gone, the chances of her being able to say a proper farewell to Mick, the chances of seeing him again, were fading. She choked back another sob, still unable to truly believe she'd lost him. The world had lost him. Maggie slung an arm around her shoulders. Jake was keeping his physical distance from her and for that, at least, she was grateful.

She was exhausted, hollowed out, emotionally drained

and petrified that things between her and Alex were irretrievably broken. Surely he couldn't really believe … Lyra swallowed, dropping her head to her hands. She could only imagine the sick, betrayed rage she'd be feeling if a video like that had been made of Alex and another woman. So she couldn't blame him for wanting a moment of distance.

Still … the video had been right about one thing. It had been the worst news of her life—a moment she needed her boyfriend to help her through. And he wasn't there. No, that wasn't fair, he'd tried to be there. But he'd also given up.

"Well, we're not going to play, right?" Maggie asked, snapping Lyra back to the present. "If we all simply refuse to go out there, they can't exactly *make* us."

Kit dashed out his cigarette and started pacing between the bench sofa seats. "I mean, are we being held against our will? Is this a situation where we could call the police?"

Jake snorted. "No," he said confidently, spreading his hands. "We're a band on tour. A tour we're being financially compensated for—pretty well, remember—and that we signed on willingly for."

"Yeah, but things have changed," Maggie said. "Lyra's not a robot. They can't make her carry on with her tour when a family member just died. There's no compassion."

"Selena doesn't have that chip installed," Kit said dryly.

"Insurance covers cancelled gigs for sickness, and some other stuff. I don't think it covers this," Jake said.

Lyra let the conversation roll on around her, her gaze still glued to her phone. She tapped out a message to Alex. *Please call me. That was not what it looks like. I know you must be pissed, but I need you.* She clicked the phone off, realising she was staring at it, waiting for confirmation that it had been read.

Maggie sat up, her eyes widening. "I've got it."

"Got what?" Lyra asked. She'd been fighting the urge to ask Maggie for more pills. The oblivion she'd spent the night in seemed preferable to the agony she was suffering right now. An all-encompassing anaesthetic. Besides, if she was passed out cold in her bunk, they could hardly *Weekend at Bernie's* her onto the stage.

"You're pretty sure they put that stuff about you and Jake on social media, right?"

"Right." Lyra studiously avoided eye contact with Jake.

"Then you make a video now. Stream it on your channels. You've got what, thirty thousand followers?"

Lyra shrugged. "Maybe?"

"Try fifty-four thousand now," Jake said, twisting his mouth as he stared at his phone.

"Oh," Lyra said blankly.

"So do a live stream. Tell your fans what's happening. *Tell* them you don't want to be performing when you've had this horrible news," Maggie said.

"Mags, that would get her fired," Kit said, stopping his pacing.

"They're not going to fire her," Maggie scoffed.

"Honestly, at this point, I don't care if they do," Lyra said. But that wasn't the whole truth. She loved that she was able to do this for a living now. She loved the three people she was holed up in the truck with, loved the music they made together and the dynamic they shared. She didn't want to lose it. She wanted to go home, be held by Alex, see Mick, talk to Kathryn, cry with Silas.

Tears pricked her eyes again. "If they could only reschedule the dates. Postpone them a bit," she said, a sob wracking her chest. "That's all I want. I can't … I cannot get up on stage tonight. Not until I've seen Mick, or until I fixed things with Alex. I can't."

"Of course not," Maggie said gently, pulling her close again.

Lyra's phone rang. Alex. She snatched it up and

immediately swiped to open the call. "Hey," she said breathlessly.

"Hey." His tone was cautious and flat.

Lyra closed her eyes. "Where are you?"

"I just got back to Aunt Kathryn's and checked my messages. Sorry, the phone was on silent as I was driving."

"It's fine. It's fine. Listen, I really hope you know that nothing is what it looks—"

"I do," he said, his voice tight. "Don't worry about it. Are you guys almost home?"

"Alex, they took us in the other direction. We're in Coff's."

"*What?*"

"Yeah." Lyra sighed. "We're refusing to come out, they're refusing to cancel the gig."

"And you've tried talk to Selena?"

"She's not answering my calls. Julian warned me the promoters will sue, then the label will sue me. Or ... us," she added, glancing forlornly at the others.

"I'm going to call Steve."

Lyra frowned. "The guy you know at the label?"

"The one who got you that first meeting."

Lyra groaned. "He still probably hates me."

She could hear a smile in Alex's voice. "He still likes me. I guess you haven't seen him much since you started. He's in the legal team now."

"Okay. I don't think it will help, but I'm willing to try anything. Alex, I don't know how I'm going to get home."

"Don't worry. I'm already back in the car."

"You are?" Lyra finally let herself smile.

"I am. I'm coming to get you, my love. Your knight in ... kinda stinky armour, actually. Haven't showered for a bit."

"Still love you."

"Good. See you soon."

40
FRIDAY

Amy was at her Bondi apartment, working from home for the morning to avoid the chaos of the Lilac Bay offices. She also wasn't sure she could keep her mind on the job, with everything that was going on with Lyra, and didn't want to be a distraction to the others.

Out of respect for her friend, she hadn't watched the social media video doing the rounds, though she *was* curious. Mostly though, she felt her friend's heartbreak. Her own heart felt battered by the news—she'd known Mick for almost as long as she'd known Lyra. It was difficult to believe the man who'd withstood so many incidents—including a lightning strike—was gone. She ached for Silas, too, knowing how much he looked up to Mick as a father figure.

The worst thing was how helpless she felt. She couldn't do anything to get Lyra out of the weird situation with her record label, to erase the internet gossip … to bring back a loved one.

She paced to her Juliet balcony, letting the light stream in and taking a deep inhale of the briny Bondi air. She tilted her face upwards, her skin gently prickling with the sun's warmth. Then she dialled the doctor's office where Marley worked.

"What do we do for her?" Marley asked immediately.

"I honestly don't know," Amy replied sadly. "There's no gesture in the world big enough to cover what she's going through."

"We can text her at least, right? I'll call her soon, but … we can text her?"

"Yeah," Amy said gently. "I already did. That's probably the best we can do. That or murder the head of her label."

"This is an unsecured line, Amy," Marley said seriously. "We can plot that in person."

Amy managed a short laugh, and then they both fell silent again.

"She's heading to Kathryn's tomorrow, I think," Amy said, recalling the text she'd got from Silas. "Maybe we can have some food sent there? Or … a cake?"

"A sympathy cake?" Marley asked sceptically. "Is that a thing?"

"No," Amy admitted, then straightened her spine as an idea hit her. "But it *is* comfort food. She loves cherry cheesecake. We could just have one sent there tomorrow? Then we just let her know we're thinking of her and that we love her, without bombarding her."

"I like that idea," Marley said. "I can search online now for somewhere that would deliver."

"Great," Amy said, then let out a small sigh. She flapped away a seagull that was angling to land on her balcony. "I'm kind of under the pump at the moment so that would really help."

"Is there anything I can help you with? For the wedding?"

"Oh, no," Amy said quickly. She knew her bluntness might have offended others, but not Marley. "How are you feeling at the moment, anyway? How are things with you and Finn?"

"Great," Marley said, instantly sounding dreamy. "We're better than ever, to be honest. I'm almost glad we went through that period apart. It actually helped us."

"I found the same with Rick. Not the accident, of course," she added hastily. "I'd do anything for that not to have happened. I mean finding our way back to each other after his untruth. I really believe it brought us closer than we would have been."

"Same," Marley said, then turned thoughtful again. "I'm so glad Lyra has Silas and Alex through this. I've been through it and I know what she's headed for. But she's survived it once and she'll survive it again."

"There's not really any choice, right?" Amy added sadly.

"No. No there isn't."

41
FRIDAY

Lyra opened one eye at the sound, then sprang upright. The others were dozing in their bunks. They'd whiled the last couple of hours away drinking and playing cards in the tour van. Lyra hated the idea of leaving the rest of the band once Alex came to get her, but they were adamant they could handle the fallout. That they wanted to, for her.

She heard the noise again—a small knock? Something hitting the window. She raced to the door and flung it open.

"Alex?" she called into the twilight, tugging on her Ugg boots.

"Lyra! Over here."

She jogged lightly around to the front of the van and saw him on the other side of the chain-link fence surrounding the parking lot. Wordlessly, she went to him, and they laced their fingers together through the wire.

"No, screw this," Alex said, and scaled the fence, dropping lightly to the other side and standing before her.

"The gate opens from the inside," she said, smiling a little from nervousness. "I could have let you in."

"Oh. But then I wouldn't have looked as cool."

For a split second, he held his distance. Then he closed the gap between them and pulled her tightly into a hug. Finally, she felt like she was home and she melted—tears springing to her eyes.

"I am so sorry, my love," he whispered over and over, squeezing her tight. "I'm so sorry I wasn't there."

"You were," she said shakily. "I'm so sorry about everything that happened after."

She felt him shake his head. "I know it wasn't you. I know you." He stroked her hair with one hand and tightened his grip on her with the other. "I know you."

"You were there?" Jake asked Alex, as the whole band stood gathered in the truck to hear his story. "You got in without a ticket?"

"Yeah, no one was scalping tickets outside, so I spoke to someone on the door—"

"And they just *let* you in?"

Alex shifted his eyes to Lyra for a second, looking sheepish. She immediately understood.

"He charmed his way in," she said, hiding a smile.

Jake looked at her in surprise, seemingly taken aback that she was okay with that. "Right," he said finally. "Then what?"

"I talked to a few of the bouncers. They said they didn't know you at all, they worked for the venue. Then I asked them where backstage was and whether there was a way for me to get there."

"And no dice," Maggie said.

"Right. So I tried to get as close as I could to the stage. I figured there was probably a way I could vault over the railing and get backstage through the wings or something."

Lyra clamped harder on Alex's arm, closing her eyes. She felt horrible that he'd gone to unearthly lengths to find her.

"But you got caught doing it," Kit guessed.

"Right." Alex nodded. "Then they asked to see my ticket, I didn't have one and security hauled me out."

"How did you get back in the second time?" Jake asked.

"I waited until the concert actually started and then explained the situation properly to the woman at the door again. She gave me a wrist band that time and suggested I get rid of my jacket so they wouldn't spot me—which was good advice. Then I made it in time to hear Lyra find out. I yelled out and tried shoving my way to her, but ..."

"We were already hauling her off stage," Maggie finished glumly.

"Right. Then my phone died not long after. I checked into a hotel, couldn't find anyone with the same type of cable as me, so I had to wait until the shops were open so I could buy one the next morning. I did think the tour would be called off, but ..."

"So did we," Kit said. "It's insane that they think she'll keep going. If anything happened to my parents—"

Maggie shot him a look that cut him off.

Jake sighed and stretched his legs out under the small table. "The question is, what do we do now?" he asked. "You leave, you're probably in breach."

"She can't keep going, and who cares about breach?" Maggie snapped.

"We might, if they sue us or cancel the contract," Jake said.

"I can't seriously believe you're thinking about yourself at a time like this," Kit said, flicking his cigarette out the door. Maggie glared at him. "I'll get it later, you know I will," he said, holding his hands up.

Jake averted his gaze as they all turned to stare at him. Lyra remembered what he'd told her on the beach that night, after their first gig. About rehab, and the band being a strong reason for his sobriety.

"Jake," Lyra began gently, sitting forward. "I'm really sorry. I *just* want to get home. I want to see Mick before …" She swallowed the lump in her throat. "And help make arrangements. I'm listed as next of kin, or at least I was. I need to be part of this. I want to plan the funeral. And be there, of course. I'd be happy to keep doing the tour at a later date. I'm … I'm not in the headspace right now. The shows would be sub-par, and I never want to do that."

Jake studied her for a long moment and Lyra felt Alex's grip on her arm tighten. Jake nodded once, briskly. "We're united then. Alex, get her out of here now. We three will stay in the van and when they come looking for her we'll try to explain. I don't honestly know what will happen. I do think they'll try and sue us."

"Good luck suing me," Kit said with a shrug. "I didn't get much of an advance, and my term was only for two years. Plus, I'm getting like three percent."

Maggie's eyes bulged. "Okay, we need to work on your negotiating skills," she said, with a short shake of the head. Then she turned to Lyra and Alex. "Get out of here."

"This feels crazy," Lyra said, momentarily getting cold feet. "Surely if I was allowed to *talk* to Selena, she'd understand? She's not a monster. She took a chance on me, and I owe my career to her. I feel bad just disappearing without trying to discuss it all with her."

Jake raised an eyebrow. "I don't really want you to go, but I get why you have to. Ly, she's the one who ordered you to keep going on the tour. Julian's not going to make that call himself. Plus, she hasn't exactly made herself available. You've tried calling her, right?"

"Ten times," Lyra admitted. "Since I got my phone back."

"Your phone got lost?" Alex asked.

"It was ..." Lyra shifted her eyes to Jake, who looked away. "Lost."

Alex frowned. "Silas called Julian earlier that day to let him know what had happened."

Anger fired down Lyra's spine. She remembered Silas telling her that, but hadn't fully absorbed it until now.

"Seriously?" Maggie asked.

Alex nodded. "Yeah. They knew hours before the concert started. I figured you weren't checking your phone because you usually don't during the day."

Jake chewed the side of his mouth, his face reddening. "I didn't know that when I handed it over."

"You handed it over?" Alex said, his voice low and brittle. "Do you know what all her loved ones were going through, trying to reach her? Are you kidding? Man, why would you *do* something like that?"

Jake wouldn't meet his gaze. "They told me she wasn't concentrating, and they just wanted to make sure she was focused," he mumbled finally, eyes glued to the table.

Alex opened his mouth again and Lyra cut him off. "Let's go," she said. "Please. I want to go home."

"Got all your stuff?" Maggie asked, interrupting Jake as he opened his mouth again.

Lyra nodded to her hastily-packed duffel and hugged Maggie and Kit in a quick goodbye. Everyone ignored Jake who sat motionless at the table, eyes still glued to the Formica. Lyra felt momentarily sorry for him. She was sure Kit and Maggie were going to let him have it as soon as they were gone. But then she remembered the distress he'd caused her—deliberately—and turned away without a backward glance.

42
SATURDAY: 4 WEEKS TO THE WEDDING

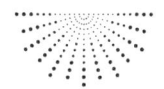

"Lyra," Kathryn said, walking to greet her as she entered the house on Alex's arm.

The two of them had spent the night in a roadside motel, to break up what would have been a ten-hour road trip for Alex, then had hit the road early the next morning, driving straight to Kathryn's.

Kathryn was obviously suffering, but Lyra marvelled that she still looked dignified and put-together. By contrast, Lyra's hair was a bird's nest, her nose was raw and her eyes were swollen to puffy slits.

"Thank goodness you're finally back," Kathryn said, pulling Lyra into a hug.

"I'm so sorry about the next of kin thing," Lyra whispered.

Kathryn drew back and held her by the shoulders. "Don't you dare be upset about that. Neither of us had made any arrangements, and he'd have been in the same position if it was me who--" She choked off, her eyes welling. But through sheer force of will, she held the tears back. "Come into the kitchen," she said. "Your brother and Ernie are here. Jenny's back to work today. She was sufficiently reassured that I had enough company."

As soon as Lyra saw Silas, the last string holding her heart together snapped. He looked horrible. His eyes were dull and hollow, with the dark thumbprints of sleeplessness bruised beneath them. She could tell he was going through hell, same as her. Wordlessly, he stood and wrapped his arms around her, and they both gulped back tears as the others looked on.

"I can't believe it," she whispered to him.

He squeezed her in response and she knew he didn't trust himself to speak. When they finally broke apart, Silas took a seat back at the table. But not, Lyra noticed, beside Ernie.

Ernie's face also looked haunted and his gaze was trained on Silas, as though no one else in the room existed for him.

"I've made a huge batch of hot chocolate," Kathryn said, bringing all eyes in the room to her. "And Lyra's girlfriends have had a gorgeous cake delivered. We have some planning to do."

Several hours later, they had the outline of a funeral planned. Mick had wanted to be buried, and Lyra had almost suggested the cemetery where her mother lay, but hadn't wanted to offend Kathryn. In the end, Kathryn had suggested it herself. She knew the place was special for him, and she also found it beautiful and dignified. They'd selected a funeral venue and decided on Kathryn's back garden for the wake.

Lyra would sing the song she'd written for Mick and Silas would deliver a short eulogy. Alex, Ernie, Silas and Kathryn's son would act as pallbearers.

They still had to tackle the slideshow that would play during the funeral, when Lyra was singing. Between them, they had thousands of photos, although none of Mick from his youth. For that, they'd need to reach out to his brother and ex-wife, who Kathryn had already notified of Mick's sudden death. Mick's brother had apparently been distraught, and Lyra couldn't help feeling a prick of satisfaction in that. After all, Mick's brother had stolen his wife and the men had never reconciled. And now they never could ... at that thought, Lyra's eyes blurred again.

"Ly. Come with me?" Silas said, once they'd all finished the last of their cups of coffee. "Alex is going to take Ernie home."

Lyra knew exactly where he wanted to go. She nodded, and kissed Alex. She wasn't sure whether she was imagining it, but she thought there was tension in his gaze as he said goodbye.

Their mother's grave was neat, the headstone polished. Silas had recently tended it and added fresh flowers. Silas and Lyra often went alone, and just as often together. They rarely saw others at the cemetery and, today in particular, Lyra was glad it was desolate.

It was late afternoon and the breeze was coming in from the nearby ocean, salting the air. The grass was lusher than it would be in summer, when all the care in the world couldn't coax it from its brittle, brown state. Now, it was soft enough to sit on comfortably. The wattle trees skirting the area were beginning to bud. It would be beautiful when in full bloom.

Wordlessly, they sat at the foot of their mother's grave and Silas slipped his arm over Lyra's shoulder. They didn't speak for a long time, the only noise the roar of the ocean.

Then Lyra heard Silas sniff slightly. She craned her head to look at him.

"I didn't reply to Mick's last text," he said quietly, clearly struggling with his emotions. "He asked me if I wanted to come over."

Lyra squeezed his arm. She held his gaze firmly. "It doesn't matter. He knew you loved him."

"Did he though? Because I called him to talk about Ernie and then I was pretty rude when he didn't give me the answer I wanted. And then ... he asked me to come over."

Lyra frowned. "Wait. What happened with Ernie?"

"Ugh," Silas groaned, wiping at his nose with the back of his sleeve. "I don't really want to talk about it."

"But you will." She elbowed him.

He bit his lip and trailed his fingers through the grass, plucking up blades and shredding them. Lyra waited.

"I proposed and he said no."

Lyra whipped her head around, twisting out from under Silas's arm. "You did *what?*"

"Can we not make a big thing about it?" Silas asked, pushing a hand through his thick hair.

"About you *proposing to someone*? You have to be kidding. How come you didn't tell me you were going to do that?" Her voice rose to a whiny pitch at the end but she didn't care.

"You were away and it kind of ..." Silas turned up his palms. "Happened."

"Okaaay." Lyra narrowed his eyes. "So why did he say no?"

"He doesn't love me, I guess."

Lyra burst out laughing.

"I'm glad my pain is so hilarious to you," Silas snapped, glaring at her.

"I'm not laughing at your pain, you idiot. I'm laughing at the idea that Ernie doesn't love you."

"Well, he said no. So you tell me why."

Lyra considered. "Has something been up between you two? What aren't you telling me? Don't keep it from us."

Lyra jerked her head at the tombstone. "Me or her. Out with it."

Silas rolled his eyes. "He thinks something is up with me."

"*Is* something up with you?"

"No! I think there's something up with him."

"Okay, this is sounding dumb. Tell me what you *actually* mean."

Silas groaned again, scrubbing a hand over his face. "I'm pretty sure he's cheating on me."

Lyra started laughing again, turning it into a cough when she saw the pain in Silas's eyes. "What. You can't be serious?"

"There's someone he's getting text messages from. Someone in his phone as four heart emojis. He's switched off the previews, and he often gets messages late at night."

Lyra frowned. "Well, that could be anyone, right? A relative, a friend going through a rough time whose privacy he wants to preserve. Who knows?"

Silas nodded, staring back out into the distance. "That's what Mick said," he whispered.

"Because he's smart … *was,*" she corrected sadly. "Anyway, what did Ernie say when you asked him about it?"

Silas studied the grass intently. Then the headstone. Then the trees. Then the sky.

"Ah," Lyra nodded, realising the answer. "You didn't. Well, I know he loves you. Full stop. And I *know* he's not cheating. So either you have to suck it up and just ask him what's going on, or you don't get to marry him." She shrugged. "Simple as that."

Silas heaved a sigh. Then he gently slid his arm back over Lyra's shoulders.

"You know, recently I found out Alex was still talking to his ex," Lyra continued.

Silas raised an eyebrow at her. "The nurse?"

She nodded. "Do you know what I did?"

Silas chuckled. "Do we need to get rid of a body?"

Lyra slapped his leg. "*No*. I *asked* him about it. In a normal way. Because I'm a normal person and I trust my boyfriend. There was a simple explanation, and it was over in a minute." She paused for effect. "You should trust Ernie."

He squeezed her shoulders after a moment. "You and Mick were always best at giving advice," he said quietly. "Suppose I should listen to you at some point."

Lyra settled her head on Silas's shoulder and traced her eyes over their mother's headstone. Delilah Beck. Taken too painfully, painfully soon. Lyra's eyes blurred with hot tears again and she swallowed at the hard lump in her throat.

"I can't believe he's really gone," she whispered, squeezing her eyes shut as tears streaked her cheeks. "I'm going to miss him for the rest of my life. And I didn't get to answer his last text either. Because they'd stolen my phone."

Silas let out a low sound, like a growl. "You should never work for them again."

Lyra tried unsuccessfully to stifle a sob. "I can't walk away. It's my livelihood now. And we've put a deposit on a house. But," she added, her voice shaking with emotion. "I can *definitely* make sure they pay for what they did."

43
MONDAY

Amy parked her car at the top of Lilac Bay's crest. Monday mornings weren't currently the joy they previously had been. She kept telling herself things would be better once the wedding was over, the new Porter Lucas team members were all settled in, once she and Rick had their own place. But she could feel herself getting close to burnout. Something needed to change, and quickly.

She turned to look at the trees—the dappled morning light streaming through them and the glimpses of the water she could catch from between them. When she rolled down her window, the scent of lilacs wafted in. Lilac Bay had a calming effect on her. It always had done. She was early, and parked outside the former Porter Lucas offices, feeling sentimental about the move. The new offices were all kitted out and Hope, Jessamyn and Amber were officially starting today. But she felt drawn to the place where it had all started for her.

She looked down at her phone, about to take a small gamble. One that might create a further stack of to-dos, but one she was convinced was right. Drawing a deep breath and hissing it out, she dialled Lyra's number.

They still hadn't spoken, but Amy felt confident that her text messages and the cake had let Lyra know how much she was on their minds.

Now, Amy wanted to let Lyra know her sympathy extended beyond cake and text messages. And that she wanted to help her through that grief in any small way she could.

"Ames," Lyra answered, her voice wobbly. "Hi."

"Hey," Amy replied gently. "I'm not even going to ask how you're doing because I know the answer. But ... are you feeling supported?"

Lyra drew a shaky breath. "Yeah. First, thank you for that cake. It was like getting a big hug. And Alex has been amazing. And I feel like it's brought me and Si a bit closer—not that we were ever not close, but since we don't live together anymore it's harder. Thank you ... for giving me space but letting me know you were there."

"I'm always here," Amy said fiercely.

"And I know it. It means the world."

Amy fiddled with the gold locket around her neck. "I really can't believe it," she said finally. "I thought he'd live forever."

Lyra gulped. "We all did. He had us fooled so many times."

"I'm so happy he had the life he did, and that you and Si let him experience being a parent."

"He's irreplaceable, that's for sure. Was," she corrected herself softly.

"Listen," Amy drew a breath. "I'm ringing to tell you that you don't need to sing or make a speech at the wedding."

There was a pause. "Why not?" Lyra demanded. "Is the wedding not going ahead?"

"Yes, yes it is. But my Maid of Honour just lost a family

member. I feel like it's selfish to ask you to stand beside me at my wedding in a few weeks."

"Amy," Lyra began in a stern tone. "No. That's super sweet, but no. I might not be as perky as I would otherwise have been, but I want to do this. For you and for me."

Amy exhaled. "Ly, I can book someone else to sing, and ask someone else to make a speech. I don't want it to be hard for you."

"No! You're not doing that. I'm not letting you. Please," she added, her tone changing. "I couldn't handle the guilt on top of everything else."

That settled it for Amy. "Okay. Alright. But do you want to drop one thing? The speech or the singing?"

"I can do both. I swear. It's not like he died at a wedding. Then we might be having a different conversation." She laughed the kind of laugh that held the threat of imminent tears. "But I love you for even thinking of this."

"Are you absolutely certain?"

"One hundred and ten per cent."

"Alright then. We go ahead."

"Good."

"Have you heard from the label?"

Lyra groaned. "No. But they have to reach out sooner or later? To be honest, I don't even want to think about that right now."

"Understood. Listen, I have to head into the office. But I love you."

"I know. And I love you."

Amy hung up the call with Lyra and sat, frowning at her old offices. Technically they were still hers as the company was paying rent for a little longer. Goosebumps rippled down her spine and she sat up straight in her seat, her head tilted with an idea that had just struck her. She pulled her phone back out and scrolled through the numbers, hitting Mrs Beckwith's. She drummed her fingers on the console, suddenly desperate to have the call connected.

"Alona," she said breathlessly, once the call was answered.

"Yes? Who's calling please?" came the tentative reply.

"It's Amy Porter. The previous tenant—actually, still current tenant at the Lilac Bay property."

"Oh, yes. Amy. Was I supposed to sign something? I received the paperwork, you're in your notice period and it's all official. No need to worry."

"No, that's not what I'm calling about. Have you put the place on the market yet? Or sold it?"

"Gosh no," Alona said, heaving a sigh. "There's been too much on my plate. I'll definitely need to do it soon though. Why do you ask?"

Amy's mind was whirring. "Can you do me a favour? Can you give me a couple of days before you make any decisions on it? We're still paying rent for a bit longer, but I'm just asking for a couple of days."

"Yes," Alona said gratefully. "Sure. That gives me a bit of breathing room anyway."

As soon as they'd hung up, Amy's phone rang again. She didn't recognise the number so she put on her most professional voice. "Amy Porter, Porter Lucas, how may I help you?"

"Hi Amy? This is Dolores, the wedding coordinator at Hunter Valley Homestead Chateau."

"Oh, hi Dolores. Am I overdue submitting something?" Amy's face burned and she tucked the phone between her ear and shoulder to fumble for her laptop so she could check her to-do list.

"No ... it's rather that there's an issue we need to discuss."

"What is it?"

"A fire in the kitchen. Burnt to the actual ground. We're not sure how long it's going to take to be repaired." Amy couldn't stifle the gasp that sprang from her. The *wedding food* squares were going back from green to red. This wedding would never be finalised. "But we do have a solution," Dolores added quickly. "We're going to bring in food from a neighbouring venue. That way there's minimal disruption to your plans. The only thing is, you will need to place new orders."

Amy closed her eyes. "Okay," she said wearily, rubbing her eyes—carefully so as not to smudge her shadow. "How close is their menu to yours?"

"Uh, well," Dolores began, and Amy knew it didn't bode well. "There are several comparable items. However, many are ... completely different. You must understand, this is a competitive business in a saturated area. Each venue tries to differentiate itself."

"Can you email me over a list then?"

"Yes," Dolores said quickly, sounding relieved.

Amy had her laptop open now. It connected instantly to her phone's hotspot and she flicked open her client project tab. Her shoulders slumped. She had no way to fit this in right now, unless she did it late at night, with Rick. Rick! This was another thing she could delegate to him. And best of all, he'd thank her for it. There mustn't be *that* many choices, and she was pretty sure they saw eye to eye on most of the food-related decisions. At least, she couldn't remember them having disagreed.

"Actually, could you please email them to my fiancé? I'll give you his email address. I'll fill him in and he can submit the choices back to you."

"Yes, certainly. They do need to be finalised before the end of the week."

"He can manage, I'm sure."

Once they'd hung up, Amy shot Rick off a quick email explaining the situation, then logged out of the file. Everything else in there would have to wait.

Realising she was in danger of being late to work, she hooked her phone up to the speaker system and dialled one of her favourite contacts—the architect Eloise Trundle. Her grin was stretched from ear to ear as she drove and spoke, and for the first time in a while, she was on a high of inspiration.

44
MONDAY

When Amy finally pulled up at Pam and Rick's place late that evening, she was beyond beat. She killed the engine and let her head drop back onto the seat rest. It was *only* Monday. And there were still four weeks to go until her wedding. How was she actually going to survive? At least they'd all had a great first day together as the new, expanded Porter Lucas. And their offices looked amazing—thanks to Kristina's foresight.

She found herself wishing that Pam would be out, or asleep, or otherwise occupied when she went inside.

Staying at that house was destroying her inch by inch. But then she remembered her calls today and brightened. She couldn't wait to talk to Rick about everything. And see how he'd gone with the food orders.

The lights were off in the living room, which she took as a good sign. She grabbed up her handbag and picked her way up the drive to the front door. Her feet were *killing* her, and she wished she could soak in her own tub at home. Whenever she used the bathtub here, Pam found constant ways to interrupt.

She squashed down the annoyance she always felt at ringing the doorbell and waited for someone to answer.

The living room light flicked on and Rick opened the door.

"Oh, thank goodness," Amy said in a low voice, leaning towards him for a kiss. He held himself stiffly and didn't return it.

Amy frowned and studied his face. He looked upset.

"Hey, what's wrong?" she asked in concern.

"Come into the bedroom," he answered, spinning his chair and heading down the hall.

Amy kicked off her shoes, her feet landing gratefully on the cool tile of the small foyer. "Well, hello to you, too," she mumbled, following Rick.

In his room, he spun to face her.

"Is this about the food?" Amy asked, dropping her handbag to the floor. "Because I thought you said you wanted to be involved in stuff."

Rick shook his head. "No. It's not about the food."

"Okaay," Amy said slowly, crossing the room to sink onto the bed. "Then I give up." She rubbed her forehead. "It's been a day, so if we can skip the guesswork …"

"Do you know where my mum is tonight?"

She held up her palms.

"She's on a date," Rick said flatly.

"Oh? Nice. Good for her."

"With your dad." The distaste in Rick's voice was clear and Amy blinked.

"Okay. Is that somehow my fault?"

"You didn't know about it?"

"No," Amy said, frowning. "But even if I did … what does it matter? She's a grown woman."

"Yeah," Rick said bitterly. "A grown woman who's now dating *your dad.*"

Amy sat up straighter on the bed, prickling at Rick's tone. "So?"

"So? Amy, he's not the kind of guy I think my Mum should be with. Especially when she's so new to dating."

Her eyes narrowed. "Why not?"

Rick threw up his hands, exasperated. "That can't be a serious question. I should have seen this coming. He's been sniffing around her for weeks. I should have been more on guard."

Amy pulled her chin back and frowned, turning her head to him. "Excuse me? *Him* sniffing around *her?* Is that a joke? Your mum has been panting over my dad like she's in heat since the first time she saw him on the phone!"

Rick froze and as the words hung in the air, Amy realised she'd crossed a line. His glare was harsh, frightening even, and he pinned her with it as he spoke. "Don't you *ever* speak about my mum that way again, do you hear me?" His voice was low and dark and so cold that it sent a shiver through Amy. He'd never used that tone with her before.

She closed her eyes, trying to think of a way to take the heat level down a notch before they both said things they'd regret. "I'm saying you're making it all seem one-sided, and I didn't get that impression."

"Amy, I don't care who started it or who's keeping it going. The fact is, we both know he's not good enough for her."

It was Amy's turn to suck her breath in. Her pulse raged as she narrowed her eyes at him. "*What* did you say?"

"Nothing you haven't said before yourself! Don't pretend to get on a high horse about it. He's trash! He let you down, ruined your childhood, gambled away god knows what, and you're probably lucky he didn't gamble *you!*"

The word "trash" was a sucker-punch to Amy, knocking the breath from her. It was all the more shocking because she couldn't believe these words were coming from Rick's mouth. From her *fiancé's* mouth. It didn't matter that she saw the grain of truth in them. It didn't matter that she knew he was angry and confused and was lashing out from some kind of misplaced loyalty to his late father. No matter what the root, he was hurting her, and the whole situation had spiralled so quickly and so dangerously that Amy felt nauseous.

As soon as Rick saw the tears in her eyes, he hung his head. "Damn it," he said angrily. "Ames, I'm so sorry. I've just been sitting here stewing and ..."

It was too late though, the tears were flowing and she didn't feel like talking through them right now. She flicked them carefully away with her ring fingers. "I'm leaving," she said, getting to her feet.

"No," Rick said desperately, reaching for her. "Please don't leave with things like this between us. Ames, *please.* I'm sorry, I don't even know where all that came from."

"I don't want it to take *tears* to make you realise you've said something wrong!"

"No, I know—I know. You're completely right." His eyes were wide and frightened. "I'm ashamed of myself. Please forgive me."

"I need to go," Amy muttered, grabbing her handbag and heading for the door.

"Please don't leave it like this!" Rick called, hot on her heels.

Amy paused at the door, her hand on the knob. Did she really want to walk out on him this way, leave this anger between them? For a split second she considered turning back around and trying to talk it out. She was beyond exhausted and hardly in the mood for the drive home.

Then she remembered his words, and the tone of his voice as he'd said them. There would be no productive discussions tonight, not while she was this hurt. She owed it to them both to take some time to cool down.

"I'll call you later," she told him, leaving no room for a reply. The sadness in his eyes stabbed at her heart, but she closed the door firmly behind her.

In the car, Amy let the tears fall as she drove. She hated fighting with Rick, hated anything coming between them, especially after all they'd been through. Still, he couldn't be allowed to talk to her that way. To talk about her father that way. After almost falling asleep at two separate sets of traffic lights, she grabbed a takeaway coffee from a 24-hour drive through. At home, she didn't even wash off her makeup, just collapsed, utterly spent, into bed.

45
WEDNESDAY

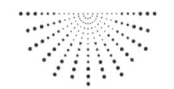

Two days later, Amy woke in her Bondi apartment with thoughts of her argument with Rick still swirling in her mind. She felt sick that they hadn't yet talked things through. But she felt strongly that he'd been in the wrong. She heaved a huge sigh as she stretched. It was nice being in her own bed, feeling the luxe softness of the high thread count on her sheets. But it was *always* nicer with Rick, no matter what the bed linen was like.

They'd been sharing text messages at least, letting each other know what was going on in their days. Amy had also texted to tell him she loved him, that she was fine, they'd work through it, and that she needed some space. He'd respected that.

She fixed herself a double espresso and a quick potato omelette—using up the last of what she had in the fridge—and then pulled her laptop towards her. It was far too early to start working, but the new team members were taking up a lot of her and Kristina's days at the moment—not to mention the new clients.

Fuelled by caffeine, and her desire to cross as many things

off her list as possible, Amy dove into her work files. Two uninterrupted hours later, she was close to finalising two projects and had made a little headway on a third.

She checked her watch. It was still early, but there was a chance Alex would be awake. He answered her video call on the third ring.

"Amy? Are you trying to get hold of Ly?" he asked, smiling into the camera. He was outside on an early walk.

Amy beamed at him. "No, it's you I wanted to talk to. I have a special project coming up and I wondered if I could send you over the plans so you could give me a cost estimate?"

"Yeah, sure! Any clues as to what it's about?"

"Nope." She grinned. "But I do need it to be top secret."

Alex saluted her before they hung up, a gesture that made her think of Rick. Her heart hurt. She *hated* being at odds with him. They'd already been through so much together as a couple. She'd really thought they were due for some smooth sailing now. Even the wedding hadn't caused any issues between them … until now. Mainly, Amy had to admit, because she had taken it all on herself.

With that thought, she logged into her wedding to-do file and gasped. *So* many squares had been turned green! Her emotions swirled between fear and gratitude and she immediately called Rick.

He answered in video mode, his hair sticking up adorably and his dimple appearing the instant he saw her face.

"I'm so glad you're calling me," he said, and the low rumble of his voice hit Amy in the belly, the way it always did. The early morning light illuminated his scar and Amy was reminded afresh of the horrible period in their lives where they didn't know if he was even going to live.

"Look, I'm sorry for leaving …" she began, but he cut her off.

"No, Ames. You had every right to. I was *totally* in the wrong, and I'm sorry. I'm really, really sorry."

Amy nodded. "I forgive you. And I'm sorry for what I said, too."

Rick grinned. "Are we good?"

"I think we probably need another discussion? But not right now. I haven't had enough coffee for that. Hey, listen, what happened to my beautiful wedding to-do list?"

"Are you missing all the red squares?"

She could see his barely-suppressed laugh.

"Kind of?" She winced. "What have you done?"

"You promise not to be mad?"

"You know I can't promise that."

"Mum and I split the remainders. Before you scream at me, I've given her explicit instructions to choose *what she thinks you would choose*, and not what she'd like herself."

"Okay," Amy said slowly, dying a little on the inside. "Oh god."

"On a scale of one to Threat Level Nuclear, how mad are you?"

Amy pretended to consider. "Like, Cold War?"

"Ames, there was *way* too much stuff on that list for one person. And it's *my* wedding too. I know I'm marrying a control freak—" He held up a hand when she opened her mouth to protest. "But when you gave Dolores my email, I took it as a sign. And Mum's a willing pair of hands. I only allocated her the items that are kind of smaller and will have less impact."

"Hmm, keep talking."

He grinned again, and Amy found herself stroking a finger over his face on the screen. "I saw your work to-do list as well. You were going to have some sort of burnout if you didn't let us help more. And I have one last argument," he said quickly, holding up a finger. "This wedding is about our two lives coming together. And we have different styles. That's how it is. You're never going to get me in like, suspenders and a flat cap with a big twirly moustache or whatever." Amy couldn't help but laugh at the image. "But our whole life is going to have to be about little compromises here and there, and about accepting one another for who we are. Don't you think that should start with the wedding?"

Amy stared at him for a second, before puffing out a breath. "Alright," she said. "Ugh. You win. That's a pretty good argument. And anyway, if something looks weird, people will assume *you* did it anyway. They'll *know* I didn't."

"That's my girl."

"Yeah, yeah. Save it for the vows, Ford."

"Listen, why don't you take another night to yourself there. Have a nice long bath, get takeout, enjoy your place. Come back here tomorrow?"

"Are you sure?" Amy pouted, touching his face onscreen again. "Usually after we fight, we have some making up to do…"

Rick groaned. "Don't make this harder than it already is!"

"That's what she said!" Amy quipped, and they erupted into childish giggles. "I'm still hurt by what you said, and how you said it," she added, once they'd regained control. "But I'm feeling much more forgiving now."

"Good," Rick said, grinning. "I love you like crazy. I was an idiot. And when you're back here tomorrow night, I'll show you just how sorry I am." He wiggled his eyebrows and Amy sighed with love.

46
WEDNESDAY

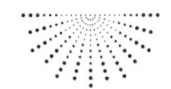

Marley worried her lower lip with her teeth as Lyra's phone rang. Finn shot her a sympathetic look, then disappeared to the kitchen to get started on their dinner and give her some privacy.

"Hi," Lyra answered finally, and Marley heard everything she needed to in her friend's tone.

A lump instantly formed in Marley's throat. "I'm sorry," she whispered, and the two of them spent a moment in silence, swallowing hard.

"Thanks for calling," Lyra said finally. "I haven't been answering many calls, but for you or Ames …"

"I'm sorry I haven't called before now," Marley said. "I remember that I didn't want to talk to anyone when I lost GamGam." She didn't add that there hadn't really been anyone to talk to. At least not anyone she trusted or felt close to.

"That's how I felt," Lyra replied. "The messages and texts and even the outpouring on social media. I mean, I don't want to sound ungrateful because it's so lovely to know that people care, but it's also …."

"Overwhelming?" Marley finished for her.

"Yeah," Lyra agreed softly.

"And it creates pressure. Like you have to get back to people, have to acknowledge that *they've* acknowledged it." For her, it had been even worse that the people of her small town had hardly paid her any attention before then.

Lyra's assent was barely a squeak.

"The ones I stressed about the most were the 'what can I do' ones," Marley added. "Although, to be honest … I didn't really have that many friends. It was mostly distant acquaintances, friends of GamGam, older people from the community. It's different with you though, people really do care."

"Oh, Marley," Lyra said, her voice cracking. "I wish I'd known you then to be there for you. This is the worst pain. It's not fair that you went through it alone."

Marley squeezed her eyes shut, a tear escaping her lashes as she thought back on the intense loneliness of the time after her grandmother had died.

"People will also try and give you a timeframe to be over it," she told Lyra. "And it does get better. But you'll get punched in the gut two years from now over something you least expect. Don't let anyone tell you that's not okay."

Lyra was quiet. "I still get that with Mum," she admitted. "And sometimes I feel like I don't have the right. Because I was so young when she went."

"You have the right," Marley said firmly. "I can't remember anything about my parents, and I grieve them sometimes. We both have the right."

She heard Lyra gulp. "I'm terrified of the funeral."

"It will help," Marley said confidently. "There's a reason those rituals have been around for so long. It's painful, but it's cathartic. And we'll all be there."

"I hope we do him proud," Lyra said, her voice wobbling again.

"Lyra. He loved you like you were his daughter. You did nothing *but* make him proud."

Marley could hear Lyra struggling with her emotions. A moment later, she hastily whispered that she had to go. Marley hung up the call and immediately texted her, saying she hoped she hadn't said something wrong. Lyra texted back a string of hearts.

Marley wiped her face and wandered into the kitchen, where Finn was in the midst of preparing spaghetti bolognese. He immediately abandoned the saucepan and wrapped his arms around Marley, who melted into his hug. She'd never felt more grateful for his love and support than at that moment.

"What kind of parent do you want to be?" she asked him later, twirling her fork through the spaghetti. She loved the small touches he brought to each dinner—always lighting a couple of candles and choosing a playlist that matched the cuisine he'd prepared. Right now, soulful Italian music drifted softly through their little portable Bluetooth speaker.

Finn broke off a crust of garlic bread and considered the question carefully. "I think it'll be hard for me to be a parent first and a friend second."

"Oh. I hadn't thought of that."

"But I think it's important that it's the other way around. I'll struggle to remember that, but it's something I'll keep working on. Most of all though," he continued, tipping his head thoughtfully so that some of his inky hair fell over his forehead. "I want them to know that literally *no matter what*, I have their back." He smiled at her and her heart swelled to twice its normal size.

"Same," she said, nodding. "Same."

That's what GamGam had been for her, and she knew it

was what Mick had provided for Lyra and especially Silas. The thought brought tears to her eyes again, but she smiled through them at Finn. She had the overwhelming sense that her life was on the right track.

Finn grinned happily at her, and the baby shifted—perhaps as contented as Marley was.

47
THURSDAY

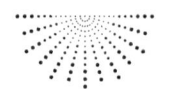

Lyra was awake but bleary-eyed when Alex returned from his early morning walk. The industrial-strength coffee she was sipping wasn't waking her the way she hoped and she knew it was because she was usually awake during the small hours, worrying.

"Hi, sleeping beauty," he said, kicking off his shoes and washing his hands in the kitchen sink.

"Hi," she replied distractedly, chewing a thumbnail.

Alex came and sat beside her on the sofa, planting a soft kiss on her forehead. She saw the shadow pass across his handsome face and wondered for the hundredth time if he was really okay about the whole situation with the Jake video. It seemed every time he looked at her, he ended up sad.

She'd spoken daily to Kit and Maggie, but she and Jake had yet to talk again. The entire band was in limbo and she lived in dread of going to the mailbox to find a note saying how much she was being sued for. Or that they were dropping her. It had been almost a week. A whole week.

The label had put out a short statement cancelling the

remaining shows and offering refunds. Their PR person had done a great job on it. *The health and well-being of our acts is of paramount importance to us at all times. Therefore, we announce that the remaining shows on Lyra Beck's current tour are cancelled, due to a family tragedy. We ask that you join us in respecting Lyra's privacy as she grieves with her loved ones at this difficult time. All ticket holders are entitled to a full refund, and the remaining concert dates will be rescheduled in due course.*

But she knew better than to take those words at face value. All she could do was wait. She'd held off posting anything on social media, though her accounts were blowing up with a mixture of sympathy messages and demands to know what was happening between her and Jake.

"Things are going to work out, Ly," he said gently, slipping an arm over her shoulders and pulling her close. "You'll see."

"Alex, if I get sued, we have to pull out of the house agreement. I don't even know if that's possible. And we'll never find another little place like that again."

"We'll find a way. I don't think it will come to that, but we'll find a way."

Lyra let herself relax into him, wanting desperately to believe his words. His phone rang and he dug into his pocket for it, his eyes widening when he saw the name on screen.

"Steve," he said breathlessly, swiping to answer the call. Lyra instantly sat up straighter. They'd been waiting for a call from Alex's contact at the label, but hadn't heard anything up to now.

"Put him on speaker."

Alex hit the button and slipped his arm tightly around Lyra. "We're both here," he said.

"Good," Steve's voice sounded harried and low, almost as though he was calling in secret. "I've got some news."

"Hit me," Lyra said wretchedly. "It can't be any worse than what I've already been imagining."

"They're not going to sue," Steve said, and Lyra and Alex let out simultaneous breaths.

"Then what?"

Steve sighed. "Actually, nothing. They want to carry on as things were. They'll reschedule the dates for the rest of the tour for after your family member's funeral. I believe it's in a couple of days?"

"It is," Lyra confirmed, pulling her head back in shock, exchanging a tentatively hopeful look with Alex.

"Good. I wanted to tie this up for you so you could attend that in peace."

"Really?" she asked, her disbelief plain.

There was a scratching noise as though Steve was covering the mouthpiece of his phone. They heard a heavy door squeak open, and then traffic noise. "I might have had something to do with convincing them this was the best path for them."

"Holy crap," Lyra breathed, setting her coffee down to grab Alex's hands. "Steve, *thank* you. What … what on *earth* did you say? If I'm allowed to ask."

"Alex told me about Jake being asked to turn in your phone. I also spoke to your brother about the calls placed to Julian once he'd learned of the … tragedy. There is a duty of care clause in your contract, Lyra. Not sure you're familiar with it, but I know that it's in all our contracts. It's relatively vague, but after some incidents in the past, our legal team were advised to add it in. It's usually only trotted out as 'evidence' that we care so much for our acts we've voluntarily legally bound ourselves to it." They could hear the sarcasm in his voice.

"Wow," Lyra breathed. "And you convinced them what? That getting Jake to hide my phone went against that?"

"It was less the argument than the very vague threat that you knew they'd done it, there was concrete proof, willing witnesses, call logs and the clause. I might also have whispered that you have access to a *very* broad audience of supportive fans. Not to mention that your popularity is, let's say *peaking*, thanks to the combo of the Jake videos and your personal tragedy. They don't think it would test very well if they were exposed for what they did. So they're letting it slide."

Lyra was silent a moment. "So … they actually shot themselves in the foot with the whole fake romance thing?"

"More or less." Steve confirmed.

"But I wouldn't have gone public about what they did," she said softly.

Alex frowned. "I would have," he said fiercely.

"Lyra, I advise you never to let them know that," Steve said carefully. "We're going to be on tentative ground for a little while. Selena isn't happy about being bested. The company did lose money from the cancelled dates, but at least some of it is covered by additional insurances we have."

"So … everything carries on?" Lyra said. "Me and the band, we get to stick together, keep playing? We all get paid?"

"Not for the dates you didn't play, obviously. But you'll make those back up when they reschedule. But, yes. There won't be any punitive measures taken."

Lyra blinked up at Alex, her eyes welling. She buried her head in his chest and he wrapped his arms protectively around her.

"Man, I can't tell you what this means to us," he said, his voice thick with emotion. "Thank you."

"No worries," Steve said hastily. "Listen, as I said. Keep it all mum, and Lyra never let them know you wouldn't have gone there. Could come back to bite you on the arse."

"I won't," she said, her voice muffled against Alex's broad chest.

"Oh, and I'm really sorry for your loss," Steve added, before hanging up the call.

Silence fell and as Alex pulled his arms tighter around her, she felt some of the tension slip from her shoulders.

"I can't believe it," she said, shaking her head. Her eyes were saucer-wide. "I can't believe it. This is like, my third life with this label. I wanted to punish her so bad … but it's almost better that she ended up punishing herself. It's poetic justice. I'm never going to do another thing wrong!"

"You *didn't* do anything wrong," Alex said firmly. "Didn't you hear Steve? They literally broke their own contract laws."

"Right." Lyra appeared to only be half-listening. "Oh! I have to call Mags."

Alex nodded, releasing her as she sprang to her feet in search of her phone, feeling the most hopeful she had in a week. Halfway to the bedroom door, she turned and flung herself back at Alex. He caught her, laughing. "What's that for?" he asked, grinning.

"For helping me. And because we can buy our house now, worry-free. And because my career isn't ruined." She tipped her face up to his, bringing their lips closer together. She pressed them together in a kiss, then pulled back to gaze up at him. "And because you're handsome and I love you."

She could almost convince herself the sadness was completely gone from his eyes.

Almost.

48
FRIDAY

Amy got home late again that evening. She, Kristina and Martha had ordered a dinner of takeout and decided to say farewell to their first offices, feeling nostalgic. It had been a bittersweet goodbye. In some ways it was unbelievable. In a little over a year, they'd already outgrown their first space—what other exciting things were in store for them? At the same time, Amy loved those offices and the memory of all her friends coming together to help her build them. She was hoping she wouldn't have to say goodbye to them forever, but it was the end of an era for her company all the same.

She collected her mail from the box downstairs, the usual stack of bills and promos, and said a quick hello to her neighbour Wilma, who she ran into in the hall.

When she put the key in her front door, she was surprised to find it already unlocked. Instantly, a shiver crept down her spine. She could clearly remember having deadbolted it from the outside that morning.

She stood back from the door, her heart pounding, and hit the hall light timer again, making sure she wouldn't be plunged into darkness. Then she took some bracing breaths, twisted the knob and kicked the door open with her heel. A surprised yelp came from inside.

"*Rick?!*"

"Yeah, Jesus Christ, Amy!"

Rick was sitting in the lit-up living room, clutching his heart. Amy's eyes bugged. "You scared the stuffing out of me. What … How? … *How?*"

"That makes two of us! Come in and shut the door," he said, grinning as he caught his breath. She obeyed. "I had Alex help me," he explained. "Turns out I can actually get up the stairs by myself, although it does take quite a while. I can't get my chair up though, so he brought it up after me."

He moved himself onto the sofa and Amy sat down beside him, swinging her legs up over his and putting her arms around his neck. "You can get up the stairs?" She was incredulous.

"Yep." His smile was proud and it made Amy's heart ache.

"So … we can spend some time here now? I don't have to always come to you?"

"Nope." His eyes twinkled as she pulled his head close to hers for a long, lingering kiss. As Rick groaned and started to manoeuvre them backwards onto the sofa, Amy put a hand on his chest to stop him.

"Wait, wait," she said breathlessly. "We need to talk."

"Right," Rick agreed, trying to slow his breathing. His pupils were wild and his hair was mussed. Amy looked at his lips, slightly swollen from their kisses.

"Forget it, we'll talk after," she said, and dove back in.

As they lay tangled up on the sofa afterwards, their heartrates slowly returning to normal, Amy laced their hands together.

"Rick … I couldn't stand our fight. We've already been through so much, and I thought we were back on solid ground. I thought we were unshakeable. Whenever I think about how close I came to losing you in the past …" She choked off, taking a moment to regather herself as he tilted his head to look at her. There was a taut, pained expression on his face as he traced his finger along her jaw. "I want the rest of our lives to start *now*," she added.

He swallowed, nodding slowly, taking her hand and staring into her eyes. She'd never get sick of the way her body responded so physically to him. "I'm so sorry, Ames. Things with Dad … I guess it turns out I haven't properly healed from everything that's happened to me over the last couple of years. Or from losing him."

Amy nodded. "I can see that. And," she drew a breath, "I can understand your hesitations with my dad and your mum. I just didn't like the way you tried to point it out. I've also been thinking that maybe the pressure I'm under didn't help how I reacted."

"You mean house-hunting, planning a wedding and expanding your business?" Rick said. "Can't see why that's a big deal."

She grinned. "Thank you for doing the wedding stuff. It was what I needed, even if I didn't know it. Thanks for knowing that for me."

Rick squeezed her hand and blew out a breath. "I can't promise we'll never fight again, Ames. But I *always* want us to be on the same side. On the same team. I never want family to come between us again. *You're* my family now, and you will be forever. Since the moment I met you, you've been all I've ever wanted, and I can't wait to get to call you my wife."

Amy gripped his hand in hers, tears forming at the edges of her lashes as she watched him try and swallow down his emotion. "Rick, how are we going to wait almost four more weeks?"

A grin broke slowly over his face. "I don't know. I think I'm going to start calling you my wife already."

"I like that." She sighed and put her head to his chest. "Why didn't we elope after all? We could have been married by now."

"Ah, but we wouldn't have learned all these new things about one another if we'd done that. Like to what extent you're a control freak and how long I'll let you get away with it."

Amy swatted him. "If I wasn't a control freak, I wouldn't be very successful at running my business."

"True, true. I guess I learned a little more about teamwork from the army than you did."

"Speaking of which …" Amy said, pulling back to look at him. "How are you feeling about leaving the army for good?"

Rick's mouth twisted. "Better than I thought I would. This thing with Alex, I'm really enjoying it. And it's starting to pick up. We're getting a lot of calls and requests for quotes. We'll need to do something official soon. And I think it's also been amazing for my recovery, as well as my motivation."

"I'm glad," Amy said, stroking his grizzled jaw as she stared up at him. "It makes me so happy to know you've found a new passion."

He ran his thumb across her lips in a way that made Amy's heart start pounding again. She loved the way he looked at her—the adoration and devotion so clear in his eyes.

"I've still got my old passions," he growled and she laughed.

"Who are you calling old?"

"My old lady," he said, grinning. "I'll be calling you that for the rest of our lives."

Amy closed her eyes, sighing contentedly. "In anyone else, I would hate those words. But from you, my love, they're music to my ears."

49
SATURDAY: THREE WEEKS TO THE WEDDING

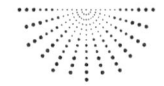

Lyra felt at ease as she and Alex walked into Kathryn's house for Mick's wake. The funeral and burial had been a fitting tribute to him and Lyra felt as though he would have been pleased with the way he was sent off. It wasn't overly mournful, it had been the right mix of truly celebrating his incredible life and paying tribute to him, while acknowledging the hole his loss would leave in their lives forever. Silas and Ernie had lingered by the gravesite, adding a visit to Lyra's mother's grave.

Lyra could see why funerals had persisted as a way for humans to bid their loved ones farewell. It was cathartic to release grief and shed tears with a community of people who'd adored Mick as much as she had. She loved that he was buried in the same earth as her mother. That she and Silas could visit both of them in one place.

Lyra also knew from experience that the ache would persist for many years to come, if not the rest of her life. But she also knew she could survive it. That she already had.

The sun was shining, but a cool breeze was rippling through the garden, ruffling the pictures of Mick on the cork board they'd set up. The wake was pot-luck and handmade dishes lined the long bench tables Kathryn had rented. Lyra and Kathryn had also spent time making Mick's favourite snacks to put out, which they were serving alongside his favourite drinks. They'd also set up an open Spotify playlist in the days before the funeral and encouraged everyone to add songs that reminded them of Mick.

As Lyra and Alex entered, one of Lyra's own songs came on and she ducked her head into Alex's chest. Reflexively, his grip tightened around her. She smiled up at him, happy that everything was resolved with the label. She just wished she could get rid of the lingering distance between the two of them.

Marley and Finn were already seated at the bench table and Lyra loved seeing Marley's head resting on Finn's shoulder as he jokingly fed her chips from the bowl in front of him and she giggled. Amy and Rick were there, too, and Lyra could see they were holding hands under the table. She pulled Alex over to sit among their friends.

"Ooh, Marley, I was thinking about something," Lyra said, once they were all settled.

"Hm?"

"The name. I had some fan mail from a girl called Nia, and I thought that was super cute. I was thinking you could also use it as a nickname for Petunia." The table fell silent and Lyra clapped a hand over her mouth. "I'm so sorry. That was really dumb to presume you wanted help. I shouldn't have said anything."

Marley's mouth had popped open in thought and she turned her gaze to Finn, who was beaming.

"I absolutely *love* it," he said.

"So do I!" Marley agreed. "Do we have our name? Do we actually have a name we're both happy with?"

"I definitely am if you are!"

"I am!"

Lyra was happy to see them so pleased. And then Marley gasped. The entire back garden turned to look at her. Finn sprang out of his chair, pulled back down quickly by Marley, who had a death grip on his arm.

"Marley, are you okay?" Amy asked.

"Fine, fine," she said quickly, waving her hand. "I felt like … there was kind of a whoosh…"

"Are you in labour?" Finn said, his voice coming out a pitch higher than usual.

"No, no," Marley said calmly. "Not yet. It's too early. She's not due for four more weeks! I don't know what that was."

Lyra spotted it first. The blooming red stain on the front of Marley's daisy-yellow dress. Her eyes widened and her hand shook as she gestured to it.

Marley flinched when she saw it and Finn sprang into action. "I'm calling an ambulance right now," he said, struggling to keep his voice calm.

As he pulled out his phone, Rick spun his chair and headed for the side gate. "I'll flag them down and lead them in here!" he yelled over his shoulder. Amy had never been so glad of army men in her life.

"I'm not in any pain?" Marley said blankly, but then her face crumpled.

By now, several others had noticed what was happening. Jenny strode quickly across the lawn, encouraging others to keep their distance. Finn hung up his call and instantly came back to Marley's side, gripping her hand tightly.

"It's probably just the womb pulling away from you a little," Jenny said, moving to crouch down beside Marley, forcing her to look at her. "The exact same thing happened to my sister. It was very dramatic and everyone was worried, but the baby was absolutely fine."

"Really?" Marley and Finn asked in unison, their eyes pinned hopefully to Jenny.

"Yes. The most perfect little baby you ever saw. Would you like to see a picture?"

They nodded. Marley was fighting tears and Finn's face was grim and frightened. Jenny passed Marley a glass of water, encouraging her to take a deep drink as she flicked her phone on and showed Marley and Finn some pictures.

The stain on Marley's dress had grown and Lyra fought tears as she looked at it, burying her head in Alex's chest. His jaw was tight and he pulled her fiercely towards him.

"Everything's going to be fine," Jenny said again, and her expression was so earnest and clear that everyone wholeheartedly believed her, at the same time as being beyond terrified.

"Ambos!" Rick called.

Finn leapt up. "Oh thank god."

As they entered the back garden, Lyra felt like the paramedics weren't going quickly enough. She wanted to scream at them for calmly taking time to ask Marley questions, check her heartbeat, gently press her in places. Finn was pushing his hands through his hair, obviously beside himself.

"Call us as soon as you know anything at all," Lyra begged Finn as Marley was wheeled out. A paramedic was sticking adhesive patches to Marley's belly and as they connected her to machines inside the ambulance, Lyra heard the paramedic say the heartbeat was there, and it was strong.

A silence fell after they left. Lyra sat down hard on the bench, Alex's arms still encircling her.

"Will they really be okay?" she whispered, and in response, Alex hugged her tighter.

"She will be. They both will," Jenny said confidently. "I'm absolutely certain of it."

Silas and Ernie entered the yard then, casting puzzled glances around. "We just saw an ambulance leave," Silas said. "Did they know Mick that well they actually attended the wake?"

Ernie tilted his head, looking at Lyra, taking in the ashen faces all around them. "I know we're at a funeral, but … what did we miss?"

50
SUNDAY

"She's so perfect," Marley breathed in awe, as little Nia squeaked and wriggled in her arms. She was bundled in a striped hospital blanket, a small mesh cap on her head and her eyes big, bright and alert, staring up at her parents. Neither of them could take their eyes off her, Finn craned over Marley's shoulder as she lay in the bed, so he wouldn't miss a second of Nia.

She'd come in a rush—a swirl of nurses and doctors—and Marley's memory was already hazy. All she could really remember was Finn clinging to her hand, talking to her gently. When Nia had made her dramatic entrance, she had been whisked off for tests. She hadn't cried immediately and Marley had struggled to sit up, panicked, but also weak with blood loss.

But miraculously, Nia had scored an eight from ten on the Apgar scale, which Marley and Finn knew was a quick system used to evaluate newborns. Five minutes later, she'd scored a perfect ten. Jenny had been absolutely right, the blood loss was nothing to do with Nia. Marley's womb had torn away a little from her body—placental abruption, the nurse had called it—a rare occurrence, and horrifically frightening. They'd both be kept in for a couple of days, and Nia would need to undergo more tests, but a long stay, or even a short one, in NICU had been ruled out. Marley and Nia would be free to go after observation.

"Nia," Finn breathed, and she slowly turned her eyes in his direction, the corners of her mouth twitching upward. Finn sucked in a breath. "She's a genius already."

Nia's eyes crossed and she grunted as a long stream of wind broke from her.

Marley burst out laughing. "Maybe not a genius. But she *is* ours and she's ..." Her voice broke off and she swallowed. "She's finally here," she managed in a whisper.

Finn squeezed her shoulder. "All my life, I'm going to remember how brave you were in there. And she's going to know all about it."

Marley twisted her neck to look him in the eye. "Her middle name should be Elise."

Finn pressed his lips together hard, emotion clear in his eyes. "Thank you," he whispered finally. "I love it."

"Nia Elise Phelps-Mayberry," Marley said, staring back down at her perfect daughter, and gently stroking the little button of her nose. "You were in a hurry."

"She just needed to hear her name and she was ready," Finn said, reaching forward to tenderly stroke her little cheek. Nia's mouth clenched and she turned her little head from side to side, squeaking as though searching for food.

"I see she has her mother's appetite," Finn joked and Marley smiled. Neither of their eyes left Nia's face.

"Hello?" Marley heard Amy's tentative whisper and sat up straighter.

"In here!" she called softly.

Lyra and Amy entered the room with an absurdly large

balloon shaped like a stork, a huge bouquet of roses, and a bulging bag of meticulously wrapped presents.

Amy practically dumped it all at the sight of Nia in Marley's arms. She and Lyra bustled a grinning Finn out of the way.

"Oh my god, you guys," Lyra breathed, her eyes glued to Nia. "She's absolutely *perfect!* I didn't know they could be this cute right from the beginning."

Amy's tone was slightly less dreamy. "She's exquisite," she admitted. "Those lashes are a work of art."

"Do you want to hold her?" Marley offered Lyra, who immediately panicked.

"No! I don't want to drop her!"

Marley fought the urge to giggle, but Finn calmly took Nia from Marley and gestured Lyra to one of the plastic chairs.

"You'll feel better if you sit down and do it," he said kindly. "And I'll show you how to hold her."

Lyra gratefully sat in the chair and posed her arms as instructed. The minute Finn placed Nia in her arms, she let out a long sigh.

"I can't believe she's real," Lyra breathed, sounding choked up.

Amy smiled indulgently, then turned back to Marley. "How're you feeling?"

"Tired," Marley admitted, sinking back onto the bed. "But pretty over the moon."

"You gave us all a scare at the funeral," Amy said, eyes wide.

"I gave myself a scare. Blame Nia when she's older."

"Oh, I will," Amy grinned. "Are you getting good drugs?"

"I'm breastfeeding her so I can't really take much, but the pain is definitely manageable."

"Good. You want to open any presents?"

Marley's eyes lit up. Finn laughed as she tore into gift after gift, marvelling at the generosity of her friends, who'd already spoiled her at the baby shower. Somehow, they'd filled in every gap she and Finn had left on their list for Nia.

Marley clutched a newly-unwrapped stuffed rabbit to her chest, closing her eyes for a moment. She had a baby. She had the best friends in the world. She had an incredibly supportive partner that she was madly in love with, and who was already a wonderful father to their daughter. Everything she'd ever wanted was in this little hospital room, and she could barely believe how far she'd come in a few short years.

"Thank you," she whispered, and she meant all four of them.

Later, Lyra reluctantly handed Nia back, wrinkling her nose as she sniffed. "Over to you, mum and dad!"

"We'd better head off," Amy said quickly. "You want me to drive this stuff over to your place?"

"We can take care of it," Finn said. "Thank you."

He hugged them both tightly and they made their exit, Lyra turning back several times for a quick final glance at Nia.

Finn and Marley grinned at one another, then gazed lovingly at Nia, chuckling as she made small, unladylike snuffling sounds.

51
TUESDAY

"Don't put her arm in like that! You're twisting it," Marley cried, as Finn tried to pull Nia's tiny knitted cardigan on. He was using the tips of his fingers and moving her arm gingerly, but still it didn't look right to her.

"Okay," he said, holding his hands up quickly and stepping back. "You show me how it's done first and then I'll do it next time."

Marley tried to put Nia's other arm into the sleeve, but worried she was bruising the baby's tiny wrist where she held it to push it through. "I can't get it on either," she said a moment later.

"Shall we wrap her in a big blanket or something?" Finn suggested.

"But what if she suffocates?"

"Good point. Okay, surely there's a way we can get this on her without hurting her? How do other parents do this every day?"

"I honestly don't know," Marley said, attempting it again and stopping when Nia's face crumpled. "Maybe we'd better call the nurse?"

Finn grabbed hold of the buzzer and pressed it multiple times. A nurse called out from the station and appeared a moment later.

"We actually can't get her arms into the cardigan," Marley admitted.

"She's three days old, isn't she?" the nurse asked, puzzled.

"You've all been doing it up to now," Marley said. "We've never had to try."

The nurse strode over to little changing table and with what seemed to Marley and Finn like a butcher's brutality, manipulated Nia's arms into the cardigan and tugged it together at her chest, fastening the little pearl button. Nia was calm and relaxed through the whole encounter.

"You can't break her," the nurse reassured them. "I know it feels like she's really delicate, but she had quite a ride getting earthside and I promise you, she's much more robust than you'd imagine. Unless you want her starting school in that cardigan, you're going to have to relax a little."

"Okay, yeah sure," Finn said, sounding confident.

"Do you want to get her hat on then?" Marley asked him.

He looked horror-stricken. "Yes?"

Marley handed him Nia's matching little beanie and he placed his fingers into it to open it out. Then he approached Nia from several different angles as the nurse watched in amusement.

"You can do it," she said encouragingly. "Just pop it on her head."

Finn's hands shook as he placed the beanie over Nia's forehead and then ever so carefully lifted up her head to slide it onto the back. He heaved a huge sigh of relief once it was on.

"Right, you can put all her hats on," Marley said, "and I'll do socks or something."

"You'll both get there," the nurse said, smiling at them. "If it makes you feel any better, a lot of first time parents are like this. She's really lucky to have a mum and dad like you two."

"Mum and dad," Finn whispered, once the nurse was gone. "I don't think I'll ever get tired of hearing that."

Marley swiped at a tear. "Am I supposed to be this emotional over *everything?*" she asked Finn.

But he couldn't answer, because he was too busy fighting his own tears.

52
FRIDAY

When Amy walked into work that Friday morning—the end of their second week in their new offices—she could sniff an ambush in the wind. Everyone was exchanging surreptitious glances. Determined to ignore it, she stifled a sigh, hoping she was imagining it. The bomb dropped shortly after lunch, with a studiously casual comment from Amber.

"Oh, so hey Amy, I was thinking … we haven't heard about your hen's?" Amber toyed with her stylus. "When's the big wild night out? You get married week after this, right? So it has to be this weekend?"

"Would have been, but there isn't one," Amy said flatly. "My best friend was supposed to organise it but a family member passed away and then she got caught up in a legal debate with her record label. So …" Amy opened her palms. "It's not a big deal."

Amber's eyes bulged. "Ames you cannot be serious. We need to do it up *big*. You're going to be sleeping with one guy for the rest of your *entire* life, which …" She shook her head in horrified bewilderment. "I mean, kudos to you and all. But your freedom needs to be *mourned.* Like, properly. With booze. And condoms blown up in a veil, the whole shebang."

"While that *does* sound appealing, I'm good. I'm delighted to be with Rick. I don't really need to go so nuts." Amy shrugged one shoulder and turned back to her screen. In her peripheral vision, she could see Amber making eyes at Kristina.

"Alright, does anyone have a good idea of a place we could go to at short notice?" Amber asked loudly.

"Everyone hates bachelorette parties," Amy said, lifting her head again to try and nip it in the bud. "If I'd been going to do anything, it would have just been to go to the Whistle Stop."

"The *Whistle Stop?*" Amber repeated in disgust. "Do you hate yourself that much?"

"Amber does make a good point," Martha said quickly. "Not about the hating thing, but it would be good for you to celebrate. You've had a lot on your plate lately."

"Seriously, you guys." Amy waved a hand and turned back to her screen. "Thanks for the thought, but I'm really okay without one."

"Kristina, tell her," Amber said on a groan. "She listens to you."

Amy relaxed slightly, certain Kristina would take her side. She glanced up at her co-founder and her heart sank. Kristina's eyes were twinkling mischievously as she tugged on a braid.

"Don't you dare," Amy said in a warning tone.

"What?" Kristina asked innocently.

"You're going to side with them and I'm not having it."

"Amy, I know a place. A *really* cool place. It's the bar where my motorcycle club hangs out."

"Ooh," Amber cooed. "I *love* me some biker."

Kristina pointed a finger at her. "See that there? That will get you banned from this."

Amber zipped a finger over her lips, but she was practically wriggling in her chair.

Even Martha looked interested. "We know nothing about your life, Kristina," she said. "This would be a great chance for us to meet your other friends."

"Not happening," Kristina said bluntly. "They won't be there and I'll take you guys to this place *only* because it's for Amy and she deserves something special for her hen's. But I'm warning you all." She eyed them one by one with such ferocity that Amy saw Amber shiver. "Anyone tries to climb on a biker, they're out. Anyone says *anything* embarrassing, they're out. Anyone puts the Macarena on the jukebox, that means you owe everyone in the bar a round. Just telling you. No one ever knows that and you really can't say no to a group of bikers. What else …" She tapped her chin. "Drinks are reasonable, the finger food is delectable, the bartender is a certified genius, and the women there *will* scratch your eyes out for ogling their men. I'll put in a call, see if we can get a big table reserved. Amy, who else do you want to come?"

"Kristina, *please.* I'm bone-tired—"

"That's why we're doing this! Zip it. Come on. Who else?"

Amy looked around the room. Amber was threatening to murder Amy with her eyes if she turned this down. Martha looked eager and excited. Even Jessamyn and Hope looked cautiously interested. And Kristina's face was pure determination.

"I guess Marley, but I doubt she'll come. And of course Lyra. And Lauren, Rick's best friend's girlfriend …" Amy hesitated. "Do I need to invite Rick's mum?"

"Do you want her there?" Kristina asked. Amy pursed her lips. "Then she's out. Okay, so that's us four, Hope, maybe

Marley, Lyra and Lauren. Max eight. I can definitely swing that for Saturday night. I'll talk to Joey."

"Joey? He sounds cute. He single?" Amber asked brightly.

Amy saw Kristina's eyes flash pure fire for a split second. "Like I said, Amber," she retorted hotly. "If you can't keep it in your pants, I'll get Hermann to throw you out."

"Hermann," Amber repeated breathily. "Ooh, I might like that."

Martha groaned. "Book us in, Kristina," she said. "I'll keep her in check."

"Amy, are you really okay with this?" Kristina asked, suddenly sounding uncertain.

Amy gave up trying to work altogether. "I don't really think I have a choice, do you?"

53
SATURDAY: TWO WEEKS TO THE WEDDING

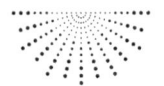

The inside of *Church of Chrome* was not what Amy had been expecting for a biker bar. She'd pictured rough-hewn furniture, peanuts on the floor and a saloon door that barely hid a filthy outhouse. Instead, the crowd for her hen's party—everyone she'd invited, minus Marley who'd had to decline, Lauren who was on a night shift but would join afterward, and Lyra who was running a little late—entered a beautiful high-ceilinged building that might actually have been a former chapel. String lights hung from the exposed beams and infused the room with warm, flattering lighting. The bar was a huge, live-edged slab of mahogany polished to a fine sheen, behind which a respectable selection of top-shelf drinks were back-lit on custom-made, geometric shelves. Polished hardwood planks lined the floor and there were several banquet-style tables along the middle of the room, with more intimate little settings dotted around the edges. They were mostly filled with grizzled, bearded men of various ages, leather-clad women and even some families. An actual motorcycle was hung on one raw-brick wall like installation art, and chrome detailing on the chairs and light fixtures added a rough, industrial feel.

Amy was genuinely stunned and Kristina hung back with her, enjoying her appreciation of the place.

"Not what you expected?"

"Not by a long shot," Amy breathed. "Just *wow*." Her eyes widened as they fell on the bartender, who was smiling in their direction. His thick, tawny hair was combed back and a neatly-trimmed beard framed sculpted features and huge deep eyes below thick brows. His mouth was pretty, almost sulky, and a tattoo peeked up from under the buttoned collar of his forest-green shirt.

"Jesus," she whispered to Kristina. "Is he real, or part of the decor?"

"That's Joey." Kristina gave her a tight, unreadable smile. "Let's head to our table."

Then Amy caught sight of the table, unsure how she could have missed it at first. It had been stunningly decorated in Kristina's unmistakeable, clashing-print style. Artfully-arranged tufts of pampas grass in cut crystal vases, a wildly-printed table cloth topped with macrame placemats, gold balloons spaced at intervals and a pineapple cocktail mug for each guest.

Amy turned to Kristina, open-mouthed. "I will still never know what sorcery you use to make all these elements come together, but I'm forever glad we're on the same team."

This time Kristina's smile was genuine. "Me too."

Two drinks in, Amber was already on her third warning. Martha was trying valiantly, but failing, to limit Amber's alcohol intake. It was hard when every time Amber went to the bathroom, she trawled by a table of bikers who took one look at her skin-tight dress, snaking hips and teased blonde hair, and pulled her into their laps to "share their beers".

Finally, Kristina got up and quietly spoke to Joey. From that moment on, whenever Amber was in spitting distance of a table, Joey let out a piercing whistle and drew his finger across his neck at the bikers.

"What's the story with you two?" Amy whispered. Kristina had nursed a single drink so far, and Amy was hoping that was enough to loosen her tongue.

Kristina frowned. "Who two?"

"You and Joey."

Her frown deepened. "I don't know what you mean."

"Kristina," Amy said. "*Anyone* can see the chemistry between you."

Kristina's eyes strayed to the bar, where Joey was already looking over at her. They broke off eye contact immediately and Kristina's cheeks reddened. "We're just good friends."

"Friends don't look at friends like that," Amy insisted.

"Look, there's no story, okay?" Kristina said, a little snippily. She took a deep sip of her cocktail. "We never got the timing right, and the moment has passed. Now can we drop it? I don't want to regret bringing you here."

Amy smiled and held her hands up. "Okay, okay. Officially backing off."

She glanced around the table, the cocktail working its magic and making her feel buzzed and blurry-edged. Kristina had been right to push her into this. It was fun to celebrate with her friends, and she realised she hadn't been out with the whole team before now. Hope was only one drink in but her cheeks were pink and she was giggling uncontrollably. Amy knew nights away from her husband and twins were rare. Not because she was stuck at home, but rather because she chose to be there. Martha looked gorgeous as usual, and Jessamyn, who Amy barely knew, had turned out to be warm and friendly. Though Jessamyn wasn't invited to the wedding, Amy was glad she was there tonight.

She looked up and spotted Lyra in the doorway, looking a little hesitant. Amy immediately pushed her chair back and crossed the room to her best friend, wrapping her in a hug.

"How are you doing?" she asked in a low voice.

Lyra managed a smile. "A bit better, thanks … sometimes. Then it gets hard again," she added. "But don't worry. Alex dropped me off and he gave me a shot of tequila in the car. So either I'll be bawling in half an hour, or I'll be doing the can-can on the bar."

Amy laughed and tugged Lyra by the hand to the table. After a quick round of introductions, Amy placed Lyra beside her. Joey came out from behind the bar with a tray of wings and another of wedges. He set them down in the middle of the table.

"You alright, Amy? Everything satisfactory with your evening?"

"Couldn't be better!" Amy said enthusiastically, looping her arm around Kristina and pulling her close. "I can't believe she pulled this off at such short notice. She's amazing!"

"She definitely is," Joey agreed with a grin.

Lyra drew Amy away from the table a few moments later, her eyes round and teary. "I should have done this for you," she said. "I'm your best friend and I didn't organise anything."

Amy tutted sympathetically, devastated that her friend felt that way. "Ly, you've just been through one of the worst things possible. This night is like a grain of sand in the ocean of our lives. I would *never* have expected you to organise it. What kind of bestie would *I* be if I did? And honestly, I was quite alright with having nothing at all. *More* than alright. But this has turned out to be fun."

Lyra glanced over Amy's shoulder at the table. The room was loud, everyone was in a good mood, and the bikers in the bar had taken very kindly to the random party in their midst. "It does look like fun. Also, holy cheese, is that bartender *hot* or what?"

"*Right?*" Amy said, unable to help spinning around again to clock another glance at him.

"He has to be a model or something."

"Speaking of which," Amy said, turning back to her. "You actually look really good. You have a little colour about you again."

"Thanks. Yes, some of my money worries are over, thank god."

A sudden squeal came from the bachelorette table as Hope clocked Lyra. She'd been in the bathroom during the introductions and flew across the room, taking Lyra by the hand.

"Oh my goodness," she gushed. "I bet you don't remember me, but we met one time when you were running a pie truck right in the middle of the city and I was looking for my husband. Well, but he wasn't my husband then, I'd only met him once and then I'd lost him. And you were there with your brother, and I remember thinking how beautiful you both were."

"Oh, thank—" Lyra began, and Amy smiled as Hope took a breath and ran on.

"And I think I asked you to put up like a picture of Connor or something? I forget. But thankfully you talked me out of it. And *then,* I went to go back to visit you guys again, I forget how much later, but you had already gone. And but anyway I found him. We're married now. And we have two big babies. He's a twin and we got twins. And *then* one time I heard your music and I absolutely loved it and then I looked up the singer and I realised it was you!"

She paused again to draw breath and Lyra managed to

quickly interject. "I definitely remember you. Hope, right? How do you and Amy know one another then?"

Amy grabbed Hope's arm and steered her back towards the table. "Come on," she called over her shoulder to Lyra. "Let's get some more tequila into you. You're going to need it."

54
SATURDAY

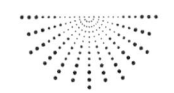

Lyra stood outside *Church of Chrome*, rubbing her arms in the late-night chill. Or was it early morning? Amy's party had ended up being exactly what she needed, completely taking her mind off everything going on around her ... well, almost. The slightly-off feeling between her and Alex penetrated even her cocktail-loosened brain. It was like a dodgy electrical connection. It wasn't going to explode, but the energy wasn't flowing freely.

Still, he was picking her up, at whatever time this was. A forty-five-minute drive from his place, but he hadn't wanted her getting a taxi home so late. Amy was still inside, dancing with a couple of her colleagues and apparently having the time of her life. Lyra had been bummed that Marley couldn't make it, but a brand-new baby was a pretty good reason and they were all glad that Nia was safe. Besides, they'd see her the following week for the rehearsal dinner and wedding.

When Alex's tires crunched on the gravel and his headlights swung over Lyra, she lifted her hand to him and jogged to the car.

"Hi," she said, immediately leaning to kiss him.

"Hello," he replied, his voice slightly croaky.

"Are you sure it's safe for you to be driving?" she asked, as they backed out of the parking lot—careful to avoid the motorbikes parked there—and joined the highway.

"Yes, absolutely," he replied, and then pretended to jerk the wheel. Lyra squealed.

"Don't do that!" She slapped him playfully on the arm. "I might be sick."

He looked sideways at her. "How much did you drink?"

"Ummm …" she giggled. "No, maybe like three cocktails? Over the whole night?"

"Lyra Beck, you lush."

"You could have drunk at the buck's night! I could easily have caught a cab."

"I didn't feel like it," he said reassuringly. "We had a nice, mild evening. I think Rick's wild days are over, much to the annoyance of his army buddies."

Lyra smiled. "I met some of them at that wedding. Remember? The one where we almost kissed?"

He grinned at her, his eyes lit up in the headlights of an oncoming vehicle. "Oh, I remember."

Lyra sighed and leaned her head back on the rest. "Do you ever wish we could go back to that time?"

A frown wrinkled his brow. "No. Not at all. Why, do you?"

Lyra shrugged.

"Is something wrong?" he asked, concerned. "I loved our time getting to know each other, but for me, it just gets better every day. I don't see any need to go backwards."

She toyed with her locket. "Alex, I know you've been mad at me, and … I hate this awkwardness between us." She could hear the tears threatening in her voice and swallowed them down.

He flicked her a puzzled glance. "I honestly don't know what you're talking about, Ly."

She rubbed her eye. "But I do. And I need to explain some things to you. Things I should have told you about before. Something happened with the label ... before I left on tour."

"Okay," he said tentatively after a moment. "What about the label?"

Lyra took his hand, needing to be anchored to him and wanting to soften the blow of her words. "Alex, they asked me to fake a relationship with Jake. For ratings. Apparently they *tested* it, like as in with some market focus groups or whatever."

"*What?*" Alex's eyes narrowed. Lyra could almost see the wheels turning in his head. Then he froze, his eyes turning to her in horror. "Wait, so on stage ... that was part of—"

"No!" Lyra shook her head firmly. "*No*. Alex, of *course* I told them where to shove it. Immediately. That's why I didn't even mention it to you. I thought my refusal would be the end of the story ... On stage, that was Jake genuinely trying to do something nice. I *believe* it was spontaneous. What definitely wasn't spontaneous were those photos that leaked of us together, as we already know. Alex, I know you know nothing happened, but I want to explain. I should have realised they would set me up. I really was in that bed with Jake, but I'd taken a bunch of pills Maggie gave me. I needed to black out, I *was* blacked out. And Maggie and Kit were in the bunk across. Also—"

"Lyra, stop," Alex said gently. "I know all this. You don't need to explain."

"But you didn't know they'd asked me about it beforehand. Maybe you could have guessed what kind of stunts they'd pull." Lyra gulped. "I feel like I broke something between us and I can't forgive myself."

Alex squinted at a road sign indicating a rest area ahead

and made a sharp turn into it, pulling the car a safe distance off the road before cutting the engine. He unclicked his seatbelt and turned to Lyra, forcing her to look back at him. His eyes were dark and fierce. "Lyra listen to me. You did *nothing* wrong. You hear me? Nothing. And nothing is broken. It can never break."

She raised her eyes to his, hopeful. "But I feel like things have been strange …"

He appeared to be struggling with something, then he shook his head in annoyance. "I didn't realise you could tell, but that's my fault. It's only that … I've hated *myself* since that night."

Lyra sucked in a breath. "What? Why?"

"Because—" He looked down and was silent for a moment. His voice was hoarse when he spoke again. "Because I wasn't there for you. The woman I love, going through the most horrible thing I can imagine, and I could *see* you. I could see it happening in real time and I couldn't get to you. I shouldn't have stopped trying. I should have kept pushing and fighting until I got to you. I just …" He drew a shaky breath. "I saw Jake with you on stage, and I was so angry at myself. I thought he deserved you more than I did. That he'd been there for you at that horrible moment, and he might be better for you than I am."

Lyra's mouth fell open. Alex held up a hand to stop her saying anything. "Don't worry. I realise now how dumb that was. And that our relationship is so much more than a single moment. But still … I've been so, I don't know, disappointed at myself since then. I didn't realise that *you* thought—"

"I thought you were mad at me," she whispered, leaning over to cinch her arms around him. "Thank god it was just you hating yourself."

A laugh escaped Alex. "You're so mean." He pulled her

roughly towards him and held her almost painfully tight. Her face pressed against his chest.

"The very idea that I couldn't be there for you …" His voice was raspy.

"You're always here for me," she said.

"I will be forever. If you'll let me …"

Lyra closed her eyes, feeling the vibrations of his voice inside his body, smelling the laundry soap that *her* clothes were scented with now too. She let out a soft hum of contentment and, a moment later, felt him stiffen against her.

"What?" she asked, pulling back.

"You didn't answer," he said, his eyes roaming her face, bright and anxious.

She frowned. "Answer what?"

"I said I want to be here for you forever, if you'll let me," he repeated, his voice imbuing the word *forever* with a significance Lyra didn't understand.

"Of course," she replied. "You're not going anywhere." She leaned across the console to hug him again, but he drew back.

"Lyra, are you trying to torture me?"

"Huh?"

"I'm *proposing.*"

She gasped, heat rising to her cheeks. "No, you're not! No, you're definitely not! Proposals involve the words *will you marry me,* or whatever. You're not even on one knee," she pointed out, her voice rising to a squeak.

"Because I'm in the *car!* Right, wait here." Before she could say anything, he sprang out of his door, raced around to her side, and pulled her door open. There, on the side of the highway, he got down on one knee.

"I know it's not the best time, with everything that's

happened recently. But …" A shy smile spread across his face, as he pulled a ring box from his jeans. "Lyra Beck—"

"Stop it!" Lyra shouted, hitting his shoulder. "Why are you even carrying that?"

"I always have it on me. I've had no idea how or when to do this!"

Lyra shook her head in amazement, a thrill running down her spine as her lips pulled into an unbreakable smile.

Alex suddenly turned serious. She noticed for the first time that his cheeks were tinged with red and his voice was wobbling. He opened the box, revealing a solitaire diamond on a platinum ring. Simple, modern and perfect. Lyra instantly loved it.

"I am *so* serious," Alex said. "I definitely didn't want to do this when you were three sheets to the wind and maybe I shouldn't take your answer as final."

"I'm suddenly feeling *very* sober," Lyra said, pressing her cool palms to her cheeks. They already hurt from smiling.

"I've had this ring for almost a year. I wanted to wait for the right moment. I don't know if I thought it was when we'd bought a house, or when we decided to try for a baby, or …" He shook his head. "But I don't want to waste another single minute of this life not being married to you. Will you do me the biggest honour of my life, and become my wife?"

Lyra's face was flushed, tears pricked at her eyes and her heart pounded. She quickly slipped out of the car, landing on her knees between Alex's legs on the gravel.

"What are you doing?" he yelped. "Get back in the car, you'll graze your knees."

Lyra giggled. "Well, apparently we're not doing this the traditional way so—"

"I'm down on one knee with a ring in my hand!" Alex protested indignantly.

She laughed, then grabbed his face with both hands,

pulling it to hers. "Yes, yes, yes. Alex. You're *it* for me. I've never had love like this, and I don't want to let it go. Ever."

"You're saying yes?" Alex asked in disbelief, his face splitting into a wide grin.

"I'm saying *hell* yes."

"Oh, thank god," Alex said. He scooped Lyra up, carried her to the back car door and gently laid her across the passenger seats, climbing in over the top of her and shutting the door.

"Alex," she sighed, snaking her arms around his neck and pulling him towards her. She pressed her mouth to his. "Now we've sealed it with a kiss. But I think you're supposed to put the ring on me."

"You haven't given me a chance," he said, his voice hazy, as though he was already lost in their kiss.

She held out her hand and from that slightly awkward angle, Alex slid the ring on her finger. It fit her perfectly. "Now come back here."

"I love you," he murmured, pressing kisses to her jawline that made her skin feel like it was ablaze. "But are you sure you want to say yes? You're a bit drunk …"

"I'm not, actually," she said, and it was true. The cold and the proposal had completely sobered her up. "There's something else," she whispered in his ear, enjoying the shiver she felt ripple through him at the tickle of her words.

"Hmm?" he replied, and the low rumble of his voice made her breath start to come quicker.

"I want a baby. I don't want to wait. I know that. I want one. With you. As soon as possible."

Alex pulled himself up on his arms to study her face.

"Are you absolutely serious?" he replied.

She beamed up at him. "Never been more sure of anything in my life."

He held himself up from her a moment longer, then

gently lowered himself back down, crushing her mouth into a kiss that instantly heated up to the point of urgency for them.

"Then let's get started …" he murmured.

It was the last sensible thought they had.

55
SUNDAY

Amy groaned and threw an arm up over her eyes, the blinding light streaming in through her window penetrating the dull fog of her hangover. And she was *Hung. Over*. Flashes of the evening came back to her. She vaguely remembered the night ending with Amber simulating a strip tease on the back of a chair she'd spun to face the other guests, and Kristina hooting with laughter at it. Hope had been teary-eyed, but Amy couldn't remember why. Lyra had loosened up a little, at one point dancing with Martha and Hope to something on the jukebox. Oh *god*, it had been the Macarena. And Amy had paid for everyone's drinks. She heaved a sigh, feeling sicker than she had in a very long time. She couldn't even remember how much she'd paid for the round. Her credit card bill that month would be quite a surprise...

She felt Rick watching her. "What?" she croaked. "Are you not hung over?"

"Nope," he said cheerfully. He'd been out for quiet drinks with Alex, Deacon and some of the army boys. Pop had even joined them for the first drink, though Rick hadn't found it within himself to invite Sean. "I had a glass of water for every beer, and I was a good boy the whole night."

"Bit self-righteous, aren't you?" Amy whispered, and the effort of talking made her jaw prickle with a warning that she'd better be careful.

"I made you an espresso," Rick said, and Amy realised she could smell it. "And there's a big glass of water beside you, too. You want me to pull the curtains closed a bit?"

"Could you?" she begged softly.

In the half-dark, Amy carefully sipped her water and her espresso as she and Rick filled one another in on bits and pieces of their evening. About an hour—and a long shower—later, Amy was ready to stomach some food. She phoned ahead to the cafe down the road and picked up bacon and egg rolls for the two of them. As they ate them, Amy started to get excited about the surprise she had for Rick today. She *really* hoped he would be as enthusiastic about it as she was.

"We're going for a drive," she told him. "But I might need another hour until I'm legally under the limit again."

"Where are we going?" Rick asked, adorably swiping a drip of ketchup from his chin.

"It's a big secret."

"A secret, huh? I thought we weren't keeping those from one another anymore."

"Last one," she grinned. "I promise."

A short nap later, they were in the car and heading for the harbour bridge. Rick had the window wound down and Amy watched him tilt his head back to enjoy the sun on his skin and the wind in his hair. She knew he still savoured little moments like that—after his dark days in a hospital bed, she couldn't blame him. She reached over the console and took his hand, threading their fingers together.

"You're handsome," she said.

"You're beautiful," he replied. "And you're all mine."

"Yep. You pretty much own me outright," she smiled.

A moment later, he sat up and frowned. "Why are we at your old offices?"

"Patience!" Amy pulled up and grabbed his chair from the boot, bringing it around. He gave her a puzzled smile as they reached the door and she fished her keys out. Inside, everything was empty. No furniture, no lighting fixtures, only the walls and spaces she and Rick had carved out and designed together. Amy took a deep breath and clasped her hands in front of her.

"What do you think about making this our home?" She played nervously with a button on her blouse as she waited for his answer.

"What?" Rick shook his head, completely baffled. "I don't get it."

"So, I've been speaking to the lady who inherited this place. They want to sell. Quick and painlessly as possible, so the price is pretty reasonable, and if we want it, they won't advertise it. I looked into the zoning with the council. It was previously residential and it can covert back. I also had my architect mock up some plans, and had Alex give me a quote. Rick ... We could *really* do this. Make it completely accessible, make it into a perfect little home for us." She brought her hands together, her eyes lit up with excitement. "It's not massive, but we can really get a lot out of the space. And most of all, the bank will approve our loan for it."

Rick's eyes had been widening as Amy talked, a slow glow spreading over his features. "Are you kidding me right now?" he asked in wonder.

"No." Amy moved to take his hand and rushed on eagerly. "It even has a little courtyard area at the back, which we never used when this was Porter Lucas. We could fit a little table and chairs, and a barbecue out there. We'd have to have a combined living-dining-kitchen area, but we'd have enough space for a big bedroom. And most importantly, a *really* great bathroom."

"Because she has to have a nice bathroom," he added, with a grin. "Oh, *Ames*."

"Do you honestly like it?"

"Seriously? I *love* it. I love the idea, I love that you did all this for us, I love this space …" His eyes narrowed. "This wasn't on *any* of the to-do lists."

"You've only got access to one file, Rick," she said with a wink. "There are multiple files."

He threw his head back and laughed, and Amy thought she had never been more in love with him than at that moment. She pulled a small bottle of champagne from her handbag, then paled as she looked at it. "I thought we might celebrate, but I think I've done enough of that for a while."

She laughed as Rick tugged her hand and pulled her onto his lap. "You are simply amazing, woman," he murmured, and the intensity in his eyes sent shivers down her spine. "I am so in love with you."

"Why don't you show me how much, then?" she whispered, letting her handbag fall to the floor as she wrapped her arms around him and put her lips to his.

56
SATURDAY: THE DAY BEFORE THE WEDDING

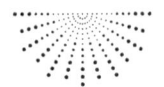

All afternoon, cars had been pulling up to the Chateau Homestead. Guests arriving for Amy and Rick's wedding weekend were first stunned with the view along the final few kilometres of their journey into Wine Country. Bland highway gave way to rolling hills of lush green streaked with rich, earthy brown between the evenly-spaced rows of stakes and vines. The vineyards alternated with fields of other broad acre crops like wheat and barley. Occasionally, plump, slow cows could be seen grazing in wide, green pastures. In the distance, the majestic mountains rose—blue and sculpted. The sun was lowering into a spectacular sunset of bright yellows, fiery oranges and deep purples, and a light mist was descending over the valley, diffusing the light and lending an other-worldly feel.

Pulling up to the Homestead, guests found a sprawling, white latticed and gabled estate. The centrepiece of the white stone circular drive was the trickling fountain, spilling layers of crystal-clear water down its scooped shelves, surrounded by bright green hedges.

Once they were checked in, they were led through the

front building and to the estate proper, which wouldn't have been out of place in the English countryside. A deep staircase framed with shrubs in aged urns led out to a huge open field, beyond which the vineyards rolled. A small lake, its waters crystal clear and its banks tree-lined, formed the centrepiece of the estate. It was circled by well-appointed, luxury cabins. Rick and Amy had booked the entire place out, and the jewel in Homestead's crown was the honeymoon suite cabin, which Amy would have to herself for her final night of "maidenhood", as Diana insisted on calling it.

Amy couldn't have designed the suite better herself. It was roomy and airy, and a wraparound veranda gave them views from all sides, accessed from wide French doors. The carpets were silk, the drapes a rich blue velvet, the furniture solid wood. A chandelier hung over the king-sized bed which looked so plump and inviting that Amy wanted to sink into it the minute she saw it. Her best friends were beside her as she explored the room.

"Whoa," Lyra breathed, setting her bag down. "Are you *kidding* me?"

"Nice, huh?" Amy said, grinning.

"I feel pretty bad for Rick slumming it in one of the other cabins until you guys are married."

"Wait till you see those other cabins," Amy said. "You won't feel so bad for him then. You guys have a good one too," she added.

They spent the next few hours exploring the grounds, lounging around the room, and sipping tea sitting on the wrought-iron outdoor furniture, feeling like royalty as they gazed over the grounds.

"I'm off for a massage and a manicure," Amy said later, stifling a yawn. "Are you *sure* neither of you have changed your minds?"

"My boobs hurt so much I think I'd punch someone if I

had to lie face-down," Marley said pressing her chest as she winced. "Speaking of which, I need to go find Nia and Finn."

"I'll go find Alex and get settled in to our suite," Lyra said, stretching luxuriously on a pillowy day-bed that had her eyes sinking closed. "Or I will in a minute."

"We need to make plans to celebrate your engagement properly," Amy said, plucking up Lyra's hand to examine the ring again.

"He did good with that," Marley said approvingly.

Lyra beamed at them both, and then looked back at her ring. "He really did. But we can celebrate me later. It's Amy's big day first. See you guys later for the rehearsal dinner?"

The rehearsal dinner was being held in a private dining area, and it looked better than Amy remembered as she and Rick entered. The parquetry floor was polished to a deep sheen and the walls were covered with rich blue wallpaper. The long banquet table was studded with leather armchairs and punctuated with fresh native flower arrangements in fine china pots. The ceiling was high, and circular fixtures shed gentle light over the scene. A decommissioned marble mantelpiece spilled over with greenery. She and Rick paused a moment, soaking it in before any of their guests noticed them.

The dinner would be intimate—parents, grandparents and best friends. That included Lauren, since they could hardly have invited Deacon and left his date sitting in her villa alone, as well as Silas and Ernie. Amy had known Silas as long as she'd known Lyra, and she thought he could use the pick-me-up of an additional night of free dinner and drinks. The other guests would arrive tomorrow. Tonight was just for their nearest and dearest. There'd be some speeches and toasts, and they'd all retire early to be well-rested ahead of tomorrow's festivities.

Amy had carefully chosen her rehearsal dinner outfit so that it would hint at her wedding dress without giving anything away. She felt beautiful in it, and Rick was having trouble keeping his eyes—and hands—off her. She wore a pair of tawny, high-waisted, tailored slacks that flared slightly at the bottom and featured a sharp crease down the centre of each leg. Into them, she tucked a cream silk blouse, open at the throat, where she'd layered several strings of pearls. Her shoes were pointed-toe faux snakeskin booties and her hair was brushed to a creamy sheen, gently curling under itself where it skimmed her shoulders. Her makeup was light, her skin dewy-looking and fresh.

Rick wore grey-blue slacks and a white shirt, his brown shoes matching his brown leather belt. He'd grown his beard a little longer for their wedding, but it was neatly trimmed, and his hair—still longer, the way Amy liked it—was styled. His dimple was visible when he smiled, and his scar gave him a handsome, slightly dangerous-looking edge. Amy had never found him more attractive, and she wasn't sure how she was going to stop herself from climbing on him during the vows the following day and scandalising their guests.

The table broke into applause as Amy and Rick approached, and Rick did a celebratory spin in his chair while Amy curtsied, both of them grinning madly. Then they took their seats on opposite sides of the centre of the table. Amy had seated Pop and Hazel to one side of her, with Diana and Bill opposite them (Bill furthest, of course), and Deacon, Lauren, Lyra and Alex on their other sides. Sean and Pam—who'd insisted on being sat beside one another—and Marley and Finn were a little further down, with Silas and Ernie rounding out the table.

The seating arrangements had caused Amy quite a few

headaches, but it would be almost impossible to talk to everyone that night anyway. She told herself she'd get up and mingle down the table once dinner was done. Little Nia was sleeping peacefully, strapped to Finn's chest in a carrier, and Marley kept sneaking little peeks at her, making sure she was okay, then getting caught in Finn's adoring gaze and stopping to kiss him. Amy and Lyra shared a delighted smile, seeing their friend so loved and in love and happy.

Right before the first course arrived, Amy lightly tapped her fork on her wine glass and stood.

"Thanks so much to all of you for being our very special guests this evening," she said, giving Pop an extra smile. "We're so excited to share our special day with you tomorrow. We don't really have any rules that we'd like to share, we just want you all to have as good a time as you can. The day is as much for all of you as for us. The weather looks like it's going to put on a very good show for us." She locked eyes with Rick, her heart flipping when she noticed him staring adoringly at her. "And for my part, I want to say how incredibly lucky I am to get to be married to that man there tomorrow. Rick, I'm going to save something for the vows, but I want to say …" She took a deep breath. "You make me the happiest I can ever remember being in my life. You support my dreams, you push me to greater things, you believe in me and you *always* have my back. You make me feel like a princess—and a porn star—" Half the table broke into laugher and Sean put his fingers to his mouth for a bawdy whistle. Pam affectionately slapped his arm and Diana and Bill exchanged a mortified look. "And I never imagined that love was like this. That love was like you."

Amy sat down, her eyes glued to Rick, who was clearly struggling with his emotions. His eyes were bright with love and his Adam's apple bobbed as he swallowed. "I'll get you back tomorrow," he whispered, leaning forward to squeeze her hand under the table. "I love you so much," he mouthed.

Amy nodded, pleased, and then waved in the waitstaff to deliver the first course. A light buzz of conversation broke out, and Amy was delighted to see everyone enjoying their meals and one another's company. Halfway through the entree, Amy noticed that Diana was stealing not-too-subtle glances at Pam and Sean. The pair were behaving almost like infatuated high-schoolers. Their heads were tipped together, Pam's colour was high, and Sean couldn't keep his eyes off her. They looked moments away from sneaking out the back door together.

Amy knew Rick must be uncomfortable, but he was hiding it admirably well. Since the fight about their parents, they'd avoided any mention of the topic.

Amy watched Diana, and Diana watched Sean and Pam. She was trying her best to be discreet, but Amy could tell she was distracted and flustered. Her normally wan cheeks were pink, and to make matters worse, Bill had noticed and kept trying unsuccessfully to get her attention. Amy guessed his spidey-senses were on full alert around Sean. He seemed unhappy with the apparent reversal of fortune Sean had experienced of late. Getting into killer shape through boxing, turning his life around, finally giving up gambling—not to mention appearing to have the very attractive Pam hanging off his every word. If Bill had been anyone else, Amy might even have felt a little sorry for him.

"Di," Bill said, having repeated her name several times.

"Hmm?" she forced her gaze in his direction.

"I said are you enjoying the squid?" He dropped his voice. "Unusual choice for a rehearsal dinner, isn't it?"

Diana blinked, as though she couldn't quite make sense of the comment. "I could do without the crumb coating, yes."

"No, but I mean--" Bill broke off, realising his wife's attention was back on Pam and Sean.

Diana lifted her wine glass, her gaze locked on the pair of them, and drank deeply.

Amy turned her attention back to her other guests. "So," she said brightly to Pop. "Are you happy with your tux?"

"He looks very dapper in it," Hazel said warmly, putting her hand on Percy's arm.

Percy rolled his eyes. "Look like a penguin. But it's for my girl, well, my *girls* actually," he corrected, laying his other hand atop Hazel's arm, "so it's worth it."

"I'm worried you're going to upstage me," Rick joked.

"Ex-army boy with a head full of hair and a scar like that?" Percy shook his head. "Not a chance."

Rick chuckled, looking pleased. "Well, as long as Amy chooses me on the day, I don't care about anything else."

"Wait, there's an option for me *not* to choose you?" Amy joked.

"Well, I'll be there, ready to step in if you need to reconsider," Deacon said loudly, picking up on the joke.

Lauren elbowed him. "Hey! I don't think so, mister."

He leaned and kissed her, chuckling, and Lauren's cheeks pinked. Amy felt happy seeing them together. They seemed to be a great couple, and things had been pretty smooth between them since they'd gotten together just days after meeting. Amy often felt bad when she remembered the way she'd initially treated Lauren—falsely believing her to be interested in Rick. But she couldn't help still feeling a prick of relief that she and Deacon were *so* smitten with one another.

Down the other end of the table, raised voices made Amy turn her head. Silas and Ernie appeared to be arguing about something. They were struggling to keep their voices low, but it was clear things were tense between them. Ernie caught Amy watching and whispered something urgently to Silas, who immediately cut himself off mid-sentence and returned to his squid.

Amy exchanged a worried glance with Lyra. Her best friend had wedged her chair as close to Alex as the legs would allow. He had his arm draped over her shoulders and Amy could see the fierce protectiveness in his grip. Lyra's cheeks were still hollower than usual, and the dark circles under her eyes made it clear she was still mourning. But there was a brightness to her that Amy hadn't seen for a long time. Lyra caught her looking, and gave Amy a secret smile. She was so pleased that Lyra and Alex were engaged, but … there was more to Lyra's glow than that, she was sure. She made a mental note to get some time alone with Lyra when they were getting ready the following day.

When dinner was over, Amy felt full, exhausted and happy. She'd be heading to bed alone tonight—she and Rick having decided to follow the tradition of not spending the night before the wedding together. Rick was bunking up with another of his army friends who'd made the trek in. She was glad he'd have the evening with his mates.

As everyone was getting ready to leave, Amy saw Pam weaving her way towards Rick to say her farewells. Diana noticed her approaching and seemed to want to make a quick getaway, mumbling something about the powder room. She stood, but had somehow managed to get her handbag snagged on the leg of her chair. Pam hurried towards her, as though to try and help her get it free, and that made Diana desperate to move faster. Her glass of red wine in one hand, Diana gave the handbag an almighty yank with the other—flinging her wine over Pam's face at the same time.

Pam gasped in shock, her mouth open as she blinked in

disbelief, red wine soaking her lashes and seeping into her blouse.

"Mum, are you okay?" Rick asked quickly, struggling to get to his feet.

"Diana, for god's sake," Sean said angrily, springing up and swiping a stack of napkins as he hurried to Pam. He tenderly patted at her face and pressed a napkin to her blouse, while glaring at Diana.

The whole table had gone silent, staring at the scene.

"I didn't mean it," Diana said weakly, setting her glass back on the table with a shaky hand.

"Sure you didn't," Sean snapped, his voice far too loud. "You've been itching for a chance to get at her since the moment we walked in. Don't think I haven't noticed!"

Diana looked mortified, clutching her chest as her cheeks flamed to a deep red.

"It was an accident, Sean," Pam said quietly, swiping at the mascara under her eyes.

"It really was, Dad," Amy added. "I saw the whole thing."

"Well, of course *you're* going to protect your mother!" he snapped angrily, and Amy recoiled at the harshness of his words.

Rick pulled himself up to his full height over Sean. "If you speak to my wife like that again, I think we can safely say you'd better not show tomorrow." His voice was low and tense and he eyeballed Sean. Amy could see Deacon shifting slightly in his chair, ready to come to his old army buddy's defence if it was needed.

Amy was caught between swooning at Rick's words, and a desire to have this whole weird situation go away. It was mortifying that it was happening, but at least it was in a room full of friends she trusted.

"Sean, *please*," Pam said urgently, tugging on his arm. "I'll go to my room and wash this off."

Sean stood firm, giving Amy a hurt look, as Rick got back into his chair. "Does he speak for you?" he asked Amy, and she swallowed before nodding.

"He speaks for all of us, Sean," Percy said in a low voice, holding his son's eye unflinchingly. In that moment, Amy saw the father he was—one struggling to set boundaries with a difficult son—instead of the indulgent, loving grandpa he had always been to her.

Sean took a deep breath. Percy's reprimand seemed to have hit home, and Amy knew from experience that he would probably storm out, ashamed, and start the whole spiral of gambling again. So she was pleasantly shocked when he pressed his eyes closed for a second, then opened them again.

"Amy, Rick. You have my sincere apologies for this. I hope you can forgive me."

"Yes," Amy said quickly, still slightly stunned. Rick nodded.

Sean turned to Diana.

"I promise you, I did not do it on purpose," she said quickly.

"I know. And I'm sorry for accusing you of it." He held her gaze, apparently completely sincere.

Diana blinked, seemingly as taken aback by his apology as Amy was by the whole thing.

"Pam, come to the bathroom and I'll help you clean up," Diana added, and Pam gave her a tentative smile, nodding.

Bill had barely raised his eyes from the table during the whole thing and Amy's blood boiled that he could be such a pig as to let his wife cop that kind of abuse and not say anything.

"Good standing up for your *wife*, Bill," Amy said sarcastically, once the women had left. The look he gave her was chilling. He stood and stalked from the room.

Pop put his hand on Amy's arm and she turned to him, taking some deep breaths to try and return her heart rate to normal.

"Just let all of this wash over you," he said, his voice low. "Nothing matters except tomorrow."

"He's right," Hazel said, leaning towards her. "Although I do think that adults should be expected to behave a little better than all that."

Amy sighed, then shrugged. "Weirdly I'm not as freaked out as I thought I'd be," she said truthfully. "I do feel sorry for Mum though. And Pam."

The two women were walking awkwardly together towards the bathrooms and Amy hoped it would at least be the start of some reduced tensions.

57
SATURDAY

Amy was neck deep in her suite's tub, a glass of red at her side and candles all around. Her last night of *maidenhood* might not have been a real thing, but a night alone in this gorgeous room certainly was. She considered ignoring the knock—maybe someone was lost on their way back to the own suite after that momentous rehearsal dinner. But the knocking persisted and Amy grew afraid something was wrong with Rick, or one of her friends.

She wrapped the thick bathrobe around her and pushed her feet into the plush slippers the Chateau had provided. She pulled back the curtain to the side of the suite's door, and was shocked to find Pam standing nervously on the other side.

"Pam? Is everything okay?" she asked in alarm, yanking the door open.

"Amy. Yes, everything's fine. Sorry to scare you … Can I come in?"

"Uh, sure." Amy stood back and Pam toed off her shoes and entered the room. Amy gestured to one of the armchairs and Pam sank into it gratefully. Amy perched herself on the end of her bed, her head tilted at the other woman as Pam sprang back to her feet and started pacing the room.

"Okay, Pam you're starting to freak me out a little …" Amy said. "Do you need a drink?"

"No. No, thank you. I came to give you something."

She made no move to hand anything to Amy and an odd silence fell.

"Okay …" Amy prompted, wondering how long this was going to take. Her bath was getting cold and she pulled her robe more tightly around herself.

Pam tucked her hair behind her ear, then quickly pulled something from the small handbag slung across her chest. "This is a wedding present for you," she said. "Just for you."

Amy made a puzzled face, but took the little box that Pam held out. She opened it, finding a single key inside. "Is this…?"

"For my place. Yes. Amy, I've been meaning to apologise." Pam was having trouble looking her in the eye, still pacing slightly around the room.

"Pam, you're making me dizzy," Amy said, trying to keep her tone gentle. "Would you be okay to take a seat?"

Pam sank back into the chair and puffed out a breath. She stared at her hands for a long moment, the raised her eyes to Amy's. "Parents aren't supposed to have favourites. But Richard is mine. I will never admit that again, and I never want it to leave this room."

"Okay." Amy nodded solemnly, wondering where this was going.

"I don't honestly think I'd have liked any woman for him, but I felt as though you came with more problems than others might have."

Amy frowned and opened her mouth to object, but Pam held up a hand, cutting her off.

WEDDING BELLS AT LILAC BAY

"I realise that's wrong. Richard shouldn't have been unclear about his job. And I know you two have worked through everything. But nearly losing him, after having lost his father … I cannot tell you what that did to me. In my mind, *you* were the danger."

"I can understand that," Amy whispered.

"This might be an inappropriate thing to say to his daughter, but getting to know your father has been … wonderful. I don't know what will happen between us, but I do know this is the first time since I lost Richard's father that I've felt anything for another man. Anything at all."

Amy swallowed, deciding to keep all feelings about their dating—and her doubts about her father's recovery—to herself.

"Since these feelings have developed in me, I feel as though I've become more aware of them in others. And Amy," Pam's gaze turned intense, her eyes pinning Amy. "My son is so madly in love with you. I've been wrong to hope it might end, or to try and throw obstacles in your path. I wanted to keep him safe, but all I've been doing is keeping him from the woman who makes him deliriously happy."

Amy swallowed at the lump in her throat, tears filling her eyes. "I love him more than anything, Pam," she whispered.

The other woman nodded, clearly struggling with her own emotions. "I know you do. I finally see it. You two are a perfect match, Amy. And there's nothing more I could want for my son. I know you two will be moving out soon, but even when you have, I want you to know that my door is always open for you."

Without thinking, Amy stood and opened her arms to Pam, who gratefully met her embrace. It was the first time they'd ever hugged and Amy was surprised by how natural it felt.

"Thank you, Pam. I promise, I will never, *ever* let you down where he's concerned."

"I know it," Pam whispered, squeezing Amy tightly. "I know it."

58
SATURDAY

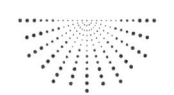

"Well, *that* was a dramatic evening!" Ernie said to Silas as soon as they reached their room and shut the door behind them.

Silas pressed his knuckles to his mouth, fighting a grin. "She did it on purpose, right?"

"I thought the same in the beginning!" Ernie squeaked. "I mean did you *see* the looks she was giving them that whole time?"

"Yes. Oh my god. *Poor* Amy."

"Right? But then I do think her mum was pretty freaked out by it. So then I wondered if it really was an accident?"

"Oh Erns, you always want to see the best in people!" Silas chucked Ernie's shoulder affectionately, then sat on the bed to pull his shoes off.

Ernie rooted through the minibar and held up two little airplane-sized bottles of vodka. He wiggled them questioningly at Silas, who sniffed.

"What do they cost? Sixty-five dollars?"

"I'll take that as a yes," Ernie said, twisting the caps off and placing them on opposite sides of the small round table in their room. He tapped the chair across from him. "Come sit with me."

Silas considered him for a moment. "This sounds serious."

"It is."

Silas gnawed at his top lip, nodding slowly. Then he slapped his thighs and headed to the table like he was on a death march. Here it was, the moment he'd been so dreading. Ernie was about to finally break up with him. Silas didn't think he had the energy to fight it any longer.

He put his hands on the table and locked his gaze with Ernie's. Ernie sprang up again, rifling through the mini bar. He set three more bottles each beside their vodkas. "I feel like we're going to need this," he said.

Silas picked up the vodka, then knocked it back in a single shot.

Ernie's eyes bulged. "Jesus. We're not in a Western, Si. You can sip!"

Silas squared his shoulders. "Let me have it. Whatever it is … I'm ready."

"Okay, what in blazes is going on with you?" Ernie demanded. His eyes were instantly fiery. Silas had never seen him look so angry. Or so desirable.

Silas clenched his jaw. "What's going on with *me?*" he repeated darkly. "Why don't you admit what's going on with *you?*"

Ernie peered at him, then threw up his hands. "I give up. What's going on with me?"

Silas twisted the cap off the next bottle—a scotch—and downed it. He made no move to answer Ernie.

"Si. Just now when we got back to our room, it was like old times. It made me really sad, because we haven't been like that for ages. You've been strange for *weeks*. Whatever it is, we need to talk about it, or …"

"Or what?" Silas asked, his hand clutching the tiny bottle so tightly he genuinely feared it might break.

Ernie's eyes dropped to the table. "Or we're not going to make it."

Silas pushed a breath out through his nose, all the fight leaving him. He twisted the cap off the third bottle. "We're not going to make it anyway," he said finally.

Ernie stared at him, eyes brimming. "Why won't you tell me what's going on? You've never opened up to me about Mick, and I *know* you've been hurting. But this was going on long before that. I don't understand. This is my last attempt at making myself vulnerable here. I want to know I tried everything I could before I lost the best thing that ever happened to me."

Silas set the bottle on the table, taking a deep breath as he raised his eyes to Ernie. "You can drop the act, Ern. I know about four-hearts."

"Huh? What the flick is four-hearts?"

Silas pointedly raised a brow and Ernie gave a small shake of his head, his mouth open in confusion.

"The guy in your *phone*, Ernie. I've seen the messages."

"What …" Ernie looked genuinely perplexed for a long moment. He stood and crossed the room to grab his phone. "There's no one called …" Then his brow cleared, as realisation set in. "Oh, you *idiot!*" he bellowed, thumping the counter. "You stupid, stupid fool."

"Jesus," Silas said, reeling back slightly in shock.

"No. You are without a doubt the *stupidest* man who has ever lived."

Silas ground his back teeth, squinting at Ernie. His mind was blank with sadness and he released a breath, staring down at the next bottle in his hands, fighting the urge to hurl it across the room.

"Silas. Four-hearts is *Alex*."

Silas snapped his head up. "You're having an affair with *Alex*?"

Ernie crossed the room quickly, taking a seat opposite Silas. "There is no affair, you gargantuan moron. I'm going to deal with the fact that you even *thought* that, later. I've been texting Alex in secret for over a year, because he wanted help choosing a ring for Lyra! And then we both realised that when dating a Beck it can help to have a wingman, so we kind of kept it up. We both need someone to help alert us to triggers, or …" He flapped a hand through the air. "Whatever. It's not always easy dating a Beck, I'll have you know. And Alex got the easier of the two by far! I helped him with this project, and I guess we've been messaging a bit more often because we were talking about Lyra being away on tour and then--" His face softened. "About how to help you guys get through Mick's … through Mick."

Silas gaped at Ernie for a moment, then dropped his head to his hands. The tension dissolved from the room and all that was left was Silas's cold regret. He really was an idiot not to have listened to Mick. And Lyra.

"I know what you're thinking," Ernie said gently, a moment later. "And yes. You will eventually, *somehow* make it up to me."

Silas groaned. "This whole time, I've been fighting so hard to keep you."

"*That's* why you've been acting so odd?"

Silas nodded, keeping his face in his hands.

"The weird smiles. The zoo trip. The flowers. The proposal…" His voice dropped. "Not letting me see your grief?"

Silas raised his eyes, looking mournful. "The proposal was real. But … yes. I thought you wanted someone sunnier."

"Wow," Ernie whispered. "You're even dumber than I thought."

Silas snapped his head up, eyes fiery. "Okay, stop calling me stupid!" he roared. "I thought I was losing you, for god's sake. I was fighting for the love of my life, and—" He broke off, mortified by what he'd let slip.

Ernie's face broke into a grin so wide it hurt Silas in the eyes and the heart to look at. He stared hard back down at the table.

"Or ... boyfriend. Whatever," Silas finished.

They fell silent and Silas could hear Ernie's breathing grow rapid.

"Si, look at me," Ernie said.

"Oh, please," Silas whined petulantly. "*Please* don't say anything soppy. I can't handle it. That was enough for a lifetime. I genuinely feel nauseous." He put a hand to his stomach, looking pained.

"*Look* at me."

Silas set his jaw, heaved a dramatic sigh and lifted his eyes to Ernie. Ernie slipped his hand across the table, encircling Silas's forearm.

"I love that you're grumpy. I love that you're often in a bad mood, except with me. Or, even with me. I love that you say what you mean and that people in general annoy you. I kind of love that you hate all my flowers and my hobbies."

"I don't--"

Ernie held up his hand. "I like that you *pretend* to hate them all. From the very first second I laid eyes on you in Rusty's Pub the night of that stupid fight, I've been in love with you. Everything about you. I *know* you, Si. I know you're not always *actually* that grumpy. But I love the charade, when it is a charade. Even when it's not. Because I'm the one that gets to have you. To come home with you. To live with you. There isn't anyone else. There never will be anyone else for me, as long as you walk this earth, and long after. I'm done. So the fact that you could even consider that I was sexting someone else, or whatever you thought I was doing ..." He puffed his cheeks, shaking his head. "You're blind as well as stupid."

Silas bit his lip, his eyes narrowed. "Okay," he said slowly. "Okay, I deserved that." He drew a deep breath. "Does this mean you'll marry me now?"

Ernie slowly, sadly shook his head. "We're headed there. Of course we are. But I don't want to do it to try and fix anything. I only want to get married once in my life. So I want to do it when we're rock solid. I think we might have some stuff to work through. The fact that you still haven't let me see you cry about Mick ... I'm not saying you need to, or there's a particular way to grieve, but you've got walls up." Ernie slid his hand back across the table, taking Silas's and threading their fingers together. "I want you to trust us more."

Silas twisted his mouth. "I'm not suddenly going to become Dr Phil or something, you know that, right?"

Ernie grinned. "I know that."

"I don't want to have to wait for a billion years to get married, because you're holding out for a Kumbaya circle."

Ernie snorted. "Fat chance. That's not what I mean, and you know it. I want you to completely trust us. I ... I really don't think you do yet."

Silas growled. "Does this also mean I'm not allowed to hug you when I'm ... in the mood?"

Ernie actually blushed. "No. That's, ahem, that's fine with me."

"Right," Silas said, giving him a significant look. "Then get over here please, because I am suddenly *very* in the mood for hugs."

59
THE WEDDING DAY

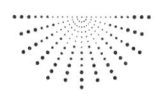

Amy pulled back the lace curtains in her room to peek at the wedding area. A team of staff from the venue were scurrying around to finalise it. As they unrolled a large purple print rug for the sitting area, Amy let out a gasp of horror.

"What?" Lyra asked, half zipped into her bridesmaid dress. She and Marley rushed to cram next to Amy at the window.

"Oh, that looks cool," Marley breathed, and Amy shot Lyra a look behind Marley's back. *See?*

"Is that one of the things Rick organised?" Lyra asked, wincing.

"Yes," Amy said. "Dear lord. I chose *wicker* furniture because it's timeless. He was meant to hire something Persian! At the very least a Beni Ourain. Not … whatever *that* is."

"Who's Beni?" Marley asked, puzzled.

"No, it's a style of … never mind," Amy said, letting the curtain drop. "We have to keep getting ready."

There was a knock on the door and Amy waved in the makeup artist. "Ly? You want to go first? Or you, Marley?"

"I need to breastfeed Nia in a minute," Marley said, glancing at her watch. "Can I have Finn bring her here, or should I pop back to our room?"

"Bring her here!" Lyra cried, at the exact moment Amy asked, "Will she be sick on any of us?"

Marley rolled her lips. "I'll pop back." She slipped on a robe and Lyra took a seat at the dresser, as the makeup artist set up her lighting.

"What a gorgeous bridal party you three are," she said, smiling.

Amy nodded, straying back to the window. "Maybe if we look good enough, no one will notice that hideous rug." She twitched the curtains back again. "Oh *no,* he added purple balloons to the arch!" She spun to Lyra, looking so horrified that Lyra couldn't help feeling for her.

"Ames, it'll be fine," she said, tucking her robe over her dress to stop from getting makeup on it. "You said you wanted a compromise between the two of you. Or … he said that."

The makeup artist gave Lyra a knowing look as she spread her wares atop the dresser. "I thought it looked beautiful when I walked past," the lady added. "If that helps."

It clearly didn't, but Amy remembered her manners enough to politely smile at the woman. She took a seat on the bed, watching Lyra as the makeup artist began to brush a creamy foundation over her face.

"Ly …"

"It's fine," her friend said automatically. "I promise. Ooh, and you can always turn the photos black and white, right?"

Amy tilted her head. "Actually, that's not a bad idea. Maybe they can Photoshop the hideous print off the carpet too."

Lyra tactfully closed her eyes.

"Oh, *Amy*," Lyra breathed, instantly tearing up as Amy stepped out of the dressing room in her wedding gown.

"That is *so* beautiful," Marley added, her eyes round. "You look like a ... Rick's going to *die*."

"Do you guys really think so?" Amy asked, suddenly anxious. She turned to look at herself in the full-length mirror. The gown *was* spectacular. Made of cream Georgette silk, the dress cinched in at Amy's waist and came up over her ample chest in a sweet-heart neckline. Her shoulders were covered with a delicate dotted-tulle overlay, with sheer sleeves that dropped to Amy's elbows, ending in a lace-trimmed waterfall shape. Victorian lace panels, embroidery and delicate beadwork added accents over the bodice, the waistline and her hips. The dress fell to her feet, ending in a short train. She did have to admit that she looked pretty exquisite.

"I've never seen a dress so gorgeous," Marley added. "Or a person."

Amy flapped her hand at her face, not wanting to get too emotional. She took a deep breath and a good look at her bridesmaids—her best friends. Her eyes widened.

"Marley! I realise now I've never actually seen you with makeup on!" Amy said.

"Isn't she a stunner?" Lyra said proudly.

Marley's chest was swollen from breastfeeding and it bulged almost indecently from the top of her dress. But she was show-stopping. Lyra and Amy had always thought their friend had runway model-like features: high cheekbones, a perfect bowed mouth and huge eyes. With the makeup on, and Marley's height, she now fully looked the part. Like a Victoria's Secret model—albeit with slightly more clothes and flesh—ready to strut down the aisle.

Amy knew Marley didn't necessarily enjoy being dolled up, so she was careful not to put too much emphasis on her looks. Besides, her friend was naturally beautiful, even when her honey-coloured hair was up in a messy bun, not artfully styled as it was now.

"I'm glad I'm walking down the aisle after you two," Amy joked. "Gives Rick a chance to change his mind."

"Well, he'd be an actual idiot if he did," Marley said bluntly.

"The set-up down there is beautiful, Ames," Lyra added. "And the weather is gorgeous."

"I'm actually too afraid to keep looking," Amy admitted. "Lest I see more horrors that Pam and Rick have dreamed up."

"Well, then I'll just tell you now about the animal straws," Lyra said quickly.

"*What?!*"

"I think that's the worst of it!" Lyra added, holding her hands up.

"Oh, I think it's those weird flower things down the middle of the table," Marley said, and Amy narrowed her eyes.

"*I* organised those."

"Maybe Rick and Marley should be getting married," Lyra joked.

They all broke off as someone tried to open the door. Lyra had locked it, so after several attempts, the rattling of the knob turned into a knock.

"Who is it?" Lyra asked, immediately assuming her Maid of Honour role.

"It's Pam," came the voice from the other side.

"Is something wrong?" Lyra asked, basing her response off the look on Amy's face.

Pam hesitated. "No. I only wanted to see the bride."

"She'll be out in a moment," Lyra said confidently. "You can go ahead and take your seat."

Amy winked at her.

"A peek?" Pam tried again.

"See you down there!" Lyra replied, cutting off any further talk. They heard her retreat. "Was she *actually* going to barge right in if the door was open?" Lyra whispered.

Amy nodded. "I kind of feel bad for not letting her in, but I want to surprise her, too. She finally gave me a key to the house last night and we had a bit of a heart to heart. There might be hope for us yet."

"She asked me if I knew about your family plans," Marley said. "When she came over to try and hold Nia without asking."

"Or not," Amy said, rolling her eyes. "She doesn't let up about that."

Amy turned back to the mirror to fuss with her veil and noticed that behind her, Lyra was tearing up.

"What's wrong?" Amy asked, spinning to her in alarm.

She swallowed, trying to blink back the tears. "I just wish my mum could be there when I get married. I keep thinking about Rick, doing this without his dad. It sucks, you know?" She sniffed. "Both the people I thought of as parents are gone."

"Same," Marley said, nodding slowly. She and Lyra crossed the room to hug one another and Amy felt a mixture of guilt and sadness. Her relationship with her parents wasn't exactly perfect, but at least she had them. And most of all, she had her Pop.

"I'm so sorry guys," she said. "I wish I could change this somehow. I won't say anything lame like, they're watching you from somewhere, because I know that's not the same. That doesn't count."

"Thank you," Lyra said, nodding. "Okay, let me pull myself together." She fanned her face. "Right, Ames. Given the purple, the animal straws, the balloons and Pam, are you sure you want to go through with this?"

"I'm having second thoughts."

And they all giggled because they knew there was nothing —not even wild horses printed on straws—that could keep Amy from heading down that aisle to her man.

As soon as Rick laid eyes on Amy, his chin began to quiver. She stood at the end of the roll of red carpet, their outdoor "aisle", her arm hooked tightly through Percy's. Percy looked proud as punch and had been quite emotional himself upon seeing her. Especially when she pointed out that she was wearing her grandmother's necklace.

Amy watched from the back row as Lyra strode confidently down the carpet, strewing petals along the way. Alex watched her hungrily and Amy saw Lyra tip her head at him to share a secret smile. Then Marley headed down and Finn's eyes almost bugged out of his head. He turned Nia around so she could "see" her mummy, and Marley quickly strayed from the path to plant little kisses on both of them.

Then it was Amy's turn.

The day would pass in a blur, as she and Rick had been warned it would. But what would stay with Amy forever was the way Rick rose from his wheelchair as she started the walk towards him. His eyes never left hers, and they were shining bright.

As she reached the front row, and kissed Pop farewell, she took both her groom's hands.

Rick leaned towards her and growled softly. "I am going to *tear* that dress off you by the way."

She let out a small laugh, then they straightened up, staring into one another's eyes.

"I *cannot* believe you're mine," he said, his voice thick with emotion.

"And you're mine," she said, beaming up at him. "Forever."

Amy's arms were looped tightly around Rick's shoulders for what would be their last dance of the evening. He'd managed two others so far and she was worried he was going to overdo it, but Lauren secretly reassured her he was up to it.

The day had gone better than she could ever have imagined and, as she sighed with contentment and hugged Rick even more tightly, she took a look around at their friends.

Kristina and Martha were locked in a tight conversation on one of the armchairs in the outdoor seating area. Amy smiled, remembering Kristina's reaction to the setting. She'd slowly gazed around, her eyes wide, and then raised her champagne flute to Amy.

"Here's to making huge compromises for the people we love."

Amy had burst out laughing. "You and Martha are the *only* ones who truly know what I sacrificed here."

"I mean … I didn't even know rugs came in that colour," Kristina said, sipping. "You really took one for the team, Amy."

Silas and Ernie were squished together on one of the

high-backed wicker chairs, seemingly quite drunk and obviously having the time of their lives as they laughed about something. Amy watched as Silas slung his arm over Ernie's shoulders and brought their heads together for a kiss. She hoped it would be their wedding next, if not Lyra and Alex's. Those two were still seated at the table, along with Deacon and Lauren, and Marley and Finn. Nia was fast asleep in the sling across Finn's chest and the three couples were sharing an easy, engaged conversation—and more than a few drinks. Nearby, Sean and Pam sat opposite Diana and Bill, the discussion seemingly flowing. From where Amy stood, it didn't look nearly as awkward as it might have been only a day earlier.

Pop and Hazel were on the dance floor, gently swaying together. Hazel was beaming, and Pop's hands were almost indecently far below her waist.

"I hope that's us at their age," Rick whispered, his eyes landing on them now.

"Me too," Amy replied. "Have you had a good day, Mr Porter?"

"I have indeed, Mrs Ford," he replied with a grin. It was a joke they'd recently started sharing, since neither of them would be changing their names. "And I don't think my rug ruined the day, do you?"

Amy chuckled, shaking her head. "It was just like you said. The perfect union of two different styles." She leaned her head on his shoulder.

"You're having it Photoshopped out, aren't you?" he asked.

"One hundred and fifty percent."

They laughed, holding one another tighter as they twirled under the fairy lights in the warm Australian evening.

"Are you okay without your dad here?" Amy whispered a while later.

Rick was silent a moment, then he nodded. "You know, most of the time it's just a blank, empty space where he was. This … ragged hole in my heart. But tonight. Tonight I actually felt like he was here. And he was proud."

Amy squeezed him tight and buried her face in his neck, breathing in his heavenly scent. She couldn't wait for what would come later, in their honeymoon suite, but for now she was perfectly happy. Basking in the glow of their love, with their precious favourite people alongside them, and their lost loved ones watching from the stars.

THE END

AFTERWORD

Dearest Reader,

Thank you so much for reading Wedding Bells! It means the world to me that you read my book, given all the choices out there. I really hope you enjoyed it, as I had a lot of fun writing it. And although I had initially planned six books in the series, for now, I'm putting down the pen on Lilac Bay.

It feels right to end the series here, with things neatly resolved for Lyra, Marley and Amy.

There are many more stories to be told, and I'm positive these characters will make cameo appearances in future series!

Until then, thank you so much for following along with their lives and loves. They've become real people to me and I'm sad to see them go.

If you enjoyed the book, I would be so delighted if you posted a review on Amazon or Goodreads. Reviews and even simple star ratings are gold dust for authors!

If you want to keep up to date on future books and series,

AFTERWORD

click to the next page where there's an offer for a free book when you join my mailing list. :)

Hope to see you there.

xoMarie

THE STRANGER FROM LILAC BAY

YOUR FREE GIFT!

When a hot paramedic saves Hope's life, she's instantly smitten. Afraid she's just feeling grateful, Connor gives her his number and tells her to make the first move. She meant to hit save, not erase ... for a girl who works in IT, it shouldn't have been that hard.

In a city like Sydney, will she ever be able to find him again?

Get your free copy at this link: https://BookHip.com/TQGLKKT

ACKNOWLEDGMENTS

Thank you so very much to my editor Katharine D'Souza, my cover designer Ana Grigoriu-Voicu, and my incredible team of beta readers.

To my friends, who believe in me sometimes more than I believe in myself.

To all my readers: you'll never know what each and every download, rating and review mean to me.

And to my family who make me the luckiest person alive.

ABOUT THE AUTHOR

Marie Taylor-Ford is a wife, mother, knitter and devoted carboholic - not in that order.

Born in Wales and raised in Australia (Newy forever!), she's recently returned to her home country after nearly 12 years in Munich, Germany.

If she's not writing, she's probably hanging out with her family or friends, traveling, knitting, reading, swearing at her FitOn app or gently coaxing her child into wearing the things she knitted for him.

You are warmly invited to stop by her website (and subscribe to her newsletter for exclusive content, offers and publication info):

www.marietaylorford.com

or connect via social media:

- facebook.com/marietaylorford
- instagram.com/authormarietaylorford
- tiktok.com/@authormarietaylorford
- bookbub.com/profile/marie-taylor-ford

Printed in Dunstable, United Kingdom